TIME BOMB

Also by Malcolm MacPherson:

Protégé (novel)
The Lucifer Key (novel)
Black Box
The Blood of His Servants

TIME BOMB

Fermi, Heisenberg, and the
Race for the Atomic Bomb

Malcolm C. MacPherson

– E. P. Dutton   New York –

Published in the United States by
E. P. Dutton, a division of New American Library,
2 Park Avenue, New York, N.Y. 10016.

Library of Congress Cataloging-in-Publication Data
MacPherson, Malcolm.
Time bomb.
    Bibliography: p.
    Includes index.
    1. Atomic bomb—History. 2. Physicists—Biography.
I. Title.
QC773.M24 1986   623.4′9119′0922 [B]   85-24568

ISBN: 0-525-24409-3

Published simultaneously in Canada by
Fitzhenry & Whiteside Limited, Toronto

COBE

Designed by Nancy Danahy

10 9 8 7 6 5 4 3 2 1

First Edition

for Annie

Contents

Illustrations follow page 176

Author's Note

What you are about to read is the author's interpretation of fact derived from his own interviews and research and from reading nontechnical works and papers on the early history of the atomic bomb. It is one interpretation only of the events that took place principally between 1938 and 1942.

The interpretation formed initially as I went into the history. I could not rid myself of the feeling that those often superb authors who had preceded me on this subject had chosen a canvas of places and names that was far too broad. I was often as lost as I was fascinated by what they had written. I came no closer to the reasons why the atomic bomb was developed than before I started reading. Except for a thirst for knowledge were there no reasons for what those scientists did? Were there no personalities, no flesh-and-blood men and women who had blown life into the drama of this extraordinary science? None at first was apparent to me, except, of course, for the much-chronicled Robert Oppenheimer and General Leslie Groves who primarily contributed to the Manhattan Project as administrators. It was then that an event caught my interest. It was the successful working of the uranium pile, without which bomb research would have been relegated to a back burner in the war years. This natural-uranium reactor contained the secrets of the bomb. Germany and America as combatants were attempting to unravel these secrets at exactly the same time. Whoever unlocked the secrets first had the better chance to produce an actual bomb with which to force the other side to sue for peace. From that point, the "characters" of the drama revealed themselves, the first being Fermi, about whom remarkably little has been written, especially considering the seminal role he played. On the German side, there was Heisenberg, clearly the most brilliant physicist in the Third Reich. Much more had been written about and by him. The parallels in the lives of these two men came into focus for me: they were almost exactly the same age, they had studied under the same teachers and attended the same places of learning, were of an equal brilliance, had won Nobel Prizes before they were forty years old, were solid acquaintances if not friends who had competed for recognition and achievement since their early twenties. One worked for the Nazis, and the other for the Americans.

The canvas narrowed itself as the drama heightened through the biographies of these two remarkable men. I chose selectively but fairly from their lives, always with the other in mind. I was limited in Fermi's case by the relatively early age at which he died, in 1954 of cancer, and by the death of Laura in 1979. I relied for personal observations on Laura's tale, *Atoms in the Family,* and interviews with Nella Weiner Fermi, his daughter, and several others, including Albert R. Wattenberg, who knew him at the time. Fermi was a man who carefully guarded his feelings. In box after box of his *Collected Papers* at the University of Chicago, there were to be found but two or three nonscientific observations; he never had the time to write memoirs and reflections, even if he had desired to do so. Heisenberg, who died in 1979, and his wife, Elisabeth, devoted their attentions after the war to setting the record straight as they saw it in her book *Inner Exile* and his essays *Physics and Beyond.*

The Allied effort to manufacture an atomic bomb has been chronicled in its smallest detail. However, the Nazi effort has not received the same scrutiny, except in David Irving's *Virus House,* notable and lasting for the thoroughness of the research. Put together in the time frame I have chosen, these stories and the competition in which the two protagonists were engaged do not try to tell the *whole* history of either the American or the German efforts. And yet, through the selectivity, it does become representative of those histories and something more: two truths that I hope that this version chronicles. The first is that war drives people to actions that they might otherwise ponder and debate in the absence of the mentality of survival. The setting for the construction of the atomic bomb was a *world* war that brought out the concept of a *world* weapon, a weapon that might destroy the enemy in one stroke. Another important truth, I believe, is that even in a war that envelops millions of people and scores of nations, the "combat" is usually reduced to the actions of individuals who are either directly or indirectly in competition for their lives or their ways of life. In the author's own interpretation, these two truths were present in World War II at the same time that scientists, after thousands of years of investigation, were very rapidly beginning to uncover the mysteries of the atom and bend them to their will, to create a device whose potential horrors have dominated our lives ever since.

Malcolm MacPherson
London
August 1985

TIME BOMB

Prologue

In the early decades of this century, an Englishman, Ernest Rutherford, and a Dane, Niels Bohr, reached deep into their genius to produce a vision of the smallest particle of matter. They were aided by great thinkers before them, from Democritus, who first conceived of the idea, to Plato, who originated a philosophy that expanded on it, making his fellow Greeks "see" through his expositions what they otherwise could not see. Bohr and Rutherford imagined a "world" with a diameter of a millionth of a millionth of a centimeter made up of protons with positive electrical charges. "Moons" called *electrons,* with negative electrical charges, raced around this tiny sphere. And just as atmosphere exists between the earth and its moon, a relatively vast empty area lay between the nucleus and the swirling electrons. Rutherford went on to imagine the way that certain atoms over time threw off their protons, changing from one element to another. Understanding this slow, natural process of decomposition and change transformed the relationship between man and his ever focusing image of the atom. Rutherford thought he saw a means of hastening the process and, thus, attaining for himself the goal of the alchemist—the centuries-old dream of changing the elements. If Einstein's new theory of relativity were true, Rutherford had theorized, splitting the atom's nucleus would unleash energy of a magnitude that was nearly unimaginable. And so he shot positively charged protons at nuclei.

Over and over he repeated the process, but nothing happened. Rutherford had to conclude that some basic component of his concept was wrong. The shield of swirling electrons could not be penetrated; Rutherford's proton "bullets" had merely ricocheted into space. Einstein told him that he had been "trying to shoot birds in the dark." Later, James Chadwick, another brilliant Englishman, discovered a third, as yet hidden component to the atom. He called it the *neutron* because it had neither a positive nor a negative electrical charge. Chadwick repeated many of Rutherford's earlier experiments. He discovered that his neutron had the capacity to slip through the shield of electrons guarding the nucleus. Overnight this third component became crucial to man's understanding of the atom and opened the path to the release of the atom's incredible nuclear forces.

Nine months after Chadwick's wonderful discovery, in February 1932, Franklin Roosevelt was sworn in as president of the United States; eleven months later, Adolf Hitler came to power in Germany. In the years that immediately followed, as Hitler marched the world toward its second world war in this century, scientists continued at a quickened pace to throw light on the atom's deeper mysteries and awesome powers. Two young and equally brilliant physicists appeared on this stage of discovery. Different from all the others, these two men, one who would flee Fascist Italy and the other a nationalist German who would stay in his country, would become the protagonist and the antagonist in the most extraordinary real-life drama in this and, perhaps, in any century. In a more abstract sense, these two men represented a mystical symmetry. Perhaps if one man had been absent, the other would have lived a life of anonymity or obscurity; it was as if each needed the other so that the special circumstances of creation could intersect. Each man came to represent the atomic physics of his nation, one Nazi Germany, and the other, America and its allies, Britain and France. In a scientific competition set within the larger conflict of World War II, they raced against one another to create the first chain reaction that would sustain itself in a uranium reactor—or what they then called a *pile.* The chain reaction in itself was a worthy discovery, but there was a war on, in which basic scientific knowledge was being channeled into the development of weapons. The pile, if it could be made to work, could be very important to the war effort. As if it were a large pot for cooking uranium "soup," the uranium pile produced a broth that had not existed in nature for billions of years. The pile had the capacity to make the element plutonium by transforming the uranium nuclei. And with this plutonium, a bomb of devastating force could be made, a bomb to win the war, for Germany or for the Allies.

Few people at the time considered it possible that Germany could lose this race; near the end of the war, it was generally believed by the Allies that Germany's lead was as commanding as its desperation was great. Hitler's persecution of the Jews of Europe left little doubt that he would use the atomic bomb on his enemies if only his scientists could develop one first. Neither reason nor morality would stay his hand. Indeed, one afternoon in the fall of 1944, he met in his Berlin bunker with Joseph Goebbels, the minister of propaganda, and Albert Speer, the Reich's minister for armaments, who later reported the event in his memoirs. Neither Speer nor Goebbels had to put into words the subject that weighed on their minds. The fortunes of war had turned bitterly against Germany. The Eastern Front was collapsing, with the Wehrmacht retreating under heavy losses. The Allied armies had opened a second front in June, and, already, American, British, and Canadian troops had liberated much of France. And yet, despite the signs of defeat, Hitler remained oddly optimistic, even bubbly on that day. The tide, he knew, might turn again. The Nazis were producing a miracle—a series of secret "X" weapons—that would give his self-proclaimed Thousand Year Reich a second chance for a real millennium.

The three men entered a special projection room in the bunker. Without preamble, Goebbels signaled a pair of SS technicians in the back to lower the lights and start the film his ministry had prepared for distribution to the Reich's motion picture theaters. As soon as the film flickered to life, the screen lit up with the image of a single Luftwaffe Stuka dive bomber sweeping down from the heavens toward the vague outline of a landmass that could only be Great Britain. A single bomb fell away from the Stuka's belly; then flames burst upward, and an explosion roared in the speakers. Almost unbelievably, the outline of the British Isles simply vanished as if vaporized by an inexplicable force contained in that single small bomb.

"*That's* what's going to happen to them," Hitler exclaimed to Speer and Goebbels. The expression that spread across his face was that of a child with a shiny new toy: "Yes, that's how we'll destroy them."

Part I

MUSSOLINI IS ALWAYS RIGHT.

BUURRRR-MMMAAAHHH SSSHHAAAVE . . .

The two-seater Bébé Peugeot convertible rolled down the autostrada between Florence and Rome, past the political billboards erected by Italy's Fascists to celebrate a recent visit by Hitler. The three occupants of the little car sang and laughed so loud that the drivers in passing cars turned their heads and stared. They did not know what Burma Shave was, but their laughter, heard distinctly from the open-top car, suggested that the three young people were ridiculing Il Duce's slogans, a dangerous act of defiance in Italy in fall 1938.

BOOK AND GUN—THE PERFECT FASCIST

BURRRR-MMAHHH SHAAVE

Riding in the rumble seat of the Bébé Peugeot, behind the driver and his passenger, a balding Swiss-born physicist named Felix Bloch led the singing in an uneven, laughter-cracked baritone. Like many of Europe's young scientists, he had recently settled in America as a refuge from the war in Europe that almost everybody, even inhabitants of lofty ivory towers, knew was inevitable. On this brief return visit to Europe, Bloch had discussed with the driver his emigration to America as well, and Bloch's arguments had fallen on receptive ears.

The driver of the car, Enrico Fermi, had so far resisted the move

to America. Only a couple of months before, during a visit to Ann
Arbor, Michigan, Fermi had talked about leaving Europe but had
decided nothing. A small man with a straight nose, quick coal-
black eyes, and a dreamy, thoroughly engaging smile, and a physicist possessed of a scientific genius that has been known only
three or four times in this century, Enrico Fermi until now had been
indifferent to the violent political tides swirling around him. Yet,
only the day before, he had mailed letters to America from two
different villages near Florence. Indeed, those letters had been the
purpose of this trip. He had wanted to mail them without detection
by the Fascist police in Rome, where he lived and worked at the
university. The letters had asked the chairmen of the physics de-
partments of Columbia University and the University of Michigan
to grant him a teaching position immediately. Further delay might
be dangerous. He now must leave Europe or risk the safety of the
person riding beside him, his wife, Laura, brown-eyed and brown-
haired and a woman of enormous gentle warmth and humor. Laura
was the daughter of Jewish parents. The danger to her of remaining
in Italy was evident. The Nuremberg Laws regulating the lives of
Jews in Nazi Germany had been introduced into Italy only a few
weeks before. Of course, Italians were among the least anti-
Semitic of peoples; Mussolini thought the racial policies of Hitler
absurd. But by now, less than a year before the start of World War
II, Hitler was forcing Italy's officialdom to do his bidding, no matter
how repellent it might have been.

To Win Is Necessary. But to Fight Is More Necessary.
BURRMMAAHHH SSHAAVE
The car's occupants did not want to understand politics. Just
so long as they enjoyed the freedom to probe the mysteries of the
universe, through the field of physics, they did not notice or care.
Never before had there been a time of equal scientific discovery,
in which major pieces of a vast unseen nuclear puzzle—the archi-
tecture of the atom, quantum theory, the theory of relativity, to
name only three—were fitting into place. By now the broad out-
lines of the atom and its function were discernible, a tantalizing
shadow that flickered on a wall. Indeed, discovery had occupied

so much of his thinking that Enrico Fermi had not until now been afraid for Laura.

It Is the Plow That Traces the Furrow, but It Is the Sword That Defends It.

BURMAAHH-SHAAVVEE

Enrico Fermi saw politics as ephemeral; governments would come, and governments would go. But what he sought to discover was immutable; once discovered, that truth could not be destroyed or changed. Fermi rode the crest of that wave of discovery; the aspect of leaving Italy that disturbed him was the loss of the precious research time that would be required to set up a new laboratory and new working relationships, either in New York at Columbia or in Ann Arbor at the University of Michigan. Fermi felt that other physicists, notably those in France and Germany, were competing against him in a race, in which the prize was greatness. One physicist especially gave him pause, one of the most gifted thinkers in Europe. This man, Werner Heisenberg, worked at the Kaiser Wilhelm Institute in Leipzig. Only a few years before, at the age of thirty-two, Heisenberg had won the Nobel Prize for a theory invented in his mid-twenties, at a time when jealousy had given rise to an enduring enmity between him and Fermi, who were only two months different in age. Given the advantage of time, Heisenberg might uncover before Fermi the mysteries that still lay buried deep inside the atom. Such was the rivalry between these two brilliant young men that the thought of losing a discovery to Heisenberg was almost as unbearable to Fermi as the Fascist attitudes on the signs they were passing.

Yet staying, no matter how desirable, was a risk Fermi could not take. But how was he going to flee Italy with Laura and their two young children? As the preeminent scientist in Italy, Fermi had been honored, feted, toasted, and proclaimed. He was a national treasure, a celebrity only slightly beneath Il Duce himself in stature. Only a few years before, surrounded by the frescoes of Raffaello, Peruzzi, and Sodoma in the ancient Villa Farnesina in Rome, Mussolini had inducted Fermi into the Royal Academy. (A modest, shy man, Fermi told Laura afterward that Mussolini had proclaimed him an "excellency" of the Academy. ("If I could say *my* excellency I probably might, just to get faster service. But how on earth can I ever walk up to anybody and say, 'I am *his* excellency'?") No, Mussolini and the Fascists would not allow the Fermis to leave and would use force against them if they tried. This was a practical reality that Fermi wished to postpone. He was not a coward. He was young and brilliant and fanciful, but he was also a man of the mind for whom derring-do, escapes, and surreptitiousness were alien. One small error, he knew full well, could spell their doom.

As the Peugeot reached a clear stretch of the Florence-Rome road, Felix Bloch, from the rumble seat, said to them, "Listen to this one." He drew up from his memory a message seen that past summer on signs on a roadside in California:

"AT CROSSING ROADS DON'T TRUST TO LUCK;
THE OTHER CAR MAY BE A TRUCK."

"BURMA SHAVE," the Fermis sang in chorus, this time without an echo of laughter.

The sound of the telephone ringing in the hall startled Laura Fermi. At that early hour of the morning, when she and Enrico were still sleeping, a phone call could only mean trouble. She threw back the covers, pushed the slippers onto her feet, and shuffled out of the bedroom, glancing at Enrico, deep in sleep. "Hello?" she said.

It was a foreigner's voice. Laura's growing concern intensified. "Is this Professor Fermi's residence?" the voice asked.

"Yes, indeed."

"I wish to inform you that this evening at six, Professor Fermi will be called on the telephone from Stockholm."

That was all. Laura hung up the receiver. "Wake up, Enrico," she said. "This evening you'll be called from Stockholm."

Fermi raised himself up on an elbow and looked at her. That his colleagues at the University of Rome had nominated him was no guarantee, but the possibility—not the probability—of winning a Nobel Prize for physics had become the key component in a plan Fermi had devised. If there were indeed to be a call from the Nobel committee, it would not come an instant too soon.

Less than two weeks had passed since the Fermis' journey in the Bébé Peugeot, and already matters in Rome had worsened. Now, there was no longer anything general, vague, or ominous about the intentions of the Fascists who had introduced new laws and procedures to identify Italian Jews. The sudden change was even more bewildering because Jews represented only 1 percent of the Italian population. There were no "Jews" just as there were no "Aryans" in Italy, only Italians, who were a mixture of Mediterranean races and bloods, anyway. Of course it was true that the Italians had blocked Jews from some professions. Laura's father had been "retired" a few months ago as an admiral in the Italian Navy, but no one was certain that his being a Jew had precipitated the sudden change.

Then, last July, the Fascists had published their *Manifesto della Razza,* a collection of absurd theories on race separation and so-called purity. Aryans existed in Italy, the manifesto declared.

JEWS DO NOT BELONG TO THE ITALIAN RACE—Of the Semites who through the centuries landed on the sacred soil of our country, nothing is left. . . . The Jews represent the only population that could never be assimilated in Italy, because they are constituted of non-European racial elements, absolutely different from the elements that gave origin to the Italians.

Since then, the pace of anti-Semitism had quickened. An institute and a magazine, *Defense of the Race,* had begun. And the first anti-Semitic laws had been introduced only two months ago. Laura wondered whether, and how, these would touch her. Her Italianness had always been emphasized. As a family, the Capons were proud of their father, Rear Admiral Augusto Capon, named Cavaliere of the Cross of Italy and Commendatore of the Crown. In World War I he had received the Cross of Merit. Roman society had reinforced Capon's stature through its acceptance of him and his family. They lived like minor royalty in a large house surrounded by park grounds and dined with the oldest families of Rome. The Capons undeniably were Jews by blood, but they were agnostic by religion.

Laura did not know when her family had first settled in Italy, or even where they had come from, but she guessed either from Spain (the Marranos and Sephardim) or earlier from France or England. For as long as history recorded, Italy had been a safe haven for Jews. When Rome became the capital of a unified Italy in 1879, Jews were granted equality and, just a few years ago, in the early 1930s, Mussolini had emphatically stated that in Italy *"antisemitismo non esiste."*

As a young, quite pretty, dark-haired woman, she had met Enrico indirectly through Il Duce: his 1926 "battle for the lira" had prevented Italians from traveling abroad. The Capon family that summer had planned to visit Chamonix in the French Alps but, because of the currency restrictions, had gone instead to Santa Cristina, a village in the Dolomites. A friend had mentioned that Enrico and his family were staying nearby. The girl friend told Laura, "The faculty of science has established a new chair ad hoc for him: theoretical physics. I think that Corbino, the director of the physics laboratory, had a great deal to do with calling him to Rome. Corbino holds him in very high esteem and says that of men like Fermi only one or two are born each century."

Laura remembered that they had met as children. He was smart, but what made him interesting was his humor. He loved games, all sorts of games, and was superb at inventing them, anywhere, anytime. He prided himself on his athletic prowess. He loved climbing and swimming and was just starting to learn tennis.

A few days later, Enrico appeared at the Capon house in a Tyrolean jacket and knickerbockers, asking Laura to climb the Valle Lunga with him "up to its top." When she asked how far that was, he looked at a map and then placed his thumb near his left eye, closing the right. He could measure anything—a tree, a mountain, the speed at which a bird was flying—by the same method. "About six miles," he said.

Throughout the climb, Fermi took the lead, rarely out of breath and always impatient to reach the summit. He told Laura that his body was custom-made, accounting for his stamina. "What about your brain?" she teased him. "Is that custom-made, too?"

Fermi thought very little about this gift. "People can be grouped in four classes," he told Laura. "Class one is made up of persons with lower-than-average intelligence; in class two are all average persons, who, of course, appear stupid to us because we are a selected group and used to high standards. In class three there are the intelligent persons and in class four only those with exceptional intellectual facilities."

"You mean to say that in class four there is one person only, Enrico Fermi?" Laura asked.

"You are being mean, Miss Capon," he said. "I place many people in class four. I couldn't place myself in class three. It wouldn't be fair. Class four is not so exclusive as you make it. You also belong in it."

Laura said, "If I'm in class four, then there must be a class five for you alone."

Two years later they were married.

They took their vows on a blistering hot day in a civil ceremony at the municipal palace in Rome. Fermi arrived late, at the last moment sewing a tuck in the comically long shirtsleeves of a brand-new shirt. As Admiral Capon in his splendid white uniform stood beside his daughter in white lace, the stitches failed as Fermi uttered his vows, and the sleeve snaked below his fingertips. For their honeymoon they braved a seaplane ride to Genoa, then traveled by train to Champoluc in the valley between Monte Rosa and the Matterhorn.

Since then, their marriage had produced two lovely children, a daughter, Nella (Fermi called her his "Bestiolina," little monster), and a son, Giulio. They had lived in peace in a six-room apartment in Rome that Laura had found and furnished. "You go ahead and buy what you want," Fermi had cautioned her. "I don't care what the furniture looks like, provided its legs are straight." Laura had expected him to fill the shelves with his books, but he owned only a few, and of these, he kept no more than ten volumes at home. Books, he told her, contained information about what had been; he worked on ideas that were not yet known; all the books in the world were of little use for that purpose.

Their first winter had been cold. The temperature never seemed to rise above forty-six degrees in the apartment, and Laura talked about fitting storm windows. Enrico did not earn a large salary, and he was practical. He undertook lengthy calculations with his ever present slide rule. He measured the fissures in the windows and the internal and external temperatures. And then made his decision. Storm windows would not keep in the heat or keep out the cold.

Several weeks later he reworked his calculations at Laura's request when the temperatures went even lower. He told her to buy the storm windows after all; he had somehow misplaced a decimal point.

By the time the spring brought warmth, the young family had settled into a routine, with Fermi's rising around five and working in his study until breakfast. He went to the university at eight. At one o'clock he returned home for lunch and relaxation—time to talk and play with the children—until three, then back to the university until eight, and bed by nine-thirty. He was rarely late for dinner, although he was once late, very late, for lunch. That was on the day he became the first man to split the uranium atom.

By January 1934, as Fermi was beginning the experiments that would lead to fission, less than two years had passed since Chadwick's remarkable discovery of the neutron, which held the key to the release of atomic power. With its neutral electrical charge, the neutron alone could enter the negative electrical field of the electrons circling the nucleus and the positive charge of the protons in the nucleus's center. But nature would guard this secret for nearly seven more years, revealing it slowly and by stages. Fermi would split the uranium atom, releasing unimaginable forces without understanding what he had achieved and would perform a series of crude experiments that would show the world's physicists the way they might build on his findings to create a bomb. But as it stood in 1934, the neutron merely offered an inventive scientific mind like Fermi's another component with which to test and explore the nature of the atom. Inspired by work then being conducted in Paris by the daughter and son-in-law of Marie Curie, Fermi thought to use the neutron as a "bullet" to shoot at metals such as aluminum and, heaviest of all, uranium. No one had thought to use the neutron in such a way before. The French team in Paris had ignored the neutron, preferring alpha particles, with which they had discovered artificial radioactivity (an accomplishment that would merit the Nobel Prize). Fermi, who had grown tired of pure theoretical physics, looked forward to hands-on experimentation. After a particularly strenuous bout of mental activity (he had just finished work on the theory of beta-ray emission from nuclei in natural radioactive processes that would later be recognized as brilliant but now was so advanced that the "bible" of the physics community, *Nature* magazine, had rejected it as unsuitable for publication), Fermi needed to turn his hand to experiments as if he were returning to the soil. He usually found himself testing, expanding, demonstrating, proving—exercising his true genius. Just as he had a need for physical action, whether it was skiing, swimming, climbing, or walking, Fermi felt compelled to experiment. And the neutron offered him a whole new field in which to expend this abundant and special energy. He hoped that the neutron, with its neutral electrical charge, might penetrate the nuclei of the metals at which he would shoot it, although the proton had failed. No one else had yet set up this experiment, but Fermi, gauging by the Paris experiments of the French team, reasoned that a particle with no charge might slip through the negative protective charge of the electrons and the positive repellent charge of the protons.

In theory the experiment made sense, but in practice Fermi was starting with less than nothing. No one in Rome had ever attempted this type of nuclear transformation. The Physics Department of the University of Rome, where he worked, had a comprehensive library, but experimental equipment was almost nonexistent. The Institute of Physics, formerly a nunnery located at 89-A via Panisperna, reflected the attitude toward physics in Rome in 1934. The institute was surrounded by gardens on a hill in central Rome. There were palm and bamboo thickets and a small fountain with carp, which gurgled lazily under the limbs of an old tree. Sparrows by the hundreds lived in the trees. The institute building itself had three floors; the first and second floors contained the laboratory, the library, and a few offices; on the ground floor were the workshop, classrooms, and the students' laboratory. Neighboring quarters housed the chief physicist at the Health Department of Rome, Professor Giulio Cesare Trabacchi.

Fermi had to start from scratch. First he built a team. He hired a young researcher named Franco Rasetti, who had by far the most experience in the laboratory; in his spare time Rasetti collected fossil trilobites and raised salamanders in the fountain behind the institute. Under Fermi, he became the chief of the laboratory; since the team soon started calling Fermi "the Pope," because to them his observations were infallible, Rasetti became "the Cardinal." Next were Emilio Segrè, whom they soon called "the Basilisk" for his flinty, obstinate character; Oscar D'Agostino; and Edoardo Amaldi. Together, they were known as "Corbino's boys," after Senator Corbino, the head of the department. Fermi was thirty-three years old that fall.

The team had nothing for experimental purposes except their inventiveness. Lacking the money to buy what they needed, they built their experimental equipment by using diagrams and self-made and borrowed parts. In 1934, a simple Geiger counter for measuring radioactivity was a novelty that could not be purchased anywhere. Fermi read everything he could find on the device and then set about constructing Geiger counters for the laboratory to help him to understand how much, if any, radioactivity he created in metals by bombarding them with the neutron bullets. Next, the team needed a neutron source. Neutrons do not merely exist in the air; they are created naturally by the combinations of different elements and gases. Fermi selected his neutron source for its utter simplicity. He knew that he could extract radon, a gas, from radium. Radon is formed when radium decays naturally, and it, too, decays, emitting alpha particles. Fermi thought to mix radon gas, once it had been extracted from the radium, with beryllium powder. The alpha particles from the radon gas would strike the beryllium powder and create neutrons. But Fermi needed the radium to start the experiment, and radium cost more than the institute could ever afford. Fermi conferred with Corbino's boys, who consulted Professor Trabacchi, in the adjoining buildings of the Health Department. Trabacchi genuinely liked Fermi and his young team members; he admired their vitality, enthusiasm, and energy. The noise coming from their laboratory, the arguments that lasted well into the night, the physical energy that they, always on the run, expended made Trabacchi feel younger. He heard them out. They explained that they needed less than a gram of radium, on loan. They would return it by the end of the year. Trabacchi did not need much convincing. He went into the laboratory's safe and gave them the full gram of radium he kept there. The "boys" nicknamed him "Divine Providence" in gratitude.

Next, they set up a neutron "shooting gallery," and, like everything else they had done so far, this too was characterized by its simplicity and inventiveness. They occupied the regular first-floor laboratory without the smallest alteration for their new work; they placed the neutron source, a tube small enough to be carried in both hands, on the marble-slab surfaces of the laboratory counters. The metals to be bombarded, always in small manageable quantities, were brought into the laboratory and subjected to the bombardment on the countertops, too. The most nettlesome problem was measuring the radioactivity that their shooting gallery would produce in the metals. The radioactivity in some of the metals, they knew in advance, would last only seconds before dying out. To measure this fleeting indication of the influence the neutrons were having on the nuclei of the atoms they bombarded in the metals, Fermi decided to separate the radioactivity-measuring Geiger counters from the neutrons and the element or metal being bombarded. He did so to prevent distortion in the Geiger readings. As things stood, there would be no chance that the neutrons from the source in the laboratory could reach the Geiger counters, which were placed in a separate room well down the central corridor of the first floor.

Their objective was straightforward. The Paris team under Frédéric Joliot-Curie had created *artificial radioactivity*, radioactivity that had been created in elements that otherwise would not emit it, through bombarding these elements with alpha particles. Fermi hoped to achieve a similar result with neutrons, and he wanted to go further. The French had produced artificial radioactivity in aluminum and other light elements, but the heavier elements had not been changed or made radioactive in the least by alpha particles.

Fermi wanted to find out through his experiments whether the new neutrons could travel where the alpha particles had not succeeded; he theorized that these neutrons with their neutral electrical charge would not be attracted by the electrons of heavier elements or repelled by the nuclei. They would speed unhindered toward the nucleus, slamming into it with their velocity and force. Their largest drawback, against all these positive advantages, was that the neutrons must be created, whereas alpha particles are emitted naturally by radioactive sources.

In short, Fermi wanted to test whether neutrons could be used as effective bullets.

Fermi's team chose to start with the lightest elements first. Artificial radioactivity had already been created in such elements as hydrogen and lithium by the French team, so the work would be starting on the safe ground of repetition. Surely, they thought, if alpha particles had created artificial radioactivity in these elements, their neutrons, if they were to work at all, would have the same effect. The first element put on the counter for the experiment was hydrogen. The neutron source was placed inside a hollow cylinder of a hydrogen compound, then placed in a lead box. After a period of neutron bombardment, Fermi removed the hydrogen "target" cylinder from the countertop and sprinted with it in his hands out of the laboratory, like a man possessed. He ran down the corridor on the first floor and into the room in which he had placed the Geiger counters, his coat flapping. He put the element in front of the counter and watched to see what the neutrons had created.

Soon, he returned to the laboratory to tell the team the news. The neutrons had done nothing to this light element, nothing whatsoever, not even a slight reading of artificial radioactivity on the Geiger counters. They discussed this unexpected result, but they could not understand the reason for it. They went forward, anyway, trying lithium, boron, then carbon—nothing. Then they tried nitrogen: still nothing.

The major result was the development of Fermi's physical stamina from all that sprinting from one room to another. He sometimes boasted that he could run the distance faster than anyone on the team, and no one bothered to challenge him. One day while he was testing a light element with a very short radioactive life, a distinguished visitor from Spain entered the physics building and asked the whereabouts of "his excellency Fermi." Somebody downstairs answered, "The Pope is upstairs." The Spaniard knew Fermi only by reputation, and he expected to see a man of imposing dignity. As the visitor turned the corner of the staircase, a short, stocky young man burst down the corridor toward him at top speed. "I am trying to find Sua Eccellenza Fermi," yelled the Spaniard. "Follow me," Fermi gasped without breaking stride.

The elements were procured by Segrè, the son of a mill owner, who had been raised with a knowledge of finance and the fine arts of bargaining. With a list of the elements they required written by Fermi in pencil on the outside of a paper bag, Segrè set out on his "shopping tour" of Rome, headed for the shop of Mr. Troccoli, who supplied most laboratories in Rome with these chemicals. Mr. Troccoli noted the list on the bag. He warned that some of the chemicals were very expensive. Segrè told him to omit those. Soon, as the bag filled up and most of the items on the list were checked off, Segrè learned that Mr. Troccoli spoke excellent Latin, having been raised by priests. They conversed for some time. And when the question of two metals, cesium and rubidium, arose, Mr. Troccoli reached high up on a shelf for two bottles. He said, "You can have these free. They have been in my store for the last fifteen years and nobody has ever asked for them. *Rubidium caesiumque tibi donabo gratis et amore dei.*"

Fermi felt almost like quitting. The lighter elements had given him no reason for hope, and if he hadn't been stubborn, he probably would have turned to other experiments. Without missing a step, the team marched up the elements, from the lightest to the heaviest, and, slowly, as they reached the middle of the periodic table, the elements started to give off artificial radioactivity, somewhere around fluorine, which showed a very strong reaction to the neutron bombardment. They now knew that they had chosen a fruitful area of experimentation. They could not know just how fruitful. They were doing something with nature that had not been done before. Yet, despite the significance of their experiments, it was as if they were playing with a new toy, the neutron. They were playing because they had the freedom to play. Their equipment cost them nothing; they did not have reputations to protect; they had nothing to lose by spending a year shooting neutrons at elements; and, being in Rome instead of Paris, London, Cambridge, or Berlin, they were far enough distant from the major centers of physics experimentation to be free of pressures to get results. Although they did not recognize them, these were the factors that led to major breakthroughs. The first breakthrough occurred when they tried to bombard uranium, the ninety-second element and the heaviest of them all.

As they had with all the other elements, they set the neutron source inside the uranium cylinder, and then inside the lead box. Then they waited while the neutrons penetrated the electrons shielding the atom's center at great speed and with a force theoretically great enough to reach the atom's nucleus. After a predetermined time with the neutron source inside the hollow uranium metal tube, Fermi removed the uranium and sprinted with it down the corridor to the room with the Geiger counters. At first, as he watched the Geiger readings, he noted a strong radioactive reaction in the uranium. The result puzzled him more than anything he had seen before.

In the other heavy elements they had bombarded, the neutrons had changed the original element to an element near it on the periodic table. From iron, for example, they had created manganese. But with uranium the process was strangely different, and mystifying. Uranium had become active; that much was certain. Neutron bombardment had produced radioactivity. But the bombardment had also produced more than one new element. And at least one of the newly created elements was nowhere near uranium on the periodic table. This new, strange creation, Fermi and the team theorized, might be an altogether new element, element 93, which had not previously existed on earth. Tentatively, Fermi called it *transuranic.*

Fermi never "announced" a breakthrough until he was absolutely certain of his ground. The team debated the findings for days; finally, they took their puzzle to Senator Corbino. A few days later, Corbino notified the world of the discovery in a speech before the prestigious Accadèmia Nazionale Dei Lincei, to Fermi's deep embarrassment.

The Fascists overnight declared element 93 a great cultural victory, proof "once more how in the Fascist atmosphere, Italy has resumed her ancient role of teacher and vanguard in all fields." *The New York Times,* under a two-column headline, reported, ITALIAN PRODUCES 93RD ELEMENT BY BOMBARDING URANIUM.

The following day, Fermi, furious, issued a statement composed with Laura's help.

The public is giving an incorrect interpretation to Senator Corbino's speech. It has been ascertained in my researches that many elements bombarded with neutrons change into different elements having radioactive properties. . . . Because uranium is the last of the elements in the atomic series, it appears possible that the element produced should be the following, namely, 93. . . . Numerous and delicate tests must still be performed before production of element 93 is actually proved.

Worried for his reputation within the tight, competitive physics community, Fermi suspended work.

He took Laura on a speaking tour to Argentina and Brazil, where he was hailed as a celebrity. Only on the ocean liner home did he begin to relax. Ottorino Respighi, the famous composer and a shipboard companion, intrigued Fermi, who had little interest in either literature or music. When he read for pleasure, his choice of books ranged from Jack London to Robert Louis Stevenson. But Fermi could not resist Respighi. During the cruise, he attempted to reduce great classical music to mathematical formulas: to sound waves and other measurable quantities. But he failed, to his dismay. For his part, Respighi had little enthusiasm for science. His single experiment had been to find with a divining rod a pan of water that his wife had hidden under the living room carpet. But they became friends.

Fermi returned to Rome with no idea of what to expect. He had hoped that the flap over the misrepresentation of element 93 had blown over. But he knew how competitive physicists could be. Any chance to discredit a fellow physicist would not be missed, and he knew that he would be a target. Yet, instead, when he returned to the Physics Institute, he found a letter waiting for him, from Ernest Rutherford, perhaps the greatest living physicist. Rutherford had written, "I congratulate you in your successful escape from the sphere of theoretical physics." Whether those words contained irony, Fermi could not say. Perhaps Rutherford was telling him that the world of theory was safer than experimentation, as Fermi had discovered so painfully. Whatever the letter meant to convey, Fermi interpreted Rutherford's words as a form of exoneration. The embarrassment of Corbino's rash announcement was now behind him. If Rutherford did not disapprove, then the damage had been contained. And with a head cleared of politics, Fermi set out to continue his experiments with the neutron.

Fermi and his associates did not return immediately to uranium, although the so-called element 93 still mystified them. They did not understand the process; what had the neutrons done to the nuclei of the uranium atoms that they had not done to the nuclei of other atoms? How had they acted? Why would a new element or an unidentifiable element be created only in the uranium atom? Unfortunately, these were questions that could be answered only with vision, for to understand the process of what they had done to the uranium atom, they needed a new theory with which to "see" it. Instead, they continued bombarding other, different elements and repeating some of the same procedures. In all the other bombarding experiments, before the recess and after, they had placed the hollow element tubes and the neutron source inside a lead box. Then they had placed the lead box on a marble slab in the laboratory. It had been the same method over and over. One morning two members of the team put the neutron source into a hollow silver cylinder and into a lead box. When they moved the cylinder from the center of the lead box to the corner and measured for radioactivity, they got different results, which they reported to Fermi. Some of the team members thought that the difference resulted from statistical error or simple inaccuracy in measurement. But Fermi was not prepared to write it off so quickly.

If the readings changed when the cylinder was placed into different locations in the lead box, what might result if the cylinder were irradiated outside the box altogether? They tried his suggestion on the silver cylinder, and the results gave rise to even more questions. The radioactivity in the bombarded silver changed according to the position where it was bombarded. Objects around the laboratory, it seemed, somehow were influencing the strength of the radioactivity. When the silver was irradiated on a wooden table, the radioactivity was greater than if the experiment was duplicated exactly but conducted outside the lead box on a marble or metal table. What followed from that point seemed logical. Take the neutron source out of the hollow metal tube and bombard the metal from different angles. Put different substances between the neutron source and the cylinder. When they placed a plate of lead, a heavy chemical element, between the neutron source and the cylinder, the radioactivity of the silver cylinder increased, but only by a little. Someone then suggested that they try a light substance, for instance, paraffin. On the morning of October 22, 1934, Fermi gouged a hole in a block of paraffin wax. He put the neutron source into the hole and the cylinder of silver on the other side, so that the paraffin was interposed between the silver and the neutron source. Down the hall with the irradiated silver Fermi discovered a hundredfold increase in the radioactivity.

"Fantastic! Incredible! Black magic!" Corbino's boys declared.

At noon, while the others were at lunch, Fermi tried to find an explanation for what had happened, something at least with a more authoritative ring to it than "black magic." He reasoned that the common denominator of the materials that had caused increased radioactivity in the metals was hydrogen. Wood contained water, which contained hydrogen. So did paraffin. Paraffin in fact contains a large amount of hydrogen, and hydrogen's nuclei are protons with the same mass as neutrons. Now it was beginning to make sense: When the neutron source was inserted into the paraffin block, the neutrons had gone out, only to collide with the protons in the paraffin's hydrogen nuclei. The collision had slowed the neutrons just as a billiard ball slows down when it collides with another billiard ball of equal size and mass. These collisions between the neutron and hydrogen protons occurred several times before the neutron emerged on the other side of the paraffin, heading toward the silver cylinder. Now these *slow neutrons* could hit the silver nuclei more accurately, as a slow golf putt has a much better chance of dropping into the hole than a very fast one, which will most likely skip over the top. "Dropping into the hole," in terms of physics, caused the artificial radioactivity, and, in the instance of the uranium atom, the slow neutron had actually split the nucleus in a manner that later would be termed *fissioning*. But for now, that process was completely misunderstood, even by Fermi. Even without fissioning, what he was witnessing seemed astonishing, but it was true.

That same afternoon, Fermi decided to test his theory further, this time with water, which is rich in hydrogen. It was a pleasant day, and he suggested that they set up the experiment in the goldfish pond behind the laboratory in the lovely private garden of Senator Corbino, where Rasetti raised his generations of salamanders. Fermi too had spent time by the enchanting little pool, listening to the lazy splashing of the carp, soothed by the sight of the water lilies in blossom, under a canopy of almond trees and perfumed flowers.

"Let's try it," Fermi said.

Knee-deep in water, their legs surrounded by the shoots of lilies and the scurrying of frightened carp, the team set up the experiment in the goldfish pond. They had taken the same silver cylinder and the same neutron source out of the laboratory. Nothing was different now except that instead of using paraffin, they were using a large quantity of water. After the neutron source had been given sufficient time to irradiate the silver—meanwhile showering the carp with neutrons—they took the cylinder inside to the room with the Geiger counters. The activity had increased, with water's hydrogen atoms' slowing down the neutrons. They had discovered beyond the question of doubt the phenomenon of *slow neutrons.*

And if they had known, they would have realized something more: They were fissioning, or splitting, atoms, too. But it would take another four long years, until 1938, before their experiments were fully understood. For now the uranium atom's behavior under bombardment caused only confusion and argument even for Fermi, who felt confident enough, without knowing exactly what he had created, to take credit for the discovery of element 93.

Four years would pass before the physics community would understand that Fermi had discovered fission, a process in nature that would become the most significant discovery since Isaac Newton's laws of gravitation in the seventeenth century. Fermi had failed to see their significance, and he was not alone. None of the great minds of physics understood a logic more unfathomable than the principles of Zen Buddhism. The slow neutron's hitting and splitting the nuclei of the heaviest elements was like a child's rolling a huge boulder with the tip of his finger. Previously, physicists had tried bombarding nuclei with electrons charged with millions of electron volts, and nothing they had done neared the effectiveness of neutrons naturally emitted from a simple source in a goldfish pond. One single, powerless, slow neutron had split the mighty atom, releasing an energy that eventually would be measured as awesome. No one in physics yet had the imagination to grasp the simple truth of Fermi's achievement.

Now, four years later, November 10, 1938, Laura and Enrico were waiting in their livingroom for the telephone call promised for six o'clock.

They had spent the day together, shopping, with royalty money from two textbooks he had written and a text for high school students written by Laura. Fermi had told her soon after they were married, "Money has the tendency of coming on its own will to those who don't look for it. I don't care for money, but it will come to me." She had believed him, and he had been right. They had wandered the shopping districts of Rome as much to distract themselves from thinking about the phone call as to satisfy needs.

They had bought wristwatches. Under normal circumstances, Enrico would have denied them the extravagance: the watches were expensive jewelry, not just time-keeping devices. But if they were to become refugees, the watches could be sold for cash outside Italy. The Fascists would not let them take their money. If they withdrew their savings all at once, the bank would notify the police.

After the watches, Laura had bought an extravagant and beautiful fur coat, her first. But for Laura, being with her husband, wandering through the city she would always love, the day held a magical quality, regardless of their extravagant shopping spree. She would never forget November 10.

Now, in the livingroom listening to the radio, Laura asked, "What if it's not the Nobel committee? Then we wasted all the money."

At a quarter to six, the phone rang.

"Well, what about the call? Isn't it coming?" asked Ginestra Amaldi, one of the "boys' " wives whom Laura had told earlier that morning about the call from Stockholm.

Laura hung up and went back to the chair. The news came on the radio. The commentator announced a second set of racial laws, which limited the civil status of Italian Jews. The announcer itemized the new restrictions: Jewish children were no longer permitted to attend public schools; Jewish teachers were suspended from their positions; Jewish lawyers, physicians, dentists, and other professionals could now take only other Jews as clients or patients. Jews were forbidden to hire "Aryan" servants or to allow them to live in their homes. Several Jewish businesses were closed.

Then, what they had feared most was made official with the broadcaster's announcement: "Passports of Jews are withdrawn. The rights, as citizens, of Italian Jews are suspended, immediately."

"What does it mean?" Laura asked. Even if the call came from Stockholm—and by now it was after six o'clock—she wondered whether she could leave.

"It means that we leave, no matter what," Fermi told her.

Then the telephone rang. Fermi answered it. The voice on the other end of the line asked for Professor Enrico Fermi. The caller was the secretary of the Swedish Academy of Sciences. He read a citation: "To Professor Enrico Fermi of Rome for his identification of new radioactive elements produced by neutron bombardment and his discovery, made in connection with his work, of nuclear reactions effected by slow neutrons."

That night they celebrated, at home with the Amaldis. They toasted and laughed, knowing that soon they would leave. Early in the evening Enrico excused himself. Alone, he went to his study, where he worked each morning. He now had the family's means of escape. As a Nobel laureate, he must be permitted to leave with his family, if only to pick up the prize in Stockholm. The ceremonies were to take place in three or four weeks. In the next few days, he would request visas from the American Embassy in Rome, and if he, Laura, and the children ever reached America by way of Sweden, he pledged to do his utmost to repay the debt of blessed sanctuary.

Part II

It hardly seemed a dignified request for a thirty-six-year-old Nobel laureate to make of his aging mother: to deliver by hand an envelope containing a letter written to the leader of the SS and the Gestapo, Reichsführer-SS Heinrich Himmler himself. But on that day in the middle of 1937 the combined emotions of fear and anger left little room in Werner Heisenberg for dignity.

His mother, the widow of a respected professor of Greek philosophy, lived modestly in a middle-class neighborhood of Munich in a small, cozy apartment furnished with oversize, comfortable chairs and sofas draped with antimacassars. Now an old, graying woman with a body as cushioned as the furniture, Mrs. Heisenberg lived for her son, understandably the pride of her life. He had brought great honor to the Heisenberg name and to the beloved memory of her deceased husband, who had been a passionate admirer of Plato, a man of "undying optimism" and "happy inner enthusiasm." Mrs. Heisenberg loved Werner for himself, of course, but she often repeated to her friends the telephone call four years ago. He had simply said to her, "Mama, I congratulate you on your son—I've just won the Nobel Prize." He had been the best son a mother could want, sharing with her his triumphs and his gifts. And now that he had come to her for help, she was ready to lighten his concern, and even some of his anger.

A recent article in the weekly SS newspaper, *Das Schwarze Korps,* had accused him of being a "white Jew," "not a Jew by race" but "a Jew in spirit, inclination and character." In the Germany of 1937, no accusation was more threatening. And there had been more, many more: "This representative of Einstein's 'spirit' in the new Germany was . . . made professor at Leipzig at the age of 26, at an age that hardly gave him any time to carry on thorough research." And so forth, with phrases such as "Jewish pawn" and "Jewish lover." The last sentence called him "a representative of Jewry in German intellectual life, and they [people like him] must vanish just like the Jews." Some of *Das Schwarze Korps*'s readers replied in letters to the magazine that Heisenberg should vanish too. One of them wrote, "A concentration camp is doubtlessly a suitable location for Mr. Heisenberg."

The pressure exerted on Heisenberg to knuckle under by espousing the so-called Aryan physics went beyond threats in the SS magazine. At one point shortly after the magazine article appeared, Heisenberg received a notification to appear at the Prinzalbertstrasse headquarters of the SS in Berlin to be questioned about why he refused to subscribe to the racially pure Nazi physics: was his reluctance due to an unpatriotic attitude, was he acting as a traitor, or was the answer something different, related to "pure" physics perhaps? The SS demanded to know. The Nazis had not actually banned the so-called Jewish physics, although the SS had espoused the beliefs of the Aryans, which ignored the contributions of Jews. It was no crime not to believe, but life and promotion would be much easier for Heisenberg if he would play along with their Aryan concepts. And there were times, like now, when he wished he had. The memory of the cellars of the SS headquarters haunted him. An SS officer had led him to a room for interrogations and seated him on a bare wooden chair facing a large, boldly lettered sign that read BREATHE DEEPLY AND CALMLY.

The psychological battering would have frightened the bravest of men, even ones who knew they were innocent of any crime as Heisenberg did, but the SS treatment affected him even more, primarily because of his peculiar disposition. Heisenberg was a man of incredible sensitivity, which was reflected in his love of classical music, in his fondness for the piano, which he played with precision and great feeling. Although he was strong physically, well-muscled and broad-shouldered, with a shock of bright blond hair swept straight back from his forehead; widely separated eyes; a narrow, refined nose; and thin, thoughtful lips, his outward appearance of the idealized German farm boy belied the currents that ran inside Werner Heisenberg. He required constant harmony. To work to its remarkable capacity, his intellect demanded of the forces around him a fine and delicate tuning. There could be neither chaos nor a complete lack of stimulation. This balance of forces, until now, Heisenberg could control himself. They had always been in equilibrium during his years in university and after, when he had done some of his best research. The charges in the SS newspaper, however, had removed that balance from his control. The newspaper charges had frightened him even more because they were so untrue. He neither loved nor hated Jews. He respected their contributions, particularly to mathematics and physics. He had used and built on their contributions, so how could he believe otherwise? But personally, he thought no more about Jews than he did about Catholics and Lutherans. That the "Aryan physicists" suddenly had declared the contributions of all Jews to science as invalid meant little to Heisenberg. One could not simply invalidate scientific fact by an SS decree. The Aryans pretended to ignore Einstein's theory of relativity because Einstein was a Jew, and, therefore, anything he had created with his mind was suspect to the Aryans. But to ignore Einstein, Heisenberg knew, was an impossible and foolish task if Germany wanted to maintain her preeminent position in science. And by its attack on him, the Aryans, through the SS, wanted Heisenberg to lend his considerable weight to their folly. He didn't care what the Aryans did; they could believe that the earth was the center of the solar system if they liked. But he did not want them to use fear and intimidation to force other scientists, like him, to subscribe to their beliefs. Any Aryan success in science would eventually be fatal for German science, and Heisenberg felt strongly about Germany. He was proud to be German. Except for certain of its excesses, he was just as proud of the new Germany that the Nazis had lifted out of the ashes of World War I and the dreaded Weimar Republic. If he had felt less for Germany, he could have emigrated to England or America as so many other German, and nearly all German Jewish, physicists already had. He still could flee. And if he did not receive the satisfaction he sought, then he still might leave with his wife and twins.

His mother was acquainted with Mrs. Himmler, mother of the Reichsführer-SS. Heisenberg's grandfather had taught on the same high school faculty in Munich as Himmler's father. Werner Heisenberg and Heinrich Himmler had not been friends, but they had traced each other's careers as politician and as scientist.

Heisenberg handed the envelope to his mother, who read the letter, at his request. It began with the formal salutation "Sehr Geehrter Herr Reichsführer! I must request a fundamental decision. I request you, as Reichsführer of the SS, for effective protection against such attacks in a newspaper under your control." He demanded "the restoration of his honor" and signed it with a perfunctory "Heil Hitler!"

His mother agreed to deliver the letter to Mrs. Himmler, who lived nearby in an apartment of equal modesty. Mrs. Heisenberg would ask her to give the letter personally to her son. That way, the Heisenbergs, mother and son, felt certain, the letter would receive the most favorable reading.

If Himmler did not restore his "honor," Heisenberg would reconsider leaving Germany; and if his "honor" were restored, he would contribute his genius in any way that the new Germany demanded.

Heisenberg heard nothing, no news one way or another from Reichsführer-SS Himmler, for nearly one year. No news, Heisenberg guessed, probably meant bad news.

Mrs. Heisenberg had explained the problem to Mrs. Himmler, who had listened with sympathy, a crucifix on the wall over the chair where she sat. "If my little Heinrich knew, he could certainly put an end to these accusations. I will talk to him and give him the letter." Mrs. Heisenberg embraced her and then put on her coat to leave. When she had reached the door, Mrs. Himmler said, "Wait just a minute. Do you think, Mrs. Heisenberg, that maybe my little Heinrich might not be on the right track after all?" She had laughed a dry, old woman's laugh.

Heisenberg, by now, had reached a peak of apprehension. The waiting had drained him. He had done everything, even degrading himself by begging powerful friends to speak with Himmler on his behalf. The Nazis owed him an apology and not only because he had done nothing wrong. He had not failed; Nazism had, and he owed it to Germany to set Nazi science right. Everything he had done was right. He searched his past, and he had found no wrong turn. Beginning in his earliest days, teachers had praised him. "He has an eye for what is essential and never gets lost in details," they had written to his parents. "His thought processes in grammar and mathematics operate rapidly and usually without mistakes." He showed "spontaneous diligence, great interest and thoroughness, and ambition." He was the best at everything he tried. He skied faster, won more often at chess. He needed to be the best, the first, the most outstanding. Then at the Munich University, he had become the protégé of Arnold Sommerfeld, then one of Germany's distinguished physicists and teachers. In the very first physics lecture, Heisenberg had stood conventional theory on its head by inventing half integers in quantum theory, where only integers had existed before. Sommerfeld had taught him all he knew. Then Heisenberg had studied in Copenhagen under the great man of physics, Niels Bohr, who taught him philosophy, essential to theoretical physics. Bohr lectured each June at what was known as the Bohr Festival in Göttingen, Germany. Young physicists from around the world competed for invitations to these festivals. Heisenberg had attended a festival and met Bohr first in 1922, and the experience had changed his life. He had discovered a true mentor, Niels Bohr himself. And he sought to become his acolyte. "He spoke softly," Heisenberg later rhapsodized, "somewhat haltingly, but behind each of his carefully chosen words was apparent a long chain of thoughts which vanished somewhere in the background of a philosophical attitude I found highly stimulating." So challenging and intelligent were Heisenberg's scientific comments that the other physicists "stared at him in wonder." Bohr had invited him on a walk in the mountains around Göttingen, an honor that was singular and unprecedented for a twenty-one-year-old student. That walk "exerted a decisive influence" on his life. Bohr taught him to intuit. "Heisenberg understands everything," Bohr said.

Another twenty-one-year-old at the 1922 festival had also sought the approval of the great man of physics. But Bohr barely noticed Enrico Fermi, who had stayed quietly in the background, wondering whether perhaps in Italy he was merely a large fish in a small pond. Heisenberg, blond with chiseled German features, was that summer's golden boy, and he had not welcomed even the potential challenge of any other young man near his age. The experience at the festival upset Enrico Fermi, who had returned to Italy with his self-confidence in tatters. Nothing specific had happened. No word was spoken about the pecking order, but neither man forgot, for different reasons, the festival of 1922.

Heisenberg had later joined Bohr in Copenhagen as a research associate at the Institute of Theoretical Physics. A year later, he "laid a big quantum egg," according to no less a light than Albert Einstein, who became enthusiastic after reading Heisenberg's discovery with Bohr of a long-sought calculus theory. "A unique excitement . . . replaced sombre resignation among we lethargic scientists," Einstein said. Essentially, Heisenberg had helped to create the new quantum physics.

Then, on November 9, 1932, Heisenberg had won the Nobel Prize for "the establishment of quantum physics." Instantly, he became a national celebrity, talked about in the press and watched by an admiring public. He basked in the limelight. One evening at Bücking's, the Munich publishers who often hosted cultural evenings, he had accepted an invitation to play piano in a trio. The audience was small, and as he played Beethoven's G-Major Trio, Heisenberg had looked across the piano into the radiant face of a beautiful blond girl named Elisabeth Schumacher. In the days that followed, the two had made much music together, in Leipzig and at the ski station at Himmelmoosalm. The daughter of a professor of economics, she was bright and spirited and Germanic. Their views fused to create a deep love, and so, in April 1937, they had married.

He had done everything right, or as right as was humanly possible. Perhaps, he had been too perfect, a model whom lesser physicists—the so-called Aryans—wanted to discredit. As the prominent German physicist, he might have expected to run afoul of these "Nazi scientists," who had been operating on the fringes of German science for years as "national researchers," led by the Nobel laureates Philipp Lenard and Johannes Stark. Their purpose had less relation to science than to race. They described Einstein's theories as "Jewish world bluff" and discredited *any* science or philosophy based on them. They tried to devise a physics counter to the modern physics of quantum and relativity theories. The Aryans did not want to create new physics so much as to return to the physics of the nineteenth century as fundamentalists were doing with Darwin's theories. Viewed generously as cranks at first, the Aryans were soon adopted by the SS. By now they were a force to be feared, if not for their numbers then for the credibility given to their movement by the SS.

In the darkest hours, Heisenberg had written to a friend, "Everything looks very bad for the moment. What is most unpleasant for me is that I don't know what will happen, whether I will stay here or not." He wrote again a few weeks later that "the situation facing us has gotten worse. I now see no other possibility except submit my resignation [to the University of Leipzig, where he was professor of physics] if protection of my honor is denied here. You know that it would be painful for me to leave Germany. I don't want to do that unless it's absolutely necessary."

Then one day in the fall of 1938, the postman delivered an envelope printed with the runic SS of the Gestapo, from the desk of the Reichsführer-SS himself. Heisenberg opened the envelope and unfolded the stationery, knowing that the words on the page would seal his fate: "Precisely because you were recommended to me by my family," Himmler wrote, "I caused your case to be examined with special care and intensity. I take pleasure in being able to inform you that I do not approve of the attack made against you in the article in *Das Schwarze Korps* and that I have insured that there will be no further attacks on your person. . . ." Himmler rebuked him only for failing to "make a clear distinction for [his] students between the scientific qualities of research work and the researcher's human and political attitudes," an unclear statement of distinction between Jews and their scientific contributions. Otherwise, outright warmth, one of Himmler's less developed qualities, characterized the missive.

The relief from the year's tension soon transformed itself for Heisenberg into gratitude. His honor, and, symbolically, that of Germany, was restored. He felt relief not so much because he knew now that the SS would leave him and other non-Aryan physicists alone. Heisenberg knew that now German physicists could move forward. They had always held a position in the forefront of physics and never more than now. Heisenberg recognized, as did Fermi and nearly every other young physicist in Europe at that time, that the great moment of discovery in physics was at hand. Reputations were being made daily. It was as if physics were a stream strewn with nuggets of gold for anyone with the energy to bend down to pick them up. Heisenberg wanted all physics to benefit from the knowledge that German physicists and he in particular would contribute. He had contracted the "fever," and now the SS had given him the freedom to explore at will. Even the SS recognized that Heisenberg might benefit Nazi Germany. As Heisenberg was reading the letter from Himmler, another letter from the SS leader was going out to his second in command, Reinhard Heydrich: "I too believe that Heisenberg is respectable, and we cannot afford to lose or to neutralize a man who is relatively young and can bring on young scientists," he wrote. The Reich needed a man like Heisenberg, especially now that so many gifted scientists had abandoned Germany in terror. Heisenberg was ready and willing to serve physics and Germany.

On the morning of July 17, 1938, Otto Hahn promised never to forget her. As a token of remembrance he placed in the outstretched hand of Lise Meitner, the woman he loved, the diamond engagement ring that his father had given to his mother. Then he said good-bye.

This gesture suited Hahn. For most of his life, as an unremarkable radiochemist, he had outwardly observed the strict nineteenth-century rules of decorum. Dignity hallmarked him, even shaped him. He was small, stoop-shouldered, with thinning black hair. His features were pinched, and he hooked a prim pince-nez across the bridge of his nose. Few people remembered seeing him in anything but a shine-worn black suit and white shirt. The symphonies of Beethoven, Mozart, and Tchaikovsky enraptured him, and he enjoyed a reputation as an avid glee singer.

He had first seen Lise Meitner nearly thirty years before, when she had come from Vienna to attend lectures on theoretical physics. He had asked her to stay for a few days, even though he knew that the presence of a woman in the Berlin laboratory where he worked would raise eyebrows. (He had restricted her to the carpenter shed; she could, of course, because she was a woman, never enter the second-floor library and reading rooms of the Institute, the Kaiser Wilhelm II Institute of Chemistry, of which Hahn was the director.) How could he not have asked her to stay? She was accomplished, one of the handful of women studying theoretical physics, and she was striking in appearance, brooding and mysterious. She pulled her long dark hair close to her head. She had strong, dark eyebrows and nearly black eyes that suited her highly independent, strong-willed character. She worked side by side with Hahn for long hours each day. In the evenings before the shops closed, she bought cheese and cold meats for them to eat at their workbenches. Before long her temporary position at the institute became permanent; after three years the institute had named her director of the nuclear physics department.

Lise Meitner was Jewish, but religion formed no more a part of her life than it did for Laura Fermi, whom she had befriended at the 1927 Lake Como Solvay Congress. She had worked without restraints as a Jew after the advent of Hitler; Nazi racial laws did not apply to her because as an Austrian, she was a foreigner. The Nazis even praised her institute as "a model institution of National Socialist Science," and she remained.

Why had Lise Meitner waited until now? Distinguished for her intellect, she too had been blind to the content of recent political change. It would have seemed natural that someone of her intelligence had heard rumors of Hitler's "excesses," the deportations, the military adventurism, or the deterioration of Germany's foreign relations. But this simply, unbelievably, was not so. Meitner and the others—Hahn, Fermi, even Heisenberg—inhabited an interior universe in which politics and such concepts of nationality meant little. Their universe was physics, a place as hermetic as its concepts were vast and expansive. For them, nothing else existed. If food were not placed in front of them they would not have noticed until they were near to starving. Politically, Meitner was now close to starving. Hahn had less of an excuse; when he thought about such things, he approved of this new German spirit. Hitler and the Nazis were helping Germany, the Germans in Germany, anyway.

Lise Meitner already had spoken to the president of the institute, who in turn had asked the Reich minister of education whether she could leave Germany for a neutral country, Sweden or Switzerland. The minister had argued that as a Jewish refugee she might spread anti-German propaganda. Nobody planned to arrest her in Germany, anyway, the minister said. She would be stripped of her official titles at the institute, but her work naturally could continue.

The Anschluss had changed all that, overnight. With the annexation of Austria, Austrians like Meitner were now under the laws of the Reich, including its sweeping racial laws. Now she might be arrested and might be sent to the detention camps at Dachau, Buchenwald, or Ravensbrück. The Anschluss had made Meitner's decision. She had no choice but to emigrate. And yet her dilemma was similar to that of other, non-Jewish scientists, men like Heisenberg and Fermi. Flight meant disruption, and disruption meant a break in the continuity of research, which gave other physicists in other countries the time to make the significant breakthroughs that all the prominent physicists sought for themselves. Meitner had reached an important juncture in her work at the institute with Hahn. The timing of her departure could not have been worse for the progress of the research. Together, she and Hahn had discovered protactinium, and recently they had fol-

lowed exactly the steps taken earlier by Fermi on the bombardment of uranium with neutrons in an attempt to solve the puzzle
of his element 93 and the transuranic elements that Fermi's neutron bombardment apparently had created. Teams in England and
France were working on the same problem. For many physicists
the enigma of the transuranic elements held the key to the behavior of the atom's nucleus. Meitner and Hahn thought that they had
identified barium as one of those transuranic elements. And yet if
barium resulted from the transformation of the uranium nucleus by
its bombardment with neutrons, then the accepted laws of nuclear
behavior would have to be reassessed. Meitner and Hahn envisioned the neutron's hitting the uranium nucleus with enough force
to crack and shatter it into several pieces. The process was still
essentially a mystery, but they felt confident enough about their
research so far to feel within reach of an answer. Meitner and
Hahn had hoped to continue this research together, working side
by side as they had for so many years. But that hope had become
an impossibility.

As Meitner had finalized plans to leave Germany, Hahn had
established a method by which they might continue their work
together. Of course, it wouldn't be the same, but it would still be
a collaboration. He would continue working on the problem at the
institute. When he had something on which he wanted to confer
with her, he would write or telephone to her either in Holland or
in Sweden. She should devote her time away from the institute to
thinking about the problem. Distance from the familiar laboratory
and the routine of such long standing would either concentrate her
attention or throw her ability to analyze and synthesize into a
tailspin.

A Dutch friend would accompany her, according to the arrangements made carefully in advance, on the train trip from Berlin to Amsterdam. From Holland she would travel alone, probably
to Sweden, a neutral country in which the leading university for
physics research had promised her a full-time position. But first,
before assuming that position or conferring from a distance with
Hahn or thinking about the problem of the behavior of the atom's

nucleus, Meitner would travel a relatively short and very perilous distance between Berlin and the Dutch border. Meitner had been warned that the train would stop at the border. The Gestapo often spot-checked passports, searching for fleeing Jews.

Now at the Berlin station as Hahn gave her the engagement ring, she cried. He was not one for public displays of affection, but he braved a kiss. Then he waved good-bye.

As she watched Hahn disappear, Lise Meitner felt as if she were dying. And part of her had died in this wrenching dislocation. Nearly her whole life was represented on that train platform, now fading into the distance so that she could barely make out Hahn's form. What she and Hahn had together was better and deeper than marriage or the traditional currents that run between a man and woman. They were partners in the best sense, each respecting and even admiring the abilities and accomplishments of the other. They knew the habits and the rhythms of the other too. Much of their work proceeded mechanically without the need for words and instructions. They knew each other so well by now that they worked on instinct and, to no small degree, deep affection. In that sense, they had become, as a couple, one person.

The separation, she felt even as the train was leaving the station, had the signs of severe trauma. Without him she felt disoriented. She might be able to get through the next few hours and the next few days with him by her side; without him, though, what lay ahead was even more terrifying, continuing as it did the specter of the SS, concentration camps, and this desperate flight. Meitner had no home now; no place to work; no friends, and one relative, a young nephew working in Copenhagen with Niels Bohr; and no one in whom she could confide her deepest fears and most dizzying confusions.

As the train headed west through the sprawling Berlin suburbs, Meitner opened a book and tried to read. Other passengers in her cabin took no notice of her, as if she were invisible. She thought that she had always considered herself strong-willed and independent, a woman who did not fit the mold of the vast majority of the world's women. That had been her pride: to have succeeded in a man's domain. She had earned her success; nothing had been given to her. But the independence, she could see now, was something of an illusion. It was the same for all physicists at the institute, perhaps all scientists in Germany who had huddled in their towers, in the holy name of science, ignoring responsibility to the society in which they lived. She might still be oblivious, if she were not a Jew.

How highly scientists—and physicists in particular—thought of themselves. The physicist reduced nature to its simplest forms, to atoms, reducing and simplifying. The worlds of people, politics, societies were beyond their comprehension. They were complicated and resisted reduction. But what a price they were paying for their isolation. Lise Meitner had reduced her world to the shadow of Otto Hahn. What she felt for him in her heart went unspoken and unacted upon. The photograph she kept of them together—taken in the laboratory, of course—reflected an aspect of their relationship. In the photo she stood to the right and slightly behind him. She was gazing on him fondly, as he stared commandingly into the camera.

Otto Hahn, her "cockerel," as she called him, was a man of patience and method. He possessed the stubborn traits required of all good radiochemists. But Lise was not suited to the harness. She had an imagination that had nearly withered; that was how willful and independent she really was. At first her imagination had trouble fitting in with his dogged persistence, like earth and fire. But as time went by, she had buckled into the routine of Otto Hahn, and her identity had fused to a large extent with his. At a conference once she had said to a colleague, "I think you have confused me with Otto Hahn."

Maybe this separation would be good for her. If this were to be a rebirth, the first few hours were going to be the most difficult, but if she survived, she could survive anything. And in survival and rebirth perhaps she might regain her independent identity and the fire of her imagination. Hahn would be fine without her. He would miss her, naturally, but his habits and routine were such by now that no separation would affect his work for long.

The train drove on through Magdeburg and Brunswick and Hannover and Osnabrück, pointing inevitably to the border with Holland at the terminus of Enschede near the Rhine. The passengers in the cabin seemed restless, either from apprehension of what lay ahead or from relief from what lay behind. No matter how one prepared in July 1938, even if every paper, visa, and document were in perfect order, the SS often decided one's fate on nothing but the glint of an eye. The conductor in the passage yelled out, "Enschede—passport control."

Meitner fished in her handbag for the little-used Austrian passport. Each entry-exit mark represented a scientific conference. She rarely traveled for any other reason. Now, the passport was nothing but a document with her name, date, place of birth, profession, and photo. It contained no magic power without a visa from the Dutch and permission from the Reich Foreign Ministry to travel across international boundaries. The passport told anyone who cared to look at it that she was a Jew escaping Nazi Germany.

The passport control officials were starting slowly to make their way from the head of the train back to the last car. Sometimes, her Dutch traveling companion told her, the German border guards handed over the whole train to the Dutch officials. Fewer Jews were trying to escape Germany now, because capture was almost inevitable. Jews sought other means than trains, and other places than the Dutch border. If she was lucky, she would not see a uniformed German checking passports on the train at all.

An official came down the passageway. A man in a uniform appeared outside the compartment door. He wore a blue cap, jacket, and pants, and around his neck, connected by a leather strap, hung a small writing surface. He knocked on the glass door, then entered the compartment.

She tried to decide whether or not he was a German as he checked the papers of those passengers nearest the door. Compliantly, she handed up her passport when her turn came. He placed it on his writing surface and flipped its pages. He looked at her, then at her photograph. He reached into a leather pouch attached to his belt and slapped a blank page with the stamp. As he handed the passport down, he said, "Welcome to Holland."

───

"Nothing can stop us now," Enrico Fermi said to Laura as their train picked up speed out of the Rome Central Station at the beginning of December 1938.

Laura searched for comfort in his assurances, but the last weeks had been so hectic that she felt exhausted, irritable, and scared. Nella and Giulio shared their *wagon lits* compartment with the nanny, and Laura and Enrico occupied one of their own. Suitcases were everywhere, making movement difficult; her new beaver coat hung on a hook. But the train was moving, and after the last few days, that they were all aboard was a miracle.

Laura had insisted that the nanny accompany them to Stockholm and onward to New York, even if the woman had nothing more helpful to do than twist strands of Giulio's blond hair into a tubelike curl. She was an ally with whom Laura could speak Italian when Enrico was not there; her presence would give Laura a measure of freedom away from the children. However, the nanny's visa had been a problem. The immigrants' quota for America was exhausted, and the nanny could not offer in return for a visitor's visa an assurance that she would return to Italy. But the Nobel Prize worked its magic, and the visa came through. The American Consul even overlooked Nella's poor eyesight; such a medical "defect" should have been corrected to qualify under normal conditions, but Nobel's authority had seemed to cover health, too.

Before giving him his visa, a young woman in the consulate had tested Enrico for intelligence.

"How much is 15 plus 27?" she had asked.

"42," he answered, pleased with his answer. No matter what he was, he still had to take the test.

"How much is 29 divided by 2?" the woman asked.

"14.5," Enrico answered.

He had passed, little Giulio was excused, and Nella and Laura answered their questions perfectly too.

They received their American visas.

They had said good-bye to their friends. Nearly everybody was scattering; the "boys" were searching for teaching and research positions abroad, and they did not know whether they would ever see each other again, let alone work together. It was a time of great anxiety heightened by the complaints of some friends that the Fermis were abandoning Italy in her hour of need. "What will become of the university students?" one of them had asked Enrico, angrily. "Do you not have a responsibility to them?"

Fermi had not argued. It was none of their business.

Enrico could say that nothing could stop them now, but Laura would not cease worrying. Many things could stop them now: this train had brakes, and it had doors through which they could be pulled. They had not yet left Italy, and the whole of Germany, from south to north, stretched before them. They might be fleeing Italy, she had told Enrico, but their route took them through the heart of Nazidom.

It baffled her how he could say things like "nothing could stop them now." He was always so sure of himself; self-doubt never haunted him, as far as she could tell. He believed in inevitability: What would happen would happen, despite anything he did—or worried about or struggled against—to change the outcome. It was fatalistic, to a degree, but this philosophy also made the world easier to bear. Fermi seemed to float through life's dangers unhindered, as if he were imitating the neutron. With no electrical charge, it had floated into the nucleus, whereas the proton propelled by 8 million volts had failed.

The source of this stoicism, she guessed, probably lay buried in his youth. Enrico was the youngest of three children. Their father, poorly educated but ambitious, had risen through the ranks of the civil service to become an inspector for the Ministry of Railroads; their mother was a stern secondary school teacher from the south of Italy. They had lived as a close-knit family in the shantytown district of Rome, near the railroad station. Immediately after Enrico was born in 1901, wet nurses in the country had raised him until he was nearly three. His father had introduced Enrico to mathematics; almost before he could read, he had understood why the equation

$$x^2 + y^2 = r^2$$

represented a circle. He showed exceptional talent in school, and in his free time, he built electrical motors and toys and conducted mechanical experiments, usually with his older brother Giulio, whom he adored. Together, they had inhabited a deeply private world, to the total exclusion of other children. When Enrico was nearly thirteen, a minor abscess had developed in Giulio's throat. He was to have it lanced, a simple procedure, and never awoke from the anesthesia. This tragedy plunged Enrico into loneliness, introversion, and brooding. He had fled the loss into an abstract, emotionless world of numbers.

At the Scuola Normale Superiore, he wrote on the "characteristics of sound" with the learning and intelligence of a doctoral candidate, when he was only a high school teenager. He would remain introverted for the rest of his life, although Laura taught him the value of humor and playfulness. She knew him better than anyone, but she did not understand the source of his utter self-confidence. He never showed fear, or even apprehension. Fear to him was a problem to be solved. Fear was not logical, and therefore its existence could not be real. He attacked fear with logic. Maybe that was why he said the things he did. To fear this voyage across the Third Reich was not logical. Ergo, nothing could stop them now.

Unless something did stop them. Laura had told the children, especially little Nella, to remain silent on the train. A chatty child, and, precocious in her way, Nella seemed to pick information out of the air. Laura did not want her to blurt out family secrets to strangers.

If all went well, they would reach the United States, but the rest of Laura's family had no hope of emigrating. Her father presented her with a serious problem. He refused to believe his own eyes; he would not see that Jews were in danger: the simplest precautions taken by every Italian Jew were anathema to him. He was flaunting his Jewishness as if to test the resolve of the anti-Semites. She feared that it would not end well for him.

The first evening out, Enrico read an Agatha Christie mystery between sessions of polishing his Nobel acceptance speech. The sun had set and the children were ready for bed; the lights from an occasional village flashed in the windows. Later that same night they crossed the Brenner Pass into Germany.

The train stopped at the border, and the Italian officials boarded. They looked at the Fermis' passports without comment. A few minutes later, the German official boarded. Formal and unbending, he asked to see their passports. Enrico's lips were pressed together so tightly that they formed a single line. Inside the compartment, Nella started to ask questions. Laura told her to be quiet. The German repeatedly flipped through the passports, as if he were looking for something in particular.

"Is everything all right?" Enrico asked him in German.

In the background, Nella shouted, "Is he going to send us back to Mussolini?"

"Be quiet, Nella," Laura said.

The German border guard looked at her.

"Why is he taking so long?" Nella asked. This time Laura took her by the arm.

"Have you visas from the German Konsulat?" the German asked.

Enrico nodded, then gestured with his hand for the passports. He showed the visa page to the guard, relieved that the German wanted nothing more, nothing that he could not give.

The German inspected the dates, then wished them good night and turned down the corridor.

It was over.

Laura went to Nella and said, "Now go back to sleep. Nothing is wrong."

Soon the train reached the shores of the Baltic. After a turbulent and freezing sea passage, they arrived in Stockholm. It was December 8, 1938.

Gustavus V of Sweden held out a small case and a diploma. Enrico Fermi watched the king from his seat above on the stage of Stockholm's Concert Hall. To his left in a high-backed chair identical to the one in which he was seated, the author Pearl S. Buck, that year's only other recipient of the Nobel Prize, waited her turn. Enrico knew that it was now that he was supposed to descend the steps, but he did not dare to move. His shirt, stiff with starch and too small for his chest, threatened to explode out of his swallow-tail coat upward into his face, as it had done when he was dressing. Any slight movement, he feared, might trigger it. All eyes were on him, and the king was waiting with outstretched arms.

He moved cautiously, as if he were twice his thirty-seven years, descending the four steps of the stage with the care of an arthritic. The top of his head came level with the monarch's chest of ribbons and decorations, such was the discrepancy in their height. Fermi took the medal, an envelope, and the diploma, then retraced his steps backward, according to the custom forbidding "commoners" from turning their backs on kings. Somehow, he navigated the stairs without stumbling, without his shirt's behaving like a spring. He sank into his seat with an expression of such relief that Laura, in the audience, thought she could hear him sigh.

Later, across Stockholm in the marbled elegance of the Town Hall, Crown Prince Gustavus Adolphus asked Laura to dance. He led her with such confidence and grace that he made the Lambeth Walk fun. Although the elegant court ladies-in-waiting and some princesses made a point of complimenting her evening gown, part of what she called her "refugee's trousseau," even asking the name of her dressmaker to help her relax, this was only and forever after "the evening she danced with a prince."

The next day Enrico called on Lise Meitner. She had stayed

only a short while in Holland before coming to Stockholm to join the laboratory of Manne Siegbahn, where she was now settled. Fermi, who had known her through years of attendance at conferences, was solicitous and kind in his own quiet way, inquiring about her and her work. He had come to see her less out of kindness than professional respect; he knew that she and Hahn had repeated his earlier experiments, and he wanted to know what they had learned, whether they had come any closer to the riddle of the transuranic elements. She was in touch by mail and telephone with Hahn in Berlin, she told him, and, somehow, they had found a means of keeping their joint research going. The arrangement, reporting findings by letter and telephone, was a dramatic break for her. As she had expected, she was finding the separation difficult.

In passing, Fermi mentioned Irène Joliot-Curie, the daughter of the two-time Nobel laureate Marie Curie and winner of a prize in physics on her own. Irène was the bane of Lise Meitner's professional existence. More than once they had called each other liars.

Lise Meitner probably had started the long contretemps, at the 1933 Solvay Congress in Brussels, when she had contradicted the French woman on a point of theory. The majority of physicists had agreed with Meitner. Nevertheless, Madame Joliot-Curie had published a paper on the theory, that everybody, led by Meitner, had doubted. "Madame Joliot-Curie," Meitner had commented, "is still relying on the chemical knowledge she received from her famous mother and that knowledge is just a bit out of date today." In a private note Hahn had suggested that Madame Joliot-Curie repeat the experiments in question. But only last summer Madame Joliot-Curie had published a second and a third paper, which Hahn had not cared to read and did not send along to Lise Meitner in Sweden. But Hahn's assistant had read it and insisted that Hahn read it too. "I'm not interested in our lady friend's latest writings," he said. The assistant told him what the paper said. Hahn put down the cigar he was smoking and went to his laboratory. As it had turned out, Lise Meitner's rival had searched out a brave new direction to answer the riddle of what Fermi had created in 1934 when he had bombarded the nuclei of uranium with neutrons to transform the element into a series of mysterious "transuranic" elements. It was thought that the process of nuclear transformation could be understood if only the transformed, new elements could be correctly identified. Now, Irène Curie thought that the bombardment of uranium produced a substance similar to lanthanum, which joined Hahn and Meitner's barium and the other physicists' nominees, herperium and ausonium, as the correct transformed "transuranic." The physicists did not so much care which element the bombardment of uranium had produced; identifying the correct element, however, could tell them what process the bombarded uranium nucleus had undergone: whether it had cracked, or split, or had absorbed the neutron to form the new, as yet unidentified, element. The search by now had assumed the form of a heated international race. To the winner would come acclaim and perhaps even a Nobel Prize.

"Are you certain it isn't radium?" Fermi asked Meitner, who had explained Hahn's idea that the bombardment created radioactive barium.

"That's what he thought at first. But he thinks it's radioactive barium."

Nobody would know until the "transuranic" by-product of the neutron-bombarded uranium was produced in large enough quantities for chemical analysis and weighing.

Fermi sensed that bombarding uranium should not create barium, unless everybody had misinterpreted what was transpiring in that tiny submicroscopic atomic universe. He asked Meitner, "In what quantities did Hahn find barium?"

"Not enough yet, I'm afraid, to be weighed," she said.

By the fall of 1938 and a Nobel Prize later, Fermi was far from unknown to the mentor of all gifted young physicists; indeed, Niels Bohr had not only spotted Fermi's unique gifts but had helped to nurture them, just as he had done earlier for Werner. Heisenberg. Yet somewhat different from Heisenberg, the Fermis and the Bohrs had established such a warm relationship that they celebrated the Christmas of 1938 together in Copenhagen. Meanwhile, Lise Meitner, alone, hit an emotional bottom and was spending her holidays in the desolate seaside village of Kungälv in southern Sweden. It was bitterly cold there, with nothing to do but walk, think, and ski across endless flats. Her nephew, Otto Frisch, one of Bohr's promising young researchers in Copenhagen, had agreed to join her providing that they not discuss physics.

Frisch had never seen his aunt quite so manic. She would not be quiet. If there had been hills on the landscape, he would have skied away, but she doggedly followed him, talking incessantly.

One day during their Christmas stay a letter came from Berlin. "We are working on the uranium substances," Otto Hahn wrote to Meitner. "It is now practically eleven o'clock at night. Strassmann [his colleague] will be coming back at a quarter to twelve, so that I can get off home at last. The thing is: there's something so odd about the 'radium isotopes' that for the moment we don't want to tell anyone but you." The substance produced *must* be radioactive barium, he wrote. He had signed off, "All rather tricky! But we *must* clear this thing up. . . ."

Clear it up, indeed. Meitner wanted that more than anything, if for no other reason than to get the better of Madame Joliot-Curie. Meitner showed the letter to her nephew, asking him what he thought. He told her that he did not want to discuss it.

She convinced him to walk with her in the snow "to clear their heads." As they progressed along the flat, barren landscape, in spite of himself, Frisch said, "It can't be barium."

"But it is. Otto is not wrong. If he says it's barium, then that's what it is."

They argued like that for the next few miles, and gradually a vague picture started to form in Meitner's head. She became more and more excited, as it focused in her mind.

"What if the atom splits into two fractions: barium and krypton?" she asked.

The atomic numbers were correct; barium had a nuclear charge of 56 and krypton of 36, equaling 92, the number of protons in the nucleus of the uranium atom!

The process was phenomenally different from what everybody had envisioned. Meitner saw the nucleus now as a droplet. When hit by a neutron, the nucleus had not shattered or absorbed the neutron. It had elongated, formed a "waist," and then split like a bacterium doubling in its reproductive cycle. Borrowing a term from biology, the atom had *fissioned*. The split, or fission, created by the neutron liberated a proportionately massive quantity of energy from within the nucleus. Frisch calculated that one tiny atomic nucleus, when fissioned, could produce the energy to lift a grain of sand in the air.

Later that same day, Frisch wrote, "Feel as if I had caught an elephant by its tail, without meaning to, while walking through a jungle. And now I don't know what to do with it." Together they sat at a desk and coauthored an article on fission for the English journal *Nature,* the authoritative physics publication. The article was published soon after, in February 1939. Hahn also summarized his findings in the January 6, 1939, edition of the German *Naturwissenschaften.*

The key to Pandora's box had been found, and it was now available, for the cost of a magazine, to anyone anywhere.

Afterward Frisch kissed his aunt good-bye and rushed to Copenhagen to tell Niels Bohr, who was packing for a visit to New York, fast on the heels of the Fermis, who were then halfway across the Atlantic aboard the S.S. *Franconia.*

Lisa Meitner immediately returned to Stockholm, as excited by their discovery as her nephew and able to derive such a measure of satisfaction from her incredible triumph that she could put behind her some of the disorientation she had felt without Hahn. If only she had known where her theory of fission would lead, she might have hesitated, even for an instant, before announcing it in *Nature.* As one who had just fled the Nazi terror, she should have known that such a scientific breakthrough might have political applications, for evil as well as for good. But for now this was her triumph, and she would not be denied. Fission soon burst into the quiet, sheltered halls of science.

———

Enrico Fermi smiled his broadest, holding Nella and Giulio close, near the rail. "We have found the American branch of the Fermi family. Look," he said, pointing. The Statue of Liberty was shrouded in the cold gray dawn off the port side of the S.S. *Franconia,* as it entered New York Harbor. Nella and Giulio peered into the far distance toward the bow-shaped outline of lower Manhattan. For Laura, whom Fermi had roused out of a warm and comfortable berth to witness the sight, the landfall meant safety.

They might have been more apprehensive if they had been total strangers there, but the Fermis had visited America on several successive summers, as guests of institutes and universities (they had grown especially fond of the University of Michigan, less for the university than for Sam Goudsmit, a Dutch physicist and a Jew who had emigrated to join the Ann Arbor faculty). On those visits they had experienced the wonderful circus excitement that a tourist feels. Enrico had driven them in a car wherever they went, from New York to Ann Arbor and back again. He loved motoring through America's open spaces, and he always insisted on taking the wheel himself. Only once, much later, would he ever relinquish control of a car. On those early visits their Ford had broken down often, and Enrico always joyfully slithered beneath the chassis to investigate the trouble; garage owners delighted him, and made Laura weep with laughter, with their offers to employ him as their mechanic. They were familiar with America and Americans. But until now, this vast country had not been their home.

They went by taxi from the docks to the King's Crown Hotel in Morningside Heights, not far from the Columbia University campus. Enrico had been brought into the physics faculty by a warm and understanding administrator, George Braxton Pegram, the head of the department, who had set aside an office and research facilities for Fermi in the Pupin Laboratories. The university Physics Department had become a sort of refugee camp; physicists fleeing Europe were pouring into New York, and their first stop was usually Pegram's office. If he could not give them a job, he let them use the university's facilities. Actually adding Fermi to the Columbia faculty had been a coup. Pegram had not known about the Nobel Prize when he had mailed the welcoming letter to Fermi in Rome.

Leo Szilard, another refugee, roomed in the King's Crown Hotel just down the hall from the Fermis. He had arrived at the Morningside Heights campus a short time before, but his reception there, as one considered brilliant but erratic and lacking the awards, credentials, and reputation, had been barely enthusiastic. However, with nowhere else to go, Pegram found room for Szilard in Pupin Hall, without, however, academic status and a salary. That Szilard and Fermi should be thrown together now at Columbia as refugees was a coincidence with far-reaching effects. Their differences, Szilard, fiery and quixotic, and Fermi, earthy and conservative, became the material of creation.

Five years earlier, in fall 1933, Leo Szilard, a physicist and a futurist, had gone into the chill of a London evening in search of support for a daring, revolutionary concept. As he had emerged from London's Holborn tube station into Southampton Row, a block or so from the British Museum, he walked deep in troubled thought, looking older than his thirty-five years, and shabby. As a refugee from Hungary, recently arrived in London, he had few means of making his suit look anything but slept in. He searched the faces of the people he passed on the sidewalk. Just now he envied them their ignorance. The world was on the threshold, he believed, of a discovery that would change it as nothing had changed it since fire. Surely, he thought, this evening's keynote speaker, Ernest Rutherford, would illuminate the neutron. Its discovery months before had burst upon the physics community with possibilities that were dazzling, and totally terrifying, Szilard had thought, if joined with his idea.

Actually, he admitted freely to friends and colleagues, the idea was not completely his own. But he took it for his own because he did not want olympians such as Rutherford to know that his theory was based on a notion found in a work of fiction by H. G. Wells. Of course, Wells had known something about the atom in 1914, when he had written *The World Set Free.* "The problem of inducing radioactivity in the heavier elements and so tapping the internal energy of atoms was solved by a wonderful combination of induction, intuition and luck," Wells had written as if he were peering at history from some future century through the eyes of a character he named Holstein.

> From the moment when the invisible speck of bismuth flashed into riving and rending energy, Holstein knew that he had opened a way for mankind, however narrow and dark it might still be, to worlds of limitless power. . . . He had launched something that would disorganize the entire fabric that held their ambitions and satisfactions together. "Felt like an imbecile who has presented a box full of loaded revolvers to a Creche,"

Holstein had said.

Szilard had read the book out of curiosity and a desire to improve his English, but the discovery of the neutron suddenly had transformed Wells's fictional vision into a real danger, as fact had transformed fiction. Of course, Szilard had hoped that his own theory was the stuff of an overactive imagination too. He tried hard to deceive himself, but he knew better. He possessed a gift, he guessed, that he shared with Wells. It had served him well and probably had saved his life.

Szilard had been born in 1898 and had reached conscription age during World War I. He had entered the Austro-Hungarian Army after a year at the Technical Academy in Budapest. After the war, he tried to continue his education in Hungary, but the chaos of postwar Eastern Europe had led him to Berlin and the Technical Academy at Charlottenburg. As he had other young European Jews in pursuit of careers in science, Einstein had influenced Szilard, who had switched from engineering to physics. Soon, people were recognizing his own special brilliance: a mercurial, highly energized intelligence that absorbed nearly everything it encountered. Working at the Kaiser Wilhelm Institute when Hitler seized power, Szilard had left for Vienna. But once there, he deduced that the Nazis would soon occupy Austria, too. After a few weeks, he had emigrated to England, en route, he felt certain, to the United States, his ultimate destination.

Szilard recalled Wells's theory now as he walked in the London drizzle. If those enormous forces that bound the atom's components were somehow unleashed, man could produce a devastating weapon. Wells had made the connection first:

> Never before in the history of warfare had there been a continuing explosive. Indeed up to the middle of the twentieth century the only explosives known were combustibles whose explosiveness was due entirely to their instantaneousness; and these atomic bombs which science burst upon the world that night were strange even to the men who used them. . . . Such was the crowning triumph of military science, the ultimate explosive that was to give the "decisive touch" to war. . . .

Szilard knew how.

Szilard kept his mind fit by conceiving new ideas through a synthesis, new ideas such as the apocalyptic vision of the neutron. He had wished that he could discuss it with people like Fermi, whom he had met and befriended a few years before at the Solvay Congress on Lake Como. Fermi's wife, Laura, had been especially kind, even solicitous. The relationship had developed through mutual respect. Szilard likened Fermi to a violinist who played new music by sight with astonishing virtuosity. Szilard was a generalist who could not stay with one idea for long, distracted as he was by a healthy and active curiosity. Fermi, on the other hand, was precise. He exercised his mind, flexing muscles on problems involving probability and mathematics.

As he had walked, Szilard tried to temper his anxiety. As Wells had said, if one man did not think up the atomic bomb, then another man would. But that was just the point. Atomic physics was the most creative of all the sciences. A physicist conceived an idea and then proved it with mathematics and chemistry. The thought came first, always the thought, the idea, the theory. James Chadwick had not merely tripped over his brilliant discovery, the neutron. It had not rolled off his workbench onto his lap. He had "seen" it in his imagination and had proved its existence afterward. A nation that made the connection would not rest until it had a bomb, because of the power that it would give it. Szilard wanted people to appreciate these dangers. Even if they thought that he was crazy, he knew that he had never been more sane.

The meeting Szilard had come through the dreary London night to attend began with a lecture by Ernest Rutherford of Cambridge's Cavendish Laboratory. An awesome power in physics whose statements even Szilard would hesitate to question, Rutherford had the chiseled features of an outdoorsman, a full head of salt-and-pepper hair, and a bristling moustache. He spoke always with a deceptive softness of tone. He began by describing the neutron that evening, mostly discussing information that was already published.

Then, near the end of his lecture, Rutherford said something that made Szilard sit up.

"There are many young physicists—" Rutherford began, "some probably here this evening—who have been talking pure moonshine about the neutron. It is pure moonshine when these young men say that the release of large quantities of energy from the atom will ever be possible."

H. G. Wells knew better, Szilard had thought. If an atom released two neutrons for every one its nucleus absorbed, then the atom would produce a mighty burst of energy. But he had performed no experiments to determine whether his idea contained any truth. Not enough was yet known about the atom for Szilard to decide where to start; besides, he lacked the stature that would make universities listen to him, and he had to find financial resources independently in order to carry out expensive research. In the sense that an ostrich finds refuge from its fears in a hole in the ground, Szilard felt a certain relief now that Rutherford had declared his idea moonshine.

A short time after their arrival, the Fermis moved out of the King's Crown into an apartment on Riverside Drive overlooking the Hudson River, and the process of adapting to America began. Giulio went to the playground each day with the nurse; Nella enrolled at the Horace Mann School for educationally gifted children. Laura made friends in the neighborhood and tried to improve her English, although she still often received birdseed when she asked for butter.

It seemed they had just settled into the apartment when Enrico insisted that they move to the suburbs. He had an aversion to living in a house that he did not own, and so they moved across the George Washington Bridge to the town of Leonia, New Jersey, where other physicists from Columbia lived. The new house had a large garden and a lawn that Laura hoped would keep Enrico occupied at home. She remembered that, soon after their marriage, he had claimed that he intended to retire at the age of forty. By then he would have "learned" all the secrets of the universe he was ever going to, he said. And he would become a real farmer, like his grandfather back in Italy. Yet, now thirty-eight, he showed not the slightest interest in the land, if the new garden was any measure. He let grass grow wild, always finding a reason to neglect it. He preferred tennis to watering the lawn and never concerned himself with the selection, pruning, and care of the flower beds.

Crabgrass was the talk of the neighborhood; it was an obsession of the suburbanites, who fought it with a dazzling assortment of weapons, from the chemical variety to a simple blunt brute hatred. In Rome, the Fermis had paid a gardener to weed and mow.

But now in America weeding was a suburban ritual. One day, Laura searched the lawn herself for the offending weed, and she found no sign of crabgrass. Later, Harold Urey, a neighbor, gardener, and Nobel Prize laureate in 1934 for the discovery of heavy water, told her, "D'you know what's wrong with your lawn, Laura? It's *all* crabgrass."

Enrico could not resist gadgets, and America was a whole fascinating souk of machines that performed commonplace duties. All the suburbanites used them. Fermi had bought a step-to-open garbage can nearly as soon as they had moved into the Riverside Drive apartment. He loved to tinker with the refrigerator, and he bought electric razors, hedge trimmers, saws, and kitchen appliances. He loved operating them, everywhere but in the garden. A young graduate student at the Pupin Labs befriended by Fermi and, by extension, the whole Fermi family, taught them American. It was proper for children to say *gosh, jerk,* and *squirt,* but not *golly,* or *This is a free country.* Children used it as license, and Enrico took the phrase to heart, using it whenever he wanted something that dictators and fanatics in Europe would have forbidden. "This is a free country" summed up his feelings about America.

Two weeks after they had arrived in America, Enrico and Laura returned to the docks to meet Bohr, unmistakable among the crowd of disembarking passengers for his unusually large head, drooping eyes, and stooped shoulders. When Enrico spied him, Bohr seemed in a state of excitement unusual for such a calm, composed man. "Enrico, have you heard?"

Fermi asked him whether he were all right.

"No," the Danish physicist replied, and, as soon as it was practicable, he told Fermi about fission.

Since the problem had been with Fermi longest, as the one who had initiated the riddle of the transuranic elements, Fermi was more astonished than anybody by the simplicity and elegance of Meitner's solution. However, he did not waste time admonishing himself for not seeing first what now seemed so obvious, as other physicists would do. Instinctively and almost immediately as Bohr described Meitner's wonderful revelation, Fermi turned to the next step: whether the fissioning of the atom released more than one neutron, and, if so, whether that would open the path to the phenomenon of chain reaction. Obviously, the same sequence had occupied Bohr's mind. Bohr explained to Fermi some of the nascent thoughts that had disturbed him—not all of them related to physics —on the long sea voyage from Copenhagen.

Like most physicists, Bohr would have happily ignored the intrusion of politics into physics. But recent events were making that impossible. Bohr knew about Lise Meitner's flight, and his heart went out to her. Otto Frisch, her nephew, was also a refugee from Hitler at Bohr's own institute in Copenhagen, which had recently taken in several other Jewish physicists as well. Bohr knew why the Fermis had fled Italy, and he had recently watched the events in neighboring Germany with growing alarm. He had nearly concluded that war was inevitable in Europe and in the Pacific too. (Only eighteen months before Bohr reached America, the Japanese had invaded China with a massive force.) And if the next event were to be war, the next step for physics would be involvement in the production of arms for war. If the theory of chain reaction proved correct, now that fission was established, then nuclear explosives would be at least a feasibility. If each fission of uranium released more than one free-ranging neutron, these newly released neutrons would search out and find other nuclei. The release of two neutrons would mean the release of four, then eight, and sixteen, and so on, until the uranium fuel was expended, and if the resulting chain reaction happened fast enough, a mighty explosion would result. If the war that seemed inevitable were to become a world war, a war that would be won by technology, many of whose prototypes such as tanks, airplanes, bombers, and submarines had been tested in the other world war of the century, then the politicians who would lead their nations into war would be receptive to the creation of a world weapon. Bohr said, "Power. Nations are seeking power, wherever it is found. The search for power will drive the Nazis and Fascists." Perhaps it would drive them even to capture the power of the sun.

Fermi as usual did not concern himself unduly with the "what if" questions. Rutherford and Einstein agreed that there was no real hope of exploiting the atom's energy even for peaceful purposes. Right now, Fermi felt stimulated by the discovery of fission, not by politics. He wanted to begin work on different aspects of proving neutron production in fission and, therefore, chain reaction. Laboratories in London and Paris and Berlin would soon start exactly the same research, and he did not want to be left behind. In the next few weeks after his discussion with Bohr, Fermi would begin work on Columbia's 15,000-pound cyclotron, with which he would compute that fission created 6 billion times more energy than was needed to liberate that energy; in other words, if fission required 1 volt, the process would release 6 billion volts. Fermi soon would prove this calculation, which the London *Times* called "the largest conversion of mass into energy that has yet been obtained by terrestrial methods." Fermi believed that scientists had their own agenda of discovery, and he could not agree with Bohr that the time was approaching when the agenda of the politicians and the physicists would become one.

In Germany, that same winter of 1939, Werner Heisenberg felt uncomfortably isolated. His life once again had achieved the necessary balance and harmony to allow him to work and think. More than six months had passed now since the SS had returned to him his "honor." But winning the battle with *Das Schwarze Korps* had not produced total exoneration. Before the article in the SS publication he had been led to expect an appointment to the coveted chair of professor of Theoretical Physics at Munich University, but that prize had gone instead to a rather dull scholar named Müller. Heisenberg thought he knew the reason why. The Aryan physicists somehow had reached the university's board with threats that they would carry out if their candidate for the chair were not appointed. Even if the board of Munich University had objected—and Heisenberg did not know whether they had argued about the appointment—he had been branded a white Jew, and the allegation, although

Himmler had supported him, had never been retracted in *Das Schwarze Korps,* and the accusation stuck. As a result, he was surrounded by silence, some of his former friends in the physics community had fled to America and to England and to neutral countries. Within Germany itself among those who had chosen to remain, people were now estranging themselves even from former friends who had not been accused of racial crimes by the SS. People were wary as never before of former friends and colleagues, even relatives, for what a slip of the tongue might bring. No one said what he believed. Talking and the art of conversation had been reduced to sloganeering, and, as the days passed, the atmosphere, especially among physicists, deteriorated.

In this isolation, Heisenberg wondered whether the choice that he had made almost automatically had been correct. It was too late now to change his mind. He knew what Elisabeth would say. She had recently given birth to their third child. She would want to stay in Germany, but he knew that whatever he decided she would agree to do, even including emigrating to England or America. It was still early in 1939. The universities of Michigan and Chicago had invited him to lecture as a visitor that spring and summer. If he visited America, using the lectures as an excuse for the trip, he could talk seriously with trusted and respected colleagues there about the question of emigration. In particular, he wanted to seek the advice of Sam Goudsmit, who had gone to America in the early 1930s, after Hitler assumed power in Germany. Goudsmit, the Fermis' friend at Ann Arbor, was a warm, gentle, wise man about the same age as Heisenberg. And he was a fellow European. If anyone could, Goudsmit would help him arrive at a decision. And the same might be true of Fermi, whom Heisenberg respected as a physicist. En route to Michigan, he would also sound out Pegram, the head of Columbia's Physics Department. He doubted whether anything said would change his mind. He wanted to stay in Germany, regardless of what happened. But he felt that he owed it to himself, to Elisabeth, and to the community of physicists in which he was once a leader to debate the question of staying or leaving. And now that he had reached a decision to make a decision, he felt that he could tolerate the silence, for the remainder of that winter at least.

———

The reporter W. H. Laurence entered room 403 of Pupin Hall at Columbia University annoyed at the two men in the front of the room scribbling mathematical formulas on the blackboard. Bohr and Fermi were about to explain fission, or what Fermi chose to call "the phenomenon of uranium bombardment by neutrons." Bohr, an old friend of Laurence, had known about fission for weeks now, but neither he nor Fermi had bothered to tell Laurence about it. As a result, the preeminent science journalist for *The New York Times* had missed a scoop, maybe the most important scoop of his distinguished career. No other journalist had reported the story, but that did not matter to Laurence. Weeks had passed in which other newspapers might have beaten him to it, and he felt betrayed.

This was *his* story, after all. Laurence had been traveling through Europe in 1934 when Fermi had first used slow neutrons to split the uranium atom. He had reported on the research of the Joliot-Curies in Paris, Hahn and Meitner, and Werner Heisenberg, whose trouble with the SS he had covered for the *Times*. He had shared the excitement gripping the physics community now that the secret of fission was out, even if he had missed reporting the big discovery itself.

Even this lecture had not been announced. It was now late in the afternoon, around five. Bohr had come to America to lecture at Princeton, not Columbia. He had agreed to share some of his thoughts with the Columbia faculty only because his friend Fermi was there.

Columbia had become the center of the world's nuclear research, transformed almost overnight by the influx of brilliant refugees from Nazism and Fascism. Laurence no longer needed to visit Europe to keep abreast in physics; nearly everybody of importance was here. He looked up into the seats of the amphitheater at John Ray Dunning, a friend and member of the university's Physics Department and went to sit beside him.

Halfway through the lecture, Laurence's ears pricked up at the sound of a new term being utilized by Fermi and Bohr: *chain reaction.* Laurence could not understand at first, then, all at once it clicked in his mind. He thought, "My God, what these men are saying is this: that for the splitting of an atom you need a cosmic ray or a neutron, and the neutrons are pretty hard to come by because they're locked up in the nuclei of atoms. But what they're saying is, if you split one atom of uranium, the split atom will give off two or three neutrons, and these neutrons will split other atoms. That goes on in a geometrical progression. It will come out the same way if you start an ordinary fire. You start a little flame by a match, but then the flame spreads and spreads and spreads, and before you know it, you have a big fire. My God, this means that you could have finally a practical way to release atomic energy on a large scale, which Einstein said could never be done, which Rutherford said could never be done, which all the top scientists have said would never be done. Here you have it!"

Laurence whispered to Dunning, "How much time does it take for an atom to split?"

Dunning looked at him. "Oh, maybe a trillionth of a second."

Laurence said, "Well, then, you could split a kilogram of uranium in something like a millionth of a second."

"Yes, sure, yes."

"Well how much energy would a kilogram of uranium have?"

Dunning figured it out in his head. "Well, one gram would have about twenty-five million kilowatt hours."

"Could it be used in an explosive?"

"Yes, sure, why not?" Dunning asked.

"How much would it be—twenty-five million kilowatt hours— in terms of explosives?"

Dunning said, "Oh, about twenty thousand tons of TNT."

"One gram?"

"Well," Dunning said, "if it's one gram fully converted into energy, that would be the case. In the case of uranium it's only one-tenth of 1 percent. So to get that amount of energy you would need a whole kilogram of uranium."

"A kilogram is two and two-tenths pounds," Laurence said.

"That's right," Dunning said.

Laurence was silenced by the enormity of the revelation. The world was heading toward war, he thought.

Dunning said,

Hold it a minute. Hear what Fermi is saying up there. It isn't uranium he's talking about. You've got to have a special kind of uranium—uranium 235, and uranium 235 is present in normal, natural uranium to the extent of seven tenths of one percent. So a pound of ordinary uranium contains ninety-nine point three percent uranium 238 and only seven tenths of one percent of uranium 235. And you have to have that uranium 235, and nobody knows how to produce it, and nobody knows how to get it out—separate it—from uranium 238.

Laurence may have needed reminding that uranium had two *isotopes:* U-238, which existed in abundance and had been the uranium used in all the laboratories of the world because the second uranium isotope, U-235, contained in U-238 was rare and considered impossible to separate from its abundant relative, U-238. No one had ever seen it alone. However, it was being theorized that U-235, if it could be separated, would be much more explosive than U-238.

As soon as the lecture finished, Laurence went down the aisle to the front of the lecture hall with Dunning, who introduced him to Fermi. Laurence asked, "If you can find a chain reaction, couldn't that be used to make an atomic bomb?"

Fermi did not want a newspaperman to write about a theory as if it were fact. Besides, Fermi thought, he certainly did not want his lecture circulated through newspapers in Germany or Italy, or even France. Fermi felt strongly against self-censorship, but this was different. He answered, "Well, not yet. I mean we don't know. We don't know," he repeated for emphasis. "A lot of work has to be done to find out."

Laurence persisted. "But on the basis of theory, on what you just said about the possibility of a chain reaction?"

Fermi said, "Yes, but nobody has ever proved a chain reaction. This is just theory. We don't know."

Bohr had discussed theory, but the hard applications had never come up. It alarmed him now to hear talk about a nuclear bomb.

Laurence said, "If it's possible, how long would it take?"

"Oh, at least twenty five years, maybe fifty years," Fermi said.

Laurence then said, *"Maybe Hitler can do it sooner than that."*

Fermi excused himself. Dunning asked Laurence, "Are you going to write about that?"

"About the chain reaction, sure. But I wouldn't dare mention about the bomb, or anything like that."

Laurence returned to the *Times*'s offices on West 43rd Street, determined to start his own one-man intelligence system. He would interview the exiled physicists from Germany. He would not mention uranium and bombs, but he would ask, "Where are the German scientists?" Eventually, if he learned that they were being ordered to work together in one single research center, rather than at their separate universities, he could be reasonably certain that their purpose was to construct an atomic bomb. Laurence mentioned the theory to his colleagues on the *Times,* but they thought he was insane.

Irène Joliot-Curie suffered from an affliction common to children of a famous parent: she feared that her mother's acclaim would rob her of her own identity. Although Irène had already won the Nobel Prize herself (making her and Marie the only mother and daughter ever to do so), her hunger for recognition and her need to exceed the achievements of her mother, a two-time laureate, could not be easily satisfied. No other spot but the limelight would do. Now having been upstaged by a second woman, Lise Meitner, she sought to recoup her losses.

Fourteen years earlier, Irène had been working with her mother at the Radium Institute in Paris when Frédéric Joliot, a young physicist and a committed Communist, arrived there. Within a year, Irène and he were married. By 1934, as a team, they had won a Nobel Prize for the discovery of artificial radioactivity. Yet since that time, their progress toward other important discoveries in physics had slowed. They had always seemed on the verge, usually only weeks or days away from some crucial discovery, when another team working independently in Rome or Berlin or somewhere else would publish first and receive the precious credit. This bad timing had started with Fermi's discovery of slow neutrons; after all, this would have been the next logical step after their artificial radioactivity. Then had come fission: Lise Meitner's fission.

More than ambition was at stake. Frédéric had been named chairman of the Nuclear Physics Department at the Collège de France. He and Irène had organized an extensive team of physicists on the rue d'Ulm, and the team needed funding. Money would mean progress, which would mean public acclaim, which in turn would generate more funds for yet more progress.

They had turned to research on chain reaction in uranium early in February 1939, days after reading Meitner's "fission" paper in *Nature.*

It was known in theory that fission might liberate neutrons, and the Joliot-Curies now focused their attention on the exact number. They made their calculations and, with a haste that later seemed reckless, published their preliminary findings: "Within the limits of error, fission in uranium released around 3.5 neutrons," they concluded. (The exact number later was closer to 2.5.)

When the paper was finished, Lew Kowarski of the Collège de France drove as if he were an escaping criminal to Le Bourget. He entrusted the paper to a French Air France pilot, who delivered it soon after he landed in London to the editors of *Nature.*

Fermi's office at Columbia was spare, nearly ascetic, a monk's chamber. No books lined the shelves. A few scientific journals rested on the desk. No print or painting adorned the walls. The furnishings consisted of a chair, a desk, a small table, a blackboard, and another chair for visitors. *Things* diverted his attention from the problems at hand.

Fermi independently had arrived at a similar conclusion about neutron production in fission only seven days after the Joliot-Curies' paper reached London (though he had estimated two neutrons). However, he had not rushed to publish the newest link that would lead to the exploitation of atomic energy. Until now discovery in the field of nuclear physics had been open to anyone with the intelligence and interest to understand. The revealed nature of physics so far was an open book. But the times were rapidly changing. Research findings, such as the number of neutrons emitted through fission, had to be weighed as never before against considerations of national interest.

Another proponent of the need for caution ever since he had read H. G. Wells's book, Leo Szilard had brought his predictions to America, without the benefit of a university appointment. If a bomb were to be built, America with its vast resources would be its builder. Szilard had roomed down the hall from the Fermis at the King's Crown Hotel, living on a shoestring and existing on the fringes of Columbia. Earlier that year when Bohr had told him about fission, Szilard had sent to England for his equipment, stored there since his leaving. He had borrowed on his own account two thousand dollars from a garment district manufacturer to rent a gram of radium for work on the phenomenon of chain reaction. The work suggested to him how this would end. Too many scientific teams of too many nations, controlled by too many different forms of government, wanted to uncover the secrets of the atom, which could only end in a flat-out, mindless sprint toward the production of an atomic bomb.

A good example was the Fifth Conference of Theoretical Physics, held late in January 1939, in Washington, D.C. Even as Bohr had been speaking that evening, some of the physicists present, dressed in tuxedos, had walked out of the conference and then rushed back to their laboratories to test fission for themselves. This physicists' "profligacy" alarmed Szilard, who had even expressed his worried thoughts in a letter to the Joliot-Curies on February 2, 1939: "Obviously, if more than one neutron were liberated (by fission) a sort of chain reaction would be possible. In certain circumstances this might lead to the construction of bombs which would be extremely dangerous in general and particularly in the hands of certain governments, We all hope that there will be no or at least not sufficient neutron emission and therefore nothing to worry about."

Then came their article in *Nature* on the emission of neutrons. They had not heeded his warning about the danger of publishing research, but it was still not too late.

Szilard sought Fermi's help, even knowing that self-censorship would be completely alien to Fermi's instincts for academic independence and freedom. But Szilard hoped to become Fermi's conscience, to appeal to his sense of responsibility and patriotism, and with Fermi's influence to put an end to the reckless publication of physics discoveries.

Fermi weighed the request respectfully. He was able to comprehend Szilard's fears, but right now, those fears still had no basis. Nobody knew whether a bomb was feasible. It was an idea with countless remaining theoretical problems, such as whether fissionble uranium 235 could be separated at all from the much more abundant, natural uranium 238. Indeed, Fermi believed that the separation was "a task that looked almost beyond human possibilities." And if censorship were so important, if fission threatened the world's security, then wouldn't Bohr himself, as the sage of the world's physicists, have suggested it instead of publicizing Hahn and Meitner's findings at the Washington conference? Would he have told the conference that a quantity of uranium 235 small enough to fit into the palm of a hand theoretically could blow up a town? Scientists had suffered and sacrificed for centuries to gain their freedom. Why voluntarily relinquish it now? Anyway, suggesting voluntary censorship by physicists was like asking children not to laugh.

"No," he told Szilard. "It is not the time."

"Then when is the time?" Szilard asked. He needed Fermi to convince other physicists to withhold their discoveries from publication, voluntarily. Without Fermi, Szilard did not have enough influence.

Fermi said, "I can only speak for myself." He could not ask other physicists to jeopardize their careers. According to the customs of the physics community, the first team to *publish* the findings was the first team to be credited with the discovery; which explained the haste of the Joliot-Curies. Fermi did not blame them for what they had done. He might have done the same at an earlier stage of his life. The system of recognition was wrong, not the scientists. And who could impose new voluntary guidelines on other scientists without seeming to be protecting himself selfishly?

For the time being, Fermi sided with Bohr and Rutherford. In theory, a nuclear bomb might be possible. But the problems were monumental. Fermi needed to be shown: Szilard would have to give him scientific proof. As for the other physicists, the ones beyond his immediate control, particularly the Joliot-Curies, he could not stop them from publishing. Szilard did not understand Fermi's attitude, with so much at stake. He decided to send a telegram this time to Paris, and if that had no effect, he would appeal to an even higher authority than Fermi to put a stop to this madness of publication.

———

Hans von Halban sat in a bath of steaming water, humming to himself contentedly. As a young scientist, he felt especially lucky to be at the Collège de France, working with the Joliot-Curies, as a German national with no love of Hitler and a resolve never to live under Nazism if he could avoid it. The college, as a place for discoveries in physics, was only slightly behind the Kaiser Wilhelm Institute in Berlin, where Otto Hahn worked, and it was closing the gap of discovery and acclaim fast. As a talented physicist who had not yet made his mark, von Halban wanted to establish his reputation, and now he had an advantage, as the team leader on the tests for neutron production, the tests that had led to the paper in *Nature*. And that had been just a beginning.

No sooner had Lew Kowarski raced with the paper to Le Bourget than Frédéric and Irène had announced the next challenge for the college's physicists, eager men and women like von Halban. Together they would be the first to discover the optimum neutron "modifier" or "brake" to slow the neutrons. The slower the neutrons, the more fissions they produced. Fermi had first discovered the phenomenon in 1934 with paraffin and pond water, and since then physicists had learned that there were even better brakes than these substances. Carbon graphite, like the lead in pencils, was one of them, as were carbon dioxide and dry ice. Any of these would work. Some modifiers, though, absorbed the neutrons, capturing them in the nuclei. That probably was true of plain water like that von Halban was bathing in, and if he were to guess, the best modifier would probably prove to be "heavy" water, which looked and felt the same as bath water but was "heavy" because it contained atoms of deuterium, or *heavy hydrogen,* naturally present in tiny quantities in all water. *Deuterium* was separated from plain water through a painstaking, slow process of electrolysis requiring large quantities of electricity; for that reason, most heavy water was being separated in Norway on a rock outcrop over hydroelectric dynamos on a fast-running river. One gallon of heavy water came from approximately one hundred thousand gallons of normal water, and there were about four thousand pounds stockpiled in Norway for use almost exclusively in nuclear research. As the Norwegian plant could produce about twenty-two pounds a month, enough heavy water was available, cheaply. Von Halban made a mental note to discuss stocking it at the college.

As he sat there thinking, a knock on the door disturbed his bath. "What is it?" he asked.

A voice came from behind the door. "There's a message for you," his wife said. "It's a telegram. It's one hundred and seventy words long."

He opened the door and stretched out a hand to take the cable, then sank back into the water. "Very expensive," he thought, figuring the cost of sending such a message.

Von Halban read the telegram slowly. It was from Szilard in New York: Would the physicists at the Collège de France please *stop* publishing their findings? Or did they want the Germans to build a bomb using the French team's discoveries? A lot of words, but the message was simple.

Von Halban let the telegram fall to the floor. He and the Joliot-Curies did not want to develop a bomb. They wanted a source of cheap, efficient energy to light the bistros of Paris, not a machine to destroy the city, as Szilard seemed to suppose. Marie Curie, the guiding light of the college, always had insisted on publishing, regardless of the consequences. Besides, von Halban wondered whether Szilard had an ulterior motive. Wasn't he also working at Columbia with Fermi on the optimum modifier for slowing neutrons? Was Szilard trying to gain an advantage by using the excuse of keeping an atomic bomb from Hitler? A bomb was not at stake here; Nobel Prizes were.

Suddenly, von Halban realized which day it was. Of course, he thought, climbing from the bath. This was a very expensive joke, but a joke all the same. It was April Fool's Day, 1939.

Admiral Stanford C. Hooper wanted his military colleagues at the Navy Department to meet his guest of honor, Enrico Fermi. As technical assistant to the Chief of Naval Operations in Washington, D.C., Hooper was on the lookout for new technology with potential military applications. This was quite innovative for the U.S. Armed Forces. Before the recent American military build-up in response to Japanese actions in China and Hitler's invasion of Czechoslovakia, the American military had not met with academics with the idea of applying science to war. The admiral had encouraged a dialogue, though, and his initiatives were bearing fruit. Only the day before Hitler attacked Czechoslovakia, declaring it a German protectorate, Hooper had received a letter from George Pegram at Columbia mentioning a new type of bomb. Its description seemed truly fantastic to Hooper, but if there were any truth in it, his military science colleagues—officers from the Army's Bureau of Ordnance, the Naval Research Laboratory, and Hooper's own Navy Department staff—would be able to help him assess the potential.

As the meeting began, Hooper said, "I want you to hear this." He held up the letter. "It's from Pegram up at Columbia." Then he began. "Experiments in physics laboratories at Columbia University reveal that conditions may be found under which the chemical element uranium may be able to liberate its large excess of atomic energy, and that this might mean the possibility that uranium might be used as an explosive that would liberate a million times as much energy per pound as any known explosive." Hooper saw on their faces interest mixed with incredulity. He continued, "My own feeling is that the probabilities are against this, but my colleagues and I think that the bare possibility should not be disregarded."

Hooper asked, "Have any of you heard anything about this before?"

Admiral Harold G. Bowen, director of the Naval Research Laboratory, answered, "We're aware of work done by two German scientists in Berlin, and we're checking on the conclusions of a couple of others, Frisch and Meitner. It seems to lead in that direction, but right now we aren't sure."

"Well, I've got someone who can answer some of our questions." Hooper picked up the Pegram letter again. "He's Professor Fermi, down here for the Philosophical Society meeting. He telephoned yesterday to say he could stop by if I wanted." He read the reference to Fermi in Pegram's letter. "Professor Fermi, Professor of Physics at Columbia University . . . was awarded the Nobel Prize. There is no man more competent in this field of nuclear physics than Professor Fermi. He's just come over from Italy and plans to stay. He wants to become an American citizen."

Before leaving New York for the Philosophical Society meeting, Fermi had discussed with Pegram the idea of approaching the military in Washington. Together they had decided that a formal meeting staffed with Pegram and Szilard and other physicists from Columbia might suggest to the military more than the scientists could deliver. Fermi still believed that a bomb was an unproven quantity. The problems even of theory were still insurmountable. He did not want to go deeply into the subject either, fearing that the military would make demands that he could not meet. He only hoped to "open a channel" through which proven scientific results could be passed. But that day, no matter what Fermi hoped, he became the first physicist in America to utter before the military the words *atomic bomb*.

He started speaking in a voice that was almost a whisper. His accent was still very strong, and his manner of speaking made him feel uneasy. He outlined superficially the work in progress at Columbia without speculating. When they came, the questions were hard, as he had feared. The officers were demanding answers that could not be given. Rather than give what he could not deliver, he answered as conservatively as he knew how.

"Is a bomb possible?" Hooper asked.

"If I had to answer now, I'd have to say no," Fermi said. "Even if our calculations prove right—that uranium 235 is indeed more fissionable than uranium 238—that still leaves us with the nearly insurmountable problem of separating one from the other."

"How much uranium is needed?" Hooper asked.

"We can't say. We just don't know. But probably less than five hundred kilograms of uranium 235."

Admiral Bowen asked, "Is there enough around to work with?"

"For the moment, yes. I know that a colleague is concerned with just this problem—securing stocks of uranium in case we need them. Most uranium comes either from parts of Africa controlled by the Belgians or from mines in Czechoslovakia. My colleague is naturally worried about the Germans' invasion of Czechoslovakia."

"Is there any suggestion that your colleagues in Germany are working on this?" Hooper asked.

Bohr had told Fermi that the Germans might be exploring a bomb, but he knew nothing more about the Germans' intentions.

"There is the suggestion, sir, but nothing more. As you probably know, Germany has lost many of its best physicists. But those who remain have a superb technical and theoretical range. Even if they are not working on a bomb—and I cannot for certain say that they are not—they are still *ahead* of us in what they know from their theoretical work." Fermi was referring to Meitner's fission and the important follow-up work being done by Hahn and his colleagues at the Kaiser Wilhelm Institute.

The discussion soon shifted from bombs to the use of nuclear fission to propel submarines. Admiral Bowen of the Naval Research Laboratory explained the present need for submarines to recharge batteries on the surface.

Fermi answered, "It is too early to tell."

There was one last question from Hooper. "Professor, if you discover how to make this thing work, how long do you think it would take?"

Fermi recalled Bohr's estimates, as accurate as the next person's. "Twenty-five, maybe fifty years," he said.

Pegram had not mentioned that point in his letter, but if that were true, a fission weapon was now nothing but a page in a science-fiction novel. Hooper was pragmatic; he dealt with real here-and-now problems. His interest in an atomic weapon suddenly wavered, then failed. And soon the meeting ended.

Fermi had done his duty, as a physicist and a refugee. He had also satisfied an obligation to Leo Szilard and those around him who saw a need for urgency. Fermi could not have honestly advised Admiral Hooper to start intensive research into the chimera of an atomic bomb.

Fermi returned by train to New York the same evening. Three days later, Admiral Bowen asked the Bureau of Engineering to finance uranium research. The Bureau gave a check for fifteen hundred dollars to the Carnegie Institution, which refused the grant.

The military let the matter die.

Edgar Sengier bounded down the platform at Victoria Station feeling refreshed. Trains always made him sleep well, and the overnight, cross-Channel trip from Paris to London had been no exception. He had come over on business, the same business that the Joliot-Curies had discussed with him yesterday, in Paris.

Edgar Sengier was very much in demand these days in England, America, Germany, and France. He produced a commodity that nations wanted, if not to own, then to control, in those early months of 1939. Sengier was director of Union Minière de Haut-Katanga, a company with mines in the Belgian colony of the Congo, where Sengier had been stationed as a young executive those many years ago when a fellow Belgian, Captain Richard Sharp, had made his remarkable discovery.

As an employee of the Union Minière, Captain Sharp had worked indirectly for Sengier. More fundamentally he worked for himself as an independent ore prospector. He had been seeking new worlds that day—January 22, 1913—as he rode out to the miners' camp on horseback with a pick and shovel in his saddle-bags. This copper-rich region of south-central Africa abounded in opportunity for ambitious young men like Sharp.

Sharp had been told to look for copper, but he had no interest in what other men had already found in abundance around Elizabethville. Sharp had heard from the Bateke natives, reputedly the most ferocious tribe in Katanga, about *mud* they smeared on their skins to make them like ghosts, dimly glowing an eerie white in the forest night. They had discovered that the substance on their skins at night instilled their enemies with fear and set them high in the tribal hierarchy, as warriors with magical powers. The mud, they said, came from holes near the area called Shinkolobwe.

From their description Sharp had thought the "mud" had to be pitchblende. Pitchblende contained a rare metal discovered first in Czechoslovakia in 1789. It had been named *uranium* after Uranus, the father of the Titans and the son of Gaea. Only a year before, in 1912, a Polish woman living in Paris, Marie Curie, had attributed great healing powers to an extract of uranium, a substance called radium. A few millionths of a gram of radium came from each gram of uranium, which in turn came from even greater quantities of pitchblende. Although extracting it was difficult, demand for radium was high and the price for even a gram was astronomical. Company directors such as Edgar Sengier would surely reward the employee who found some.

That morning, Captain Sharp had ridden across the savanna through the acacias, toward a hill he had sighted the day before. The hill was eroded into a smooth curve with "rusty" topsoil. He noted with satisfaction that vegetation grew on the upper belt of the hill, but after he had dismounted and inspected several hundred yards of terrain, he did not find the diggings of the Bateke warriors.

Captain Sharp had been ready to move on, when a fragment of bright yellow mineral caught his eye. The dolomite revealed an intricate network of glowing red, yellow, and green seams that flamed garishly against the gray and brown rock. He stopped digging when, at the bottom of this pit, he saw a gleaming black mineral.

Captain Sharp had discovered the largest concentration of uranium in the world. Besides Shinkolobwe, deposits existed only in Czechoslovakia and in Canada. The Canadian deposits, however, were separated by a thousand miles of rugged country from the nearest rail link.

Nearly twenty-six years after Sharp's discovery, Sir Henry Tizard, the rector of Imperial College and the director of the research department of the Royal Air Force, called this meeting, attended by Baron Cartier, the Belgian ambassador to the Court of St. James, Lord Stonehaven, a British director of Union Minière, and, of course, Sengier himself. The meeting came at the end of an interesting chain of recent events.

Professor George Thomson, the head of the Physics Department at Tizard's Imperial College, not long before, had read an article in *Nature* by the Joliot-Curies that had raised in his mind the idea for an atomic bomb. Thomson had not conceived of fission and chain reaction as anything but a means to a weapon with which to threaten Hitler, from the start. War seemed imminent, and the Germans were a frightening adversary. The British did not have the luxury of distance from the Nazis. They could not employ the same long list of "maybes" that Fermi had used with Admiral Hooper. Neither could the British deceive themselves, as did the French, into believing that fission and chain reaction might be used only to light the cities of the world cheaply and cleanly. Fission in the British mind triggered thoughts of a superweapon that they would drop, if necessary, on the Germans.

Of course, in spring 1939, Thomson only wanted to be prepared. He had asked Tizard to purchase a ton of uranium for six shillings, four pence a pound. The request had gone to the Lord Privy Seal, who had studied nuclear physics at Leipzig. Thomson had told him about the bomb, and the Lord Privy Seal had sent the request to Sir Henry Tizard at the Air Ministry. Fission might make a bomb. Bombs were dropped by airplanes. Therefore, atomic bombs were the Air Ministry's affair.

Many months had passed with Tizard deeply absorbed by secret research on radar, a technology that had seemed incredible only a few years before. Thomson finally had gone to see Tizard, feeling slightly ridiculous. There was still much to learn about the uranium and its preparation, but if successful, a uranium bomb would give England a large advantage. Thomson was not the only person in England who had made the connection. Coincidentally, a few days before his visit to Tizard, Thomson had received a letter that said, "as a result of a recent discovery in nuclear physics . . . there is a chance that an explosive might be produced setting free an amount of energy ten million times greater per gram than the highest explosive known." The writer, a physics professor from Bristol who had been reading *Nature,* had ended with the words, "Such a weapon in the hands of one nation might be quite decisive."

Sir Henry evaluated Thomson's proposals with interest. Only recently, he had heard rumors that the Germans had banned the export of uranium from the Czechoslovakian mine; furthermore, the War Ministry in Berlin was supposedly looking into alternative sources of uranium. Presumably, the Czech mines were nearly exhausted.

Sir Henry opened his meeting with Sengier by stating his ministry's interest in uranium. He asked Sengier the disposition of known supplies. Union Minière controlled almost all the world's uranium: both the tonnages in sealed drums in Brussels, transported by steamer through the African port at Lobito, and the reserves at Shinkolobwe.

Sir Henry then asked, "Have the Germans approached your company?"

"No," Sengier replied.

"Has *any* source indicated a heightened interest in your uranium?" he asked.

Sengier shook his head. He did not count the seven tons of uranium and the loan of one gram of radium promised only yesterday to the Joliot-Curies. They had confided in him about the wartime application of uranium: that an atomic weapon was not impossible. More probably, they had told him, uranium could be made to produce nuclear energy. They, and Sengier, would profit handsomely. Informally, they offered him a share in return. Nothing prevented him from "investing" in a new, potentially profitable source of natural energy.

However, he did not want his company's uranium to fall into the hands of the Germans, whom he hated for their slaughter of his countrymen in World War I. But as a man of great practicality, he knew that a historical invasion route between Germany and France cut through Belgium. If Hitler went to war, as events suggested, then Sengier would have to deal with him.

Sir Henry asked, "Will you grant the British government an option on each ton of ore which you extract from the Shinkolobwe mine, including the ore that is already in Belgium?"

"I won't be able to do that," Sengier said, thinking of the Germans.

Sir Henry did not complain. The Germans had not acquired

Union Minière's supplies. Yet, as the meeting broke up, Sir Henry warned Sengier, "Be careful. Never forget that you have in your hands something that may mean a catastrophe if it were to fall into the hands of a possible enemy."

In the summer of 1939, only one characteristic of Werner Heisenberg, having no relation to his brilliance or his ambition or his achievements, truly mattered to Fermi, who was waiting for him in his office. Now that war seemed imminent Heisenberg might lend the Nazis the use of his genius and talent in the coming conflict. He would become his enemy.

Fermi agreed to talk with Heisenberg during his visit to Columbia about Heisenberg's value to the Nazis if he chose to return. Fermi had known Heisenberg longer than anybody else at Columbia, and Dean Pegram had asked him to see whether he might convince Heisenberg to take up the standing invitation at Columbia to join the faculty of the Physics Department. It was a proposition of offering him anything to prevent him from returning to Germany. Pegram and Fermi respected Heisenberg's intelligence and judgment; however, they wanted him to know his options, clearly presented. If he chose to stay in America, Heisenberg would be made comfortable; a means for helping his wife and children to join him as soon as practicable would be found, and he would have the freedom of the Columbia campus, including its physics laboratories and libraries.

There was nothing charitable in their solicitude. Pegram and Fermi knew better than most Americans how Heisenberg could benefit the Nazis' war effort. Fermi possessed talents equal to those of Heisenberg: anything that Fermi could achieve, Heisenberg could also achieve with equal ease, all other factors being equal. If nuclear weapons of some variety and type were made feasible within the span of the war years, Heisenberg would have the intellectual and scientific capacity to grasp them and to put them to use. Of course, there were other physicists and scientists of considerable note still in Germany, Hahn, for example. But as a radiochemist, Hahn, like the others, did not possess the same breadth of understanding, the same utter confidence and mental flexibility as Heisenberg.

If Heisenberg returned to Germany, he could become a menace. Indeed, these were the thoughts of another physicist, Sam Goudsmit, who had talked to Heisenberg only days before at the University of Michigan about waiting out the war in America. Goudsmit, a Dutch Jew who had emigrated to America in the early 1930s to teach at the Ann Arbor campus, counted himself as a good, loyal friend of Heisenberg. He had almost begged Heisenberg to stay away from Germany. Goudsmit felt that Heisenberg could not resist pressures to work on a bomb for the Nazis. Heisenberg had said no to Goudsmit, and the chances were that he would say no to Fermi too.

When the time came, they greeted one another with stiff formality and then entered Fermi's spartan office, shutting the door behind them. They seemed to be strangers. But there had never been warmth between them; they did not necessarily like one another, but they were held in a bond of mutual respect, even admiration, regardless of the difference in their outward characteristics. Heisenberg (and to an even greater extent, Elisabeth, his wife) saw Fermi as uncultured, poorly educated, and inelegant in appearance with his short, olive-skinned torso, dark curly hair, and unrefined, peasant face. Fermi did not truly understand opera and the great symphonies; he did not read great literature, study philosophy, or feel in some way thrilled by a magnificent sculpture or painting. For his part, Fermi saw before him a man who had never had to struggle. He did not envy Heisenberg's blond, handsome good looks or his cultivation. He didn't think much about it at all. However, both men acknowledged the other's talent; it was the source of their mutual respect. Fermi was a physicist with the exceptional gift for experimentation; Heisenberg counted theory as his strong suit. They were geniuses, Nobel laureates at young ages. Few on earth could successfully compete with them.

Once they had settled down, having exchanged pleasantries

about families, mutual acquaintances, and details of Heisenberg's visit to Sam Goudsmit in Ann Arbor, Fermi asked, "Whatever makes you stay on in Germany?" Before Heisenberg could answer, he expanded on the question:

You can't possibly prevent the war, and you will have to do things which you will hate to do. Here you could make a completely fresh start. You see, this whole country has been built up by people who fled their homes. In Italy, I was a great man; here I am once again a young physicist, and that is incomparably more exciting. Why don't you start anew? Why renounce so much happiness?

Heisenberg could have replied that Elisabeth wanted to stay in Germany, but he knew that would be a self-deception. Elisabeth would agree with what he decided, even if that meant leaving Germany. The truth was that he could not bear to live anywhere else. Besides, he had responsibilities to others. He had doubts, naturally, that he was doing the right thing. But the system in Germany for the last six years under Hitler had led to the attitude "when in doubt, do nothing." Doing nothing is safe. He replied, "I've told myself the same thing many times. Perhaps I ought to have emigrated ten years ago. The idea of leaving the confines of Europe for the expanses of the New World has been constant temptation."

"Then why not give in to it?" Fermi asked.

"Because I have collected a small circle of young people around me in Germany. If I abandoned them now, I would feel like a traitor."

"Isn't it preferable to be a traitor to a small circle of young people than to support Hitler?" Fermi asked.

"I am not a Nazi," Heisenberg replied. "I am a nationalist. I believe in Germany, not in Hitler or the Nazis."

"But aren't they indistinguishable?"

"For now, *yes*. I just hope that the war will be a brief one, if there is to be a war. It is quite possible that the German people will make short shrift of Hitler and his followers. But I admit it doesn't look like that at the moment."

"But don't you have a responsibility to your young people to set an example? If you were to leave Germany, wouldn't they follow?"

"They cannot emigrate as easily as we can. They would have quite a hard time finding jobs abroad, and I would feel it quite improper to take advantage of my greater experience."

"I'd think it would be better for them to take any job here rather than to work in physics there."

"They are anxious to make certain that uncontaminated science can make a comeback in Germany after the war."

"Contaminated science," Fermi realized, was the so-called Aryan or Nordic physics. Heisenberg had been hurt by their accusations. As much as being called a "white Jew," distortion of the truth of physics distressed him. He wanted to show that his physics was right. It was a personal crusade. Heisenberg was so vain that he might even attempt to construct a German atomic bomb to prove himself and his science right.

Fermi said, "There is another problem. You know that Otto Hahn's discovery of atomic fission may be used to produce a chain reaction. In other words, there is now a real chance that atom bombs may be built." Heisenberg started to speak, but Fermi stopped him. "Once war is declared, both sides will perhaps do their utmost to hasten this development, and atomic physicists will be expected by their respective governments to devote all their energies to building the new weapons."

"That danger is real enough," Heisenberg replied. "You are only too right about participation and responsibility. But is emigration really the answer?"

"I can't think of anything better."

"The war will be over long before the first bomb is built. The war will certainly be finished before then. However hard governments clamor for them, atomic developments will be rather slow."

"What if they are not? Are you willing to take that chance?"

"Modern wars call for vast technological resources," Heisenberg said. "Hitler has chosen to cut off Germany from the rest of the world. Our technical potential has grown incomparably smaller than that of our probable opponents. I sometimes have the vague hope that Hitler may have a second thought about starting a war. But this is probably pure wishful thinking on my part. He is irrational and simply shuts his eyes to anything he does not want to see."

Heisenberg was shutting his eyes to everything that he did not want to see. "And you still want to return to Germany?" Fermi asked.

"I don't think I have much choice in the matter," Heisenberg replied. "History teaches us that sooner or later, every century is shaken by revolutions and wars, and whole populations obviously cannot migrate everytime there is a threat of such upheavals. People must learn to prevent catastrophes, not to run away from them."

This was exasperating. Heisenberg was not part of a "whole population," and he had not done anything so far to prevent a world war, so why not run away? Pegram had offered him a teaching position at Columbia, begging him to stay, at least until the end of war.

"There are no general guidelines to which we can cling," Heisenberg was saying. "We have to decide for ourselves. We cannot tell in advance whether we are doing right or wrong. Probably a bit of both."

He was willing to live in Nazi Germany through a war and maybe even work on the Nazi atomic project. He wanted to succeed among the only people that mattered to him, his fellow Germans. He was not a true Nazi, but what difference did a membership card make?

"I have decided to stay on in Germany," Heisenberg said, "and even if my decision is wrong, I believe I ought to stick to it. I know there will be great injustice and misfortune."

With real feeling, Fermi said, "That's a great pity."

The next day, Heisenberg boarded the S.S. *Europa*. Once at sea, he walked the decks. The ship steamed out of sight of land.

He returned to his stateroom and read, then he went out again. The weather was clear, the seas were calm, and the ship was sound.

That first evening out, Heisenberg dressed in black tie and headed toward the first-class dining room. Besides Heisenberg, the ship's officers, and a single table of passengers in this large room, usually filled with bright happy faces, there was no one else, as if to confirm Fermi's comment that the time for preparations was over. People were now as ready as they could ever be for war.

Leo Szilard had been driving around for two hours without getting nearer to where he wanted to be. For that, he could thank Eugene Wigner, a fellow physicist and Hungarian refugee who was sitting beside him in the passenger's seat. Wigner was hopeless as a navigator. They were looking for an address in Peconic, on the south shore of Long Island, but the address did not seem to exist, and neither Szilard nor Wigner, recent emigrés, knew the area well enough to get back on course. The heat of the summer day and the Long Island humidity heightened Szilard's nervousness.

Of course to Szilard anything, even being lost, was better than doing nothing. The work at the laboratories was at virtual standstill. Fermi had gone with his family by car to Michigan, and without Fermi, and now that the 1939 summer holiday was in full swing, Szilard had nothing to do. He hadn't even had anywhere to go, until now. And now he was lost, in search of Albert Einstein.

Szilard had learned about the Navy's indifference to atom bomb research and blamed Fermi for being too balanced, too cautious, too afraid to venture beyond the confines of fact. Fermi maddened Szilard. Conjecture did not exist for him. Something was either a fact or not a fact. And if it was not a fact, it did not exist in his mind. If Szilard had met with the military, they would have jumped into action. This once, Szilard thought, Fermi should have taken a stand.

Increasingly Fermi and Szilard were coming into conflict over the nuclear threat and what to do in response to it. Fermi was placid and cautious about the prospects and Szilard volatile, almost as convinced now of the need to build an atomic bomb as he had been worried about the concept of nuclear power in 1934 in London. Fermi's reluctance to support Szilard's censorship scheme had divided them even further; Fermi sent his technical papers to *Physical Review* with instructions that the editors date and verify the papers but hold them until some future time, a compromise that allowed him to compete for prizes and deserved recognition while denying the Nazis access to the information.

Fermi's reasonableness annoyed Szilard. Fermi seemed unperturbed by the recent news that the Germans had blocked the export of uranium from their Czech mines. Szilard wanted to warn the Belgians either to remove their uranium stockpiles to a safe place or to destroy them. Unfortunately for him, private citizens, much less aliens, did not as a rule make demands of sovereign governments.

Albert Einstein was undoubtedly the preeminent scientist in America. Even children knew his name. People in America loved his "eccentric professor" look. Furthermore he was linked with the atomic bomb through his theory of relativity. He was also a close friend of Queen Elizabeth, the queen mother of Belgium. In the 1920s he had participated in her salon of intellectuals and artists. The queen mother could pass a personal letter of warning from Einstein to the king, who in turn would deliver it to the Belgian government, if only Einstein agreed.

Szilard had decided not to wait for Fermi's return in the fall. Obviously, if Fermi had understood the urgency, he would have stayed in New York. As a fellow Nobel laureate, he could have approached Einstein on a nearly equal basis. Szilard did not have anything like Fermi's credentials, but what he lacked, he hoped to make up in commitment.

"Are you sure it's Peconic?" Szilard asked Wigner, who had called Princeton University himself for Einstein's summer address. Einstein's secretary had said Peconic: "Dr. Moore's cabin." Dr. Moore was a colleague of Einstein at the Institute for Advanced Study. "Maybe it's Patchogue," Wigner said. "They sound the same."

If the secretary had said, "Peconic," why didn't anybody they asked in Peconic know the location of Dr. Moore's cabin? "Maybe we should give up and go home," Szilard offered, disgusted.

"It's our duty to find him."

"Maybe if we simply ask where Einstein lives," Szilard suggested. He stopped the car and motioned to a boy standing on a curb. "Hey, kid, do you know where Professor Einstein lives by any chance?"

"Yeah," the kid said. "If you want, I'll take you there."

It was just around the corner. "Do you know him?" the kid asked.

"No," Szilard answered.

"He's nice," the kid said.

They knocked on the screen door. They heard muffled sounds from within. Einstein shuffled onto the porch wearing house slippers. He invited them in.

Szilard felt no less certain of himself and his "cause" in the presence of Einstein, as he explained the theory of chain reaction in uranium.

Einstein said, "I was not aware of that."

There probably was not another physicist anywhere by now who did not know. Szilard realized that Einstein might not have studied the behavior of atoms, much less nuclear power, in his search for higher truths, such as the formulation of a unified field theory of physics. But Einstein understood what Szilard asked, and he agreed to help. For personal reasons, he did not want to sign a letter to the queen mother. But he would write to the Belgian government.

Wigner asked, "Should we send a copy to the State Department? We'll give them three weeks. If they do not want the letter sent, they will tell us."

"Isn't this really their responsibility?" Einstein asked.

Szilard said, "Maybe we should just tell them [the State Department] what we want: to start an atomic bomb project immediately. Maybe we should tell them about Germany's getting an atomic bomb first. Everything then falls into place."

"Tell whom?" Wigner asked.

"The president," Szilard responded.

Szilard asked Einstein whether he would be willing to write to Roosevelt.

"Who will take it to him?" Einstein asked.

"I have somebody who can fix it," Szilard replied.

With Wigner's and Einstein's help over the next few days, Szilard wrote drafts of what he wanted to tell the president. The final letter began:

Sir,

Some recent work by E. Fermi and L. Szilard, which has been communicated to me in manuscript, leads me to expect that the element uranium may be turned into a new and important source of energy in the immediate future. Certain aspects of the situation seem to call for watchfulness and, if necessary, quick action on the part of the administration. I believe, therefore, that it is my duty to bring to your attention the following facts and recommendations.

He described the release of large quantities of energy through chain reaction.

This new phenomenon would also lead to the construction of bombs, and it is conceivable—though much less certain —that extremely powerful bombs of a new type may thus be constructed. A single bomb of this type, carried by boat or exploded in a port, might very well prove to be too heavy for transportation by air.

The letter went on to ask for the president to appropriate public funds for further research and close coordination between the government and physicists. It concluded, "I understand that Germany has actually stopped the sale of uranium from the Czechoslovakian mines which she has taken over. . . . Some of the American work on uranium is now being repeated at the Kaiser Wilhelm Institute in Berlin."

Before Einstein signed, he wrote as a postscript in his own

hand, "For the first time in our history, man will use energy that does not come from the sun."

On his return to New York, Szilard visited Alexander Sachs, a trader with Lehman Brothers on Wall Street and an old friend of Roosevelt. Sachs had heard Rutherford speak in England in the mid-1930s and had kept abreast of developments in nuclear physics. As Sachs listened to Szilard, he recalled the lines from a book he had read several years earlier: "I think there is no doubt that subatomic energy is available all around us," the author had written in *Forty Years of Atomic Energy*. "And one day man will release and control [the atom's] infinite power. We cannot prevent him from doing so and can only hope that he will not use it exclusively [for] blowing up his next door neighbor."

Soon after Sachs called the White House.

———

On the first day of September 1939, with the German blitzkrieg of Poland, World War II began, and the tensions of war, like ripples in a pond, reached across the Atlantic to the Fermis and those around them. Their neighbors in Leonia were branding a German neighbor a spy, speculating that when he had inspected the roof of his house he was measuring for an antenna with which to communicate with U-boats. Enrico's work also brought the war into their home. He never told Laura what he was doing at the laboratory. In the best of times he disliked talking shop. Yet now that war had been declared in Europe, he was saying even less. He started to leave New York on overnight trips, saying only that she should call his secretary at Columbia if there was an emergency. Laura stopped asking questions like "How was the office today?" She even caught herself once looking at the mud on his shoes to find out where he might have been. Not long ago, the wife of another physicist at Columbia gave her a copy of *Public Faces* by Harold Nicolson, without saying why. It was about a diplomatic incident caused by the dropping of an atomic bomb. Enrico never mentioned a word about bombs, and she no longer asked, because she now knew.

The summer vacation of 1939 had been wonderful, probably because Enrico and she now sensed it might be the last one for some time. Enrico had given seminars, leaving plenty of time for picnics and outings. Nearly every afternoon, the family drove to a lake, where Fermi swam as though he were in training.

Fermi had played tennis with equal drive. Everybody laughed at his game, except he, making it funnier. God had not endowed him with the coordination to swing a racquet with grace. He lunged at the ball, swatted at it, and often exhausted himself in a few games. He looked comical on the court and knew it. Yet, he played at every opportunity, usually against better opponents. Enrico did not mind any of this for one reason: he usually won. Once Laura overheard him explaining to their friend Sam Goudsmit, the Dutch physicist, "Sam, you think the object of the game is to hit the ball beautifully and place it accurately, do you not?"

"Yes, that's the game," Goudsmit had said.

"Well, I think you're wrong. It seems to me that the object of the game is to get the ball back over the net, every time."

That carefree summer had now turned to an autumn of deep concern for Laura, as long as her family remained in Rome. The Fascists in Italy had forced on Jews patterns of stealth and deception; fear had become a part of their daily existence, the Capons reported to her in their infrequent letters. Her father, the admiral, still refused to hide, and stealth was quite impossible for him. Yet without protection, Laura felt certain, he was in great danger. She had asked earlier whether he wanted to leave. He had said no. Enrico had brought what influence he could to bear, but now that war was declared, no one could help them any longer.

She discussed the events in Europe with their neighbor, an American chemist on the Columbia faculty who was married to a German physicist. With Hitler's swift triumph in Poland, all Europe might soon fall. If the Nazis then attacked America, their husbands would be in grave danger, with no choice but to flee. The two families started to imagine themselves in the role of Robinson Crusoe on a desert island. The neighbor would command the ship on which they would escape, and Enrico, with his knowledge of currents, winds, tides, and the like, would be the navigator. Enrico soon started planning seriously, learning to use a navigational sextant. Laura read about agriculture and learned how to make clothing. They would not sail east—it was too close to Europe—but to one of the islands in the Pacific Ocean. One night after the children were asleep, Laura and Enrico buried a pipe stuffed with "getaway" money under the furnace coal in the cellar.

One day Enrico recalled an incident. He remembered it now because events seemed to be repeating themselves. Back in 1935, Emilio Segrè, one of his "boys," had come to him for advice. The work at the nunnery had slacked off, and he had asked Enrico, "You are the Pope, full of wisdom. Can you tell me why we are accomplishing less now than a year ago?"

Enrico said to him, "Go to the physics library. Pull out the big atlas. Open it. That's where you will find an explanation."

Segrè found the atlas, which fell open to the most consulted and dogeared page, a map of Abyssinia, which Mussolini had invaded in October. Abyssinia had no minerals, no agricultural bounty worth mentioning, no important ports or boundaries, nothing to warrant invasion. This event had overshadowed everything else in Italy, preoccupying Italians and turning them against each other. It was the end of cooperation, in the laboratory as well as in society.

Now war was distracting their thoughts again from more important matters. At lunch, the physicists at Columbia started to talk more about their fears of Nazi terror than about research.

Before the summer holiday, Enrico had taken his research at Columbia as far as money and time allowed. The end result of his work was a rough estimate of the neutrons emitted by the fissioning in uranium, a duplication of the work done in Paris by the Joliot-Curies. Many important breakthroughs were yet to come before the atom would be understood in all its simplicity, and even more research was necessary to apply that knowledge. But of these problems two in particular seemed to defy solution by research teams anywhere in the world: the first was to find a modifier that effectively slowed down the neutrons, enabling them to hit the nuclei, without actually absorbing them. Fermi had discovered *slow neutrons,* neutrons slowed by the modifiers paraffin and water. It seemed now that the best modifier would be water, graphite, or heavy water. Unlike heavy water, which was expensive and difficult to acquire, graphite was available and cheap, but the impurities in existing industrial graphite tended to absorb too many neutrons. Until Fermi found a means of extracting the impurities, graphite could not be used reliably in research.

The second major problem involved the uranium itself. Fermi wanted to determine whether he could create a chain reaction in the common isotope, uranium 238, of which uranium 235, the highly explosive isotope, constituted a very small percentage. There were also the large, unanswered questions of the shape and form uranium should take in the experiments and the quantities required to make the chain reaction occur. Should the uranium be cast in pellets or spheres, or should it be cast at all? And in what quantity and in what position, should the uranium be placed in relation to the modifier in order to give the neutrons the best chance to succeed?

Far on the horizon Fermi conceived of establishing in natural uranium 238 a chain reaction that would sustain itself. Fermi had fissioned the uranium nucleus with slow neutrons in 1934, but the action had not been sustained. Nobody knew whether a self-sustaining reaction was possible, but it was now the dream of physicists the world over. One neutron would fission one atom, releasing more than two new neutrons, which would collide with two other nuclei, break apart, and release, in turn, their own two neutrons, and so on. This infinitely simple engine would at the very least create heat that could be used to drive a turbine to generate electricity, or, in its military application, turn the crankshafts of submarines. An atomic bomb was far off, even in theory.

To begin with, Fermi filled large vats on the seventh floor of Pupin Hall with ordinary water and uranium 238 in which he placed a radon-beryllium neutron source, identical to the small tube used in Rome in 1934. It soon became evident that the hydrogen in the water was "capturing" too many of the neutrons, thus preventing them from reaching the nuclei of the uranium atoms. He then tested different configurations to lessen the incidence of neutron capture. The team working with Fermi lumped the uranium and flooded the spaces between the lumps with the modifying water, but no matter what, they concluded that water did not work. It was a beginning, and the failure with water encouraged Fermi to test graphite next, except that he did not have six thousand dollars to buy the minimum amount of graphite needed.

The modifier research reached a sudden impasse. Unless Fermi convinced the government to give him the six thousand dollars, nuclear research in America would fall further behind the Europeans.

A few days later, on October 11, 1939, General Edwin M. "Pa" Watson, the secretary to President Franklin Roosevelt, accompanied the Wall Street trader, Alexander Sachs, into the Oval Office. Considering the problems that weighed on the president, he looked well, Sachs thought. Seated behind his desk, with the long rays of autumn light falling on his shoulders, Roosevelt appeared his usual jovial self, sparring with jokes that hid another reality. The Congress was fighting to block his repeal of the arms embargo; Americans were not moved by Britain's declaration of war or by Germany's invasion of Poland. The noninterventionists were winning the early political rounds; war in Europe was Europe's business, they believed. America had gone to war in 1917 and had lost its men, but not again. Now, after an economic depression, there would be no volunteering.

Sachs did not know whether the president would believe this pie-in-the-sky scheme of Szilard's. Earlier, Pa Watson had asked him to explain his plan to two ordnance specialists from the Army and Navy who had seemed to understand. Once they privately told Pa that Sachs was worth listening to, he showed Sachs into the Oval Office.

Sachs tried to explain what he wanted to FDR in florid language, as if he hoped to entrance the president with fancy words.

He read aloud from *Forty Years of Atomic Theory* and the Einstein letter, then showed FDR supporting scientific material supplied by Szilard. Sachs wanted to counter the impression in official Washington that an atomic bomb could not be produced before the war in Europe was over. Sachs reiterated to Roosevelt what he, Einstein, and Szilard wanted. It was not much, but it was a beginning: a system of cooperation between the scientists working on the atom and the government with an "unofficial" governmental appointee to help appropriate raw materials, such as uranium and graphite. Sachs knew that the American government was wary of a permanent scientific establishment. Even in times of national emergency, the federal government had not embraced pure science. The relationship had lacked mutual confidence.

Suddenly, as Sachs was still explaining, President Roosevelt said, "Well, you mean that you don't want the Nazis to blow us up."

Sachs replied, "Yes, that's precisely so."

Roosevelt turned to General Watson.

"This requires action," he said.

"This requires action" was translated only hours later into deeds, with Pa Watson asking Lyman Briggs, the director of the National Bureau of Standards, to chair what Watson called "The Committee on Uranium" and what everyone else soon was calling "The Briggs Committee."

If it seemed too good to be true, it was too good to be true. Once outside the White House, the proposal fell into a void. Except for refugees like Szilard and Alexander Sachs, nobody, especially in the military, really believed in the bomb. Every good military man knew the axiom that a new weapon required two wars for its development. Besides, the morale of the soldier, not newfangled arms, made armies victorious.

"If that's true," Sachs argued later, "if armaments are comparatively so unimportant, then why doesn't the Army cut its budget?"

The skeptical response did not surprise Fermi when he heard. He had succeeded in Rome with a small bit of borrowed radium and a goldfish pond. He was accustomed to working that way. Yet, his research at Columbia had reached a virtual standstill for want of money that no amount of his inventive genius could replace. Nuclear research required sophisticated equipment, raw materials, and machines that even he could not rig together from visits to the junkyard. He sought a solution to this dilemma; one day soon after, when he was walking up the stairs in Pupin, from the lecture hall to his office, emanating a characteristic dreaminess, his secretary told him that Sachs had phoned, asking him to call when he arrived. And, she said, Szilard was waiting in his office.

Szilard was sitting in a chair. "Did you hear?" he asked, as soon as Fermi opened the door.

Fermi asked what he meant.

"We've just heard that the Germans opened a research center to work on a bomb. It's in Berlin-Dahlem, at the Kaiser Wilhelm Institute."

If this were true, then the Germans would be working all out. Once committed, they always seemed to move at full speed and with full resources. Fermi placed a return call to Washington to Sachs, who told him the glad news that the Briggs Committee was going to fund the uranium project.

"How much?" Fermi asked.

"Six thousand dollars," Sachs replied: enough for the graphite and nothing more.

Part III

Werner Heisenberg breathed in the fragrance of wildflowers and the scent of pine borne on the breeze, as he surveyed the grandeur of the Karwendel Mountains. Below, the sun was pulling back the heavy blanket of mist from Lake Walchen; above, the bluish, majestic peaks of the mountains seemed to rise higher with the hours of the day.

He had decided to buy in this place after he had returned aboard the *Europa*. He and Elisabeth did not know what the future held, and they wanted to own a house far in the German country-side. Now, back in Germany only two weeks, with the house settled, there were no second thoughts, no inner turmoil. No matter what, they would stay, if not in Leipzig or Heidelberg or Munich, then here in Urfeld, a village of ten houses and two hotels high in the Bavarian Alps, where a war could not reach them.

These mountains invigorated him as powerfully as the music of Beethoven. Heisenberg had first come here two years ago, when, like all other German men his age, he had become a military reservist. For the last two years he had served two months each summer in the Mountain Rifle Brigade. Last year he had stood by, expecting to be posted to the Czech border. While he had waited for the call that never came, he explored Germany's forests.

Only a few villagers were stirring at this hour of morning, when it seemed as if he alone inhabited the world. Nearing the village, he saw a man run toward the post office. He seemed excited, and Heisenberg wondered why. It was September 1, 1939. Nothing more was expected on the news than the latest condemnations from abroad and from Berlin, the latest claims of the Propaganda Ministry.

When the man saw him, he came running up. "Did you hear?" he asked, out of breath.

Heisenberg asked, "Hear what?"

"War against Poland has started."

Heisenberg looked surprised.

The man said, "Don't worry, it will all be over in three weeks' time."

Heisenberg doubted that. He guessed that this would mean a world war. He immediately wondered how the news would affect him personally.

Back at the house, he told Elisabeth. She asked whether he would be posted as an officer in a combat unit, or, because of his accomplishments, in some scientific research center? Naturally, she preferred that he not fight, but stay close by with her and the children. He did not know, and there was no way to find out. They would have to wait, just like thousands of other Germans.

On September 16, a little more than two weeks later, Heisenberg received an official letter. He was ordered to report to the War Ministry in Berlin. Elisabeth packed a small suitcase with just enough personal clothing to last until his uniforms were issued; he was to become a soldier. He could not complain, if that was what his country asked.

Earlier that same year, 1939, unknown to Heisenberg and months before war was declared, a group of German physicists in Göttingen met to discuss the theoretical use of uranium in the production of energy. Two physicists present had written the minutes for the Reich Minister of Education, who had seized on its implications by funding research and providing laboratory facilities at the Army's Ordnance Testing site at Gottow. At the same time, after reading the Joliot-Curies' article in *Nature* on neutron production, two other German physicists warned the Reich War Ministry of a new development, which, they wrote, "will probably make it possible to produce an explosive many orders of magnitude more powerful than the conventional ones." They added in their official report, "That country which first makes use of it has an unsurpassable advantage over the others."

On April 29, 1939, the president of the ministry's Research Council on Physics had called a meeting at the ministry building in Berlin. Those who attended criticized Otto Hahn for publishing his findings on fission earlier that year. They asked what the British and Americans had learned about fission from reading *Naturwissenschaften?* Something had to be done, and soon, to stop the publication of German scientific research. The second item on the agenda that day was a "uranium burner," or pile, which the ministry decided to fund. Last, the meeting urged the ministry to ban the export of uranium from Germany, and, with equal urgency, to acquire uranium from the Czech mine at Joachimsthal.

Not long after, *Naturwissenschaften* published an article under the provocative headline CAN THE ENERGY CONTAINED IN THE ATOMIC NUCLEUS BE EXPLOITED ON A TECHNICAL SCALE? The author simplified the article, which he then sent to the leading German national newspaper, *Deutsche Allgemeine Zeitung.* Chain reaction offered unimaginable powers to the side that first exploited it. He wrote,

> One cubic meter of consolidated uranium-oxide power weighs 4.2 tons and contains 3,000 million-million-million molecules, or three times as many uranium atoms. As each atom liberates about 180 electron-volts . . . a total energy of 27,000 million-million kilogram-metres would be liberated. That means that one cubic metre of uranium-oxide would suffice to lift a cubic-kilometre of water (total weight: 10 million-million kilograms) 27 kilometres into the air.

Even if the readers of *Deutsche Allgemeine Zeitung* had not comprehended the exact magnitude of "millions" or had not been able to imagine millions of tons of water being flung into the air by no more than a square yard of chain-reacting uranium oxide, they would have understood that this was power that the Reich must be the first to harness.

The War Ministry had moved quickly after that. It ordered the Army to explore the explosive potential of uranium at a special center inside the Army's research testing complex near Berlin. It described its new project as "the creation of new energy-sources for R. (rocket) propulsion." But the physicists who knew better were soon calling it simply "the Uranium Club."

The first German military task force on atomic energy, under Kurt Diebner, a young physicist and Nazi Party member, met on September 16 to recruit research personnel. Diebner sought to find the best scientists available in Germany for this specialized research.

Principal among the German physicists was Otto Hahn. Little that he now said about radiochemistry and physics was disputed. True, he had been reluctant from the start to cooperate with any agency that sought to develop fission for use as a weapon and had avoided previous meetings with the War Ministry. But Hahn had failed to use his stature to dissuade the authorities from the notion of developing a bomb even before they had begun.

Otto Hahn had spent that spring and early summer traveling, first to Göthenburg and Stockholm, where he had discussed the implications of fission with Lise Meitner. Later, in London, he had met Professor Frederick Lindemann, the éminence grise to Winston Churchill, later known as Lord Cherwell. Lindemann understood nuclear physics, and eventually their conversation had turned to the potential of an atomic bomb. Hahn had been candid. He did not believe there was anything to fear, he had told Lindemann, but he was surprised by Lindemann's interest and the quality of his questions. Obviously, the British were thinking about fission as a weapon too. The thought had unnerved him.

Even before Diebner had solicited the views of those attending the first "staffing" meeting, Hahn had raised an objection that he hoped might obviate the need for the Uranium Club. The American physics digest, *Physical Review,* Hahn said, had recently published a technical paper pointing out that only the rare isotope of uranium 235 might be fissionable. Only seven parts in every thousand of natural uranium 238 consisted of this isotope 235. Isotope separation, even when the parts were relatively equal, was consummately difficult; the work was delicate, painstaking, and almost universally unproductive. Something on the scale of an industry was needed for the production and separation of an isotope that might not produce energy for electricity or for bombs. In his opinion, isotope separation presented science and engineering with insurmountable problems.

At another time, Hahn's attempt to dissuade the authorities might have succeeded. But careers, reputations, and standings within the party and with the Führer were now at stake. If these best and brightest young German physicists and chemists could deliver to Hitler a weapon with which to spread Nazism without further conflict, they would be hailed as heroes. And in that fall of 1939, optimism permeated the air in Germany. This was not a time for Germans to say what could not be done; everything was possible in the new Germany, and, in some respects, the more difficult the problem, the more satisfying the ultimate solution would be. Diebner typified the attitude; he was a Nazi, a member of the party, and a scientist who had started his career with the Ordnance Department. He reported to the SS and Gestapo; he insisted that others share his loyalty to the Führer. Right now Diebner brushed aside Hahn's objections. "If there is only a sliver of a chance," he told him, "it is vital that we follow it up."

Meanwhile, Heisenberg journeyed by train from Urfeld to Berlin. His small suitcase contained so very little: photos of Elisabeth and the children, a shirt, a change of underwear, socks and toilet articles, and books he hoped to read on the fighting front.

When he entered the War Ministry at number 12 Hardenbergstrasse in Berlin, he looked around for the "call-up" section. An officer there told him to report next door to the Army Ordnance Department, where he met Diebner, whom he neither liked nor trusted, considering him too avid a Nazi. Diebner told Heisenberg that he had been drafted "to work on the question of the utilization of atomic energy together with a group of other physicists . . . to give the matter some thought, whether under the known characteristics of uranium, you think a chain reaction is a real possibility, and if so, then please write down what you think about it." In the vaguest of terms he was being asked to explore a self-sustaining chain reaction in uranium.

The sheer gladness of avoiding a combatant's role overshadowed everything else that day for Heisenberg. He could now spend the war in Germany, and he could be near Elisabeth and their children, near his laboratory in Leipzig and his getaway house in Urfeld. This assignment during the war meant hardly any disruption at all. Only later, on his return to Leipzig, he realized that he was being ordered to help produce what might result in an engine of destruction, an atomic bomb. Yet what concerned him was not connected to responsibility and morality, or even to the issues Fermi had asked him about in New York. It had to do with the sign BREATHE DEEPLY AND QUIETLY in the cellars of the Gestapo headquarters. The "white Jew" affair had ended a little more than a year ago, and the images were still fresh in his mind. He knew what the Gestapo would do if he failed to cooperate with Diebner, a committed Nazi.

Everything weighed heavily in favor of obeying orders.

There were examples he could follow if he chose to. Otto Hahn, for one, had told the ordnance people that he would not help. Hans Euler was not going to follow his orders, either. A young physicist in poor health, Euler had volunteered instead for the Luftwaffe. Euler had told Heisenberg before leaving, "I have not volunteered because I want Germany to win. I don't believe in that possibility." The cynicism of the Nazis filled him with despair. "I have not volunteered for a unit in which I might be asked to kill people," he said. "I may get shot down myself but will never have to fire a gun or throw a bomb. And in this ocean of senselessness, I can't really see what good I would do by working with you on the exploitation of atomic energy." (Soon after, the Luftwaffe sent him for training. He was then posted with a reconnaissance unit in Greece. One day his airplane never returned from a mission over the Sea of Azov.)

Heisenberg had told Euler,

We can do nothing about the present catastrophe. But after the war life will have to go on, here, in Russia, in America, everywhere. Before then many people will have died, good people and bad, innocent men and guilty. And the survivors will have to try to build a better world. It won't be a particularly good one either, and people will quickly realize that the war has solved few problems.

He soon was working on the idea of using heavy water as a moderator or "brake" for neutrons. He knew the positive characteristics of the other possible moderators, such as graphite and water, but, above all others, heavy water captured his attention as a substance with a low quotient of neutron capture, a high quotient of supply, and fewer inherent impurities. Money was one early obstacle to the acquisition of heavy water; it was expensive, but the Ordnance Department had agreed to permit the expense because its auditors had been told how a chain reaction might produce energy by alternating layers of uranium oxide with layers of heavy water. Creating a working pile, a heap of uranium put together with a moderator in a great enough quantity to create a self-sustaining chain reaction, was by now everybody's goal, but so far, nobody had found the correct components to start a self-sustaining (and therefore energy-producing) chain reaction in uranium.

Heisenberg began by working through the theory, always his greatest strength as a physicist; only after he had perceived the feasibility of a theory would he turn his hand to actual experimentation. After two months of intensive thought Heisenberg was able to report his theoretical conclusions to the Ministry of War:

The uranium fission processes discovered by Hahn . . . can on present evidence be used for large-scale energy production. The surest method for building a reactor capable of this will be to [use] the uranium 235 isotope. It is, moreover, the only method of producing explosives several orders of magnitude more powerful than the strongest explosives yet known. For the generation of energy, however, even ordinary uranium can be used . . . if the uranium is used in conjunction with another substance [a moderator] which will slow down the neutrons from the uranium, without absorbing them. Water is not suitable for this. Heavy water and very pure graphite would, on the other hand, suffice on present evidence.

Of course this was theory, and Heisenberg still had to prove its truth in practice by constructing and operating a uranium pile. Yet, he had cracked the theory long before anyone else. Suddenly the nuclear genie was out of the German bottle.

Heisenberg had nominated graphite or heavy water in the letter to the War Ministry as the likely moderator in a uranium pile. However, heavy water seemed to him the better choice not only because it was available and already free of impurities, but equally and unrelated to physics, because of another German physicist, Walter Bothe.

Diebner had failed to convince the physicists in the "club" to come together at the Berlin-Dahlem Institute in Berlin to use its advanced experimental equipment and cyclotron. The physicists would not even discuss moving to Berlin. Working as a single cooperative unit in Berlin threatened their independence; they knew their own research centers best, and besides, they did not want their lives disrupted. By staying in their universities they could work on specific assignments, as individuals, and receive recognition and rewards as individuals too.

The most important consequence of this dispersion was a singular deterioration of communications, which became most apparent between Heisenberg and Professor Walter Bothe, a physicist at Heidelberg University. Bothe had written to the War Ministry soon after reading Heisenberg's optimistic report appraising nuclear energy; in his memo, Bothe pointed out errors in Heisenberg's theory. Bothe, as it turned out, was experimenting with graphite as a moderator. Graphite, he thought, offered several advantages. It was available and could be purified at a relatively low cost. Further, handling solid bricks of graphite would be easier than sloshing containers of heavy water.

Aside from the scientific arguments, Professor Walter Bothe personally disliked Werner Heisenberg. Bothe, at the "staffing meeting," had argued against including Heisenberg in the Uranium Club, maintaining that the club could get along nicely without him. Heisenberg was a prima donna, Bothe believed. He was too much of everything: too accomplished, too brilliant, too well recognized, too far above the fray. Heisenberg seemed to hold researchers like Bothe in contempt. Bothe saw in Heisenberg a broad streak of arrogance, too. Last year they had squabbled over the supply of uranium then available. The uranium had gone to the more accomplished physicist, and Bothe was left almost with nothing. Bothe had felt so discouraged, he had nearly lost the will to continue.

Then, worse still, Heisenberg had met the challenge in a longer reply to the War Ministry, implying that Bothe's graphite research was unworthy, although he did not realize that Bothe had poured himself into the graphite experiments, and the work was paying off. The early tests had indicated clearly that graphite functioned as a moderator. Impurities in the graphite probably absorbed neutrons, but in time those impurities could be removed. His report caught the attention of the Army Ordnance Department, he knew, because he had pointed out that graphite was cheap and readily available. If the use of graphite as a moderator were feasible, researchers could eliminate heavy water and concentrate on more advanced research, leaving the question of the modifier behind.

The Army Ordnance Department, good as their word, delivered a new load of the purest graphite that the Siemens company could make to Bothe in his Heidelberg laboratory. Bothe set up the simple test with confidence; he thought he could smell success. But when he measured the absorption qualities of this pure graphite, they were lower than those of the impure graphite. He tested again, almost in disbelief, and again the results were disappointing.

Bothe was forced to conclude bitterly that graphite was not an effective moderator. Its *diffusion length* (the capacity of the modifier to absorb neutrons) was simply too short. He dutifully reported his dismal conclusions, which were accepted without question at the Army Ordnance Department and by Diebner at the institute in Berlin. From then on, the majority of German physicists working on atomic energy perceived graphite as an unsuitable modifier. If Bothe had reworked his calculations, he would have discovered a disastrous mistake: graphite was indeed the most effective of all uranium modifiers.

Meanwhile, a few hundred miles away in Belgium, Edgar Sengier, the chairman of the Union Minière de Haut-Katanga, was paying a rare visit to the company's uranium storage site outside Brussels, a large covered building, filled from floor to ceiling with eight hundred tons of natural uranium oxide in sealed sixty-gallon drums, each neatly labeled URANIUM ORE: PRODUCT OF THE BELGIAN CONGO. The sheer bulk illustrated Sengier's predicament.

In that winter of his visit, there was war, but there was no war. Over in England they were calling it the "Phony War" because no new armies had moved, and the Germans had conquered no new territory. Sengier feared that this peace was temporary. Soon, perhaps when the weather improved in the spring, Hitler would move again, this time to the west, into Holland, Denmark, Belgium, and France.

The Germans had invaded Belgium once before in this century, with tragic consequences for Belgium's young men on the fields and in the trenches of Ypres and Passchendaele. The German armies would come and this time they would stay.

This Phony War gave Sengier a feeling of anxiety. The Berlin firm of Auer and Company had been awarded the Reich War

Ministry's contract for the acquisition of uranium. Already, Auer had built up a complex at Oranienburg to cleanse the Czech uranium of its rare-earth impurities. And it now appeared to Sengier that Auer and Company was near to exhausting the Czech stocks or, worse, was in need of larger supplies of uranium. So they had come to him. On his desk back at his Brussels office, the purchase order from Auer for uranium stored in this warehouse read to him like a declaration of war. The order suggested to him the existence of secret German "X" weapons, and the earlier warning of Sir Henry Tizard rang in Sengier's ears: "Never forget that you have in your hands something that may mean a catastrophe to your country . . . if it were to fall into a possible enemy's hands." Since then, Germany had become England's enemy and soon would be Belgium's.

Sengier was a patriot, but he was a pragmatist, too. Decisions in the copper and uranium trade often took politics into account, and although the thought of Hitler's spreading his madness further was abhorrent to Sengier, Hitler just might succeed, and if he did, Union Minière de Haut-Katanga would have to do business with him. To prepare for that contingency, however repellent, Sengier had already refused the British request for uranium options. It had not been in the interest of Union Minière to invite Germany's ire.

Sengier himself would not see the occupation, if it were to come. Union Minière rented offices in North America on 42d Street in New York, near Grand Central Station. The instant that the German armies moved, he would move, too, by airplane or boat to Southampton or London, and from there by whatever means to New York. There, far from the hostilities, he would wait out the war. His business would recover later, ready to trade in good faith with the victor.

In the meantime, he made three decisions. He would cooperate with the Germans; the stocks of uranium in Belgium would remain where they were, in this warehouse within their reach. That decision covered Union Minière in the event of a German victory. Second, he would send an order to the company office in southern Africa that the Shinkolobwe mines be flooded with water and closed. Sengier knew better than most the scarcity of uranium. By this action, he might prevent the Germans and the British from producing the "catastrophe" hinted at by the Englishman.

Sengier looked around him in the warehouse, then returned to downtown Brussels. He told Madame Hamoir, his private secretary, to order the office in Shinkolobwe to start closing down. Then before he finished with Madame Hamoir, he made his third decision. Consistent with his other articles of faith as a businessman, Sengier held that what was fair for one customer was fair for all. Now he acted on it.

———

Two outcast physicists were wasting time one dreary February night in 1940 in Birmingham, England. One of them, Otto Frisch, the newphew of Lise Meitner, was in England because he had been visiting London when war broke out. He had mailed his resignation to Niels Bohr and stayed in Britain, but the British so far had shown him little of their famous hospitality. He carried a German passport, and in their eyes, he was a German, even though a German Jewish refugee from Nazism. He had offered to help the British war effort, but the authorities forbade him to use his learning and experience as a physicist on important war-related research. However, Sir Henry Tizard had permitted him to conduct to his heart's content nonpractical "theoretical" research on an atomic bomb.

Frisch had accepted an appointment to the science faculty at the University of Birmingham, in the heart of the English Midlands, where he had met a similar "outcast," Rudolf Peierls, a thirty-two-year-old German Jewish physicist who had abandoned Nazi Germany for Britain soon after 1933. Peierls had applied for British naturalization papers for himself and his wife, and until the papers came through, his status was no different from Frisch's. Sir Henry had thrown him the same bone.

Frisch rented rooms in an old Georgian house occupied by Peierls near the university in the Edgbaston district of Birmingham.

The declaration that had made them "enemy aliens" had also made them inseparable; the strict regulations governing aliens prevented them from venturing outside the house at night, after ten o'clock, even to visit a movie house or a local music hall. They could not travel outside Birmingham without special police permission. Nearly everything they did was watched. These tight restrictions forced time on their hands, time in which there was little better to do in the evenings than sit around the living room discussing anything that entered their minds.

Earlier Peierls had approached the question of the atomic bomb as a mathematical exercise. Until now, nobody had tried to calculate the size a bomb would need to be. Many physicists and most war planners thought either that a bomb would be too large for practical use, or, if it were small enough, less than the superpowerful explosive it was conceived to be. Einstein in his letter to Roosevelt had suggested a bomb of a size on the order of a ship; it could be floated into a harbor and detonated, leveling most of the port city. Other theorists had figured roughly the same. Certainly, even the most optimistic calculations had not considered an atomic explosive device small enough for delivery in an airplane.

Peierls had reached a similar conclusion earlier that the weapon would be "on the order of tons." Less than a month ago, in January, Frisch's independent calculations concurred with Peierl's. "There are now a number of strong arguments to the effect that the construction of such a super-bomb would be, if not impossible, then at least prohibitively expensive and that furthermore the bomb would not be so effective as was thought at first," Frisch had written.

But on that evening with nothing better to do, Frisch and Peierls took a second look. They had been lounging around the house, reviewing the work sheets of the original calculations. Together they began to play with the concept of size. It was all an exercise. All their former calculations were based on natural uranium 238. But what if they were to calculate only with the superfissionable isotope 235, that rare element of only seven parts in every thousand of natural uranium? As yet only submicroscopic specks of uranium 235 had been separated from natural uranium. They asked how much U-235 was needed for a bomb? What would be the explosive characteristics of a U-235 bomb? Would it be worthwhile researching, or would it ultimately be only an expensive curiosity? These were simple, logical questions. But nobody seemed to have asked them before.

Using scrap paper for their calculations, they estimated for the first time the *cross section* of the uranium 235 nucleus, a physicist's term to describe whether a neutron splits the nucleus or merely caroms off into space. The more nuclei the neutrons split, the more extensive the chain reaction and the more powerful, therefore, the resulting blast. The conclusion Frisch and Peierls reached that night staggered them. A bomb in theory would not need to be the size of a ship or weigh in hundreds of tons. An effective weapon of U-235 alone, Peierls said, "could be less than one pound" and about the same size as an orange. But, they asked next, how would such a bomb explode, with a blast of unimaginable force or with a pop or a bang or a swelling like rising bread? Again, the answer surprised them.

The next morning, they bicycled to the university, mulling over a new problem en route. They were classified as enemy aliens, and yet they now possessed such highly secret information, if only of a theory that had not been tested in any way in the laboratory, that Sir Henry Tizard would not have told them about it if they had not thought of it themselves. They went immediately to the chairman of the Physics Department, who recommended that they write directly to Sir Henry, laying out their findings in simple terms. If there were merit to their theories, Sir Henry would see it. The chairman imagined that Tizard would remove them from further work, even of a theoretical nature, at least until their status as aliens changed.

Soon after, they sent two papers to Sir Henry in London, "On the Construction of a 'Super-bomb': Based on a Nuclear Chain Reaction in Uranium" and "On the Properties of a Radioactive 'Super-bomb.'"

Sir Henry acknowledged their theories and the supporting materials, and felt that these new ideas helped to eliminate a new and growing problem. Recently, a number of fanciful aspects had infused questions of an atomic bomb with an air of silliness. Sir George Thomson had proposed sending bogus reports to the Germans through secret channels, hinting that the British had already tested an atomic device that had proved so powerful that tests had to be temporarily abandoned until an island was found to test a bomb. The bogus report would conclude, "It is therefore of the first importance to complete the arrangements for the island, as we must get some idea of the delay required to give the aeroplanes a reasonable chance of getting clear."

The fake report was never sent. When Winston Churchill learned about it, he turned the scheme on its head. If the Germans were talking about "superbombs," then they were merely doing to the English what Thomson intended to do to them. Besides, Churchill ridiculed the idea of a bomb with the conventional wisdom, probably gleaned from his advisers, that "the chain process can take place only if the uranium is concentrated into a large mass." Churchill wrote, "As soon as the energy develops it will explode with a mild detonation before any really violent effects can be produced."

Sir Henry was less skeptical. On the basis of what he had heard from Sir George Thomson and the theories of Frisch and Peierls, he decided that he had a basis to "get the ball rolling with a committee to weigh the scientific validity of some of these questions." Peierls and Frisch did not sit on the committee that resulted, but Sir Henry at least got them security clearances, "even as enemy aliens," for continued atomic bomb research.

French physicists, too, started to work in unison with their Ministry of Munitions. Minister Raoul Dautry became a quartermaster for the Joliot-Curies' uranium research. Frédéric and Irène continued to move forward without a pause. Earlier, during the fall of the previous year, 1939, they had started research on a self-sustaining chain reaction, by testing modifiers. By now, they had tried and rejected ordinary water and carbon dioxide. Dautry had ordered ten tons of graphite brought from Grenoble with which to build a crude pile, shaped in a sphere, with water and graphite as modifiers. Their Geiger counters clicked with the first faint heartbeat of a reaction, until the water and graphite captured too many free neutrons to sustain the life. Now, they wanted to test heavy water.

Dautry had an amazing grasp of nuclear physics for a cabinet minister. He understood almost intuitively how energy from the atom could transform a society; if the French realized this "miracle" first, France would attract buyers from all over the world. Perhaps as a bonus, the French might contain this energy in a bomb casing to conquer the Germans.

Dautry saw all this and acted.

He knew that the Norwegian company Norsk-Hydro was the only practical source of heavy water. The single use for heavy water was physics research, and the Norwegians would surely demand to know why the French Minister of Munitions wanted it. Dautry looked into the matter rather carefully. He noticed that Norsk-Hydro had certain partners: I.G. Farben, the German chemical giant, owned shares, as did the French Banque de Paris et des Pays-Bas.

Dautry was acquainted with an officer of the Banque de Paris, Jacques Allier, a man of resourcefulness and bravery. Allier was anything but a gray banker, surely not one to inspect balance sheets and return to his family in Neuilly each evening at six. There was something different about him; he was too fit, too alert to be merely a banker. And indeed he was not entirely, for Allier "moonlighted," giving his mind during daylight hours to the Banque de Paris and his brilliance at night to the Deuxième Bureau, France's secret service, where he worked as an undercover officer.

The two men, Dautry and Allier, discussed this mutual "problem" of heavy water. Allier told Dautry that he would see what he could do.

Now, in early March 1940, Allier reported distressing news. His sources told him that only two or three days before, the German War Ministry, through a representative at I.G. Farben in Frankfurt, had telephoned Norway with an order for Norsk-Hydro's entire stock of heavy water, around four hundred pounds. The caller had evaded the question of its use, and Norsk-Hydro had refused him. The German had sweetened the offer with the promise of more orders in the future, but Norsk-Hydro was still not interested.

Dautry did not need the Joliot-Curies to realize that the Germans were working on a uranium bomb, and their interest in heavy water indicated progress on a bomb far in advance of that of the Collège de France. Dautry could not stop the Germans, but he could slow them.

Soon afterward, Frédéric Joliot-Curie told Allier about the characteristics of heavy water, that it behaved no differently from ordinary tap water in the normal course of a day: it melted, it froze, it boiled, it turned to steam, it sloshed back and forth. But, if it were to be transported, it required special containers to prevent its contamination. Boron or cadmium weldings on the containers, it turned out, would render it worthless.

Days later, a submarine of the French Navy left the pens at Brest, while Allier, along with three colleagues in the Deuxième Bureau wearing bankers' hats, boarded an Air France flight for Oslo, Norway. During the flight, Allier pondered the odds for success, which depended almost solely on the Norwegians. He would not appeal to their sense of profit. They would be insulted. But he would appeal to their "better feelings." Perhaps their tie to France would prove closer than their tie to Germany.

From Oslo, they went by car west to Rjukan. Snow blanketed the countryside, weighing down the branches of the conifers in profusion on the steep sides of the mountains. Allier had received a briefing on the terrain around Rjukan, but he was nevertheless surprised by what he saw. The six-story Norsk-Hydro plant was cantilevered over a sheer cliff face, several hundred feet above a ravine of fast-running water. The outcrop below the factory jutted like the prow of a gigantic ship.

The plant's general manager, a Norwegian named Axel Aubert, greeted Allier and his companions warmly. Allier knew that he could not lie; he could not even avoid telling the truth. Aubert was equally direct. He asked why the French wanted the heavy water.

"As you know, it has only one use," Allier replied. "The Joliot-Curies want it for their research into uranium at the Collège de France. The possibility exists that a powerful explosive can be produced from uranium, and your heavy water might be used in the process."

Aubert replied, "Convey my best wishes to Monsieur Daladier [the Prime Minister of France] and say that our company will not accept one centime for the product you are taking, if it will aid France's victory." Aubert not only provided Allier with all the available stock, which weighed around four hundred pounds, but promised all future heavy-water production as well.

Allier returned to Oslo, careful not to approach a welding or container company. The specifications were so precise, and odd, that they would surely arouse suspicions. German intelligence agents in Oslo would know why the containers were needed.

Instead Allier went to a one-man forge. The Norwegian owner took his order without a hint of interest, and within two weeks, twenty-six containers were waiting at the forge. Transported to Rjukan, they were filled by Allier's colleagues with the precious liquid; then back in Oslo, the men hid them in the cellar of a "safe" house acquired by the French Embassy. There they waited for the submarine.

The timing had been arranged to avoid delay, but the Norwegian government, ignorant until now of the transfer, sensed with alarm the reason for the Quai d'Orsai's request for permission to dock the submarine up the fjord in Oslo. The submarine was too obvious; the Germans would have figured that out, too. Just now, Norway's government did not dare to risk Germany's enmity, even if it meant refusing a friend's request to dock a submarine.

The heavy water had become a potential diplomatic problem. Norway's passing it into French hands could be interpreted as a hostile act and provide Berlin with a pretext for invasion. Understanding the urgency, Allier and his colleagues rushed the containers to the Fornebu Airport near Oslo. Dressed in civilian clothes, Allier and his partner, Lieutenant Mosse, bought tickets on a regular flight to Amsterdam, then surreptitiously bought a second set of tickets. When the time came, they put thirteen of the canisters into the cargo hold of the second flight, which they boarded under assumed names.

As they climbed through the clouds, Allier waited for an interception by a Luftwaffe aircraft. What better way to destroy the heavy water without a trace? The airplane would fall into the North Sea, and everything—the pilot, crew, passengers, Allier and Mosse, and the heavy water—would disappear forever.

"We are French officers in civilian clothes," he told the pilot.

Their destination was Edinburgh, Scotland, directly across the sea from Oslo, the shortest route from Norway. As they passed the Norwegian coast, an aircraft followed them. The pilot could not identify it, but it was on the same course and at the same altitude. Allier ordered the pilot to descend into the clouds. The aircraft dropped several thousand feet. The pilot decided to change their destination from Edinburgh to Montrose. The question of the other, following aircraft was never resolved.

They landed with the hazardous transport only half over. Back in Oslo, the remaining two Deuxième Bureau agents also booked double flights, as Allier loaded his thirteen cans aboard a British Rail train for London, where the French Military Mission waited to hide them. They put the cans into the Mission's cellar overnight, and in the morning of March 15, Allier again moved them, this time to the Channel coast at Dover, and from there by boat-train to Paris.

Immediately, and in great secrecy, Irène and Frédéric Joliot-Curie and von Halban started to test the effects of neutron bombardment of uranium, using sparing amounts of Allier's heavy water. They knew that it would have to last.

Just two weeks after Allier's return from Norway, the Germans invaded, beginning the military occupation of Norway and Denmark. The Phony War was over.

In Rjukan, Axel Aubert, the general manager of Norsk-Hydro, reported to the German military command in Oslo. He told disbelieving Wehrmacht and SS officials that Norsk-Hydro did not have even one drop of heavy water. I.G. Farben knew that there had been more than four hundred pounds in storage at Rjukan less than three weeks before. The SS demanded that Norsk-Hydro, now under the control of the Nazi occupying forces, increase its production to the plant's maximum capacity of two hundred twenty pounds a month. In the meantime, the now certain knowledge of French interest in heavy water raised German fears, while in Paris the German conquest of Norway soured Allier's victory.

Allier went to see Dautry. Even in so short a time, the French had progressed toward a successful pile, step by step. But now that Germany seemed likely to invade France, something had to be done to safeguard France's atomic research. Allier and Dautry formulated a plan.

———

The men converged on Piccadilly from their lunch tables at Whites and Boodles and the In and Out, as chauffeured cars deposited others at the same address on that spring day, April 10, 1940. They were due to attend the inaugural meeting, called for two-thirty sharp, of Sir George Thomson's "British Subcommittee on the U-Bomb of the Committee for the Scientific Study of Air Warfare," convened in the hallowed, darkly paneled ground-floor committee room of the Royal Society, looking out onto the gardens of Burlington House.

In a less formal period before the war, these same men had met regularly at Balliol College, Oxford. Then they had called themselves the "Balliol Beagles" because, like beagles, they seemed to bound from one fantastic scheme to another, without stopping long enough to give anything careful consideration. But now with far more urgency to their work, Balliol Beagles were setting out to explore new weaponry and defense technologies. Now, too, they were pausing in quite unbeaglelike fashion to consider a uranium bomb. Even though their primary, private concern was to stop the

Germans from developing a bomb first, their orders from Sir Henry Tizard were "to examine the whole problem, to coordinate the work in progress and to report as soon as possible, whether the possibilities of producing atomic bombs during this war, and their military effect, were sufficient to justify the necessary division of effort for the purpose."

By now they had digested the Frisch and Peierls documents on the size and explosive qualities of a U-235 bomb. Sir George, the committee chairman, proposed that "Frisch should be informed that his proposal was being considered." He should not be told the details, but there was no reason that he should not continue to work "on his own lines." The committee was updated on another breakthrough, one that curiously had gone unreported in the scientific press.

James Chadwick, the discoverer of the neutron and the head of the Physics Department at Liverpool University, had displayed the usual initial skepticism about a bomb, estimating its size anywhere from one to forty tons. But then Chadwick had used the university's cyclotron to determine the explosiveness of uranium 235 when its nucleus was irradiated with *fast neutrons,* neutrons that were not slowed by a moderator. U-235 attracted neutrons more speedily than the nuclei of the isotope U-238; therefore, it was thought, in order to create a chain reaction in pure U-235 a moderator to slow down the neutron would not be necessary for fission to take place. In theory the idea of fast neutrons and U-235 worked fine, but most physicists recognized the near impossibility of separating enough U-235 from U-238 to make a bomb. However, after his cyclotron experiments, Chadwick felt that in theory a bomb could work. At the time of the meeting Sir George still shared the majority of his scientists' skepticism about the bomb's feasibility with the majority of Americans, whose indifferent attitude was summed up in a letter from an attaché in the British Embassy in Washington:

It would be a sheer waste of time for people busy with urgent matters in England to turn to uranium as a war investigation. If anything likely to be of war value emerges they [Americans] will certainly give us a hint of it in good time. . . . They feel that it is much better that they should be pressing on with this than that our people should be wasting their time on what is scientifically very interesting, but for present practical needs probably a wild-goose chase.

Contrasted with the American indifference was what Sir George considered French hysteria. The Foreign Office had been consulted when the Norwegian heavy water had crossed Britain. Sir George recognized the French vulnerability, but he did not understand their panic, considering it unseemly and unmanly. However, he kept these opinions to himself in deference to the only foreigner among them at the meeting that day and waited simply to let the visitor explain the purpose of his visit.

Jacques Allier of the Deuxième Bureau and the Banque de Paris thanked his hosts, when the time came for him to speak. Before he proceeded, he requested from them, much to the annoyance of Sir George and the other Englishmen, a pledge of secrecy on their honor as gentlemen for what he was about to say. He then told them that the Germans were trying to learn about the work by the Joliot-Curies at the Collège de France. They sought as well to control the Norwegian heavy water, which meant that their nuclear energy research probably ran parallel to the French. And how far along were the French? Their water and graphite piles had given birth to the first faint stirrings of a self-sustaining chain reaction; the Joliot-Curies could state with some confidence that their aim, a self-sustaining chain reaction, could probably be realized in the not too distant future.

"I hope that the British and French will agree to cooperate," Allier told the committee. "A collaboration seems to be the only way to achieve a uranium bomb before the Germans."

Later, after the meeting adjourned, Allier warned Sir Henry Tizard about a German atomic bomb. But since Sir Henry had heard nothing from Edgar Sengier, who had promised to report any German requests for the Belgian uranium stocks, he did not share

Allier's alarm. "If Germany is trying to buy heavy water and not trying to buy uranium," Sir Henry wrote soon after, "I cannot think why they want the heavy water. It may be, however, that they are terrified at intelligence of our own in England and think they had better corner the heavy water so that we should not have it."

The French were "unnecessarily excited," in his opinion.

Finally, the committee tried to find a more appropriate name for itself. *British Subcommittee on the U-Bomb of the Committee for the Scientific Study of Air Warfare* took one's breath away, and, besides, it revealed its secret purpose in fifteen words. Before Sir Henry allowed discussion to begin, the committee pondered a message received from Niels Bohr. Bohr, who had refused to be evacuated from Copenhagen, had sent a message to a physicist friend in Britain, who in turn had given it to a member of Sir George's committee. The friend had transmitted it this way: "Met Niels and Margarethe [Bohr's wife] recently both well but unhappy about events please inform Cockcroft and Maud Ray Kent."

Sir George asked whether anybody knew Maud Ray Kent. Who was she?

This new, unknown name raised suspicions. Bohr, they assumed, must be in some danger. But, John Cockcroft said, the message stated clearly that Bohr and his wife were well, though unhappy. This message, the committee agreed, had to be a code; otherwise, the reference to Maud Ray Kent made no sense. The words *Maud Ray Kent* revealed Bohr's secret message: the three words contained the anagram *radium taken.* Was that what Bohr wanted to say?

Another committee member offered another explanation. The three words also formed the anagram *make ur day nt.* Bohr could be warning them about a German "ray" weapon. Sir Henry Tizard thought the explanations were science fiction, but "just sufficiently reasonable to make one worry."

As time passed, the mystery deepened. But for now, the committee had a new name. "In order to avoid having to make all letters about the subcommittee secret," Sir George explained, "we have decided to call it by the initials M.A.U.D."

Lord Cherwell wrote him to ask, "What meaning?"

"We have not been able to find out what the letters represent," Thomson replied.

Jacques Allier returned to France, shattered by the British attitude. They had not listened to a word of his warning. Now, of course, his predictions were coming true. The Germans were almost at the gates of Paris.

Allier had decided to remove the heavy water and radium from the Collège de France. If the German occupation forced the team of physicists at the college to suspend work, the enemy would not benefit, either by capturing French supplies or through the theoretical and experimental experience of Frédéric or Irène or von Halban.

Von Halban was to leave first.

German artillery guns roared in the distance, to the north of the city, as he loaded aboard his Citroen the twenty-six cans of heavy water. He arranged the cans around a small, one-gram container of radium to shield him, his wife, and baby daughter from radiation. Scientific papers were packed in boxes and placed in the trunk. Then they entered the heavy, steady stream of evacuating Parisians on the main autoroute south.

Allier had instructed von Halban to lock the cans of heavy water in the vault of the Banque de Paris in Riom in France's Massif-Central. If the French stopped the German invasion at Paris, the physicists from the college would join von Halban in Riom, still safely within France. Otherwise, they would be evacuated to England.

As part of their plan, Allier had told von Halban to stop in the small resort town of Mont-Dore, a spa for the taking of restorative waters, and wait there until he received further orders. Perhaps the transport all the way to Riom would be unnecessary. The French had held the German Army north of Paris in 1914. However, by the end of the first week in June, the Germans were fifty miles from Paris. The French government had declared the capital an open city; then the government abandoned the City of Light altogether.

When he reached Mont-Dore, von Halban went to the town hall. The mayor, a patriot who had fought in World War I, listened to von Halban with suspicion and alarm. There had not been any time to arrange for official papers with impressive colored seals and ribbons for von Halban to show him. The mayor, however, demanded such an authority, a document providing authorization for what he saw as a thoroughly unbelievable request.

It was, indeed, an unusual petition. Von Halban needed a cell in the local prison, preferably on death row, where he could stay with the secret war materials that could not remain unprotected, in his car. Von Halban hoped to sound convincing, but he was not. The mayor tried to call the Collège de France, but the lines were jammed: French telephone communications required luck at the best of times. Overcoming his suspicions of von Halban as a fifth columnist, the mayor finally took him on trust. That the Germans would want to invade Riom did not make sense. Nothing was there but hotels, a spa, and elderly invalids.

The mayor spoke to the prison warden, and soon, inmates from death row were carrying the containers to their cell block, locking the doors behind them. Meanwhile, von Halban went in search of a lodging for the other physicists. The Clair Logis, the place he settled on, suited the scientists' requirements well.

Back in Paris, the twentieth earl of Suffolk, the scion of a most distinguished British family, a friend of the king of England, an avid sportsman, and an eccentric swashbuckler, was removing £2.5 million in raw industrial diamonds, valuable handmade machine tools, and whatever scientific and nuclear-research hardware still remained in the city. The earl had been assigned this task by the British Ministry of Supply, who did not trust the French to take care of these things for themselves. The earl brought along Miss Morden, his "secretary," who was always ready at the right instant with a lighted match for his cigars, and Fred Hards, his faithful chauffeur, bodyguard, and friend. The earl wore riding boots and carried a Purdy gun, as was his custom. When he rolled up his sleeves, he revealed a gallery of tattoos acquired in distant

South Seas ports, to which he had sailed as a common seaman after running away from home at an early age. Together, the earl, Hards, and Morden were known in the British popular press as "The Holy Trinity."

The earl did not hold with the Joliot-Curies' peculiar brand of Communist patriotism; their expertise was needed in London, regardless of their desire to remain in Paris. The earl would take them there, no matter how they complained. The earl himself would bring the diamonds and machine tools to Bordeaux, where he would wait for Allier, the physicists, including the Joliot-Curies, and the heavy water. The French government had not provided a ship to take them to Britain, but the earl had never commandeered a boat before and looked forward to the adventure.

Allier reached Mont-Dore on Sunday, demanding to see the prison warden, who was attending mass. He went to the church and told the warden why he had come, but the warden refused to release the heavy water and radium.

"Where are your orders?" the warden asked.

"I have none, at least not in writing," Allier replied.

"I'm afraid then that you'll have to get some."

Such a request would take days, and the Germans were likely to occupy Paris in hours. Allier argued with the warden. Finally, he pointed a nine-millimeter pistol at his stomach. "This is my authority," he told him.

"Your authority is sufficient," the warden replied. The inmates loaded the cans from death row into Allier's Simca.

Allier next went to the Clair Logis, where the Collège de France scientists, now joined by the Joliot-Curies, were enjoying an elaborate lunch. Reunited, they were celebrating what they hoped was the imminent resumption of their atomic research, including the achievement of a self-sustaining chain reaction. Allier explained that the defenses were not holding in northern France, that the French Army was in no position to counterattack, and that the British Expeditionary Force (BEF) was being evacuated from the Continent at Dunkirk. The time had come to leave France, Allier told them. They could help defeat the Germans from England. The scientists needed little convincing. Joliot-Curie, however, refused to leave France in his desire to fight with the *Maquis* and help the Communists within the competing resistance groups.

After lunch Allier and the scientists set off in a southwesterly direction, toward Bordeaux and the Gironde estuary. The time was short, and the convoy of scientists riding in the cars behind Allier's own Simca with the heavy water already was overdue for the rendezvous with the earl of Suffolk. The car carrying the Joliot-Curies swerved out of line. Allier guessed that the Joliot-Curies had decided to defy his orders and head back to Paris.

For his part, the earl had commandeered the coaler *Broompark,* a small coastal freighter, and its crew. The coaler had been scheduled to leave the day before, and the only means at the earl's disposal of holding the ship in port was to keep the crew occupied with rum and the sheer force of his personality. Desperate people crowded the docks, looking for a boat to take them away. Families were separated, and frightened women and children seemed to be everywhere, abandoned and hopeless. Meanwhile, the earl, Miss Morden, and Fred Hards drank with the crew. There was little else to do, once the earl had supervised the construction of a wooden raft, a highly buoyant platform to which he lashed the diamonds and the machine tools. If a German U-boat or bomber attacked and sank the *Broompark,* a likely event, the strategic supplies would not be lost.

In harbor the captain of the *Broompark* felt vulnerable to an enemy air attack, and he did not want refugees to overrun the decks. He steamed his ship into the estuary, to wait at anchor before heading out to sea. The earl damned Allier.

Finally, as the crew was readying the *Broompark* for sea, Allier arrived, sending word by radio for the ship to return to the docks. They loaded on the heavy water and the scientists. The earl inquired about the Joliot-Curies.

"What if the Germans get them?" he asked.

"They will not cooperate," Allier replied. "Remember, he is a Communist."

The *Broompark* left the dock once again, steaming past its

former anchorage in the estuary. As it neared the mouth of the river, another ship came abreast. It took the lead over the slower *Broompark,* then hit an underwater mine and sank. The *Broompark* picked up the survivors, then headed for the Falmouth Roads.

Before they reached Paris, the Joliot-Curies heard about a ship's sinking. Confused about its identity, they assumed that it was the *Broompark;* and they mourned the fate of their colleagues.

Back in Paris, which was now being occupied by the Germans, they continued experimenting with their cyclotron, expecting an inevitable visit by a German. But weeks passed without a single visitor, and they thought perhaps that the Germans did not know they were there. Then one day a German came to the college introducing himself as Doctor Kurt Diebner. He told them that the Kaiser Wilhelm Institute of Physics in Berlin now was officially in charge of the college and its scientists. The college laboratory equipment, including the priceless cyclotron, the men and women remaining, and the Joliot-Curies, were now the property of the Nazis. The time eventually would come when the equipment would be transported to Berlin, but right now there was no time to waste in dismantling, transporting, and then setting up again. Diebner then asked the Joliot-Curies where the other physicists had gone, von Halban, for example.

"They left," Frédéric told him.

Diebner already knew about the heavy water "stolen" from the Germans by the French from Norway. He wanted to send it at once to Germany. He asked where it was. "It left with them," Frédéric said, considering this the first, but not the last, of their victories.

Later, Diebner authorized the Joliot-Curies' interrogation by the SS. When asked again about the heavy water, they repeated what they knew. It had been loaded onto a ship at Bordeaux. When questioned further, Frédéric said, "As far as we know, it was sunk. Their ship, along with the heavy water, went down in the estuary. We don't know their fate. But you can check on it yourself."

The SS soon learned that a ship had hit a mine in the Gironde. The heavy water probably was lost. And the scientists? If they had survived, eventually they would return to Paris.

Diebner was disappointed, but, in truth, the loss of the heavy water did not much matter to him. He had France's cyclotron. Heavy water was being separated now in Norway on a priority basis, and the precious liquid had been promised for later that year. Thousands of tons of uranium oxide were in Brussels, which the Germans now occupied, too. In fact, sixty tons was already being sent to Auer in Berlin. As far as Diebner was concerned, he had everything he needed.

Carl-Friedrich von Weizsäcker, a young theoretical physicist at the Kaiser Wilhelm Institute and a close colleague of Werner Heisenberg, read scientific journals the way that other people read newspapers. He consumed them with great speed, for his understanding of physics was unusual and broad. Indeed, while other Germans poked their noses into their morning *Deutsche Allgemeine Zeitung,* commuting to and from work, he read *Naturwissenschaften,* or the British *Nature,* or the American *Physical Review.* Despite the war, the output of journals was never greater. In England and America, governments had not yet censored the publication of sensitive information. Physics was still a strictly private, academic affair. The physicists themselves could not tell for certain where the research might lead, and therefore they would have condemned government censorship as the behavior of dictators.

In Germany physicists and politicians understood that papers on theoretical physics such as those papers published in America and England had helped them to make their own breakthroughs. If Reich officials did not fathom nuclear physics, they nevertheless saw clearly that enemies might use German scientists' discoveries against Germany. They approved of censorship.

So voracious was his consumption of scientific journals, that von Weizsäcker had nothing to read that morning in July when he headed for the subway that took him to the institute. Delivery of the American physics publication he had been waiting for was delayed because of the war. He satisfied himself with a newspaper and watching his fellow commuters and by thinking, which he did very well. As he went down into the subway station, he thought that Germany showed few signs of being at war. The German armies had conquered France, the Low Countries, Norway, and Denmark. The country had never been stronger, and its industrial war output was enormous. Yet, looking around, people were going about their morning routines as they had been doing for years. Only the headlines of the newspapers in their hands reflected a change.

It made von Weizsäcker proud.

Von Weizsäcker was not a Nazi. Few of the physicists had joined the party, but as an ardent nationalist, he had not disapproved of what the Nazis had accomplished before provoking war; they had helped to give Germany a renewed sense of self-esteem after the worst national crisis in Germany's modern history, during the years of the Weimar Republic. Von Weizsäcker now saw far fewer of the same expressions of defeatism that were so prevalent during the Weimar era. This renewed national spirit bolstered von Weizsäcker's confidence as a scientist. The Nazis were leaving scientists in peace to conduct their work as usual. Von Weizsäcker, for example, enjoyed as much time as he had before the war to think about physics.

For days now, a new concept had occupied his mind. It had not been anything conscious, but it was generally related to uranium 235 and uranium 238 and the way to fuel a self-sustaining chain reaction, the experimental goal that everybody, it seemed everywhere, was trying to achieve.

Then, on his way to work that day, a new concept came to him all at once. Uranium 238, the abundant isotope, absorbed neutrons, often without fissioning. If the nuclei absorbed neutrons, then the atomic weight of uranium 238 would change, creating a new element. This new product, created through the process of chain reaction in natural uranium 238, just might turn out to be fissionable: explosive, even more explosive than the material from which it was derived. This theory sprang from von Weizsäcker's genius: the by-product of the process that bombarded fissionable elements would itself be fissionable. Until this thought occurred to him, he had examined only the potential of uranium 235, the rare uranium isotope, as the material for a bomb. Physicists and chemists in Germany, England, and America were exploring ways to separate the 7 atoms of uranium 235 in every 1,000 atoms of natural uranium 238. Those seven superfissionable U-235 atoms were identical to the 993 other atoms of U-238, except in their atomic weights. Most of the physicists and chemists involved in that line of inquiry knew that the separation of the two uraniums, although not impossible, was unthinkably expensive and would require the creation of an industry.

The new element that von Weizsäcker proposed now, the element resulting from the process of chain reaction in natural uranium, was the same transuranic element discovered by Fermi in 1934, the one that scientists had largely misunderstood. Von Weizsäcker called his element 93 *neptunium* after the planet Neptune. But what was truly extraordinary about von Weizsäcker's theory was the application and interpretation of Fermi's discovery. Von Weizsäcker soon confirmed his idea, at the same time that the postman delivered the overdue June issue of the American *Physical Review*. The *Review* contained an article by a young physicist at the University of California at Berkeley, Glenn T. Seaborg. Independently and many thousands of miles apart, Seaborg had hit on the same idea for a way to produce bomb-grade, superfissionable atomic material from uranium. Von Weizsäcker asked himself as he read the American physics journal whether the Americans could possibly have grasped the implications for war weaponry, for a bomb. Otherwise, why would the American government have so freely allowed Seaborg to publish his findings?

The Kaiser Wilhelm Institute somehow had to manufacture a working pile, a reactor, before the Americans and the British. Success with a chain reaction in a uranium pile might mean the production of element 93. It would give Germany the material with which to fuel a bomb.

Soon afterward, von Weizsäcker wrote a five-page report that brought the news of neptunium's properties to the attention of the Reich War Ministry. The irradiation of uranium in a pile theoretically created a new fissionable product with gigantic explosive potential.

———————

In the West African port of Lobito, a Panama-registered freighter prepared to cast off for sea. Unremarkable looking, the ship had been tied bow and stern to the docks for more than a week while Angolan stevedores grappled with heavy cargo drums that were now loaded and lashed down in a full hold. Oddly, considering the usual pace in this subequatorial region, the freighter had been leased on the spur of the moment, a crew had been assembled hastily, and the harbormaster had given priority loading to the cargo, which had been brought to Lobito by rail from the African interior. The steamer pulled slowly away. When it cleared the port, the captain opened a sealed envelope. The letter inside instructed him of the ship's destination. Now three people knew what it was: Edgar Sengier, his secretary Madame Hamoir, and the captain.

———————

Werner Heisenberg very much wanted to announce a concrete, historic breakthrough. So certain was he now of his ability to create a self-sustaining chain reaction that he had become anxious. He wanted to be first, to rob anybody else—Professor Paul Harteck in Hamburg, or Walter Bothe in Munich, or better yet, some foreign physicist—of the honor. As much as the tributes, he wanted this to garner for himself the reputation of an experimentalist.

But there was one problem. He had asked the Ordnance Department in Berlin to provide him with between 500 and 1,500 kilograms of uranium oxide, but they had given him only 150. Each physicist at each major university was competing to be the first to produce a self-sustaining chain reaction, and each needed the same, or similar, supplies of uranium. And just now there simply was not enough to go around. Diebner had recommended that Paul Harteck, the chemist in Hamburg, and Heisenberg—Hamburg and Leipzig—join forces. Neither man agreed.

Heisenberg had asked Harteck for part of his uranium. The Nobel laureate had written his lesser colleague, "Of course if there is for any reason any urgency in your experiments, you can go first by all means. But I should like to suggest that for the time being you content yourself with just one hundred kilograms."

Harteck was experimenting with the moderator dry ice, which *sublimed* (went from the solid to the vapor state), so of course there was urgency. I.G. Farben had shipped tons of dry ice by special express train to Hamburg, and there was no time to lose if it were not to sublime. Certainly there was no time to lend the uranium to Heisenberg. For Harteck, the ice dictated the test schedule. Once the shipment arrived, I.G. Farben had earmarked all further dry-ice production for the military.

The Ordnance Department tried to placate both physicists, ultimately disappointing both. Just before the dry ice arrived in Hamburg, Army Ordnance sent Harteck 50 kilograms of uranium, then a day later added another 100 kilograms to the insufficient stock, with a warning that Harteck take care not to "damage" the uranium. Harteck had acquired about 185 kilograms of uranium by the time the dry ice arrived, but it still was not enough for his experiments. However, he tried to muddle through, alternating layers of dry ice and uranium oxide. He instructed his team to stand by with counters, but when the moment arrived, the pile construction did not produce any fissioning, almost certainly because so little uranium had been made available. Harteck felt crushed; he found it difficult to accept the pettiness of Heisenberg; who had shown so little magnanimity toward a fellow physicist that the spirit of cooperation completely went out of Harteck.

. But Diebner had not given Heisenberg enough uranium either, and the shortage had also caused failure. Heisenberg blamed Diebner and Harteck, who he thought should have deferred to him, not only because he was a Nobel laureate, but because he could get the job done. If he were given unlimited supplies of uranium and heavy water, he would build Germany a working atomic pile, which might lead to an atomic bomb. He despised the environment of chaos that Diebner had created.

Diebner was a Nazi, a member of the party, a devotee of the Führer, and a problem. Heisenberg had cooperated with him in the Ordnance Department. Until recently, the Dutchman Peter Debye, a noted physicist, had been the director of the Kaiser Wilhelm Institute's Physics Department, and he had earned Heisenberg's respect. But Debye had been forced to resign, and Diebner had nominated himself as the "provisional head."

But Diebner did not have the stature to run the institute. He was a laughingstock to qualified physicists like Harteck, Bothe, and Heisenberg. As a fanatical member of the Nazi party, he had an allegiance to the Führer, not to physics. He would not hesitate to report to the SS and Gestapo, those physicists who lacked the proper fervor. He played one physicist against another, insisting on personal loyalty.

The time had come for Heisenberg to unseat him, now that Diebner had left for Paris to supervise the takeover of the Collège de France personally.

Heisenberg partly moved his research to the institute's laboratory in Berlin-Dahlem, commuting every few days to Elisabeth and the children in Leipzig. The problem of the pile obsessed him. Together with von Weizsäcker, he started building a uranium pile in a separate wood-framed laboratory, next to the larger, older Physics Institute building. Despite all the theory, all the brilliant insights on subways and the like, he and von Weizsäcker still did not know whether a pile would work.

They had calculated a particular configuration of moderators stacked in layers alternating with uranium oxide. Although the design was simple, many variables had to fit perfectly if the uranium were to "ignite." They guessed that heavy water was the most suitable moderator. Until eighty-five gallons arrived from Norway, they would improvise with second best, with paraffin, cautiously entering the world of the unknown, with definite, known dangers. They wore masks and goggles, gloves and boots against the highly toxic uranium oxide, which would kill if absorbed by the lungs or stomach even in microscopic quantities. They did not know how the pile would behave, if it ignited: whether it would explode violently and spew poisonous oxides over the neighboring community.

First they constructed an aluminum cylinder a yard and a half wide and equally tall to contain the moderator and the uranium. Then they alternated layers of uranium with layers of paraffin, submerging the whole container in a pool of plain water. When they thought themselves ready, they lowered a neutron source into a shaft in the center of the sphere, then waited, watching their Geiger counters.

But absolutely nothing happened. The pile failed, which meant that the moderator, either the paraffin or the plain water, was capturing too many neutrons.

Later, they added more uranium and more paraffin; by now they had more than enough supplies of everything except heavy water. And again, when they lowered in the neutron source, the Geiger counters failed to register a chain reaction.

Heavy water, Heisenberg and von Weizsäcker knew, was the key. When the heavy water arrived, they would have their pile, a chain reaction that sustained itself, and the resulting element 93. Despite the failure they were still far ahead in their theory. No physicist outside Germany was likely to catch up.

Part IV

Six thousand dollars wasn't much, but Fermi and Szilard did not complain.

"You look like a coal miner," Szilard remarked, as Fermi climbed down the side of what looked like an immense domino. Black from head to toe, he was smiling, happy with his work: away from the classroom theory and doing what he loved most, tinkering. His teeth, the whites of his eyes, and the tip of an ivory slide rule in his breast pocket were very nearly all of him visible in the dimly lighted room.

Some weeks ago, Fermi had asked Dean Pegram to find him a space in which to construct a pile. He needed a large space, unlike anything the university had been asked by any of its professors to find before.

"A church isn't the best place for a physics laboratory," Pegram had cracked. In fact a cathedral was exactly what he needed, Fermi had thought. He had followed Pegram around the campus, like a dog in search of a lost bone. They wandered into empty classrooms, dark corridors, book stacks, athletic facilities, until finally they emerged from under a low row of heating pipes, into a high-ceilinged room the size of a church's nave in the Schermerhorn building. The space was dim as a cave, but it had looked right to Fermi.

"How do you plan to carry the bricks?" Pegram asked.

Fermi hadn't addressed the problem yet. He was strong, and so was Szilard. The other two team members, Zinn and Anderson, were young and fit. "We'll do it ourselves," he said.

"I have a better idea," Dean Pegram said.

Columbia had not enjoyed a winning football season last year. Maybe, he thought, the team could work itself into shape for next season by hauling graphite bricks. The players were mostly on scholarships, anyway, and could use the extra money, and there was plenty to do.

Szilard had found forty tons of graphite at the United States Graphite Company, which now was trying to meet his requirements for "pure" graphite. The idea of graphite as a moderator had originated with Szilard, and no one knew better that "impurities," such as boron, absorbed neutrons, inhibiting a chain reaction.

Another physicist had set up a milling assembly line in the physics workshop. He adapted an old, unused band saw to cut the chunks of graphite unto uniform "bricks" that the football players then hauled into the basement "cathedral" room of the Schermerhorn building. To shape the uranium oxide, another physicist used a press found in a junkyard across the Hudson River in New Jersey. Once the graphite was cut into bricks, holes were drilled at even intervals and filled with the shaped uranium; then each brick was stacked against another, up and out, until the eventual structure reached four feet by ten feet high, literally a "pile" of graphite bricks.

The sawing, the milling, the pressing, the stacking, and the theorizing took months before what Fermi called an "exponential pile" was ready for testing. They had started to build the pile in the fall, two months after war was declared. It was now January 1940. And only now that it was done did Fermi realize how he had reveled in the work, particularly the teamwork. He liked the physical exercise, the hefting of the heavy bricks, the side-by-side labor with the football players, many times taller and broader than he, with whom he had vied to lift the most bricks. They had responded to his unusual brand of leadership, knowing that he would not let them do anything that he himself had not already done. At the end of each day, they all resembled coal miners, a badge of distinction, especially for Fermi. He had always dreamed of becoming a farmer, when he retired from physics. This work on the pile had contained the physical, healthy labor of the farmer and the mental, theoretical work of the physicist.

Fermi still fundamentally disagreed with Szilard that man could harness practical nuclear energy, either as electricity or, as Szilard insisted, in a nuclear bomb. The work went slowly, step by step, and not just because Fermi saw no immediate need to rush. Haste created dangers for him, his team, and, potentially, the city around them. Besides, Fermi hated to make any move without knowing in theory exactly how that move would turn out. To behave otherwise, he believed, was experimentally reckless.

Fermi was serious about his work, but he wasn't as grim as Szilard, who preached about the dangers of this, the threats of that. Like Chicken Little, to Szilard the sky was always about to fall on his head. Fermi paid little attention, knowing that he was the better seer of future events.

A club in the Physics Department called The Society of Prophets met over lunch in the Men's Faculty Club the first day of each month. They chose a set of ten probable events: whether the Nazis would invade Great Britain, whether the British would defend Tobruk, whether Roosevelt would convince the Congress to end its noninterventionism, and so forth. Everybody these days, it seemed, was trying to predict the same, with or without the imprimatur of a society. Such momentous events were at hand, in the Pacific and in Europe, with America sitting neutral in the middle that it was difficult to imagine that the world would not change, cataclysmically, some believed. The society members made their guesses each month, then handed them to a "secretary," who saved them until the next month's meeting, when the answers were often verified by actual events.

In the Society of Prophets there was only one real prophet: Fermi, who saw the future with astonishing accuracy (97 percent). As always, Fermi enjoyed the competition, and his accuracy helped augment his aura of genius. He based his answers on his conservatism: nothing ever happened as fast as people liked to imagine, even though Hitler's bold diplomatic and military moves were sorely testing the axiom.

If Szilard was correct about the future of atomic bombs, Fermi asked, why was his standing so low among the "prophets"?

The graphite experiments continued at Fermi's pace. When he slipped the radon-beryllium source into the hole, he removed rhodium foils from the upper sections of the pile; then, his feet sliding over the graphite dust on the floor, he ran down a corridor to another room with the Geiger counters, as he had done in the days at the University of Rome. The *half-life* of rhodium is forty-four seconds, meaning that detectable radioactivity died out in that short time. To get a reading of the pile's function—whether it fissioned nuclei, producing neutrons, or merely absorbed them— he had leeway of around fifteen seconds.

He was measuring three quantities that Fermi called *eta, f,* and *p.* Their sum needed to be 1 or more, even factoring for inaccuracies, if the pile were to go "critical" in a self-sustaining chain reaction. He had hoped to measure the three quantities to an accuracy of 1 percent. Any number under *1.0* would signify that graphite was not an effective moderator.

But with their crude instruments, a measurement of such pinpoint accuracy as 1 percent was improbable. The reality was closer to 20 percent, a fifth of a chance to misunderstand what they were doing. If he compounded only three errors by 20 percent, the likelihood of inaccuracy would rise to 35 percent. Even if he found neutron production at 0.90 with a 20 percent accuracy and a 0.3 plus or minus margin or error, the reading would be meaningless. The same applied if the reading were 1.1.

"Push the likelihood high," Szilard urged him, knowing that a high probability made as much sense as a low probability.

Fermi preferred always to underestimate. He would make it more difficult for them; until they were more certain, they would assume that graphite did not have the proper moderating qualities.

Finally they reached an accurate reading.

It was 0.87.

"It's too bad," Fermi said, who started to work on the 0.13 needed to reach the 1.0 before graphite could be targeted as a workable pile moderator.

"What should we do?" Szilard asked.

"There are many things yet to be done," Fermi replied. They had a long way yet to go.

Dr. Peter Debye, the Dutch scientist whom the Nazis had expelled as director when Kurt Diebner took charge of the Kaiser Wilhelm Institute of Physics in Berlin, reached New York with the news that the Germans were working at full capacity toward the development of nuclear energy, toward a bomb. Debye knew firsthand that the talent, brains, and engineering and chemical genius existed in Germany to perfect a nuclear bomb. Once manufactured, there was no question in his mind which course the political leaders would take.

Debye hoped to awaken America to this threat. First he talked with Fermi, who had feared this outcome when Heisenberg left America. Debye said that the Germans were spread out, each in his own university, meeting from time to time at the Kaiser Wilhelm Institute. Fermi, on the other hand, knew since the days with "the boys" that collaborations worked better than separate individuals. Only when the Germans were living and working together would he really start to worry.

Debye next took his message to Leo Szilard; it was all Szilard needed to hear. He was already frustrated by Fermi's rate of progress on the exponential pile. The White House had not mentioned the subject of bomb research for months. The amount of money forthcoming from the Briggs Committee was hardly adequate to buy the materials for testing. Considering Debye's message, the pace seemed dangerous to Szilard, who partly blamed himself. Perhaps the Einstein letter had seemed too technical for nonphysicists such as "Pa" Watson. Szilard asked Einstein to write yet another one that was more direct and even more alarming. Einstein agreed that too little was being done in Washington. It was time that America put its effort on a par with Germany's.

Einstein composed the new letter to Roosevelt himself. "Since the outbreak of war," he wrote,

> interest in uranium has intensified in Germany. I have now learned that research is being carried out in great secrecy and that it has been extended to another of the Kaiser Wilhelm Institutes, the Institute of Physics. The latter has been taken over by the Government and a group of physicists under the leadership of C. F. von Weizsäcker who is now working there on uranium in collaboration with the Institute of Chemistry. The former director was sent away on a leave of absence, apparently for the duration of the war.

Then he added,

> Dr. Szilard has shown me the manuscript which he is sending to the *Physic* [sic] *Review* in which he describes in detail a method of setting up a chain reaction in uranium. The papers will appear in print unless they are held up, and the question arises whether something ought to be done to withhold publication.

In other words, Szilard was threatening to give valuable information to Germany if the White House did not formulate a policy about nuclear energy research. If the White House allowed the paper to be published, it would then be evident that the Briggs Committee was window dressing. Once they knew where they stood with the government, Einstein, Fermi, Szilard, Sachs, and physicists such as Edward Teller, also working at Columbia, and Eugene Wigner, at Princeton, could plan accordingly.

In the meantime, Szilard made Debye's information public.

W. L. Laurence, *The New York Times*'s science reporter, had fulfilled his earlier promise to interview German scientists arriving in America. He had learned from them that the "club" of German scientists working on atomic power was very small. He had asked, "Where are the scientists?" to determine whether Germany were working on the atomic bomb, and then who was involved. It was obvious that the top men, Heisenberg, Hahn, Harteck, and Bothe, were involved. He had asked the exiles, "Where is this one; where is that one?" The latest answer: in Berlin. The Nazis had recently started to concentrate all these scientists in one laboratory, in one institution.

Earlier, Laurence had interviewed Albert Einstein at Princeton on the mathematician's sixtieth birthday. Laurence had a solid lead to go on, and he asked, "How about this discovery of uranium fission? Doesn't that change your opinions about the possibilities of utilization of atomic energy on a large scale?"

Einstein had answered, "No," he did not think so.

But other information contradicted Einstein's "opinion." Privately, Laurence felt certain that Hitler "will make an atom bomb and make it ahead of us, and if he succeeds in doing that, it will be the end of the free world as we know it."

But he had not yet reported that in *The New York Times*.

Szilard told Laurence about Debye, whom he then interviewed. What he heard alarmed him. He wrote the story at unusual length, reporting in detail facts related by Debye and augmented by his other interviews. He wanted to explain the magnitude of the German effort. Nearly every German scientist, physicist, chemist, and engineer, Laurence wrote, had been told "to drop all other researches and devote themselves to this work alone. All these research workers, it was learned, are carrying out their tasks feverishly at the laboratories of the Kaiser Wilhelm Institute at Berlin."

Public reaction to the story surprised Laurence.

There was none.

Laura Fermi was more in the dark than before. She was physically distanced from her husband, across the Hudson, just as she was distanced from his work. Although she thought the work had some relation to nuclear energy, or perhaps a bomb, she did not understand why he arrived home every evening looking like a chimney sweep. And she didn't ask, because her questions were usually met by a shrug. He had explained to her once, and that was enough, that she should keep any information about him to herself. The war in Europe forced people to be secretive, especially the immigrants. It was good enough for her to support him, even if it meant not knowing. The other wives largely felt the same. Harold Urey's wife, Frieda, and Laura discussed this estrangement. They felt that their silence supported their husbands' work. In the meantime, there were children to raise, a house in the Palisades to maintain, and, worst of all for Laura and Enrico, weeds to pull.

Fermi had wondered aloud why all the people in Leonia seemed so preoccupied with their gardens, particularly the front gardens. What was different about crabgrass? It was green and it filled the space where the lawn was supposed to grow. What then distinguished grass from weeds?

Harold Urey, their neighbor, answered him, "Weeds grow spontaneously, without being planted. They take up space, air, and food from good plants and kill them. At the end of the season they die and nothing is left."

Fermi retorted, "Therefore, a weed is an unlicensed animal."

The definition did nothing to solve the "problem." He was content to watch the crabgrass grow. But its presence embarrassed Laura; it made her house different. As an immigrant, she wanted to meld into the new society. Her strong accent was bad enough, and her daily habits set her apart too. She was happy in America. Returning to Rome after the war was never discussed, and she guessed that they would become Americans. "It's a free country" seemed to say it all. Europe would always be torn by upheaval. Wars had been fought there twice in thirty years. America had always been safe.

The children loved it, too. Despite the change, Nella and Giulio had learned flawless English. Nella had scored close to 100 percent on an intelligence test. Laura had asked the teacher what question she had missed. She had not been able to identify a small animal with a white stripe on its back. Laura had asked the name of the animal. "A skunk," the teacher said. Of course. Skunks did not exist in Europe.

There were days, though, when she missed Italy. America was so complicated. There was so much to learn. The Anglo-Saxon culture ignored Italian history and culture. No one knew what she was talking about when she named Meucci as the inventor of the telephone, Leonardo as the creator of the airplane, and Dante as the greatest author of all time. The Americans had never heard their names.

She and Enrico mentioned her family in Rome less and less, although she thought about them more. As far as she could tell, Rome was still bad for Jews, but not yet intolerable. According to what she had heard, her father persisted in his blind belief. She prayed that he was right. There was no secret among German Jews in New York about the concentration camps at Dachau and Bergen-Belsen. There was no secret about who was sent to them. There were rumors about what the Nazis did to Jews, but everybody said that it was too preposterous. The Nazis were not killing Jews in these camps. But the rumors frightened her all the same.

Whatever Enrico was doing at Columbia, she hoped it would help bring an end to the war soon.

In late April 1940, Fermi, Szilard, and Sachs attended a meeting at the National Bureau of Standards in Washington. Lyman Briggs, the chairman of their Committee on Uranium, had felt the pressure from people like Laurence of *The New York Times,* Szilard, Einstein, and Ernest Lawrence, the Nobel laureate and inventor of the cyclotron: the atomic energy project simply could not survive without government funds. Briggs had called the meeting to ask whether anything would result from the expense. There was a scarcity of money. America was providing Britain with the material and finances to fight the Battle of Britain, and nobody wanted a scientific fly-by-night project to take resources from their chances to defeat the German Luftwaffe.

Fermi had only agreed to attend reluctantly. He knew he would be asked for opinions again.

Einstein had declined the invitation. But he had put what he wanted to say in a letter: "I am convinced as to the wisdom and urgency of creating the conditions under which that [atomic energy] and related work can be carried out with greater speed and on a larger scale than hitherto."

When it came his turn to speak, Szilard was his usual politically pessimistic and scientifically optimistic self. Speaking like a salesman for nuclear research, he said that the self-sustaining chain reaction in a pile was all but certain. He could not say for sure whether it might lead to the construction of a bomb, but his opinion about the pile served to counterbalance the straight factual account given by Fermi.

Sachs offered a unique proposal. Sachs was an economist, a businessman, a financier for whom nuclear power offered a profit potential. Investors would not demand the same assurances Briggs did. If the government were not interested, then, Sachs told Briggs, private enterprise would get the job done.

Fermi told Briggs that the work on the exponential pile was going slowly. For now, however, it was irresponsible to recommend large-scale research. It might be throwing good money after bad. Privately, he appreciated one point that Szilard and Sachs did not understand: that if after he promised Briggs success and the experiments failed, he would never again be trusted. He would not allow himself to be pressured by colleagues or friends. Facts, the truth: nothing more, nothing less mattered to him.

Sachs said that if the government funded large-scale research, Fermi's doubts would be overcome. But as things were, they had locked themselves into a circle of self-defeat. The experiments failed because they were starved of funds. The circle needed breaking, either by the government or by private investors. As long as they continued with six thousand dollars here, a few thousand there, they would not know the truth until it was too late.

Briggs listened closely. Although their opinions were all very interesting, nothing in fact had changed since the committee first met. They had not discovered anything new. Nothing had occurred to change his opinion that nuclear energy was still a fantastical idea, a million miles from reality. He would not recommend that the president appropriate more funds, unless, perhaps, Fermi's graphite reactor somehow cleared the impasse with real, concrete results. He set up a time to visit Fermi at Columbia.

Other people in America were less cautious than Briggs. They were seeing what they thought were dark shadows on the wall. Vannevar Bush, the chairman of the Advisory Committee on Aeronautics and former vice-president of the Massachusetts Institute of Technology, an inventor, scientist, and administrator, believed that science had a responsibility to defeat Hitler. This war, he sensed, much more than the last one, for which he had developed a submarine-detection technology, was going to be decided by advanced technologies: aircraft, submarines, new weapons. Science was war machinery; there was no sense in pretending that it was not. If the United States were to join the Allies, the country's scientists in the university and military laboratories should be prepared to invent war-winning weapons.

Bush had already presented this argument to the president, who gave him the authority to establish the National Defense Research Committee (NDRC) to coordinate, fund, and oversee all aspects of science in war. The top priority, of course, was radar, followed by other defensive technologies: sonar for the underwater detection of submarines and jet-engine development. Well down the list was Briggs's committee. The NDRC now became a second and far wealthier source of funds for projects created by the committee, independent of the military.

Soon, the NDRC sent Fermi an unexpected forty thousand dollars.

The money brought the Columbia team no closer to an understanding of graphite as a neutron brake. Back at the laboratory in the basement of Schermerhorn, Fermi continued to test his pile. He wanted to understand the 0.13 deficit for the benchmark figure 1.0 for neutron production in a self-sustaining chain reaction. Somehow, he said, they had to "squeeze" out the extra 0.13, "or a little bit more."

The initial 0.87 figure had been a disappointment, that much was true, but it signified little about the actual potential of graphite. They still had not quantified the impurities that reduced the production of neutrons through nonfissionable absorption. Which absorptive materials could be eliminated from the pile, thereby reducing nonfissionable absorption? One was the iron used in the bulwark holding together the piled graphite and uranium oxide.

Shifting variables; testing the new, purer materials; shaping others; chemically analyzing the results took weeks of painstaking, eighteen-hour days in the laboratory. Fermi was thorough, but he acknowledged that luck played an important role. Luck had been largely responsible for his prize-winning theory of slow neutrons. Luck to him, though, was trying again and again, every possible angle and use, until an idea was proved right or exhausted. Luck required work.

If the graphite acquired by Szilard were pure enough, all the signs so far indicated that the exponential pile would show the first faint stirrings of life, and with that to encourage him, Fermi could then speak to Briggs and Vannevar Bush with more certainty than he had so far. Right now, it came down to his ability to squeeze the 0.13 deficit down to 1.0 or anything greater than 1.0, a benchmark Fermi designated with the letter k.

To anyone observing Fermi and Szilard in the basement of Schermerhorn, short tests for purities punctuated frantic bursts of pure physical labor as the bricks were machined and stacked. The real drama took place mostly in the mind; outwardly, there was little to see. Methodically, Fermi adjusted the variables, so that he could get the most accurate measurement of the graphite, eliminating what he could and substituting where he could not. During a test, after he had introduced the neutron source into the exponential pile, he would sprint with the measuring foil into a separate room with the counters lined up on a table and read the gauges for a sign that they were closer to the magic k. It was wearisome, plodding work with no promise of success.

And yet the signs calculated on his slide rule encouraged Fermi, for the deficit fell from 0.13 to 0.11, then to 0.09. They were on the right track, after all, and he saw no reason now that they should not succeed, if only they could eliminate enough materials that absorbed the neutrons without fissioning from the pile. Finally, they reached a state of purity that they could not improve with the existing technologies and supplies. They had come as far as they could go. Now they tested again.

Fermi slid the neutron source into the pile and waited for the neutrons to "cook," rising in the pile from the source outward. The fissioning, he knew, could not sustain itself. That was not the question now. Many months and a lot of luck would be needed before that point could be even approached, but if they had a positive result from graphite, an important hurdle would have been cleared.

No laboratory in America was farther removed from Fermi's Schermerhorn than Gilman Hall at the University of California's Berkeley campus, across the bay from San Francisco. No laboratory could have *seemed* farther than the one in room 307-A, where a twenty-eight-year-old teacher of freshman physics worked his modest side of nuclear physics. Because of his age and his reputation among physicists, the university had relegated Glenn T. Seaborg to a "lab" no larger than a walk-in closet.

Seaborg, the six-foot, three-inch son of a blue-collar worker, had entered a physics career almost by accident. Fermi's early work had fascinated him; in particular, he had puzzled over the transuranic elements. Then Meitner and Hahn's solution to the puzzle of fission had amazed Seaborg for its utter simplicity. It was so obvious that he wondered how he had missed it. The night after the news reached Berkeley, he had tested fission himself.

During the day, he taught first-year physics, stealing time from his normal course work for research. In the evenings, he courted a Berkeley woman and discussed the exciting advances in physics with other young teachers and graduate students who gathered at the Varsity Coffee Shop on the corner of Telegraph and Bancroft. Late at night, Seaborg slept in a dormitory at the Faculty Club, a rambling, shingled building in a grove of spruce trees on the edge of the campus, within the sound of the bells in the famous Berkeley campanilla.

Ernest Lawrence, the Nobel laureate and inventor of the cyclotron, dominated Berkeley's Physics Department. Lawrence seemed larger even than his achievements: dashingly handsome and possessed of an unbending personality. Students revered him, and each hoped to be singled out to join his research team. Because that dream for the moment seemed beyond Seaborg's reach, he lived less in Lawrence's shadow, enjoying more freedom of choice and the unrestricted use of this cramped laboratory. Lawrence's absolute belief in the future reality of atomic energy, nevertheless, had influenced the direction of Seaborg's research.

Physicists had known for many years that heavier elements than uranium probably existed. The existence of neptunium (Fermi's element 93) had been proved by irrefutable chemical means in Germany and England only months before. The next element, he theorized, should have ninety-four protons in its nucleus, but researchers so far had not found the ninety-fourth element because it, like element 93, did not exist in nature. Scientists surmised that once, many billions of years ago, it had been present in the swirling mists that had collected from the debris of exploding stars to form Earth. But it had decayed out of existence after only a few billion years to form the most mundane of elements, lead. In the meantime, the technology to create elements by synthetic means with accelerators and simple neutron sources and to separate them by chemical means had been developed. To Seaborg, element 94 was "logical," but finding it was by no means easy.

Seaborg had tried for months to find out whether neutrons

absorbed by natural uranium created another, heavier element besides element 93. Last spring—it was now December—a colleague at the university had found traces in bombarded uranium of a heretofore unidentified, heavy radioactive substance. The colleague had written about the discovery in a subsequent issue of *Physical Review*. He too had suspected the existence of yet another, heavier element, this one with 94 protons in its nucleus, which formed as a by-product of element 93, but he could not be certain either.

Glenn Seaborg had started last summer by bombarding bits of uranium with *deuterons* (the nuclei of deuterium, heavy hydrogen, atoms), in a powerful cyclotron. Now, on the afternoon of December 14, he plastered uranium oxide on a copper plate, which he placed gently into a vacuum-creating bell jar. He bombarded the plate with 16 million electron volts of deuterons constantly from eight that night until midnight. The next morning, Seaborg took the plate out of the bell jar and carried it to room 307-A of Gilman Hall.

The lab was on the top floor. A bare sink with a cold-water faucet hooked to a rotting rubber tube stood to the left of a door. Opposite the sink was Seaborg's desk, where he wrote out his research notes in a small black notebook. Because of the lack of space, Seaborg had built a glass shelf on a balcony outside the window on which to "cook" compounds without overwhelming himself with the smell. Nevertheless, a sour odor pervaded the air. A quartz-fiber electroscope and the Geiger counter to detect radioactivity were tucked into a shelf under the beams of the roof that hung so low that Seaborg bent over to move around.

Seaborg next scraped the copper plate with the end of a rusted ice pick for twenty minutes, then dissolved the filings in hot nitric acid, which turned them green. As the quiet hours of that Sunday passed, with most of the university faculty spending the morning in church or at home with their families, Seaborg waited for the scrapings to dissolve and precipitate into their component parts. Later that day, Seaborg searched the split samples for radioactive traces.

At two fourteen on Monday morning, he exposed sample 93-7-2

to an FP-54 electrometer, which indicated the presence of a new element, 94. Exhausted from his weekend's labors, Seaborg wanted nothing more now than to fall into bed. But before leaving for the Faculty Club's dorm, he transferred the new element onto a strip of platinum, then searched around for a container. He spied a box of his boss's cigars. It had contained Alhambra Casinos: "Wooden Box N. 50 'Claros.'" He lifted the lid; it was empty, except for the printed advertising message, "Real 10 cents Value 5 cents." Seaborg placed the platinum plate on a cotton wad inside the box. Last of all before heading downstairs into the early morning, he wrote a warning, which he taped to the top: VERY VALUABLE SAMPLE, DO NOT DISTURB IN ANY WAY.

Days became weeks after that night, as the word of his discovery went out. Still called *element 94,* it needed a name. As the "father," Seaborg thought of *extremium.* But a tradition that had begun with the discovery of uranium, of naming new elements after the planets, existed among chemists. Element 93 was named after Neptune, the next planet after Uranus. Seaborg decided on *plutium,* for the planet Pluto. Plutium became *plutonium.*

Seaborg was not then aware of the irony. Pluto, the deity after whom the planet was named, was the Roman god of death, and the Greek lord of hell. The irony was that plutonium had only one reason to exist: as fuel for an atomic bomb.

Emilio Segrè, one of the former "boys" of Senator Corbino in Rome, walked beside Fermi down the esplanade that borders the Hudson River. The two old friends from Rome in 1934 were in such deep conversation that neither looked toward the Hudson to Grant's Tomb or to the docks where they had first landed in America. In the preceding weeks Segrè, as a professor of physics at Berkeley, had followed Seaborg's discovery. When Seaborg had finally proved plutonium's existence beyond a doubt, Segrè had analyzed its properties. He had found that plutonium, like U-235, was fissionable. So far he could state with utter certainty that plutonium was 1.7 times more fissionable under certain conditions than the isotope uranium 235!

This discovery had awakened Segrè to the imminent reality of an atomic weapon. Ironically, it was Fermi who could produce bomb quantities of element 94. Fermi's pile was the key. Work on the pile suddenly had become immediate, almost urgent.

Segrè earlier reported his analysis to Ernest Lawrence, who also recognized the new importance of a uranium pile. He wrote, "An extremely important new possibility has been opened for the exploitation of the chain reaction with unseparated isotopes of uranium." With this new, highly fissionable plutonium, there was less need to pursue the expensive and elaborate separation processes of the rare isotope uranium 235 from the heavier isotope uranium 238. "It appears that if a chain reaction . . . is achieved, it may be allowed to proceed . . . for a period of time for the express purpose of manufacturing element 94 [plutonium]," he wrote. Indeed, if Fermi's pile were able to produce a self-sustaining chain reaction, then a self-sustaining chain reaction would "cook" the uranium 238 into the precious broth of plutonium. A bomb would be nearer to reality, and no skeptic would doubt it. The government would pour money and talent into its rapid development. "If large amounts [of plutonium] were available it is likely that a chain reaction with fast neutrons [neutrons unhindered by the braking effect of a moderator] could be produced," Lawrence continued. "In such a reaction the energy would be released at an explosive rate which might be described as a 'super bomb.' "

"If large amounts were available . . . ," Lawrence had written. Perhaps, assuming that Fermi succeeded in manufacturing plutonium, only a small quantity would be necessary for an explosive. If that were so, then surely they could manufacture an explosive in time to change the course of the war. Fermi discussed this question of quantity on his walk with Segrè.

Even an approximate answer meant everything to Segrè. He had watched the triumphs of Hitler and heard rumors of a Nazi nuclear lead. In the nunnery days, Fermi had nicknamed him "The Basilisk" for the speed of his angry reaction to personal remarks, even those made in jest. Fermi knew that he had resigned as the director of the physics laboratories at the University of Palermo in Sicily because of the Fascists and, by extension, because of the Nazis. Segrè, as a Jew, had been forced into exile.

Fermi stopped to face the Hudson, but hardly to embrace the sight. He took from his breast pocket a small slide rule with which he made several fast calculations. Then he turned toward the esplanade and resumed his walk. Fermi used the so-called uranium 235 cross-section calculations, applying them to plutonium.

Finally he said to Segrè, "We can do it."

Both men stopped and turned to each other.

"We need only pounds, on the order of six pounds," Fermi said.

They changed direction, east, toward Riverside Drive, where they hailed a taxi back to Morningside Heights. There, in the Pupin Hall offices, they met with Dean Pegram and Ernest Lawrence, who had come east with Segrè. A bomb now required only unseparated isotopes of natural uranium 238 cooked in a pile. Now it all depended on Fermi.

Part V

By the fall of 1941, Heisenberg had a "feeling" about the nuclear research. Everything in the past had seemed to conspire to slow him down, but those obstacles were now disappearing, leaving a clear, straight road ahead. The first shipment of the Norwegian heavy water, about 725 pounds, had arrived in Germany, the first of 3,000 pounds guaranteed by the Army Ordnance Department before the end of 1941. Auer and Company was processing about a ton of uranium metal a month. And the war was going well too. German troops had invaded Russia, with nothing to stop them from reaching Moscow, everybody imagined, by Christmas. An optimistic mood prevailed, for no one more than for Heisenberg.

Shortages, particularly of heavy water, had been the reason that Heisenberg's experimental pile had not yet performed as anticipated according to theory. A success was a function of proportion and shape: enough layers of heavy water between enough layers of uranium stacked together in a pile and a chain reaction would become self-sustaining. Nobody had proved or even completely tested it yet. But Heisenberg knew that he could succeed.

He felt optimism too because of recent changes at the Kaiser Wilhelm Institute in Berlin. The director's chair, since the Nazis had forced Debye out, had not been filled. Heisenberg was succeeding in his effort to prevent Diebner from becoming the permanent director. How long he could keep out the Nazis, represented by Diebner, he could not say. The Nazis' influence, particularly in physics, with their dangerous Aryan fantasies, continued to worry him. The more successful their nuclear research, Heisenberg knew, the more the Nazis would want to make decisions for them.

Heisenberg started to ask himself questions he had never thought to ask before. What would be the consequences of a super-bomb? How would it be used, against whom, and what would its effects be, should it be made? Aloud he wondered,

The psychological situation of American physicists, and particularly of those who have emigrated from Germany and who have been received so hospitably, is completely different from ours. They must all be firmly convinced that they are fighting for a just cause. But is the use of an atom bomb, by which hundreds of thousands of civilians will be killed instantly, warrantable even in defense of a just cause? Can we really apply the old maxim that the ends sanctify the means? In other words, are we entitled to build atom bombs for a good cause but not for a bad one? And if we take that view . . . who decides which cause is good and which is bad? All in all, I think we may take it that even American physicists are not too keen on building atom bombs. But they could, of course, be spurred on by the fear that we may be doing so.

He had received some intelligence about the progress of Allied research. Besides, he felt certain that those physicists who had fled Nazi persecution would not rest until they had manufactured a uranium bomb, and naturally, their target could be the heart of Germany, maybe even Berlin itself. There was a solid rationale of self-defense, Heisenberg felt, in continuing his own research. Unless he worked hard, he and his family might soon become the victims of his own laziness and moralizing.

He set up a second pile in the Leipzig laboratory. The first pile there had failed to chain-react for want of enough heavy water. He gave the second pile a spherical shape in an aluminum casing. Two layers each of uranium oxide weighing a little more than 300 pounds and heavy water, weighing about 350 pounds, surrounded a neutron source buried in the center of the sphere. The whole apparatus rested in a pool of natural water in the corner of the lab.

The Geiger counters told Heisenberg whether the pile was "manufacturing" neutrons or chain-reacting. He knew the number of neutrons emitted by the source, or "starter." If the uranium engine were working, the Geiger counters would detect more neutrons than the neutron source had produced initially.

Once he had activated the neutron source, nothing happened. The counters indicated no neutron production.

Heisenberg thought that perhaps the reaction was too small to be read by the counters. Or perhaps the aluminum casing had absorbed the newly manufactured neutrons on their outward path from the central neutron source.

So he had compensated for this effect and then counted once again. This time he extrapolated a positive reading. The pile indeed had produced neutrons, weakly, barely stirring, but neutrons nevertheless.

The next, larger pile, he knew, would sustain itself. And the immediacy of this goal gave Heisenberg pause to contemplate its implications, and he sought a friend to give him advice. Heisenberg decided that he would not take that final, irrevocable step, without first getting absolution from the great man himself, Niels Bohr.

For Bohr in Denmark, life under the Nazis went on much as before the occupation. The Germans gave him considerable freedom to visit his summer house in Tisvilde. On occasion he sailed his small sloop in the Kattegat, that narrow body of water between Denmark and Sweden. He sent messages to the Allies in London, and from there to America, via an effective and secure underground network. He was not allowed to travel abroad, and for Bohr that prohibition was difficult to bear because the Nazis had forced so many of his colleagues and friends into exile. He missed the healthy intellectual exchange of before the war.

Bohr now lived between two worlds. He had close friends and respected colleagues in Germany and in England and America, physicists on both sides of the conflict. The young man he had taken under his wing in 1922, Werner Heisenberg, had stayed in Nazi Germany. Heisenberg had been his protégé, a young man who had seemed to understand "everything at once." Thanks largely to him, Heisenberg had climbed fast in physicists' circles.

Enrico Fermi had entered Bohr's life later than Heisenberg. That conference in 1922, when they had first met, Fermi had been quiet and reserved, seemingly outclassed that summer. Bohr later understood why. Fermi, almost completely self-taught in physics, did not trust pure theory; ideas needed testing every step of the way. And 1922 had been a summer of pure theory.

Since then, Fermi had become Bohr's favorite. Bohr respected him for the balance of his genius: his theoretical ability matched the experimental. Even more, although he admired both men, he genuinely liked Fermi.

Bohr did not question either man's motivations, but he had wondered about Heisenberg. Before they had fled to America three years ago, staying for Christmas at the Bohrs' home in Copenhagen, Fermi had told Bohr why he and his family had to leave Italy. They had not discussed Nazi treatment of Jews, but Bohr as a Jew had understood. Anyone who would *choose* to remain a part of that system must be as flawed morally as the system itself.

Heisenberg suggested a meeting with Bohr through the German Embassy in Copenhagen under the guise of a lecture at Bohr's institute. When they finally met, they talked frankly about what weighed on their minds as Bohr, accompanied by Heisenberg, took a constitutional under the stars.

Heisenberg asked, "Do you think it's right for physicists to devote themselves in a war to the uranium problem?"

Bohr, his large head resting on his breast, asked in reply, "Do you really think that uranium fission can be used for the construction of weapons?"

"In principle, yes."

Bohr was so shocked he could barely speak. Heisenberg, he felt, had come to Copenhagen for the single purpose of conveying to him this information about a German bomb. He wondered whether Heisenberg was trying to trick him. Was he trying to find out what he knew about the Allied nuclear program, or perhaps spread disinformation through Bohr? Bohr said, "The involvement of physicists in war is unavoidable. And it is justified. It is not possible for physicists to unite in a cause against the will of their governments."

Heisenberg asked Bohr to use his influence with the Allied physicists to stop their nuclear research. Heisenberg promised to try to do so in Germany. But would he? Or was Heisenberg's visit a plan to persuade the Allies to quit? Before the war Heisenberg had been offered security and the promise of work in America, but he had refused. Wouldn't he now be working hard, Bohr asked himself, to ensure Germany's victory? Wasn't he perhaps playing Bohr, an old friend, as a pawn?

The Germans must know the secret of an atomic bomb, Bohr concluded from this conversation. Unless the Allies did something, and fast, they would be at the receiving end of this discovery. Frightened, Bohr broke off the conversation. A silence fell between the two men, master and protégé.

Heisenberg could not understand how he had offended Bohr. He had come from Berlin to seek his advice. Yet, no matter how much he wanted to continue talking, he could not be honest and open for fear of the Gestapo. However, Bohr seemed removed, as if to say that he knew about an Allied effort to produce an atomic bomb. If the Allied project were of such infancy that the comparison with the German effort startled Bohr, then the Germans were well ahead. He had not received the absolution he sought from Bohr, but Heisenberg did not return to Berlin empty-handed. He could now be certain that the Americans and the British were at work on a uranium bomb. They had not progressed far, but they knew about the potential use of uranium as a weapon of war.

One morning a few months later, the directors and scientists of the Kaiser Wilhelm Institute escorted a group of guests into the ground-floor meeting room of the institute's Berlin physics building. The room had been arranged with a table like a stage for the chairman and seven other featured speakers, watched by an audience of distinguished guests including representatives of the Reich, the high command, the SS, the Army, and the Navy who would listen to the scientists' presentation, then either vote to step up the commitment to a bomb or to continue as before.

Heisenberg and his fellow scientists envisaged this conference as an unusual scientific "sales conference." No speeches were to be too long, too complicated, too boring, too far from the comprehension of the simplest of the guests to confuse or bore or annoy. Everything had been geared for the nonscientist to show the product in its best light. As if to underscore the sales character of the meeting, Heisenberg, when the time came for him to speak, used a simple analogy to describe the theory of creating energy from uranium fission. He told the guests,

> The behavior of neutrons in uranium can be compared with the behavior of a human population sample—taking the fission process as analogous to "marriage" and the capture process as analogous to "death." In natural uranium [U-238], the "death-rate" exceeds the "birth-rate," with the result that any given population is bound to die out after a short time. . . . If one could assemble a lump of uranium-235 large enough for the escape of neutrons from its surface to be small compared with the internal neutron multiplication, then the number of neutrons would multiply enormously in a very short space of time, and the whole uranium fission energy, of 15 million-million calories per ton, would be liberated in a fraction of a second.

Next he offered his audience a description of a pile, or reactor, as a collection of natural uranium 238 and a chosen modifier in a shape and quantity to allow the neutrons to multiply, thus producing energy; he explained his reasons for believing that heavy water would produce the best results as a modifier, and, then, once he had laid out the basics before them, he lectured on the applications of atomic energy. If German physicists could achieve a self-sustaining chain reaction in a uranium pile, he said, then several possibilities would be open. Specifically, the pile could be transformed into an engine; the heat from the chain reaction in the uranium could produce steam to drive a turbine, which could propel a submarine for long distances without the need in wartime of surfacing. The pile had another application as well, he told his audience:

> As soon as the pile begins, the question of producing the explosive receives a new twist: through the transmutation of uranium [U-238] inside the pile a new element is created [plutonium] which is in all probability as explosive as pure uranium 235, with the same colossal force. The Americans seem to be pursuing this line of research with particular energy.

Others spoke after Heisenberg, but none conveyed the same immediacy. Not only was Heisenberg's speech a model of simplicity and directness, but he was a Nobel laureate sharing dark secrets with his audience. Until now the scientific priesthood alone possessed the knowledge that Heisenberg had shared. The secrets were no longer chalked numbers and signs on a blackboard that only physicists could understand, but applications that could help Germany win the war. The audience could nearly feel the imminent reality of nuclear electricity to power the Reich, of U-boats plying the Atlantic for months underwater without the need for oxygen and the implications for their enemies. Less tangible and yet more exciting was Heisenberg's vision of bombs with energy a hundred million million times that of chemical explosives.

But if Heisenberg was a persuasive salesman for nuclear energy, the men in the audience that day were unfortunately not the prime buyers of his goods. Heisenberg had been surprised by the caliber of the audience before him; he thought he had the influence to attract men of more power from within the Reich. His presentation had been simple and illustrative, but it had fallen on the wrong ears. He had not known until he had entered the conference room who they were; none of the faces had been recognizable to Heisenberg, but he still did not think that the ministries would have sent men who were no more significant in terms of policy than secretaries and junior executives. Their bosses had not appeared that morning, perhaps to avoid what they thought would be an impenetrable, boring scientific symposium in which the priests of the temple would mumble incantations to their peculiar gods. Politely but firmly, Himmler, Speer, Göring, Field Marshal Wilhelm Keitel, among others in charge of the SS, the high command, and the Reich, had simply canceled at the last moment with such transparent excuses as previous engagements, illness, and out-of-town trips, sending their underlings in their place. The nature and timing of the refusals being such, Heisenberg asked the institute administrators to find out why. They later reported that a dreadful clerical mistake had been made by one of the secretaries, who had slipped the agenda into the invitation envelopes for another, purely scientific meeting that few of the people invited would have been able to understand. No wonder the ministry leaders had refused the invitations.

Another date was set, and this time, after the correct agenda was sent, Minister of Munitions Albert Speer agreed to attend. The acceptance excited the physicists at the institute, who knew that nobody in the Reich, except perhaps Hitler, carried more weight in the area of procurement or was better placed to be an advocate for nuclear energy. Intelligent, with a technical background, forward-looking, and yet realistic, he could be talked to intelligently, and he had the power to reach Hitler. If he advocated nuclear energy, research would be funded on a scale that made sense.

The physicists showed Speer and his ministry's top officials into the institute's Harnack headquarters in Berlin-Dahlem. When it came his turn to speak, Heisenberg approached the rostrum with the knowledge that if this attempt to gain support failed, Germany could lose its lead in the race for nuclear energy. And so he went skillfully through his paces, this time emphasizing the bomb. He ticked off U-boat propulsion, energy, and finally, plutonium as an explosive element more readily acquired than uranium 235.

Before he stepped down, Heisenberg asked his audience for

questions. A general asked, "How large would an atomic bomb have to be if it were to destroy a large city?"

Heisenberg raised his arms and made a circle with his hands. "As large as a pineapple," he said.

Speer was impressed and later said so. Within days, he reported the essence of the meeting to the Führer.

Soon after, large-scale construction projects received the ministry's approval. A bombproof shelter was authorized for the construction of a pile at the Berlin-Dahlem Institute. A new Reich Research Council was established, this time with Himmler and Göring as members. The nuclear project received the highest priority in the Reich, which even the V-1 and V-2 rocket programs did not have. It was much more than Heisenberg could have hoped. He returned immediately to Leipzig with a renewed sense of mission, this time to construct a new pile.

Coded *L-IV*, his most ambitious pile so far, its size and shape were the key. L-IV was a little less than two feet in diameter and spherical. Two layers of heavy water, weighing around three hundred pounds, and nearly three-quarters of a ton of uranium metal fit inside the aluminum casing. A radon-beryllium neutron source was designed to slip into the heart of the sphere through a pipelike channel running half its diameter. The whole pile resembled a large upside-down lollipop.

After months of preparation—scooping the uranium into the designated layers, then waiting for further supplies of heavy water to arrive in Germany—Heisenberg and his assistant were ready to test L-IV. He lowered the pile slowly into a tank of plain water, then introduced the neutron source into the pipe. Heisenberg watched the Geiger counters and listened for their telltale clicking. Soon, he started to feel elated. This pile was producing neutrons, without a counteracting absorption by the heavy water, the aluminum in the casing, or the air. This indeed pointed the way to a self-sustaining chain reaction, which now lacked only a supply of heavy water. Everything finally tested out beautifully.

As soon as Heisenberg had rechecked his calculations, he wrote to the War Ministry. In guarded, confident language, he said that "a simple expansion of the pile configuration described would lead to a uranium reactor from which energy approximating to the energies within the atomic nucleus can be extracted." In so many words he said that once he had received five tons of heavy water and more solid uranium metal, he, Heisenberg, would usher in the nuclear age.

Heisenberg reported the news to Elisabeth; then, as he did most evenings at home in Leipzig, he played his Blüthner grand piano. He felt curiously at peace. He had come to terms with his dilemma. Everything that could be done, he had done by taking the warning to Niels Bohr, and, in a sense receiving the great man's absolution. With that meeting he had satisfied whatever obligation he owed to his old friends. By speaking out to Speer, he had served his other master by explaining nuclear possibilities so that even the simplest person could understand, and his voice had been heard. Now Allied nuclear weapons could not catch Germany off guard; he was giving Germany a strong position in the race. Of course the bomb would be used only as a political deterrent. It might even *save* lives. And last, as he sat at the piano, he knew that he had arrived at the very brink of achievement. He was within sight of harnessing the power of the atom. If events outside his control in the last few months had pushed him off that balance, that harmony and peacefulness that he tried so hard to maintain, it did not matter now.

Minutes after he had left the Leipzig laboratory, however, bubbles started to appear in the water tank, floating up from the bottom of the aluminum sphere. Heisenberg's assistant noted this "fish-tank" effect as nothing more than a reaction of the uranium and the water to a small leak. The bubbles soon stopped, and the assistant winched the container out of the water tank and inspected to determine the precise amount of water that had seeped into the sphere. A second technician used a wrench to loosen bolts joining the two halves of the sphere; a sucking sound indicated a partial vacuum inside the sphere. But a hiss soon replaced the sucking as air rushed out of the container. The stream of air intensified into a jet of hot particles of uranium.

Seconds later, a bright flame the length of a man's arm flared out of the opening. Alarmed, the assistant released the winch chain, dousing the container in the water; then quickly, as the jet subsided, he siphoned off the heavy water inside the sphere. He lowered the sphere back into the water tank, with the idea that the water would continue to cool the aluminum until the whole pile could be handled manually.

Heisenberg was told, but he did not see reason for concern, and he told his assistant so. Uranium was highly pyrophorous in a powdered form and could easily ignite when exposed to nothing more than air. But with the container now immersed in water, the threat of fire, or worse, had passed. Or so he thought.

A few hours later, the temperature of the pile was still rising at a rate that alarmed the assistant, enough to call Heisenberg back to the lab. When he arrived, the two of them peered at the shiny globe inside the tank of water.

Heisenberg understood the principle of pyrophory: all labs using uranium powder tried to guard against fires. However, he did not know what to expect after a fire. This was a potential explosive with an energy several million times greater than an equivalent tonnage of TNT. The heavy water had been removed from the sphere, so that the neutrons, if loose, had nothing to slow them down. Some neutrons might have remained in the sphere, without being absorbed or spirited into the air, and revived a chain reaction slowly at first, then faster and faster. Heisenberg and his assistant did not know what to do, or how to stop the temperature from steadily rising, except by doing the obvious: ventilating the aluminum sphere with holes punched with a hammer and chisel. As the assistant worked with his hands and arms underwater, Heisenberg monitored the temperature gauges, which showed no signs of lowering. He went back to the tank, and as he watched, the sphere seemed almost to shudder, to heave of its own energy. Then the sphere started to swell.

Neither Heisenberg nor his assistant wondered any longer. They ran from the lab a second before the sphere exploded, shooting a fountain of red-hot uranium twenty feet into the air and up through the ceiling. The flames burst through the room, licking at their backs. They did not stop running until they were well clear of the lab. Then they turned and waited. Either the flames would die out or the uranium pile would explode, perhaps even endangering half of Leipzig.

Part VI

S. S. Smith thought about the billboards, as he thought about nearly everything that passed before his eyes. The research director of the metals division of the British company Imperial Chemicals Industries, he was observant as a matter of course. However, one particular billboard on his route each morning to the company offices in Witton, just outside Birmingham, England, had caught his attention. Each day he found himself looking at it with a special interest. He did not study it, but it fascinated him more and more, and not because of the product it advertised, something related to soup.

S. S. Smith was by now accomplished at solving mysteries. Earlier, the Thomson Committee on Uranium, now called MAUD—nobody had yet learned what Niels Bohr in Copenhagen had meant by the term—had assigned Smith's company the task of devising an industrial means of separating uranium 235, the highly fissionable but very rare isotope, from its more plentiful brother, uranium 238. There was no chemical difference between the two, only atomic weight. So the problem really had seemed beyond man's grasp until someone had proposed a process using gaseous uranium compounds. But uranium gas (*uranium hexafluoride*) was highly corrosive, attacking and breaking down metals. Even worse, the gas solidified at temperatures below 50 degrees Fahrenheit and when it came into contact with other materials such as water.

S. S. Smith addressed a truly formidable problem. For the machinery to separate uranium 235, he sought to create a metal membrane with no less than 160,000 holes to the square inch, each with a diameter of $\frac{3}{10,000}$ inch, with a tolerance of only 10 percent. These holes had to withstand contact with the corrosive uranium hexafluoride without clogging or tearing from hole to hole. And millions of square feet of the membrane were needed.[1]

Although Smith did not know it, he might well have guessed that by now his government was taking decisive, confident steps toward the exploration of atomic energy. With Hitler just across the Channel and every indication that the best German physicists were at work on atomic energy, too, the MAUD committee began the full-fledged pursuit of an atomic bomb.

"The committee," MAUD had reported, "considers that the scheme for a uranium bomb is practicable and likely to lead to decisive results *in the war.* It recommends that this work be continued on the highest priority and on the increasing scale necessary to obtain the weapon in the shortest time." A memo to this same effect went to Churchill, who had written in reply, "Although personally I am quite content with existing explosives, I feel we must not stand in the path of improvement, and I therefore think that action should be taken." Britain would forge ahead, even if it meant stretching its overtaxed resources to the limit, now to encompass an expensive and time-consuming project for the success of which no guarantees could be given.

In terms of security, the sudden pace of the project created new hazards, and new opportunities for German spies working in Britain. At the universities, scientists circulated papers without restrictions. A British publication, *The Fortnightly,* talked about bombarding uranium 235 with neutrons, which "might act as triggers for starting a chain of atomic explosions, making an atomic bomb." The "secret" was discussed even in Parliament. Dr. Haden-Guest, an irascible Member of Parliament, told the House of Commons,

I learned the day before yesterday to my astonishment that
the Prime Minister either in his capacity of Prime Minister

or as Minister of Defence . . . has been conducting a series of experiments of a most amazing character, investigating some new weapon, and that a large sum of money has been spent. I do not know whether it is £10,000,000 or £20,000,000 or £30,000,000. I hope the Leader of the House will . . . let the House know what authority there is for this conducting experiments of that kind and spending that amount of money without Parliament knowing anything about it.

While Haden-Guest was broadcasting his announcement, the government obliged men like Peierls and Frisch, the "enemy alien" physicists, to secure "late passes" for work after dark and special orders from the local police to travel to London for technical conferences. (Once Peierls sent technical papers by train to London, which did not arrive. Scotland Yard searched for them without success, and Peierls restenciled the reports. The papers later were found on the platform in a mailbag at Euston Station.)

If the German Intelligence were as active as the British, then the war planners in the United Kingdom had much to concern them. The Secret Intelligence Service was monitoring the whereabouts of Germany's better-known physicists, men like Heisenberg, who, the service learned much to its chagrin, erroneously had been listed by British Immigration as still in England: his presence at a prewar lecture at one of the universities had been noted, but not his return trip to Germany.

From the undergrounds in France, Norway, and Denmark, British Intelligence learned that the Germans had ordered several thousand pounds of heavy water, something scientists in Britain knew to have no other use than in atomic pile research. An agent in Norway, a plant engineer at Norsk-Hydro, heard from the Germans themselves about work in Germany on atomic research. The Special Operations Executive (SOE), which Churchill had formed to carry out all manner of "dirty tricks" on the Germans in the occupied countries of Europe, weighed this intelligence, trying to decide what to do.

In October 1941, the British government reached a decision to coordinate bomb research with the Americans through a new committee based in Old Queen Street, London, which called itself *Tube Alloys* and was funded for six months with £100,000. Britain did not share America's ambivalence toward atomic research; Britain needed help, and America was the only friend to whom she could turn. A bomb required a commitment of money and staff far more immense than Britain's overstretched resources could bear. And since the Battle of Britain, a bomb industry for isotope separation and plutonium production, among others, was no longer safe from German attack on the British Isles. America, so far distant from the German threat and so rich in scientists and raw materials, was the logical place now to build the Allied "laboratory."

As S. S. Smith already knew, British-American "exchange" programs were increasing, and the Americans had opened a liaison office in London at the urging of the British. Still, the American sentiment was honestly contained in one report written in Washington, which stated, "If the problem [of atomic research] were of really great importance, we ought to be carrying most of the burden in this country [America]." The "British are doing as much in this field as the Americans if not more," the report continued. But the writer of the report, playing it safe, was more concerned that the research didn't make him appear foolish. Certainly, the report concluded, "no clear-cut path to defense results of great importance lies open before us at the present time."

However, in fall 1941, MAUD laid out a detailed plan to construct a bomb during the present war, and the Americans took serious notice for the first time. A week after President Roosevelt and Vice-President Henry Wallace, as well as Henry Stimson, the Secretary of War, read the MAUD assessment, Dean Pegram at Columbia and Harold Urey, the neighbor who had instructed the Fermis on the etiquette of American gardening, went to England to see for themselves.

In Liverpool, James Chadwick, the discoverer of the neutron, toured them around the Physics Department, where they studied his detailed analysis of fast and slow neutrons and their interactions with uranium isotopes. At Oxford University, Peierls told them about the work being done on isotope separation. In Cambridge, they read a technical paper supporting the theory that a self-sustaining chain reaction in a pile would generate the by-product plutonium. The British hosts even gave Urey, who had discovered heavy water but had never seen more than a droplet of it, a whole gallon from the supply that the Deuxième Bureau had taken out of Norway and the twentieth earl of Suffolk had brought from France. Von Halban told Urey, with a mixture of humor and admiration, that during the voyage the earl had handed around bottles of vintage champagne to cure the ladies aboard the *Broom-park* of their seasickness.

The Americans were impressed. Pegram wanted to return to the States quickly, as much to tell Fermi what he had seen as to report to the president.

Meanwhile S. S. Smith continued to address the problem of holes, millions upon millions of them, all exactly the same minute size. One morning while passing the billboard again, his sub-conscious interest in its design finally surfaced, and he stopped for a closer look. The billboard advertisement had been printed by the halftone process, in which microscopic dots of differing sizes were joined on a surface to create an image, in this instance for an advertisement, with the dots enlarged to suit the size of the sur-face, the billboard. Why, he asked himself, couldn't a process similar to printing in halftones be used to make his millions of uniformly sized, uniformly spaced holes on metal sheetings?

While Smith was in Wales finding a printer, in London the MAUD Committee met to discuss the plight of Niels Bohr. Bohr's mind was considered so important to physics that it was in effect a weapon of war. Since April 1940, the Nazis had occupied the territory inhabited by this "weapon," but repeated attempts by MAUD to convince him to leave had failed. Now, however, events in Denmark were making such reluctance unwise.

Bohr based his refusal to leave Denmark on selfishness and obligation. He loved Copenhagen, its comforts, the familiarity of the surroundings, the country house, and, naturally, his Danish coun-trymen. Leaving would disrupt the pattern of his life. But his leaving would also betray many of his fellow researchers at the institute who were not Danes. They had sought refuge from Hitler in Copenhagen as Jews and political refugees. Since the Nazis had overrun Copenhagen, they depended on Bohr for their continued safety.

The British offered to help him escape, communicating through the underground by means of microdots hidden inside a hollowed-out key. Bohr replied that he now saw how war threatened to abuse his laboratory with politics, terror, hardship, violence, and perhaps even death. A diplomat in the German Embassy had warned him that the Nazis planned to "transport" the Danish Jews, about six thousand in all. The Nazis would avoid arousing non-Jews by making the arrest en masse in the middle of the night. The same informant had told Bohr that his life was in danger because he was a Jew. The British Secret Intelligence Service could not help him. The Nazis were arranging for the mass arrests during three nights, beginning October 1, less than a week away. Bohr would be treated the same as every other Danish Jew.

The night before the arrests, thousands of Jews took prearranged routes to the Copenhagen docks, where Danish fishing boats ferried them to safety across the Kattegat Channel to the shores of southern, and neutral, Sweden. Bohr and his family—his wife and son, Aage—went by car to the dock on the assigned evening. They boarded a boat on the quay already filled with other Jews. One by one, the craft left the moorings and headed into port waters, as quietly as shadows, then into the open channel. The night of their crossing, a violent storm threatened to wreck the small boat. After several hours, they reached the safe shore, then waved good-bye to the seamen, whose purpose and daring had saved them. A young naval officer on the docks introduced himself as their escort. For the Bohrs' safety, and other reasons that his superior officers never fully explained to the young man, anonymity was advised. If the Germans learned of Bohr's escape, they would try to kidnap or kill him. En route to Stockholm the Bohrs and their escort stopped for lunch. The young officer inexplicably ignored his orders, telling all and sundry. Soon, even before Bohr reached Stockholm, all Sweden seemed to know the identity of the old man with the large head and droopy eyes.

AN END TO INNOCENCE: Enrico and Laura Fermi in their Peugeot Bébé, circa 1938, about to leave Rome for exile in America. The Fascists' laws governing Jews left them with no other choice. *(Courtesy American Institute of Physics/Niels Bohr Library)*

GERMANY'S FINEST: Werner Heisenberg, circa 1928, on a prewar visit to Ann Arbor, Michigan. Already, at the age of twenty-seven, Heisenberg towered above the other physicists of his generation. *(Courtesy AIP/Niels Bohr Library)*

A CONVINCING EXCUSE TO LEAVE: Enrico Fermi sits beside Pearl Buck awaiting the call from the king of Sweden to receive the 1938 Nobel Prize for Physics. He would not return to Italy. What lay ahead for him and his family was a mystery, but at the ceremony he worried only that his starched shirt front might spring up into his face. *(Courtesy AIP/Niels Bohr Library)*

FRIENDS AND FUTURE ENEMIES: Sam Goudsmit (far left) and Fermi (fourth from left) tried to persuade Heisenberg (third from left) during a visit to the Ann Arbor campus before the war to remain in America. They did not want him to contribute his genius to the Nazis' effort to create an atomic bomb. *(Courtesy AIP/Niels Bohr Library)*

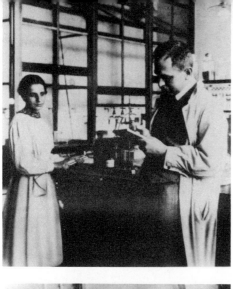

LISE MEITNER AND OTTO HAHN: He was her "cockerel," and together they unraveled the mystery of fission, which led immediately to the possibility of atomic energy and to an atomic bomb. (*Courtesy* Otto Hahn: A Scientific Autobiography, *New York: Charles Scribners' Sons, 1966*)

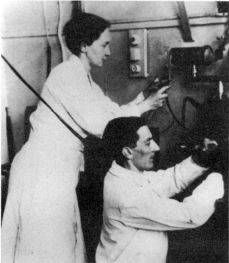

THE GERMAN INVASION ENDED THEIR RESEARCH: Irène and her husband, Frédéric Joliot-Curie, in their Parisian laboratory on the rue d'Ulm. The Gestapo thought that their researchers and the precious heavy water for atomic research had gone down with the *Broompark*. (*Courtesy Société Française de Physique, Paris*)

THE PRESIDENT NEEDED TO BE WARNED: Albert Einstein (left) and Leo Szilard reenact the drafting of the letter of the summer of 1939 urging President Roosevelt in the strongest terms to fund research for an atomic bomb. (*Courtesy G. W. Szilard, AIP/Niels Bohr Library*)

LAUGHTER DISGUISED THEIR
UNCERTAINTY: Until Fermi built a
reactor for them, the administrators
of the early atomic bomb project
(left to right: Ernest O. Lawrence,
Arthur H. Compton, Vannevar Bush,
James B. Conant, Karl T. Compton,
and Alfred Loomis) could only
hope that the government was not
wasting its money. *(Courtesy
Lawrence Radiation Laboratory,
AIP/Niels Bohr Library)*

NOWHERE ELSE TO GO:
When a strike among construction
workers delayed the Argonne Forest
Laboratory, Arthur Compton
and Fermi chose to build the pile
in a squash court under the
West Stands at the University of
Chicago's Stagg Field. *(Courtesy
AIP/Niels Bohr Library)*

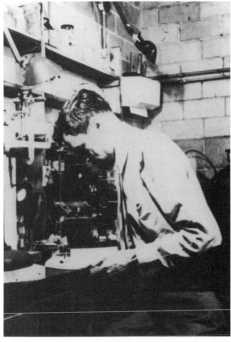

A MACHINE OF AWESOME SIMPLICITY AND POWER: A model of Chicago Pile Number One (CP-1), formed of graphite and uranium, rose from the floor of the squash court almost to the ceiling, and by December 2, 1942, it was ready for its final test. *(Courtesy AIP/Niels Bohr Library)*

A SUBSTANCE NAMED AFTER THE LORD OF HELL: Glenn Seaborg at work in the University of Chicago's Jones Chemical Laboratory in the summer of 1942 when he devised a means of extracting plutonium (which he had discovered and named after the planet Pluto) from Fermi's CP-1. *(Courtesy AIP/Niels Bohr Library)*

▲ THE DAY MAN ENTERED THE NUCLEAR AGE: December 2, 1942, Fermi looks down on CP-1 as it reaches the point of criticality, a self-sustaining chain reaction in uranium. The researchers at the far right hold bottles of cadmium sulfate solution to pour over the pile in the event of its going out of control. Later, they would drink from a bottle of Chianti and silently hope that they had beaten the Nazis to this momentous breakthrough. *(Painting by Gary Sheahan. Courtesy AIP/Niels Bohr Library)*

WOULD THE BOMB IGNITE THE UNIVERSE?: Fermi (center) with Ernest Lawrence (left), director of the Radiation Laboratory at the University of California, and the physicist I. I. Rabi (right). Before the Trinity test, the physicists at Los Alamos placed bets whether the plutonium bomb would fizzle, explode as planned, or perhaps do the unexpected. *(Courtesy Lawrence Radiation Laboratory, AIP/ Niels Bohr Library)*

THEY RAN THE SHOW: Robert ▼ Oppenheimer (left) and General Leslie Groves, the scientific and military leaders of the Manhattan Project, inspect the remains of the steel tower at Alamogordo on which the world's first atomic bomb was exploded in July 1945. *(Courtesy AIP/Niels Bohr Library)*

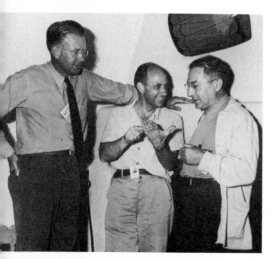

WAS IT A RACE AGAINST TIME?: Colonel Boris Pash directs the search, code-named *Humbug*, for the Nazi atomic research facilities in southern Germany. *(Courtesy Brookhaven National Laboratory)*

IT WAS HARD FOR THEM TO BELIEVE: The German physicists were captured (Otto Hahn is being taken prisoner by the American Alsos officers) and sent to England. When the bomb was dropped on Hiroshima on August 6, 1945, the news caused disbelief, confusion, and anger. *(Courtesy Brookhaven National Laboratory)*

HE HAD BEGGED HIM TO STAY: Before the war, Sam Goudsmit had used every argument he knew to convince Heisenberg to stay in America; as a member of Alsos' Humbug raid, he searched for Heisenberg in southern Germany. *(Courtesy Brookhaven National Laboratory)*

UNDERNEATH THE CHURCH: Heisenberg and his team of physicists from Berlin had set up their heavy-water pile in this limestone cave beneath the rococo church in the small, picturesque Württemberg village of Haigerloch. *(Courtesy Herlinde Koelbl; insert courtesy Brookhaven National Laboratory)*

THEY FEARED WHAT THEY WOULD FIND: The men of Alsos dismantle the Nazi reactor vessel in Haigerloch. *(Courtesy Brookhaven National Laboratory)*

British Intelligence in Stockholm ordered Bohr to maintain a low profile until the darkest phase of the moon, several days away, when they could fly him out to England over German-occupied territory. But contrary to British Intelligence's wishes, the Swedes wanted to celebrate the arrival of Niels Bohr. The king invited him to dine at the palace.

Not wanting to appear rude, Bohr accepted. Newspapers reported the event, while British Intelligence fumed. To all appearances, Bohr was acting as if he didn't know about the war. Vague, dreamy, and forgetful, he exasperated the British. Finally, he was told that his wife and son were to remain in Stockholm, eventually to follow by boat. Now that the moon was right he was driven to a grass airfield several miles outside Stockholm. A Mosquito, dimly lit and camouflaged, waited near where the car had stopped. When he looked inside the small attack bomber, Bohr did not believe that the airplane could be meant for him. Mosquitos were designed for war, not passengers, not even one passenger. The narrow cockpit allowed space for a pilot and copilot. The rest of the aircraft was fitted with now-empty bomb racks over a wide hydraulically operated bay door.

Bohr was put aboard as if he were a bomb. While the crew prepared the aircraft for takeoff, an Intelligence agent pointed Bohr to a three-legged milking stool placed over the crease in the bomb-bay floor. He was shown how to work the headset to communicate with the crew inside an oxygen mask: the Mosquito pilot would try to maintain altitudes at which the oxygen was not necessary, but if a German interceptor approached, they would climb for altitude. As a last desperate resort, the crew had orders to open the bomb-bay doors. Bohr would fall to earth beneath a parachute that opened automatically by a static line.

After takeoff, the airplane gained altitude and set a course for England. At one point in the flight, the pilot brought the aircraft to an altitude where oxygen was needed. He put on his mask, then pressed the intercom to tell Bohr behind him in the bomb bay. But Bohr did not respond. The pilot and the copilot could not leave their seats. Again and again they called. But no reply came. As soon as practicable, the pilot descended to an altitude where the oxygen was rich. He called Bohr again on the intercom. Now when Bohr did not reply, the alarmed pilot took swift action.

He diverted from their planned course, landing at an emergency field in Scotland. As the Mosquito rolled to a stop, the pilot unstrapped and went back to the bomb bay. Bohr was slumped over on the floor, near to death, or so the pilot thought. Only later did he understand why. The canvas headpiece with the earphones had not fitted Bohr's head, and he had decided simply to ignore it. The oxygen mask sat nearby, unused. Bohr had been starved of oxygen, near to the point of dying.

Bohr recovered without permanent damage, and soon he was en route to London, where he exchanged information with the anxious officials in Old Queen Street. He was not told the details of their practical progress on the bomb, only asked to comment whether the general theory was correct. His answer would be regarded as definitive. If he found flaws, the program would be reappraised. The leaders of Tube Alloys and MAUD knew that if Bohr subscribed to the theory, then they could proceed.

First, Bohr elaborated the details of Heisenberg's visit to the Copenhagen Institute. Bohr told what he had inferred: the Germans were working on atomic energy less as a general concept than as a bomb.

The directors of Tube Alloys asked Bohr whether the message he had sent MAUD earlier had been meant to warn them. MAUD had not been able to decode Bohr's secret anagram. Had he meant to tell them that the Germans had taken radium from the Copenhagen Institute?

If MAUD had read that meaning, Bohr thought, then they were truly worried about the Germans. The message, "Tell Maud Ray in Kent," meant exactly what it said. Maud Ray was an old nanny, a woman who had practically raised the Bohr children. She now lived in retirement in Kent. He had wanted to allay her fears after the Germans occupied Denmark, nothing more.

Finally the time came for Bohr to give Tube Alloys his judgment on the theory of a bomb. "Of course it will work, but what will happen then?" he said. They sent the first part of his reply to Churchill, but no one was in the mood to consider "what will happen then."

Some time after his escape, unknown to the British, the SS ordered Bohr's assassination in Stockholm. When they learned that he had left Sweden for Britain, the SS planned to kill him there.

But by then, Bohr had left for New York, far out of reach of SS assassins. In the United States he lived under the watchful eyes of two Scotland Yard Special Branch detectives and later, two FBI agents, with *Nicholas Baker* as his nom de guerre.

Fermi again was the first person he saw when he reached New York. By now, Bohr had other considerations than physics that he wanted to discuss with his protégé. Fermi, he thought, no longer needed his advice on nuclear theory, but everybody, it seemed to him, needed his help on questions of morality. He asked Fermi what he thought the world would be like once the nuclear genie was out of its bottle. He wanted physicists and politicians to think before they went further with their research. Later Bohr would take the same warning to Felix Frankfurter, the Supreme Court justice, and to President Roosevelt, but by then there was no time. By then Bohr might have done better arguing with the wind.

Constance Babington-Smith had discovered in herself an extraordinary aptitude for the war work that the British Central Intelligence's photo-analysis cell assigned to her. The cell was based in Medmenham, near Henley, the mecca of the world's oarsmen, where each July after Wimbledon and the Derby, the Regatta was one of the events of the "season." She was a young woman, and few things had delighted her more than parading in her bonnet, watching the boats on the Thames and the young ladies and men in their summer dresses and blazers. But that was before the war. Now she spent most of her time watching photographs, hundreds of them, taken over occupied Europe by high-flying reconnaissance aircraft.

She scrutinized the photos spread out on a table illuminated by a bold light, under a strong magnifying glass. They were of German military installations, and not everything about them was clear. She "interpreted" them for what they suggested about enemy capabilities. A German tank in an area was not just a tank; its existence in a photo could suggest German intentions, strengths, and weaknesses. She stared at the photos sometimes until her vision blurred, but her doggedness had earned her a reputation as someone to whom the toughest problems were given.

She didn't mind that she saw only her part of the puzzle. Once she had spotted an unusual configuration in the photos, her reports went to London, where intelligence officers with more knowledge of the total German design mulled them over. Because she hoped that her work was helping to defeat the Germans, Babington-Smith tried not to let blurring vision, headaches, and frequent sore necks interfere with her work.

Her cell leader had recently given her a set of photos that particularly fascinated her. Under the glass she saw what her cell leader had identified as factory buildings, low, long sheds that the Germans had constructed a few hundred yards inland from the Baltic beaches. The vehicles near the buildings signified nothing unusual or important. By the looks of the construction materials that lay near the sheds this was a recently built installation. But it wasn't enough merely to guess its general purpose. Her cell leader wanted her to explain what the factory produced, if anything at all, or what the sheds housed. But she was not convinced that it was a factory at all. The location was unusual, for one thing, on this barren, windswept stretch of sand and dune grass. Usually with factories like this one, Babington-Smith expected to find railroad spurs connecting main lines for transporting raw materials in and finished materials out. Another thing: the photos indicated that few people worked there, which also might argue against a factory. It looked to her more like a laboratory of some sort.

She pushed one photo aside for another taken with a higher-resolution camera, magnifying the site even more. Bending over the glass, she looked more closely at one of the buildings. Beside it, she could tell from shadows the sun had cast on the ground that day, a dark, elongated shape resembled a ramp of some sort, a ramp with rails. Near the rail-ramp she saw what appeared through her glass as a white dot, nothing more. She noted her interpretations, then returned the photo to her cell leader.

Analysts in London soon were scrutinizing her report; they had intelligence reports about German plans to build rockets, Buck Rogers contraptions of a somewhat crude design, and therefore had a better idea of what to look for. They concluded that rockets were being built at this site, which they coded *Peenemünde 30.*

The Peenemünde 30 photos then went to an Intelligence branch with even more overall knowledge of German activities and plans, and it was at that level that the photos created alarm.

After much conversation and argument, the British Intelligence analysts deduced only one purpose for these rockets at the Peenemünde base. They were clearly intended as unmanned bombers. And only one explanation of why the Germans wanted unmanned bombers presented itself: The ordnance intended for the rockets was too dangerous to carry aboard piloted aircraft. The rockets were meant to transport radioactive material with which to poison Britons or perhaps even atomic bombs across the Channel to Britain.

If the conveyance were indeed for one type or another of nuclear weapon, they concluded, then the Germans were further along on their uranium project than anyone in Britain had imagined.

This intelligence went to the planners within the Special Operations Executive (SOE), the saboteurs and "dirty tricksters" working between the British military and British Intelligence. Through British Intelligence and with the authority of Combined Operations, SOE had learned of the flow of heavy water to Germany from the Norwegian plant at Rjukan, now being produced at a rate of about three hundred pounds a month. A Norwegian underground agent actually inside the Norsk-Hydro plant reported that the Germans had awarded heavy water a high priority. All this evidence formed in the minds of British Intelligence a clear picture of German physicists (1) working at a rapid pace on nuclear energy and therefore a nuclear bomb, and (2) relying on heavy water for their plutonium-producing reactor.

The destruction of the heavy-water source, a "hard" target, could perhaps slow the German project enough to give the Allies time to catch up.

SOE's planners wanted to attack before the Germans could be reasonably sure that the British knew about their interest in heavy water. They designed a plan code named *FRESHMAN* and handed it back to Combined Operations for implementation.

FRESHMAN could not involve bombing the Rjukan site for fear of endangering civilian lives. The raid had to be carried out surgically, or not at all, by sappers who were parachuted in without the Germans' knowing until it was too late. Already Combined Operations had trained four Norwegians in its secret camp in Scotland in the techniques of stealth, reconnaissance, survival, explosives, and close combat. When the decision to start the initial stages of FRESHMAN was made, the Royal Air Force (RAF) flew the four Norwegians at night over the North Sea and inland from the Norwegian coast, then dropped them on an icy, windswept plateau. Minutes after they landed, as they collected equipment dropped after them, a severe storm hit, covering the equipment in a deep blanket of new snow.

The men walked for nearly three weeks to reach a preplanned rendezvous point with the Norwegian underground, who were to supply them with the most recent intelligence on the Germans. The whole length of the trip, about thirty miles, they labored beneath heavy packs and with the knowledge that they could be spotted easily by German patrols and aircraft and reported by Norwegian collaborators. They had no way, though, to reduce the risk. When they finally met, the underground gave them the worst possible news: the Germans had fortified the security of the Rjukan plant. The Norwegians tried to radio this information to Combined Operations, but their transmitter failed. Several days later, by erecting a high antenna, they got through. But by then Combined Operations had already committed itself to a main assault.

Further problems arose as the two Halifax bombers towing the thirty-four volunteers in two Horsa gliders took off from Wick, Scotland. The weather over the North Sea, unpredictable and hazardous at the best of times, closed in once the Halifaxes reached the Norwegian coast. They were towing gliders without oxygen, forcing the bombers to fly below and through the weather, rather than above it. Communications between the gliders and the bombers also failed.

The sky cleared over Norway, but the pilot could not see the markers set out on the white, flat plain by the four advance commandos. Near the target of Rjukan, they again ran into heavy clouds. Low on fuel and having ice on the wings, the pilot decided to abort the mission. As the bomber neared the coast again, the tow rope slipped its mooring or snapped, and one of the Horsa gliders was on its own, without power, falling. The second glider-towing bomber, its wings also iced, went low to avoid the clouds. Some few miles inland from the Norwegian coast, it crashed along with its glider into a mountain, killing the pilot. Fourteen of the volunteers on the glider survived the crash.

Norwegian police found the first glider, which had disconnected from its towing aircraft, about a hundred miles from the proposed landing site near Rjukan. Several of the volunteers aboard died in the crash, but those who had survived were interrogated shortly afterward. They told their SS interrogators where they had intended to land.

The commandos in the gliders all wore khaki uniforms without insignias of rank or unit, over snowsuits that were to help them survive a run for the Swedish border after the attack. Because of their irregular uniforms, the Germans treated them not as prisoners of war, but as spies. After their interrogations, they were put up against a wall and shot.

The commandos of the second glider, fourteen in all, were captured without a fight by German troops, along with the equipment in the gliders, including explosives, skis, packs, radios, tents, and automatic weapons. The Germans also shot these men as spies without even interrogating them.

What FRESHMAN's failure revealed to the Germans made the loss even more appalling to Combined Operations back in London. The Nazis now knew that the British had intended to attack the heavy-water plant; it followed that the British knew enough about the German nuclear energy research to risk the lives of nearly forty men and the organization of the whole Norwegian underground. More than just aware, the British were afraid. It had to follow, then, that the British too were working on a bomb and believed themselves to be trailing the German effort.

It did not matter to Heisenberg that the audience of mainly Swiss physicists listening to him now was less distinguished than those he was accustomed to addressing. Their invitation had offered him an excuse to leave Germany for Switzerland, if only briefly, and he needed a break from the laboratory, the waiting, and the backbiting. Heisenberg and his assistant had survived the dangerous flames of the Leipzig L-IV pile, which mercifully had not exploded after catching fire. The new pile bunker at the institute in Berlin-Dahlem was still under construction; the five tons of heavy water projected by Heisenberg as necessary for criticality in a pile had not arrived from Norway. Further, the physicists were getting on each other's nerves. The "Aryans" had raised the issue once more of the correct form of physics for Nazism, accusing Heisenberg of propagating the ideas of "half-Jews" such as Niels Bohr. Until now, Heisenberg had kept the Kaiser Wilhelm Institute free of Nazi domination. But the SS and Gestapo had started to support the Aryans more actively as atomic research achieved respectability through the support of leaders such as Speer and Göring.

The achievement of a self-sustaining chain reaction in a pile motivated Heisenberg as a physicist. These attacks by the Aryans made him want the achievement even more. He felt that he needed to show them who was right, who was the most talented, the most irreplaceable. He had recognized months ago that his Nobel Prize meant nothing to the vast majority of Nazis, who despised the Nobel institution for its recognition of the achievements of Jews and other non-Aryans. The one thing that did matter to them was achievement for the Reich according to its bizarre, racist principles. This was a self-devouring attitude, Heisenberg knew, yet, regardless of the rules or the frequency with which they changed, he could not relinquish his position as German doyen without a fight.

Heisenberg had wondered why he had not achieved criticality in a pile before now. The theory, at least, had been fully laid out before him for more than two years; yet, so far he had come closer to disaster than to hearing the constant, telltale clicking of the counters that would signify criticality. The L-IV pile he had built in the Leipzig laboratory had nearly destroyed the physics building before the local fire brigade extinguished the flames that at first had seemed to come from nowhere, bubbling up from the small pile's interior through the water in the surrounding tank. After the firemen had eliminated the danger from the flames and packed their equipment to go, scratching their heads in bewilderment at the cause of the fire, Heisenberg's assistant had peered into the ashes and issued the hysterical warning "Hundreds more will fall for the supreme goal—the atom bomb!" But since that time, hundreds had not fallen, and hundreds would not fall, not even one, as far as Heisenberg was concerned. The near disaster that had been L-IV was not the experimental disaster that it had seemed. The experimental pile had spawned yet another experimental pile, the B-III, employing paraffin instead of heavy water as the moderator. B-III had been designed by Heisenberg specifically to answer questions of control that he needed to understand before making any larger-scale attempt at criticality in the underground bunker then being built in the Kaiser Wilhelm Institute's Berlin-Dahlem facility. Heisenberg had started pile B-III in the Berlin laboratory to determine whether fission in a self-sustaining chain reaction in uranium might increase at such a rate as to cause an explosion, a nuclear explosion. In its simplest definition, Heisenberg recognized, the pile was nothing but a crude bomb that employed neutrons slowed by a modifier instead of neutrons (fast neutrons) that did not collide with a modifier, and natural uranium 238 instead of the rare isotope uranium 235 or plutonium. The use of slow, or *thermal,* neutrons, which a moderator had braked from their natural high speed, in theory prevented fast fissioning, or explosions. Using B-III, Heisenberg tested the concepts in small measure to see whether his theories would prove correct. As part of the control experiments, he tested cadmium as well. Cadmium is a strong absorber of neutrons, which can "smother" the fissioning of a pile, just as carbon dioxide smothers a flame by removing the oxygen needed for the flame to flourish. And yet for all the answers that B-III had provided Heisenberg, no matter what tests signified and no matter what scientific reason suggested, one fact seemed irreducible in nuclear physics: nothing was certain until full-fledged tests proved it certain. Some unknown quantity could always defy the experimenter, denying the prize of full understanding and the thrill of discovery,

In preparing for this lecture, Heisenberg had taken pains to avoid specific comments about German pile research. He was discussing only theory, including no details of experimentation. He knew that the Gestapo mistrusted the "Jew-loving" physicists at the institute, and he therefore surmised that they had sent an officer to take notes on the "correctness" of his speech. If he were even to imply anything about Germany's research, the SS would inevitably "invite" him again to the cellars at Prinzalbertstrasse. Certainly no agent had appeared in uniform, even the Gestapo would not be so obvious. However, one young man near the front row of the lecture hall seemed to hang on his every word. Heisenberg had never seen the man before, but his intensity set him apart. Heisenberg wondered whether he were the watchdog.

The head of the Swiss institute was to host a dinner after the lecture at his house; he had checked the details in advance with Heisenberg, who had accepted with pleasure, requesting only that the group remain small and include only trusted members of the institute. He did not want to worry about strangers' interpreting his unguarded words. He had also asked his host to avoid discussing politics. He knew this would not be easy. Everybody, particularly here in neutral Switzerland, talked of little else. For them it was not dangerous.

After the lecture, Heisenberg was surprised to find the intense young man from the front row among the dinner guests. He introduced himself in German as a Swiss student of physics who greatly admired Heisenberg's achievements. In a sense this adulation by the young completed a circle. Back in 1922, he had been equally admiring and outspoken about his admiration for Niels Bohr, basking in the great man's warmth. He had flattered him a little, as this young man was doing now, not so much with words as with the way he listened.

Naturally, they talked about physics, more animatedly than at any time in Heisenberg's recent memory. To be safe, he slightly underrated the work in Germany. If this attitude were interpreted as an expression of humility, then all the better. He stayed away from opinions or guesses about what might be. And, of course, he mentioned nothing about the weapon of nuclear energy. If the other guests did not know yet about the feasibility of an atomic bomb, then he should not be the person to tell them. No one mentioned the topic.

The dinner had been agreeable, and when the time came to leave, the young man, with the approval of the institute director, offered to walk Heisenberg back to his hotel. Feeling more at ease, Heisenberg accepted gladly.

As they walked through the narrow, dimly lighted streets, the young man continued to question him. But now, away from the others, the questions hardened. Heisenberg interpreted this as intense interest. At least the young man had the courtesy to wait until they were alone to ask about his institute's work on atomic energy. However, Heisenberg skirted the questions about experimentation, mentioning nothing that his companion could interpret as the destructive applications of his nuclear research, not indicating even that the thought had crossed his mind. The one question about a bomb that seemed to be on every physicist's mind did not arise. They parted with a handshake at the hotel entrance.

As the young man turned away, he reached up to his rib cage

and shifted the weight of a pistol concealed under his jacket. Moe Berg was his name, and he was not a physics student. Neither was he Swiss. He had been an athlete, a star catcher for the Boston Red Sox and the Washington Senators, before William Donovan, the head of the Office of Strategic Services (OSS), had recruited him and sent him to Switzerland to get the measure of Heisenberg. Donovan had ordered him to ask leading questions. If Heisenberg even hinted that he was working on an atomic bomb, Berg was to kill him.

Berg felt relieved. He had never killed a man.

When he returned to his hotel, Berg wrote his report and then sent it to Washington. As far as he was able to tell, Heisenberg's research was aimed at the production of nuclear energy, not of a bomb.

Some time later back in Berlin, Heisenberg went to a lecture at the Air Ministry and listened to the speaker theorize that the shock waves of exploding conventional bombs could create lethal embolisms in the human body through a rapid rise in air pressure. As the meeting was drawing to a close, the air raid sirens warned of an imminent Allied bomb attack, among the first over Berlin. Along with the others in the lecture hall, Heisenberg rushed down into the ministry's basement shelter. Above, they heard the thuds of exploding bombs and felt the earth shudder. For a while they joked about the bombs, until they started to explode on the ministry building itself. The walls above crumbled, and flashlights eerily lit up the basement, as stretcher bearers carried the wounded down into the shelter. Nearby, Otto Hahn whispered to Heisenberg, "I bet [the lecturer on embolism] doesn't believe in his own theories right now." Heisenberg smiled in spite of himself.

Once the bombers had turned back for England, Heisenberg climbed out of the cellar, around and under twisted steel and crumbled concrete. The night sky was orange with fire, and pools of phosphorus burned in the streets.

Without transportation, Heisenberg set out on foot for the suburb where he was staying with Elisabeth's parents. The children were there, too, celebrating their grandfather's birthday. Elisabeth had remained in Leipzig. He was understandably anxious, until he saw that the bombers probably had spared the suburbs because there was nothing of strategic value in them. Yet, the farther he walked, the less certain he became. Houses burned on nearly every street, and the fire brigades could not keep up.

As he walked, a colleague beside him asked, "What do you think are our chances of doing scientific work after the war?"

Heisenberg took the question seriously. "There's good reason to hope," he said. "Many Germans will remember the work of reconstruction after the First World War. Our people will probably come to see quite quickly that modern life is impossible without fundamental research." He stepped in a pool of burning phosphorus and doused his burning shoe in a puddle of water left by the fire brigades, then went on talking.

> What we see before us, this destruction, is only the natural consequence of that myth of the twilight of the gods, of that "all or nothing" philosophy to which German people have time and time again fallen prey. Their faith in the Führer, a hero destined to lead them out of danger and misery into a brighter and nobler future, free of all external constraint, or else, if fate should have decided against them, ready to march resolutely to their doom—this terrible creed is our greatest scourge. It replaces reality with a gigantic illusion and prevents any real understanding between us and the nations with whom we have to live.

Heisenberg was repeating what he truly believed, although he rarely discussed the concept of Hitler as a grotesque. The Führer's excesses threatened to destroy everything he had given to the German nation. He had gone too far.

His colleague agreed:

> A glance at the map, at the gigantic territories under the control of the United States, Great Britain and the Soviet

Union, and at the tiny little area that is Germany, ought to have been enough to warn us against military adventurism. But we Germans find it extremely difficult to think logically and soberly. We are certainly not lacking in intelligent individuals, but as a nation we are inclined to be dreamers, to prize the imagination above the intellect, to exalt emotion above reason. Hence there is an urgent need to bring scientific thought back into honor, and that should not be too difficult during the unromantic times that are bound to follow this war.

Heisenberg added,

We Germans tend to look upon logic and the facts of nature—and even this debris all around us is nothing but natural fact—as a sort of straitjacket which we must wear, but only for lack of anything better. We think that freedom lies only where we can tear this jacket off—in fantasy and dreams, in the intoxication of surrender to some sort of utopia. There we hope, at long last, to realize the absolute whose existence we dimly suspect and which spurs us on to ever greater achievements, for instance in art. But we fail to appreciate what "realization" means. Its very basis is reality; it can only be attained through the combination of facts or thoughts in accordance with the laws of nature. But even making due allowance for our strange propensity for indulging in fantasy and mysticism, I really cannot see why so many of our compatriots should find the scientific approach dull and disappointing. It is a common mistake to think that all that matters in science is logic and the understanding and application of fixed laws. In fact, imagination plays a decisive role in science, and especially in natural science. For even though we can hope to get at the facts only after many sober and careful experiments, we can fit the facts themselves together only if we can feel rather than think our way into the phenomena.

Heisenberg thought for a second, then went on:

> Perhaps we Germans, of all people, have a special part to play in this area precisely because the absolute exerts so strange a fascination on us. Abroad, pragmatism is far more widespread than it is here, and we need only to look at our neighbors or at history—that of Egypt, Rome or the Anglo-Saxon world—to appreciate how successful this approach can prove in technology, economics or politics. But in science and art those philosophical principles which the ancient Greeks developed to such magnificent effect have proved more successful still. If Germany has made scientific or artistic contributions that have changed the world —we have only to think of Hegel and Marx, or Planck and Einstein, of Beethoven and Schubert—then it was thanks to this love of the absolute, thanks to the pursuit of principles to their ultimate consequences. But only when the hankering after the absolute is subordinated to appropriate forms —in science to logical thought; in music, to the rules of harmony and counterpoint—only then, only under this extreme constraint, can it reveal its full power. The moment we try to explode these forms, we produce the kind of chaos we can see all around us. And I myself am not prepared to glorify this chaos with such concepts as the twilight of the gods or Armageddon.

Heisenberg could rationalize his position, but his doubts about the political environment did not change his mind about his research. Indeed, as the two men parted, the destruction all around spoke eloquently to an urgent need. He had no doubt, none at all after the intense and indiscriminate nature of the Allied bombing raids, that their enemies would not hesitate to explode an atomic bomb over Germany, if they achieved the invention first and if an atomic blast would shorten the war by even a day and save even one Allied life. As long as Germany was being pounded night after night, his research at the institute was even more urgent. Naturally, he wished that none of this were happening now, not to him or to Germany. But he had approved of the Nazi miracle and now he would live with the consequences.

He walked alone into the Berlin suburb of Fichteberg, where his in-laws lived in a wood-frame house. He walked faster, seeing that houses were on fire here too. The house neighboring his parents-in-law's was aflame, and glowing cinders were landing on their roof. Almost certainly it, too, had caught fire. As he ran past the neighbor's house, he heard a cry for help, but he did not stop when he saw that the house with his children and their grandparents had been hit, the shutters blown off, the windows shattered, and the doors torn from their hinges. And he saw no signs of life inside. He ran upstairs, then down to the ground floor. There was nobody. He went down into the cellar. His mother-in-law, wearing a steel helmet to protect her from falling debris, was fighting the flames with uselessly small buckets of water. He asked about the others. Their grandfather had taken the children to a house that had not been hit. As far as she knew, the children were safe and asleep.

Then Heisenberg thought about the cry for help. He changed out of his business suit into a tight-fitting track uniform, then went to see. The cry had come from a young woman who was fighting the fire on the ground floor. The upper floors were ablaze, and there was no hope of saving the house. Some of the roof had collapsed, and those beams that remained would soon collapse too. The young woman told him that her father, an old man, was in what remained of the attic, fighting a battle that he could not win with buckets of water from a dying tap. He could not come down, she told him, because the staircase had collapsed. Heisenberg climbed a pipe fitting and, finally, after a tremendous effort, reached the white-haired old man, who was standing in a closing circle of flame. Heisenberg startled him.

The old man bowed and said, "Most kind of you to come to my aid," with a formality and stiffness that surprised Heisenberg. Finally, with what strength remained in him, he carried the old man down the same way he had come up.

The narrowness of their escape sobered Heisenberg. From that moment he resolved that their lives would not be endangered again. They would have to leave the cities; even Leipzig would not be safe.

A few weeks later he moved the children and Elisabeth to Urfeld, the country house in the Bavarian countryside he had bought just after returning from America.

———

Some time later, another emergency demanding heroism confronted Heisenberg, but because he had the luxury this time to ponder the implications of his actions instead of responding instinctively, Heisenberg's natural conservatism and caution and his fear of the Nazis all came to the surface at once. This emergency was a request from an old colleague, Sam Goudsmit at Ann Arbor, who had asked him through friends to intervene on behalf of Goudsmit's elderly parents, recently transported as Jews by the SS from their home in The Hague to a concentration camp.

Goudsmit, a feisty and particularly imaginative physicist, had learned about his parents' fate through a network of friends still in Holland. He had immediately contacted other friends in Germany, asking them to reach Heisenberg. With his influence as a Nobel laureate, Heisenberg surely could convince the SS to leave Goudsmit's parents alone. It was a simple and humane act that Goudsmit felt confident that he would perform, if not out of some deeper instinct, then at least out of friendship.

The timing of the request, though, could not have been worse from Heisenberg's point of view. The Aryans with the support of the SS were again on the attack, and anything he did to save Jews would strengthen their arguments against him, would perhaps even turn their suspicions into criminal charges. He had talked over what he should do with a colleague, whom Goudsmit's friends had also asked to intervene. The colleague was equally afraid, but he had written a letter to the Nazi Gauleiter of Holland but he had not signed it.

Heisenberg still had his private, family channel to the Reichs-führer-SS, Heinrich Himmler, who could save those two lives with the utterance of a word. But writing to Himmler was something that Heisenberg did not want to do. Himmler was too powerful to approach on such an "insignificant" matter having nothing to do with science or principle. Heisenberg did not know why the Goudsmits had been transported, and there was no easy way to find out. He had heard rumors about the extermination of Jews. Probably their "crime" was just that: being Jews. But it would be suicide for him to question the SS laws. All the same, Sam Goud-smit *was* his friend, and he genuinely wanted to help. A photo-graph on his desk of him at Ann Arbor with Goudsmit attested to his deep feelings toward Goudsmit.

Heisenberg agonized over a decision for weeks, until he finally felt that he had found a method that would not provoke harsh accusation. He wrote a letter, using guarded language, asking the authorities not to "inconvenience" the Goudsmits. Their son, Sam, had shown himself to be a friend of Germans, even sympathetic to their cause. He did not know why the Goudsmits had been arrested. His precise words were *for reasons unbeknownst to me,* which avoided the Jewish question. Then, feeling that he had done for them everything in his limited power, Heisenberg signed and mailed the letter.

Heisenberg never knew whether his request might have saved the old couple. His delay in writing had made the exercise point-less. Five days before he mailed the letter, the SS gassed Goud-smit's mother, who was blind, and his father, who on the day of his death would have celebrated his seventieth birthday.

Heisenberg could not have known then that Sam Goudsmit would exact a peculiar form of revenge before the war was over.

Heisenberg increasingly felt the need to develop other heavy-water sources than the Rjukan plant in Norway, without which progress on a working pile would continue to falter. He and others explored several production alternatives, one in the Tyrol, another near Munich, expanded facilities in the Rjukan region of Norway, and a plant in Italy at Merano. But by now, for immediate research purposes, the plans for alternative sites for heavy-water production were too little too late because to nearly everyone's surprise every other aspect of the basic research had outstripped the production of heavy water. As a matter of policy, the German physicists had all but officially designated heavy water as the pile moderator; perhaps they could have switched to another moderator, but they were not yet desperate enough to abandon their initial direction; besides, sufficient quantities of heavy water were continually promised for next month, or the month after. They did not need such large quantities of the liquid; Heisenberg estimated five tons for the construction of a successful pile. But five tons, given the slow nature of the separation of heavy water, might just as well be five hundred tons. There was nothing for Heisenberg to do but wait and wait longer still. German research on atomic energy enjoyed a considerable lead over any other country's effort. Germany had ranked number one at the outbreak of the war. And since war had been declared—by England and France in September 1939 and by America in December 1941—the enemies of Germany had been preoccupied, Heisenberg had to assume, by considerations of defense that were far more conventional than atomic bomb research. Germany's lead in the atomic race was secure, or so he had to presume. He saw the daily progress being made on the underground pile bunker at the Kaiser Wilhelm Institute; by any standard, the bunker was a magnificent structure, a testimony at the very least to the commitment of the Nazi hierarchy to nuclear energy at last. Six-foot-thick walls of reinforced concrete surrounded the pile room. Originally intended as a shield against escaping radioactivity, it now also protected the room from bomb damage from above. The corridors contained airtight steel bulkhead doors, which further limited damage from falling bombs. In the center of the pile room itself was a large circular well set in the floor. There were electrically driven pulleys overhead to lift and move the heaviest equipment; in neighboring chambers were ventilators, pumps, air conditioners, and decontamination devices of extraordinary sophistication. Other chambers were designed for smaller-scale experimentation and for offices, in which Heisenberg had started to work eighteen-hour days.

The physical grandeur of the pile bunker was threatened by the Allied bombing, which was becoming so intense that the institute had formed contingency plans for the eventual evacuation of the scientists and their equipment. Heisenberg, who thought these plans prudent, pushed himself while there was still time to work in such ideal laboratory conditions. No amount of his energy and commitment, though, could produce the heavy water they had come to rely on so desperately, though delivery of sufficient stocks was expected soon. For the moment, Heisenberg could do little more than wait.

Later, when the order to evacuate the Berlin bunker finally came, it was a mixed blessing. Like most other physicists, Heisenberg worked best in a familiar environment and a routine. Change signified initial delays and, worse, disruptions to the steady, calm processes of the intellect. But a threat of change now was preferable to the threat of annihilation from Allied bombs that were reducing Berlin to rubble. Heart-pounding panic electrified the pile-bunker air when the bombs fell, squeezing out what room remained for thought. When the bombing stopped, Heisenberg's thoughts raced to his family's safety and to the larger questions of the implications of the bombing for his future. Morale among the scientists at the Berlin-Dahlem Institute, as a result of the bombing, had deteriorated to such an extent that there really was no other sensible option. For the moment, he could forget a successful pile in favor of dismantling the equipment in the pile bunker, and after a brief disruption, the physicists would regroup in a place as far distant from the rumble and blast of war as any in Germany. There they could proceed with the science. There they would enjoy the best possible odds for success.

They had chosen for their relocation an area about thirty miles south of Stuttgart in Württemberg, a place of rolling farmland and pine copses dominated by a massive castle built by the Hohenzollerns. Nothing there could in any way attract the interest of Allied bombers. The region had been "scouted" and the arrangements made. The physicists would lodge themselves in the towns of Hechingen and Tailfingen, where they would also set up laboratories. A third town, Haigerloch, between the other two in a nearly straight line, would become the new home of the heavy-water pile. A magnificent rococo church sat on the top of a limestone ledge about two hundred feet above the Eyach river that ran through the town. The church had a pipe organ, on which Heisenberg could play fugues. Near the bank of the river, in a direct line from the soaring bell tower of the cathedral, there was a cave in which the monks had laid down their devotional wines. That cool, damp-walled cave, deep and wide enough to serve as an enclosure, would protect the pile.

That they had not moved until now partly had justified the expense, effort, and time expended in the building of the pile bunker in Berlin. But now, while they still waited for the arrival of the heavy water from Norway, the moment seemed opportune for a complete move. As the convoy of trucks carrying the equipment and physicists drove out of Berlin-Dahlem, Heisenberg had every reason for optimism. They were leaving behind them the Allied bombs and the Nazis' meddling and interference. In that new location, Heisenberg could do his utmost, finally, to attain his goal.

Part VII

I f *they* want me to travel for them, *they'll* have to find a way to let me do so freely," Fermi told Laura, without specifying who "they" were.

Because he was an enemy alien, now that America had declared war on the Axis powers, the government was restricting the freedom of Fermi's movement to such an extent that he had even dropped his much-beloved phrase "It's a free country." To take a trip outside Leonia and New York, he was obliged to file a statement with the United States Attorney General in Trenton, New Jersey, at least seven days before his departure. He also had to carry with him on those trips "an endorsement of the United States Attorney General," like a pass. What made the regulations especially nettlesome, Fermi thought, the United States Congress had enacted Alien Laws that, among other restrictions, forbade him and all other aliens to "undertake any air flight or ascent into the air." This particular enemy alien, however, was deeply engaged in secret war research. The policy seemed just as much a contradiction to Fermi as it had to Peierls and Frisch in England.

By "they," of course, Fermi meant Vannevar Bush, the director of the Office of Scientific Research and Development (OSRD) and Briggs and his Committee on Uranium, which by now was being called simply *S-1*. "They" had done virtually nothing to relieve Fermi's bizarre set of circumstances.

Fermi was not being a prima donna, stamping his foot petulantly. If the rules applied for one Italian alien, he thought, they applied for all. But "they" should not then have placed such demands on him, ordering him to travel with increasing frequency from New York to Washington and, more often now, to Chicago. The burden was not on him alone. At home he lied about his work to Laura, something that he had never done before and did not like doing now. "They" had explicitly forbidden him to tell her anything about his travels, even that they were vaguely related to the war effort. She had stopped asking questions about why he came home looking like a coal miner, where he went for days without telling her, and about his experiments. She understood physics better than most people; after all, she had written a textbook on the subject. For his part, Fermi could make the most complex problem seem simple. She could understand and she had tried to keep abreast of physics. His research was consuming almost the entire part of his waking day, and besides the children, it was about the only thing in their lives that they had to share anymore. It wasn't that they did not love one another as much as they had, but this secrecy was driving a wedge between them.

"They" had forced him to make unrealistic demands on other people, as well, and that upset Fermi. Just a short time ago, when "they" had ordered him to go to Chicago again, there were only hours left before the train was due to depart, and he had not yet received the travel permit from Trenton. A telephone call to the Attorney General's office confirmed that the document was ready. Could he travel just this once without it? he had asked. He was told flatly no. He would have to pick it up in New Jersey or cancel his trip. The secretary in the Columbia Physics Department had rushed over to Trenton herself, and Fermi had caught the train with only minutes to spare. He felt angry that his personal dilemma infringed on the lives of others.

Fermi saw less of his children than he would have liked, and at least little Giulio had reacted to his frequent absence in a peculiar and, Fermi thought, troublesome manner: he had been telling his schoolmates that he hoped Mussolini and Hitler would win the war. There was such paranoia at that time that Fermi was afraid of what his teachers might be thinking: that Giulio might have acquired this treasonous prejudice at home. Fermi was brilliant and distinguished. The community of Leonia felt proud to have the Fermis among them. But he was still an alien. He had talked with Giulio, who could not say why he had said such a thing. Enrico and Laura believed that because Giulio had seen Mussolini and Hitler together in a parade in Rome, the grandeur and ceremony of the event had impressed him. Enrico had said to him, "Suppose a responsible citizen reports you. Suppose an FBI man overhears you. What do you think they would do? Wouldn't it be their duty to put you in jail?" The admonition had been effective: Soon afterward Giulio was singing "We'll wipe the Japs off the maps."

Enrico was sufficiently worried about his status to inspect the house for anything that the authorities might construe as suspicious or incriminating. He could not be certain whether the FBI would search the house, confiscating the things from his past as evidence of his present attitude toward America. As an enemy alien, he enjoyed limited civil rights; the FBI could do with him pretty much as it pleased. He had heard rumors that the homes of enemy aliens were regularly searched and their telephones tapped. He went on an inspection tour of the house with Laura. He would never forgive himself if "they" diminished his authority on the atom project or removed him from it altogether simply because the FBI found something that it did not understand from his past, such as a second-grade reader that Nella had brought from Rome that contained a number of flattering photographs of and references to Mussolini.

Fermi naturally worried for himself and his family, his reputation, and, perhaps, his place in history. But even more than these, since America's entry into the war, he worried about the real threat to his adopted country. When he and Laura had acted out their fantasy about Hitler's invading America, planning to flee west toward the Pacific, they had not been playing a game. Fermi knew how much he might contribute to the development of an atomic bomb, a bomb that might win the war. He did not feel at all confident that the OSRD could finish the job in time without him.

And by now, there was a job to finish, rapidly. It was true that the research at Columbia had been more or less desultory, as it was everywhere in America, with nuclear energy guiding the research, and even that had been painfully slow, until the fateful afternoon of December 6, 1941. It was one of the strange coincidences of history that Vannevar Bush should call a meeting in Washington for that day, to decide, after all the months of prevarication and delay, what America should do about an atomic bomb.

Six months earlier, in July 1941, Seaborg and Segrè had demonstrated that plutonium was more fissionable and more easily attainable than uranium 235. This finding, coupled with Fermi's work on exponential piles at Columbia, led to one absolute conclusion: America, along with the Allies, could produce an atomic bomb for use as a weapon in this war. On the morning of October 9, 1941, Bush had visited the White House, outlining to President Roosevelt and Vice-President Henry Wallace the significance of the British research on a *bomb* and the cost of producing one. Success was by no means assured, but if America could not succeed with her seemingly limitless resources, then the Germans would also fail.

The president had ordered Bush to proceed, on one condition: The research was to be expedited in every way with the full authority of the White House, but Roosevelt wanted to stop short of actual production outlays. Bush conveyed the president's wishes to the scientific administrators whom he had called to the December meeting, asking them how they thought the project should proceed, which research responsibilities should be parceled out to which universities, and so on. When the meeting broke up, the men went home to their families, to be awakened the next morning by the news of Japan's attack on the American Pacific Fleet at Pearl Harbor, the so-called day of infamy.

The responsibility for organizing the bomb research initially fell to a missionary's son and Nobel laureate, Arthur Holly Compton, chairman of the Physics Department of the University of Chicago. Compton studied the problem. One route to the construction of a bomb at that moment appeared to be uranium 235, despite the difficulty and expense of separating it from uranium 238. An explosion in countless atoms, each releasing the energy of 200 million electron volts, was likely to result from the joining of two subcritical masses of uranium 235 to form one supercritical mass. U-235 was difficult to acquire but easy in principle to detonate. Plutonium, on the other hand, young and relatively unexplored, was easier to acquire and difficult to detonate.

Fermi supported the plutonium potential and argued its cause. With a pile of natural uranium and graphite he could produce the plutonium to fuel a bomb. Fermi told one of his research assistants, "If you stick with me we'll get the chain reaction first. The other guys [working on uranium 235] will have to separate those isotopes first, but we'll make it work with ordinary uranium."

Compton permitted funding for both isotope separation and pile-plutonium research.

By the start of 1942, the project had expanded beyond the administrative control of the OSRD. Within two or three months of Pearl Harbor, America had grasped the potential, scooped it up with incredible energy, and determined to make it fact. America applied such speed that there was no time whatsoever, virtually none, to ponder questions of morality.

Fermi felt the pressure; it was unfamiliar, annoying, spectacular, disarming. Until now he had worked alone in nunneries and university basements with borrowed, jury-rigged materials costing next to nothing, with little interest in his peculiar discoveries outside the confines of the tight, eccentric physics community. Until now he had known little about timetables; coordination of one discipline with another; urgent, often hysterical demands from people who knew nothing about the details and theory of what he was trying to achieve. He was not familiar with the role of a cog in a machinery of a dimension that the world had not seen. It was as if he had tumbled from the ethereal heights of academic physics into the real world, and the landing was bumpy. Sometimes he did not know where he was or what was happening to him. The change often set his nerves on edge because he had lost direct control. As one who had always insisted on surveying every aspect of an experiment before it began, he found the new methods disorienting. Although he was gaining all the support a wealthy nation could give, he was losing what had become familiar. He was a tinkerer, and tinkering had always helped to clarify his theory. He was forced to enlarge beyond a scale with which he felt comfortable; he had to relegate experimentation to his associates after outlining the theory to them. At first he had followed orders to the letter, but he had then realized that he had to be consistent with himself. He was no administrator, and he would not be one now. If he were to usher man into the nuclear age by creating a self-sustaining chain reaction in a pile, he would have to proceed as he always had, with his own hands and his own mind. He shut out the noise and clamoring of the administrators and concentrated on one problem at a time: the first and perhaps the most important obstacle was the moderator. Fermi wanted to determine once and for all whether graphite, as Szilard had so confidently suggested, worked in a pile as an effective moderator. (Although Fermi could not have known, the Germans had already abandoned the idea of graphite, choosing instead to rely on heavy water, on the grounds that graphite in tests had absorbed too many neutrons for its efficient pile application.)

A porous material, graphite naturally held tiny bubbles of air in its honeycombed spaces. The air absorbed neutrons once the process of chain reaction was started by an artificial neutron source, such as the radon-beryllium device used by Fermi. Capturing the neutrons prevented them from reaching the uranium nuclei that they otherwise would have fissioned, creating more than twice the original number of neutrons and a chain reaction. Although air was not the only inhibitor to the process potentially present in graphite, it seemed the most obvious, and, Fermi thought, the most easily tested.

Fermi was still working at Columbia's Pupin Laboratories on the problem of squeezing out the additional 0.13 to reach the coefficient k. Fermi was acting as a nuclear dressmaker: The test pile was the form of the dress, made up of the fabric of uranium and the moderator, in the present instance, graphite. Once he had realized the pattern of the dress and gathered together the fabrics, he went about putting it together. He had done just that by now, but it had not fit: by a factor of 0.13. And so he went about tucking here, trimming there, cutting and shortening, lengthening, until he decided that perhaps the fabric did not suit the fit of the dress, causing it to drape or sag. So far his test "dress" had sagged by 0.13, if k represented a perfect fit. Right now, he wanted to see whether "tucking"—eliminating air—would bring him closer to that perfect fit, and he asked himself how he could enclose the space around the pile to create a vacuum. He thought about the problem for days before hitting on the right idea, which his colleagues at Pupin had to admire for its originality, its boldness, and, characteristically of Fermi, for its simplicity. He decided to can it: to place the whole pile into an enormous tin can, an inspiration based on the assumption that if a vacuum in tin cans preserves food from going bad by totally eliminating air, then the same process might be effective with a uranium pile.

He hired a small army of tinsmiths from the New York City area. They were recruited through their unions, which in normal times might have created problems if Fermi had not explained to the union bosses that the tinsmiths would be engaged in war work. The tinsmiths certainly had never done anything quite like this before, nor would they ever again, and they soon became caught, up in the spirit of the project by Fermi's presence in the laboratory, measuring, calculating, advising, encouraging. Many of the tinsmiths did not speak English, and for those who did not speak Italian, the problems of communication at first were acute and troublesome. The dimension of the can was to be more than twenty feet by twelve feet square with thousands of joints and solder points holding the sheets of tin together. Fermi decided to instruct the tinsmiths by a series of simple symbols painted on the tin surfaces. Each new section of the can was marked with the stick figure of a standing man. Without reading instructions or being told, the tinsmiths knew which end was meant to be fitted up or down, and together, they worked on thousands of seams, testing as they went along for airtightness. Finally, when the world's then-largest tin can was finished, Fermi and his team checked that the pile, completely surrounded by the tin can, had not been damaged. The graphite bricks had retained their shape, and the uranium metal cubes latticed in the graphite seemed as perfectly positioned as they did when the tin can was started. A vacuum pump pulled the air out of the sealed tin can. After several hours, once the maximum quantity of air had been expelled from the interior of the can, Fermi slipped a neutron source into the pile's center. Remembering the deficit from k of 0.13, he hoped for the best.

The Geiger counters told him that the vacuum in the tin can had reduced the deficit to 0.09. Of course the desired k quotient still eluded him, but Fermi was a patient man. If the quotient had remained the same or had increased, he would have known that he had guessed wrong, that it was not the air but some other variable that was influencing the k factor. But the initial tin can tests proved beyond a doubt that impurities, such as air, in the graphite inhibited chain reaction. If the deficit could be reduced from 0.13 to 0.09, then it could be reduced further to zero, Fermi believed, through the careful elimination of impurities in the graphite and, perhaps, through different configurations of the uranium in the lattice contained in the tin can. The elimination of the 0.09 deficit did not entail a mystery; it simply involved a lot of hard work.

And so Fermi and his team set out to accomplish what needed doing, barely complaining about the eighteen-hour days at the laboratory. Szilard demanded purer graphite. The executives of the commercial companies tried within the limitations of their production equipment to eliminate the impurities in the graphite; new shipments to Pupin were tested for purity, which varied widely. But the effort started to pay off as the deficit dropped even further than 0.09.

Finally, Fermi came to understand that the team could go no further, regardless of how hard they worked and how Szilard badgered the graphite manufacturers, or how Fermi mixed the different factors. In one last test, if the deficit did not disappear altogether, graphite would have to be abandoned as a pile moderator, and Fermi and his team would have to ask the government for adequate stocks of heavy water with which to modify a pile.

When the day of the last test finally came, the routine did not change. One of the team members slipped the neutron source into the pile. Then everybody waited while the "cooking" began. At a calculated moment not long after, Fermi removed the foil from the pile and ran with it to the counters in a nearby room. He watched the Geiger counters and listened to their clicking sound. Very rapidly, the deficit, he saw, went from 0.09 to 0.07, then to 0.05. Within seconds, as he watched, the deficit went from 0.03 to 0.02. There was an instant when he wondered whether the 1.0 figure or k were physically possible. Perhaps it was akin to the sound barrier; the closer, the stronger the resistance. And then, as he watched, the Geigers indicated the magic k and more. They did not stop at 1.0 but continued their upward course, ending with a reassuring surplus of 1.73.

Beyond all doubt, graphite was the answer. The answer and more. It was going to be easier to handle than heavy water; it was cheaper and could be supplied in great quantities right in America; and it could be shaped in whatever way Fermi finally decided for a pile with the goal of producing a self-sustaining chain reaction in uranium.

The proof of graphite's effectiveness gave Fermi direction. But for the moment, he and Szilard paused to discuss what they should do with their findings on graphite. In normal times, they would have published them at once. Szilard argued that any information, no matter how distant from the actual production of an atomic bomb, could help the Nazi atomic program. Fermi asked him to explain in what way it would help them; Szilard replied that he did not know, and that was exactly the point: the Nazis had built a wall of secrecy around their nuclear energy projects. Szilard felt that the Nazis' insistence on secrecy indicated just how far along and how far in advance of the Allies the Germans were at that time; otherwise why bother with secrecy? Fermi and he should follow exactly the same procedures as the Nazis. For Fermi, who had actually experienced life in a Fascist country, the inhibition of freedom of scientific information was abhorrent, and he was less certain about the course of secrecy being followed. If publication of their findings were prohibited, although with their acquiescence, what would this mean for other physicists in the country who might benefit from their findings, who might expose one more clue to the mystery of nuclear energy by reading Fermi and Szilard's conclusions about graphite? They argued to the point of acrimony and decided to leave the decision to Dean Pegram.

They visited him and expressed their opinions, ending by asking him what he would do. Pegram did not deliberate for long. He said that he would surely withhold publication until after the war. The decision was made.

Fermi, Szilard, and Pegram could not have known at that time that if they had elected to publish their findings on graphite, the outcome of the war might have been very different: for surely Heisenberg and the German physicists at the Kaiser Wilhelm Institute would have immediately switched from heavy water.

Meanwhile, Fermi had been fighting Dr. Arthur Compton on a matter of where to locate the first full-scale atomic research laboratory in America. Fermi wanted New York. He knew the facilities at Columbia and the working habits of the researchers there, and he saw no reason to leave. Compton, on the other hand, argued that the University of Chicago better suited their research requirements for now and in the future. Housing for the physicists' families near the university was abundant there, and vastly increased numbers of researchers were going to be needed. The university also allowed for expansion of research space. If the pile worked, the program would expand, perhaps enormously, with large factory piles for the bomb-quantity production of plutonium. With that concentration of experimental equipment and brainpower, Chicago was safer, far less vulnerable to attack from the air if either Hitler or Hirohito decided to bomb America. The benefits, in the long run, Compton told Fermi, far outweighed the inconvenience.

Fermi had nothing against Chicago. He simply did not want to move. He admitted that disruptions upset him personally. The shift from Rome to New York had aroused in him similar feelings of disorientation and confusion. Now he and Laura considered Leonia their home, and the children had settled comfortably into new routines. It was unfair to change so soon.

But the whole nation was mobilizing, and the inconvenience of uprooting from New York was nothing compared to the sacrifices being asked of some. Besides, by living in Chicago, Fermi would eliminate the need to travel there. In April 1942, Fermi moved for the duration of the war—or what he was told would be the duration—to bachelor quarters in the International House at the University of Chicago, starting work for the code-named *Metallurgical Laboratory* (the "Met Lab") under Arthur Compton. The Met Lab had virtually no association with metals, and no metallurgist was to be found among them. Its simple duty was to create a pile of graphite and uranium in which a self-sustaining chain reaction could manufacture plutonium.

"They" had won, Fermi supposed, but what mattered now were the pile, chain reaction, and plutonium, and then the bomb.

In the early months of 1942 at one of the first organizational meetings of the Met Lab, Compton was telling the physicists who had gathered in Chicago that he had moved the chemists out of the University of Chicago's Eckhart Hall to provide working space for Met Lab. So that nobody else at the university would know the purpose of their work, a security wall had been erected between the half of Eckhart Hall occupied by teaching physicists and the Met Lab people, who by now included Fermi, Szilard, Walter Zinn, Norman Hilberry, and Herbert Anderson, essentially the same team that Fermi had organized three years before at Columbia.

Compton explained that the university would provide space for the initial stages of Fermi's research on subcritical exponential piles, until a final critical pile could be built and tried in the Argonne Forest, twenty-five miles southwest of Chicago in a secluded wooded area run by the Cook County Parks Department. The Argonne Forest lab was expected to be ready at precisely the moment when the tonnages of graphite and uranium needed for a pile arrived. The purpose of all this organization, Compton told the physicists, was to create enough plutonium for use in a bomb during the probable duration of the war, within the next three to five years. It was an extravagant challenge for the conservative physicist, who knew that with Fermi and Szilard—and soon, with Seaborg, who was arriving from Berkeley to work on the chemical process of extracting plutonium from a pile—Met Lab would either meet the deadline or concede that the job was not humanly possible.

Fermi took over the meeting after Compton spoke, to describe the way Met Lab was to proceed with its experiments. Each batch of graphite arriving at the university would be tested for purity and density. He had worked out a technique for what he called a *sigma pile*, four feet by four feet and eight feet high. A neutron source would be placed in the small subcritical pile, and counters would indicate the quality of the graphite by its absorption properties. To test the uranium, other piles were to be built, eight by eight by twelve feet high with a lattice of uranium and graphite bricks. A neutron source would then be introduced and measurements made to gauge the decrease in the neutron intensity at distances from the neutron source.

To explain the fundamentals, Fermi used math formulas chalked on a blackboard in the front of the university conference room. Soon, as the discussion turned to the question of quantity— the amount of fissionable material an atomic bomb would need— each of the physicists contributed ideas, using the blackboard as well to show their reasoning. The blackboard was nearly covered with symbols and equations, when a stranger in their midst, whom none of them remembered ever seeing before, spoke up.

"Excuse me," he said.

Most of the physicists had forgotten that he had been sitting among them from the start of the meeting. He wore an army uniform with the silver eagles of a colonel on his epaulets. He was tall, and he must have weighed close to two hundred fifty pounds, which made him seem older than his true age, forty-six.

"I don't understand how you got from equation five to equation six," he said. "How does ten-to-the-minus-six become suddenly ten-to-the-minus-five?"

They turned from him to the blackboard.

He was correct, of course, about the miscalculation. But the simple mistake held absolutely no significance to the problem. That he had pointed it out embarrassed them, giving them the uneasy feeling that this man wanted to prove himself their equal in theoretical physics by demonstrating his grasp of addition and subtraction. No physicist, surely, would have made a point of the error, unless to chide a colleague. Indeed, it seemed a joke, but by the expression on his face, it wasn't to the stranger.

Colonel Leslie R. Groves, a member of the Military Policy Committee that would soon assume absolute control of the whole bomb project, did feel himself to be their equal. He reasoned, as he told them later when he knew them better, that he had received ten years of formal education after entering university. That time, he believed, was the equivalent of two Ph.D.s, whereas most physicists had earned only one. He had shown these "crackpots," as he called them to their faces, that they, including the Nobel laureates, were capable of making errors. He knew that they would not easily forgive him, but they could not deny that he was correct. Perhaps a little mistake was of no importance now, but, he asked, when might it be? When might one small error in calculation—perhaps the miscalculation of the k factor in graphite—throw off track the entire, burgeoning program, causing the bomb effort to lose valuable time?

The physicists, Groves thought, needed constant supervision. And he was the man for the job. The son of an Army chaplain, he knew only the military and its strict codes of discipline. He had attended West Point, where classmates tagged him "Greasy," then he had slipped into a career as an Army administrator. He had distinguished himself as one who got things done, no matter what the job, through practicality and stubbornness, if not diplomacy.

He had constructed whole cities of military barracks, and, a short time ago, he had built the War Department's new Pentagon building on the banks of the Potomac. But he had never heard a shot fired in anger.

Groves did not care what the physicists thought of him personally, so long as they did what he asked. Being liked was not high on his list of priorities. He did not like them very much personally. In his estimation physicists were weird people: hopelessly vague and barely responsible in his world of life and death, victory and defeat. Groves dwelled on facts, and the physicists, he thought, concentrated on probability and theory. They were strangers to supervision and discipline, the Army way. They could not even take orders without asking why they were necessary and then talking the matter to death. He expected their worlds to clash, even forcefully. But the job would get done before the war was over.

All his career Groves wanted a field command, to hear just one shot fired in anger. He had lobbied hard and performed well for the assignment he so coveted and then his superiors had withdrawn it by offering him the job of becoming head of the Manhattan Engineering District, the so-called Manhattan Project. Other field commanders—hundreds of them now that the Army was mobilizing—eventually would distinguish themselves in combat with Medals of Honor and Purple Hearts, but Groves would win the war by making the world's most powerful weapon of war.

The physicists discussed the critical mass of a bomb until they reached a conclusion.

"How accurate is the figure?" Groves asked.

"By a factor of 10," someone answered.

Groves expected them to work within a 10 or 20 percent margin of error. But a factor of 10, anywhere from 10 times more to 10 times less? This was exactly the problem with physicists, he thought. Neither he nor the Army, but *they* were going to have to change, and not just with their factor-of-10 guesses.

Groves had noted that the physicists were "loose," anxious to talk about their work, no matter what the need to know. They believed that their scientific discoveries were free to be shared among other physicists, wherever they were, whatever they believed, however antithetical were the policies of their countries' leaders. They thought that discoveries in physics were common to everybody, like the air. Groves's duty as a military commander was to run a military campaign, using scientists as troops. Under his command they would learn unquestioned obedience or would be removed from the project. He wanted them held in check, through organization. No small research group was to be told about the work of any other small group. If they talked, then the damage would be limited.

Groves could not help but think that the Germans, with their scientific capacity and army of first-class physicists, were ahead of the American atomic bomb program. The Germans, from what he knew of them, would research a bomb without regard to the safety of the workers involved. Intelligence reports from England warned that the Germans would rain radioactive poisons on their enemies, contaminating millions, causing widespread panic, and forcing the evacuation of whole cities. With such a strategic advantage, they then could complete their bomb project before the Americans.

By communicating these fears, Groves hoped to convince the scientists to cooperate with him in any way he asked. Even if they did cooperate, he would still find trusting them difficult. These men —Szilard, Fermi, Wigner, Teller—formerly were citizens of countries now occupied by the Nazis. Groves could not be certain whether they secretly believed in Hitler, whether they were men of divided loyalties, whether they were indeed spies. This world of foreign-born scientists was as alien to Groves as anything fate could devise. But in spite of his natural suspicions, he had to trust them. If Fermi could make a pile work, the project would blossom to a point at which trust would be the only practical response.

Groves ordered the top alien physicists to use code names. He did not want German Intelligence to blackmail them by holding relatives and friends in Europe hostage unless the physicists in America sabotaged the program. Fermi became "Mr. Farmer," with a constant "companion," an Italian-speaking bodyguard named

John Baudino. Fermi protested, but he acquiesced, soon recruiting Baudino as a handyman in Met Lab.

Uneasy at first and never smooth, the relationship between Groves and the physicists worked, out of necessity.

Fermi's exponential and "beta" test piles proved that with sufficient materials—a great amount of purest graphite and shaped uranium, either in the form of an oxide, or, better yet, a metal—a pile should go critical. Encouraged by these results, he laid out a schedule leading up to the final push, predicted for late fall 1942. The OSRD, also encouraged by the beta tests, accelerated the whole program, including planning huge, expensive factory piles, all on the basis of tests that were barely conclusive: The tests had indicated the success of the final pile; but they had proved nothing. Fermi saw the racing ahead of the OSRD as imprudent. It might turn out to be a monumental—and, for Fermi, embarrassing— waste of money. The difference of opinion brought him into conflict with Colonel Groves. Groves's demands were opposed to all his better, time-tested instincts.

If the Army galled Fermi with its assumptions, the physicists working in Met Lab gave him a confidence he otherwise would not have had. In Arthur Compton he recognized a fascinating anomaly. A devout Christian, Compton went against the grain of scientific philosophy in his unshakable belief that science served to illuminate religion. "Science is a glimpse of God's purpose in nature," Compton wrote. "And the very existence of the amazing works of the atom and radiation points to a purposeful creation, to the idea that there is a God and an intelligent purpose back of everything." Strong-jawed and dark-browed, handsome and with great physical vitality, Compton believed in routine exercise—nearly always beating Fermi at tennis with his superb, stylish racquet strokes— as a means of paying respect to his body as a creation of God. He never hesitated to bring the Bible into the laboratory when he sensed a need for inspiration. Strong and supportive, he fought

Fermi only once over an important issue, and he fought with grace and character.

The conflict arose when Compton sided with Groves against the Met Lab physicists, from whom it seemed that the Army wanted to wrest control of the project. Groves wanted an old-boy-network of Army cronies to work with Fermi on the construction of so-called factory piles, which eventually would churn out plutonium. The Met Lab physicists had listened to representatives of the construction firm chosen by Groves to build the piles. The firm had built bridges and barracks for the Army, the physicists thought, but building factory piles posed special problems that exposed the ineptness of the company.

The physicists had not agreed that the choice of the company was the Army's responsibility. One evening they met to discuss the problem in Eckhart Hall. Compton arrived, carrying a Bible. Before anyone was allowed an opinion, he read to them from Judges (7:7): "And the Lord said unto Gideon, By the three hundred men that lapped will I save you, and deliver the Midianites into thine hand; and let all the *other* people go, every man unto his place."

This once, the physicists would not back down; they voted to force on the Army a change of construction firm. Both Compton and Groves found themselves with little choice, and the Army approached E.I. du Pont de Nemours with the offer. Du Pont was by far the best suited for the work, but it was highly skeptical about the project. Its engineers had more urgent war work, and until Fermi provided proof by building a sample pile that achieved criticality, du Pont would wait to commit itself.

Yet, in spite of this small victory, the military was encroaching to an unprecedented degree on the scientists' turf. Before this, the military had cooperated with scientists infrequently in the military applications of science. The scientists worked by consensus, building discovery on discovery. The military worked by the imposition of commands. And now neither worked comfortably with the other. Sometimes the military surprised and delighted the physicists with a peculiar, often bizarre view of the world. At other times they caused alarm. Few of the Met Lab physicists ever thought about an atomic bomb as anything but a discovery. So specific was their research that they did not view themselves as the creators of an instrument of destruction. Norman Hilberry, Arthur Compton's assistant and a well-regarded physicist and member of Met Lab, for one, was robbed of his innocence on the day that an Army officer told him, "Now, look, Hilberry. There is clearly a major misunderstanding here that has got to be straightened out. It seems to us that all you folks are thinking in terms of making one or two bombs. Isn't that true?"

"Yes," Hilberry answered. What possible use could there be for more than one bomb?

"That's all wrong," he was told.

There is a fundamental principle in military matters which —and I don't care how fantastic this atomic device may prove to be—is *not* going to be violated. This is one's ability to continue delivering a weapon, and it's this that determines whether the weapon is useful. If you folks succeeded in making only one bomb, I can assure you it would never be used. The only basic principle on which the military can operate is the ability to continue to deliver. You've got to sit down and get re-oriented. The thing we're talking about is not a number of bombs; what we're talking about is *production capacity* to continue delivering bombs at a given rate. That, you will discover, is a very different problem.

Leo Szilard had not changed his attitude at all since the government had finally accepted what he had urged them to do. The physicist-visionary, correct from the start, Szilard wanted the bomb, desperately, and he wanted *scientists* to control its development. In Chicago, Compton assigned him to procure pure, abundant graphite and uranium.

Szilard, conferring with Fermi, knew that uranium was an important variable. Natural uranium cast into metal produced a smaller pile. The first uranium shipments came from the Westinghouse Company in a metal powder that was volatile and dangerous when exposed to the air. John Marshal, a young physicist who had just joined the Met Lab team in Chicago, lined fifty-gallon oil drums with asbestos and heated them with silicon carbide elements. Then he lined them up in the narrow hallway of Eckhart Hall's basement. These makeshift "furnaces" worked beyond expectation, changing the pyrophoric powder, the same substance that had burst into flames in Heisenberg's laboratory, into solid cast metal.

Of all the physicists at Met Lab, Fermi worked most closely with Herbert Anderson, who had been with him since Columbia. Anderson, younger than Fermi and a native of the Bronx, had helped the Fermi family learn the ways of America, starting with idioms. As Fermi's protégé, Anderson worked on neutron research, and now at Met Lab he was developing a new, more efficient neutron source for the final test pile. Fermi found that he could always rely on Anderson. As an experimenter he could see clearly the process through which theory was translated into fact. Without much interpretation from Fermi, he put together the supplies that the pile would need: items like machines for lathing the graphite, presses for the uranium, and control devices. In the weeks up to the fall of 1942, Anderson became a steady and valued customer of the Sterling Lumber Company in south Chicago, which delivered large quantities of four-by-six timbers for the construction of the square cradle to hold the spherical pile.

Anderson conceived the idea of a rubber balloon filled with carbon dioxide to prevent neutrons from escaping, as the tin can had earlier. Anderson asked the directors of the Goodyear Rubber Company in Akron, Ohio, for a huge balloon, especially made, a *square* balloon. The directors asked why; Anderson said that he could not tell them. They shook their heads and set to work.

Although Anderson was Fermi's friend and confidant, Walter Zinn, a former physics professor at the City College of New York whom Szilard had recruited, earned Fermi's deep respect for his natural understanding of the components the pile required in order to work. When he had been with Fermi at Columbia, Zinn had noticed that the exponential pile would operate closer to k if the uranium oxide were cast in lumps of a partial spherical shape (called *pseudospheres*). Working beside an immigrant tool and die maker named Di Costanze, Zinn had created at Columbia a die with such polish that it eliminated the need for oils, which threatened to contaminate the uranium. Because of his feel for the pile's needs, Zinn organized the half dozen young physicists, whom he worked without mercy.

Usually Zinn got more from the Met Lab physicists than he asked. An "older" Met Lab team member returned to Eckhart Hall one morning only an hour after he had finished the night shift. He looked exhausted, but he said that he could not bring himself to rest, knowing that the Germans were at work on an atomic bomb. The Germans would not be resting, he told them, so why should he? "We're in a real race," he told them. Everybody seemed to understand.

They worked eighty- and ninety-hour weeks from then on, sleeping and working, working and sleeping, sometimes without taking the time to eat. At the best of times they snatched quick meals, usually at a lunch counter on campus where a doting waitress served the house "specialty" of mashed potatoes and thick, greasy gravy. They smoked harsh Fatima cigarettes to diminish their hunger.

When they had the chance, they talked about the war. Listening to the news on the radio in the mornings while they shaved and reading headlines kept them abreast of developments in Europe and the Pacific. They even talked about what would happen if the Nazis won the war. As individuals they would be shot, they concluded, a belief that infused their work with a definite immediacy.

The rigors of sleepless nights and nutritionless food had less immediate impact on Fermi's team than they might in older persons. Volney Wilson, a graduate student at the University of Chicago, was responsible for the pile's control and measuring devices that Fermi would use to decrease and increase the fissioning in the pile, as a driver might regulate the speed of a car with the accelerator. Wilson also had to devise a means to "extinguish" the fissioning pile if it went out of control. Nobody knew for certain how a pile, once critical, would behave. Would the reactions increase so fast as to cause a violent, massive explosion? Would the pile, once it had exhausted the fissioning uranium, burn with such intensity that it would seek out new fuel, perhaps the air itself? Would the pile in fact detonate the heavens? Neither Fermi nor Szilard nor Zinn nor Compton could say for certain. If something went wrong, could Wilson shut down the pile? Men could not operate the controls faster than the fissioning of the uranium nuclei. Therefore, the buildup would need to be gradual. Once it became critical, if Fermi could not push the pile back down to a subcritical state, Wilson would have to "drench" the graphite and uranium in neutron-absorbing chemicals.

Physicists even younger than Wilson had been recruited by Met Lab. Fermi asked Leona Woods, a pretty, dark-haired graduate student in the university's Physics Department, to devise special neutron counters to measure the pile as it approached criticality. Woods went about her work with enthusiasm and humor, and, as the only woman on the team, became their "younger sister." Leona organized picnics and swimming parties to the Michigan Dunes. She provided a willing audience for Fermi, who clowned with her sometimes when they worked late at night. Once, something she did or said ended with Fermi and some of the other physicists' emptying chemical fire extinguishers at each other, much to the annoyance of the janitor. Leona followed Fermi to lectures and took notes as his secretary. She joked with him, and he with her, more naturally than the others because of her age.

The Met Lab relationships derived from Fermi. He never asked anyone to do what he would not do himself. He often helped with the most menial jobs, such as milling and machining graphite. Because Laura was still in Leonia, waiting for the children to finish their school year, Fermi, outside the laboratory, spent leisure time with the young physicists. He played table tennis and chess and concocted games to sharpen their minds. Sometimes out of the blue, he would ask them, "How many piano tuners do you suppose there are in the United States?" Once, pointing to the fireplace of the International House, he asked them to calculate the vacuum above the fire in the flue. When he saw a dirty window pane, he wondered at what thickness the dirt could accumulate. He wanted his team, through these absurd-seeming problems, to understand the use of the fundamental constants in nature. When the team struggled with answers, he gave them clues, with which they narrowed and refined their answers. They sometimes verified his results, and his accuracy amazed them. A Chicago guild for piano tuners later confirmed that Fermi's calculation of the number of tuners in America had been accurate to within a few.

To keep the team sharp, Fermi encouraged them to work and play together. Outside the laboratory, he drove himself to run faster in races on the beach, swim farther, and climb higher. And despite the age difference, he nearly always won, more through desire than natural ability. The team appreciated the effort he was making. He was like one of them, and they did everything in their power to please him.

Fermi as team leader lectured once and sometimes twice a week on an aspect of the theory of the pile, reducing complex problems to their simplest form. He never used complex formulas or convoluted language. Simple metaphors often described what he perceived in nature. Once he explained why the control rods created a low density of neutrons. The rods were coated with cadmium, which absorbed neutrons in the fissioning process, preventing them, naturally, from seeking out and fissioning other nuclei. When the rods were inserted into a pile, they attracted the neutrons and rendered them useless to the chain reaction, and in this way Fermi and the Met Lab team planned to control the fissioning in the pile. Fermi had learned in school in Italy the history of the Black Death, which had infested Europe in the fourteenth century. Reaching for a method of explaining the control rods, he compared a European city to the pile, the control rods to the Black Death, and the fissioned neutrons to the inhabitants of the city. When the plague approached the city, the inhabitants either fled or died.

These simple explanations inspired more than their best efforts. Quite surprisingly for a man of his stature, Fermi managed to inspire their love, too.

Fermi was worried less right now about criticality than about the procurement of materials and research space. What uranium existed in America was now being sent to MIT for processing, but there still was not enough, and he did not know when more would be found. As for research space, Compton had planned for the "center" in the Argonne Forest as the site for the first pile, but the construction workers' union had called a strike, interrupting construction.

"Let's hear your analysis," Compton asked Fermi.

The pile could be built at the university, he said, to Compton's surprise.

His team already had constructed the "beta" test piles under the bleachers of Stagg Field near Eckhart Hall, a structure of stone and masonry used for athletic events before the university had suspended its intercollegiate football program. The highest point of the stands was crenellated to resemble a medieval castle wall. Underneath, there were singles and doubles squash courts, locker spaces, and long, winding corridors in which Met Lab could build the pile experiment. What about the doubles squash court, Fermi asked?

"What if some new, unforeseen development should occur?" Compton asked. The pile might release energy such as no human had ever before seen. Was it safe to play with such forces as those in the middle of a large city? Even if a nuclear blast did not occur, the radioactive material in the pile could poison the whole city of Chicago. Compton thought out loud that he should raise the question with the president of the university, but he reasoned that the president, as a nonscientist, could not evaluate the hazards. In terms of safety considerations alone, Compton said that he should order Fermi to wait until Argonne was completed, regardless of the length of the strike.

"You must assume the responsibility yourself," Fermi said.

Compton told him to use the doubles squash court under the West Stands.

———

Laura Fermi arrived with the children in Chicago in early summer 1942 with the suspicion that their lives would not be the same. She had loathed the disruption, content as she had been to make Leonia their permanent American home. Enrico had promised her that they would live in Chicago only for the duration of the war, but as far as she could tell, "duration" meant the time the OSRD needed to move all the scientists from the West Coast to the East and all the scientists from the East Coast to the West and back again in an unbroken circle. Nothing ever again would be permanent as she understood the term. She had visited her neighbor, Harold Urey, in Leonia before leaving for Chicago. He was staying behind at Columbia to head up a team to research isotope separation and, understanding better the demands made on scientists by the government, had told her, "Laura, you'll never come back to Leonia."

The impermanence was all the more difficult because she had been raised to expect quite a different life. In the Italian tradition, a woman lived with her family until marriage. Then she moved, once, to her husband's house and his city. Children were raised, and parents grew old in familiar, safe surroundings. In America, on the other hand, everybody seemed to move constantly without a care. She could not make that adjustment so easily.

Despite her misgivings, she found a house for rent near the Met Lab on University Avenue. The government was moving its owner from Chicago to Washington, D.C., also for the duration of the war. The transaction went smoothly until the owner learned that the Fermis were enemy aliens. The house, which was to be rented furnished, contained a large Capehart radio with shortwave channels, and enemy aliens were not allowed to own shortwave. Spies used shortwave.

On July 11, 1942, Laura dressed in her Sunday best and Enrico in a suit and necktie, they went together to the District Court of the United States in downtown Chicago, where they joined a crowd of other immigrants. A judge in robes told them to raise their right hands and in unison to solemnly swear allegiance to the United States. With those words they became American citizens. A few days later, they moved into the house with the Capehart, the most visible proof that they were no longer "enemy" or "alien."

In many respects, their new status made life easier, but Laura found it difficult to escape from an environment of fear and suspicion. She was now an American, but one whose husband was engaged in secret war research. As such, she attended seminars given by Arthur Compton's wife on security, and what she learned disturbed her. She was told to remain aloof from anyone not associated with the Met Lab. She watched the film *Next of Kin,* which graphically showed the dire consequences in war of breaches in security, that a slip of the tongue could cost lives. The film showed the German Luftwaffe's bombing Britain. Words were not needed.

To occupy their time, Mrs. Compton encouraged the Met Lab wives to volunteer for war-related work. Laura did not feel that she wanted to cheer up lonely soldiers at the USO, so she signed up with the Red Cross in a Southside Chicago hospital. At home she continued to live a quiet life. The Fermis preferred to spend what time they had together as a family. Besides, they were not "party people." Neither she nor Enrico really approved of drinking, except the rare glass of port after dinner to celebrate an "occasion," and they considered smoking a foul habit.

However, Fermi told Laura that he wanted to encourage camaraderie among the Met Lab physicists. Reluctantly, she hosted parties at the house, which usually ended for her on a depressing note. Secrecy separated the scientists from their wives, even on social occasions. Couples who had never kept secrets were now being forced to erect a wall of silence between them. The women had always lived in their husbands' shadows. Before the war, they had been proud of their achievements, shared their enthusiasms, listened to their problems, and tried to understand the nature of their work. Now, at parties the men huddled in corners, talking physics, abruptly changing the subject when a wife joined them. The pattern embarrassed everyone, the men as much as the women.

Beyond these new, nettlesome concerns, Laura carried a heavy extra burden, shared with Enrico alone: the concern about her family. About this, too, there was nothing she could do, except wait and hope. Her attitude changed day by day: from the belief that no news was good news to the opposite or somewhere in between. Watching the film *Next of Kin,* she had imagined Rome, not England, and her family inhabiting those bombed houses. She translated every news item about the war into her own personal frame of reference. The war meant that her own family was being torn to pieces. She and Enrico talked, first one and then the other, about her family until there was nothing left to say; then days of complete silence on the subject would follow, as if the trouble would go away if unspoken. And yet the more life in Rome deteriorated for Jews, the more it occupied their minds.

Occasionally, Laura received news sent by friends. Her father still would not hide himself in the Italian countryside, where many Catholic Italians were sheltering urban Jews. Laura could not understand what he was trying to prove, or whom he was trying to defy, because if he continued, it would not end well for him. What the Nazis were doing to European Jews was no longer a secret, although in the absence of any confirmation, American Jews found the stories hard to believe.

Then, later, the suspense ended for Laura. She would not know for certain until well after the war, and she kept some hope alive. The Fascists had tolerated her father's defiance, but the Nazis had noted it and quickly sought to destroy it before he served as an example to other Jews in Rome. Without so much as a hearing, and despite all that the admiral had contributed to Italy during his career, he was arrested by the SS and placed among the initial one thousand Italian Jews transported east by train. He made his final stop in the southern Polish town of Auschwitz, and there, along with 4 million other Jews, he was exterminated.

No rumor, no invasion, no defeat could have brought the threat of Hitler closer to the Fermi home. Admiral Augusto Capon had been murdered by madmen whom Enrico was working to destroy. He did not need Colonel Groves's descriptions of the Nazi threat; he knew better than Groves. Hitler would not hesitate to explode an atomic bomb on men, women, and children, on his family. If Hitler could exterminate innocent people as he was in places like Auschwitz, nothing would restrain him if he were to acquire an atomic bomb. There could be no rest for Fermi, no excuses, no needless delays. He had to sweep everything else aside. As he saw it, he and his family were running the same risk, and he did not plan for them the same end his father-in-law had had.

Captain Kenneth Nichols, U.S. Army, had no desire to fail Groves on his first assignment for the Manhattan Engineering District, the official code name for the U.S. Army's Manhattan Project that President Roosevelt had created on September 17, 1942, to coordinate and oversee all aspects of the construction of an atomic bomb for the federal government. But success to Nichols seemed a long shot, given the problems. Nichols's new boss, now General Groves, who commanded the Manhattan District, had ordered him to visit the office building on Forty-second Street, eight blocks from the Manhattan District's headquarters in the Empire State Building. Groves did not tolerate failure. As far as Nichols was concerned, Groves was the most hard-nosed, tenacious, driven general officer he had ever known. From the Empire State Building, Groves had spread the Manhattan District's influence in just weeks from Washington state and California in the west to Illinois, Tennessee, the District of Columbia, New York, and Boston in the east. The development work on a bomb spanned the country. Yet, none of this breadth meant anything if Nichols failed to carry out orders that he considered impossible.

The shortage of uranium in America was so acute that it threatened the project. There was virtually none besides the small amounts being used for lab experiments. The Congo mines of Union Minière had been flooded and the work force scattered. There were other mines in Canada, but these were too far from railroad lines for any practical use. If Groves collected the total available supply of uranium in America in one place, it would not be enough to make a working pile, let alone produce a bomb. And nothing on earth acted as a replacement for uranium. Ounce for ounce, it was more precious than diamonds. No one knew this better than Captain Nichols.

It was September 18, 1942, one day after the official creation of the Manhattan District, that Nichols entered the doors of the American offices of Edgar Sengier and Union Minière de Haut-Katanga. Nichols vainly hoped that Sengier could tell him where to find a few extra tons of uranium; if Sengier couldn't, nobody could. Sengier, who had emigrated to New York shortly before the outbreak of war, knew nothing other than rumor and gossip, of course, about the American atomic bomb project. Earlier, the Joliot-Curies had referred vaguely to the use of uranium for a nuclear weapon, and Sir Henry Tizard in London had hinted of a threat if the Belgian company's uranium should fall into German hands, which by now had happened.

Nichols had been told to try to bring the conversation with Sengier around to the subject of uranium delicately, but he was to stop short of telling him that the Army wanted uranium for a bomb. He was to sound him out. If Sengier did not get the point, it would be unfortunate, but he would know nothing more than he had before the conversation about the most highly classified military secret in history.

Once in Sengier's office, Nichols found himself sitting across from a man of late middle age with graying hair; dark, almost hooded eyes; a moustache in the manner of Old World Europeans; and a substantial paunch. His dress was as impeccable as his manner. Almost before Nichols had settled in a chair on the other side of the desk, Sengier spoke in his light accent.

"I've been expecting you," he said, to Nichols's surprise.

It was not a statement meant to suggest that Sengier expected

Nichols at this prearranged, particular meeting. Nichols glanced at his wristwatch in spite of himself. He was exactly on time. Sengier raised his hand. "You've come about uranium," he said.

"Yes," Nichols said, even more nonplussed.

Sengier, of course, could not imagine any other reason that the U.S. Army would contact him except to ask questions about his company's uranium.

"I have some," he said.

"You *do?*"

"You see," he explained, "in August 1940, I instructed our people in Africa to ship discreetly to New York, under some kind of name, an existing stock of rich ore. A tonnage of 1,140 metric tons was shipped from Africa in 2,000 steel drums. The two shipments left Lobito Bay in September and October 1940, arriving in New York in November and December 1940. These are stored in a warehouse right here in New York, in Staten Island."

Three miles away from where they were sitting, Nichols thought, a feast of uranium only three miles away.

"What would have happened if I hadn't come here?" Nichols asked.

"I would have waited," Sengier replied. "It is no secret that I am here. It's no secret either who I am. Eventually, someone would have come—or not. And if not, then there would have been no need. The uranium was only a precaution on my part."

Within one week the Congo uranium was taken from Staten Island aboard railroad freight cars to MIT in Cambridge, Massachusetts, for processing from its natural 238 isotope state to an oxide; then it would be loaded aboard other freight cars and shipped to Fermi at the University of Chicago. It had already traveled long distances, over many, many years. And yet it would not end its journey for some time, until it obliterated itself first in a New Mexico desert and then, finally, in the skies over Japan.

The Twentieth Century Limited pounded through the night of a slumbering rural America, en route from New York to Chicago.

It was the early autumn of the same year, 1942. The express train carried General Groves, Captain Nichols, Fermi, and Robert Oppenheimer, a physicist from Berkeley. In the cramped space of a sleeping compartment, they talked in hushed voices about a vision of an "atomic city."

Groves had recently recruited Oppenheimer for his organizational skills, potentially as the leader of the entire science division of the project, but right now on this trip, "Oppie" was still just another physics researcher. Tall, gaunt, and soft-spoken, he had watched the rapid advances of nuclear research from a distance since 1939, when Bohr had announced the fission concept of Otto Hahn and Lise Meitner. Fission had so electrified Oppenheimer that he had started right away to calculate the critical mass of uranium 235, paralleling the work in England of Frisch and Peierls, at the Berkeley Radiation Laboratory. He had caught the eye of Arthur Compton, who asked him to concentrate on fast fission. So far, he had impressed everybody working on the Manhattan Project as capable, industrious, and talented, even charismatic.

It had been purely a coincidence that Fermi was returning to Chicago at the same time as the others, after a short visit to New York. Oppie more than admired Fermi; he once said that if he could be any man in history for only one day, he would choose to be Fermi. Yet, they could not have been more unlike. Fermi was earthy and materialistic; he worked with his hands. Fermi was direct and concrete in his language, reflecting the working of his mind. Oppenheimer, on the other hand, an intellectual fond of abstraction, a philosopher-physicist who read widely, could say things like

Both the man of science and the man of art live always at the edge of mystery, surrounded by it; both always as a measure of their creation have had to do with what is familiar with the balance between novelty and synthesis, with the struggle to make partial order in total chaos.

. . . Everything can be related to anything; everything cannot be related to everything.

What Oppie perceived as his own personal failure as a physicist
made Fermi stand out for his success even more in Oppenheimer's
opinion. During the 1920s, while studying in Germany at Göttingen,
Oppenheimer had shown great promise as a physicist, but that
promise was never realized. His contemporaries—Fermi, Heisenberg, Joliot-Curie—had achieved greatness in physics; as one measure of their success, they had each won a Nobel Prize. Oppie
could not say what, but after a promising start, something had
changed in him, scattering his promise in myriad directions. Now,
the moment for brilliance in physics had passed. Physicists rarely
achieved greatness in their forties. Theoretical physics was a
young man's discipline. Yet, as one opportunity had dimmed, Oppenheimer's ambition had blossomed to be named the scientific
head of the Manhattan Project: the achievement of the bomb
would be his Nobel Prize.

Already Oppenheimer saw a way to give birth to a bomb in the
shortest possible time. In those early months of the Manhattan
Project, Groves had established research centers all over the country. Planning seemed to progress on an ad hoc basis, at best. This
style, Oppenheimer felt certain, had to change. To proceed swiftly,
the scientists needed to be located in one place, in an "atomic
city," if for no other reason than communications. Oppenheimer
could understand why Groves wanted to build an isotope separation plant at Oak Ridge, Tennessee, and the plutonium factories at
Hanford, Washington. Engineers could easily operate the industrial end of the project. But why, he asked, were the chemists and
physicists scattered, too?

As the train rolled west, Oppenheimer suggested northern California as the site for the new city. But Groves said, "No, the War
Department will never approve." The U.S. Navy had not recovered
from the devastation at Pearl Harbor and the West Coast was
thought to be vulnerable to Japanese submarine attack. No, the city

had to be located inland from the coasts, ideally some distance from a major city, hidden from civilian eyes, a secret city that did not officially exist.

As Groves itemized his requirements, Oppenheimer recalled his days in a place of boyhood adventures; of a rugged, parched countryside; of old Navajo caves and scented pines. His parents had sent him to the Los Alamos Ranch School for Boys, about seven thousand feet above sea level on a mesa forming the Little Bird Plateau in the Jemez Mountains. Except for a few school buildings and a dirt road leading to Santa Fe, no sign of humanity existed there.

Oppenheimer mentioned Los Alamos to Groves, for whom the place inspired another, different vision. Out there, at the end of the world, he could keep the "crackpots" tightly under his control. Even better, such a wasteland, when the time came, would be ideal for a test of the new superweapon.

———

In a hotel in the center of Liverpool, Rudolf Peierls, Otto Frisch, and other MAUD and Tube Alloys' physicists, were stuck without transportation to the *Andes,* which was to sail in minutes for New York. Their luggage and cases of technical papers surrounded them in the lobby, but unless somebody did something fast to find them a ride, they were going to miss the boat.

They had decidedly mixed feelings about that eventuality.

Since the early months of 1942, the leaders of Tube Alloys and the prime minister at 10 Downing Street had agreed that the British research on an atomic bomb had to be moved in its entirety to America. Yet, as the day had dawned for the move, problems threatening to embitter the British scientists arose. Immediately after Pegram and Urey had conducted their inspection tour and had left England for America, cooperation between the two allies had lacked nothing. Yet, once the president had committed the United States to making a bomb, the Americans had turned less than generous. Vannevar Bush had written as a guideline, "We will continue, on this matter as well as on other phases of OSRD work, to adhere to the principle that confidential information will be made available to an individual only in so far as it is necessary for his proper functioning in connection with his assigned duties." Only the very few men at the very top in England were going to see the whole picture, for reasons, the Americans said, of security. But the British were not convinced.

As far as they were concerned, the American concept of security far exceeded the level needed to keep secrets from reaching the Germans. Indeed, the Americans' concept of security seemed to have less relation to the Germans than to the British. While failing to give proper recognition to the British for their contribution so far, the Americans even suspected that Britain aspired to sell nuclear energy as a commodity after the war.

In fact Britain was only protecting its own interests, summed up in a memo written by the Ministry of Aircraft Production. "Since we are passing to the USA all the knowledge gained over here on this matter, it has been suggested that steps ought to be taken to ensure that this country shall obtain an appropriate share of any benefits resulting from the immense industrial developments which will arise if this work is successful." A further memo, this one sent to Churchill, pointed out a further deterioration.

It appears that [the Americans have decided] that information must be withheld from us over the greater part of the field of Tube Alloys. At the same time the United States authorities apparently expect us to continue to exchange information with them in regard to those parts of the project in which our work is further forward than theirs. This development has come as a bombshell and is quite intolerable.

Britain's reaction to America's attitude was easy to understand: MAUD and Tube Alloys had been first to conceive of nuclear energy as a weapon of war. Earlier, in the face of American indifference, MAUD had begun bomb research, without any certainty of a payoff, expending priceless time and resources on what then had seemed fanciful. Yet now that a bomb was feasible, the Americans were being coy. Churchill wrote to the White House, "Time is passing and collaboration appears to be at a standstill. We have made some progress in the last three months and I shall shortly be forced to take decisions." When this entreaty failed, Churchill wrote again: "That we should each work separately would be a sombre decision." Finally, during a wartime meeting in Washington, D.C., Churchill raised the matter directly. "The President," he wrote later, "agreed that the exchange of information on Tube Alloys should be resumed and that the enterprise should be considered a joint one, to which both countries would contribute their best endeavors." Translated, this became the "Articles of Agreement Governing Collaboration between the Authorities of the USA and the UK in the Matter of Tube Alloys," known as the *Quebec Agreement.* Henceforth Britain and America would pool brains and resources in America; each country promised not to use the bomb against the other or against a third party without the other's consent or reveal information about the bomb to a third party without mutual consent.

The British finally were getting what they wanted for the war, and no more. America insisted that

in view of the heavy burden of production falling upon the United States as the result of a wise division of war effort, the British Government recognize that any post-war advantages of an *industrial* or *commercial* character shall be dealt with as between the United States and Great Britain on terms to be specified by the President of the United States to the Prime Minister of Great Britain. The Prime Minister expressly disclaims any interest in these industrial and commercial aspects beyond what may be considered by the President of the United States to be fair and just and in harmony with the economic welfare of the world.

Britain signed away the proprietary right to postwar atomic energy. Churchill had no other choice.

The agreement brought only dismay to researchers like Frisch and Peierls, without whose work there would have been no reason for the Quebec Agreement. They worried that their American counterparts would treat them as poor relations. It was like contesting a will before the relative had died. All the agreements and regulations meant next to nothing because nobody knew whether America or Britain, alone or together, could manufacture a bomb, let alone apply existing theories of the atom to commercial nuclear energy after the war.

However, Peierls did know one thing, as he milled around the hotel lobby. They were about to miss the *Andes* sailing time. They had to find transport from the hotel to the docks soon.

Then Peierls had an inspiration. He marched out of the hotel and up the Liverpool High Street to the first undertaking establishment. He told the funeral director what he needed and the amount he was willing to pay. There was no funeral scheduled, so the director agreed with alacrity. Soon, a "cortège" of somber black Daimler limousines pulled up in front of the hotel. Before getting inside, the scientists stacked their baggage and technical papers into the hearse with etched windows where the casket rode. In this practical but bizarre manner, Britain's team of bomb researchers departed for the New World.

———

In the north of Scotland, Claus Helberg and five other Norwegians in the commando training section of the Special Operations Executive (SOE) were about to board the four-engined RAF plane that would take them over Norway. Their SOE commander had already briefed them on the tragic failure of the first Combined Operations sabotage mission on Rjukan. He then had issued them each with small, liver-colored cyanide capsules, telling them, "If any man is about to be taken prisoner, he undertakes to end his own life." They knew the stakes and were still eager for the mission to succeed, not only to right the failure of the first commando raid, but because after months of training in the harsh Scottish Highlands, their initial drop over Norway had been aborted when the advance party—the same men who had waited earlier in Norway for the arrival of the ill-fated passengers of the Horsa gliders and since had stayed, foraging for food and living primitively in hunters' huts—had failed to light the drop zone. That same advance party had reported by radio that the Germans had reinforced their defenses around Rjukan in expectation of another Allied raid. All of these mishaps and obstacles inspired a feeling of discouragement among the men of the commando. They were not exactly being sent to their deaths, yet the chance of success was remote.

The RAF bomber this time dropped them over Lake Shryken, about thirty miles to the northwest of Rjukan, above the wind-swept, barren Hardanger Plateau. The need to cover that distance on skis with sixty-five-pound packs, demolition equipment, radios, food, and personal weapons, under life-threatening weather conditions nearly ended the mission at the start. Then a fierce storm swept across the plateau. They struggled to collect the supply containers, dropped separately, when the storm reached its peak, forcing them into a shelter near the frozen lake for two days. The wind and cold brought another threat to "Gunnerside," as their mission was code-named, from an unexpected quarter: the glands in their necks swelled painfully. Everything so far had conspired against them. They were consoled only by the awareness that they had already done better than their doomed predecessors.

When the storm blew itself out, they skied toward Rjukan and, despite their exhaustion, understood the SOE's decision to drop them so far from their target. No German patrol had been anywhere near the drop; even German airplanes did not patrol the skies so far north. The only other living thing they encountered were herds of caribou and the wolves that fed on them. On the second morning, the sight through binoculars of two men on skis startled them. They sent one man to reconnoiter, while the others hid behind drifts, their rifles pointing out. Later, shouts of joy, then laughter, told them that they had rendezvoused with the advance party.

Claus Helberg, who was born and raised there, went into Rjukan to learn what he could about the Germans' defenses. As he neared Rjukan, he surveyed the gorge, about five hundred feet in depth, between the village and the heavy-water plant, spanned by a narrow bridge that the Germans guarded at both ends. Using the bridge, Helberg knew, would require killing the guards, but there seemed to be no other approach. The cliff seemed impossible to climb; however, Helberg resolved, if trees and shrubs found room on the cliff face to shoot down roots, then surely there were footholds for the commandos to climb down and then up the other side, if only they had the stamina. On the climb down, they would be laboring under the weight of their gear, and later they might have to carry wounded. But, without killing, there was no other way in.

Helberg moved among relatives and friends in the village: all enemies of the German occupiers, even more since the Germans had staged a fake air raid after the earlier aborted sabotage mission, searching houses and interrogating the men. Afterward, the Germans had clamped down on the village as if it were a concentration camp.

They told Helberg that the Germans had erected searchlights and machine guns on Norsk-Hydro's buildings and mined the approaches; a dozen or so guards patrolled the area between the bridge and the plant. Luckily, though, the Germans, on the assumption that their defenses were impregnable, had not placed guards in the buildings themselves, although, Helberg learned, they locked the door to the target electrolysis plant at night.

Helberg and the commando unit agreed to begin the raid just after midnight, when the guards would least expect them. It was still little short of a suicide mission, with each man imagining the whine of the electricity-generating plant as the last sound he would ever hear.

They skied down from the hillside to the edge of the cliff, where they stripped off their white camouflage suits. Now in British Army uniform, they could not be executed if they were captured alive.

They loaded their weapons and strapped on the packs, then climbed down into the gorge. The sounds of the electricity plant, the wind, and the rushing water covered the noise of ice and snow dislodged by their boots from the cliff ledges. They climbed up the other side and waited until the guards had changed shifts and settled down. Dim lights twinkled in the windows of the plant itself; the area otherwise was bathed in darkness.

When they thought the guards were dozing, the commando team cut through a wire fence with half the group covering the half constituting the demolition party. To avoid German land mines, they followed the narrow-gauge railroad track leading up to the plant. A German guard had left his footprints in the snow.

As the covering party fanned out to preassigned locations, the demolition crew crept up to the building with the high-concentration cells for the separation of heavy water, entering through a conduit crammed with electrical cables and pipes. A bespectacled Norwegian technician was alone in the room, monitoring the cells. They slithered out of the conduit and covered him with a machine gun; then they wrapped plastic explosives around eighteen of the stainless steel cells. Just as they touched off the fuses, the Norwegian said that he had lost his eyeglasses, and if he did not find them he could not get another pair until the war was over. The commandos searched the room as the fuses shortened. Finally, they found the glasses, then ran for safety.

Thirty seconds later, the charges shattered the cells. Nearly a half ton of heavy water poured onto the floor. The "shrapnel" of stainless steel punctured the cooling pipes; ordinary water polluted the heavy water beyond any hope of reclamation.

The raiders retreated, as a confused lone German searched the night with a flashlight. A siren wailed. The Germans trained the floodlights on the railroad tracks as the team rappelled the gorge and climbed the other side. They retrieved their skis and set off toward the original drop zone, en route to Sweden.

The next day, ten thousand German troops searched for them in the region around Rjukan. The raiders paused only long enough to radio London. "High Concentration Installation . . . completely destroyed on the night of 27th–28th. 'Gunnerside' has gone to Sweden. Greetings."

All of Gunnerside escaped overland to the Swedish border except Claus Helberg, whom the German patrols had spotted. At the peak of physical and mental fitness after months of training in Scotland, Helberg had thought that he could ski faster than the three German soldiers chasing him. He had felt confident when two of the Germans, the members of a large, sweeping patrol, dropped back exhausted. But the remaining German was gaining. He skied better than Helberg and had not spent the previous night on a sheer rock face. Helberg looked behind him. The German was closing the distance between them. Helberg doubted that he had the stamina to continue.

Helberg did not want to use the .32-caliber Colt pistol in his parka. He had taken great pains to avoid encounters with the German guards, even when he could have killed them easily, fearing reprisals the Germans might take on the local Norwegian people, on his friends and relatives. The raiding party had agreed beforehand to kill only as a last, desperate act.

Helberg was having trouble drawing breath, and his legs felt numb after two hours of hard, nonstop skiing. He stopped and turned his body to face the oncoming German. He could make out the man's features, and by the rhythm of his movements, Helberg knew that he could not outdistance him. He reached into his parka for the Colt. The German stopped, and they stared at each other, trying to read each other's intentions. Helberg saw the German draw his pistol too. Helberg enjoyed a slight advantage. The German carried a Luger, a wildly inaccurate weapon over such a long range. Helberg stood there, the Colt at his side, as the German aimed.

He pointed the Luger and shot eight times, slowly, and then he lowered his pistol. He made a halfhearted attempt to turn as Helberg raised the Colt. He pulled the trigger once, and the German slumped over the ski poles. Helberg did not check to see what damage he had done or try to kill the man. He had stopped his pursuers, and that was enough.

Part VIII

In Chicago, under the stands of Stagg Field, the first graphite brick was laid on the balloon cloth on November 16, 1942. Chicago Pile Number One (CP-1), Fermi's heap of graphite bricks and uranium, began to rise from the floor of the doubles squash court with the adjoining spectators' balcony as the control point. Supervised by Fermi, Zinn, and Anderson, the physicists machined the bricks in a space formerly used as a rifle range for student competition; the pressing of the uranium and the machining and drilling of the bricks proceeded in the maze of corridors under the stands. Fermi could not predict the precise height that would give criticality, somewhere, he thought, around fifty-seven layers of graphite bricks. If it needed more, the pile would not fit into the squash court. The other dimensions were less critical: he planned for a spherical shape to give the pile a minimum surface area through which neutrons could escape into the air. Anderson constructed a square "cradle" of wood to hold the graphite and uranium spheroid.

The rubber balloon had arrived on schedule from Akron, and Fermi supervised its unfolding. At first he was not able to see the top of the balloon from where he was standing on the floor of the court. He moved to the portable "elevator" that the physicists used to carry the graphite from the rifle range to the squash court. He climbed on board and raised the elevator to just below the ceiling, where he could look down on the balloon's unfolding as a ship's captain on a bridge would look down on the decks.

"All hands stand by!" Fermi yelled, as the physicists started to maneuver the balloon.

"Now haul the rope and heave her." The balloon, with a rope fastened to its top through a pulley, started to expand upward from the floor.

"More to the right."

"Brace the tackles to the left."

One of the Met Lab physicists yelled up, "All right, Admiral." And they all laughed.

Once it was in place, they secured the balloon on five sides and laid the flat end of the sixth side on the floor, allowing them access with the bricks and the uranium. When they had finished for the day, one of the physicists searched for a nautical wheel for Fermi, the "admiral of the S.S. *CP-1*."

When the West Stands of Stagg Field were originally constructed, the planners had not included heaters in the honeycomb of corridors beneath. Fermi estimated that they would complete the fifty-seven layers of the pile around the end of November; the autumn cold might reduce the heat generated by the pile. Theoretically, the pile could become so hot that it would explode, spewing fiery chunks of radioactive uranium against the squash court's white, wood-lathed walls.

Fermi wanted the pile ready for criticality by November 28, the day that General Groves was scheduled to visit the university with the Reviewing Committee, which included an executive from the du Pont Company, Crawford Greenwalt. If Greenwalt were actually present for the momentous event, he could no longer doubt the feasibility of a plutonium-producing pile.

But for now the task that lay before Fermi was considerable. The four-inch-by-six-inch timbers were arriving daily from the Sterling Lumber Company. Gus Knuth, a local carpenter, built the cradle for the pile without knowing what strange device the cradle was meant to support. He cut and hammered, asking few questions. Fermi admired Knuth's "feel" for wood, lathes, and nails. As one of the physicists said, noting the accented speech of Knuth, Fermi, Szilard, Wigner, and others on the project, Met Lab seemed like "one big happy accent."

According to Fermi's estimates, CP-1 would need around four hundred tons of graphite, which reached Chicago by boxcar in bars that ranged in size from four-by-four-by-seventeen to fifty inches in length, with rough, saw-cut surfaces. Thirty young Chicago high school dropouts, called the "back-of-the-yard kids," loaded the bricks onto trucks, then from the trucks into the rifle range. Before milling, the graphite was tested for purity in the exponential piles. The bricks then were planed smooth and cut to uniform size, $4\frac{1}{8}$ inches by $4\frac{1}{8}$ inches. Next, about every one in four bricks was drilled with holes exactly $3\frac{1}{4}$ inches in diameter with a lathe-spade made from old files. The physicists drilled a hundred holes an hour, with the spades either breaking or dulling every seventy.

As for the uranium, they needed twenty-two thousand pseudospheres, which they pressed on the same machine that one of Fermi's group at Columbia had scrounged from the New Jersey junkyard. On a good day, they could press twelve hundred lumps, working around the clock in two shifts. The pseudospheres then were inserted into the holes in the graphite, and then at last the bricks were stacked on the balloon cloth in the squash court.

No matter what they did, the work was monotonous, and very little saved the physicists from boredom. They swore and sang at the top of their voices to be heard over the rasp and whine and clatter of the machines. Graphite dust coated their butchers' jackets, working itself into their skin. They showered at night and in the mornings after their shifts, but their skin still oozed graphite. Under graphite-coated light bulbs, only teeth, eyes, and the glowing tips of Fatimas appeared, as if they were spirits in a corner of hell.

To the man they were willing to drop one job and help on another. One day a new shipment of graphite was dumped at the stands' entrance, and one of the physicists told Anderson that they would get around to it later. "Hell, no," yelled Anderson. "We'll *all* do it now." Another day, when a shipment of graphite reached the railroad yards and the high school dropouts were busy on another job, four of the physicists unloaded the bricks themselves in less than a day: two thousand bricks weighing fifty tons. Then, barely stopping for a breath, they returned to their "normal" work under the stands.

A team of doctors arrived one day with cages of white mice. The physicists stopped their work and stared. Because they had refused to wear masks, they had been breathing and even eating uranium for weeks without knowing whether they were slowly poisoning themselves, and only now had someone thought to determine in what way the environment would affect mice. But from then on, they looked in on the mice, which survived. But the graphite turned them black, too.

The graphite made the floor slippery, and periodically the physicists' legs went out from underneath them as they carried an armful of bricks or pseudospheres. With the coming of winter, the corridors turned unseasonably cold. Physical exertion helped to keep the physicists warm, but the two university policemen on guard at the door to the stands were chilled to the bone. Walter Zinn took pity on them. He searched the athletic lockers in the dressing room and found two raccoon coats. The "raccoons" gave a certain "collegiate" look to the whole enterprise.

On those days when the temperature dipped well below freezing, the physicists rigged Rube Goldberg electric fire-simulating heaters that barely worked. They tried burning charcoal in oil drums, but the smoke choked them, and gas-burning heaters sucked the oxygen out of the air and burned their eyes. Finally, they resigned themselves to the cold, working harder to keep themselves from freezing.

In more ways than one, their work was dimly lighted. Fermi had guessed at the optimum size and configuration of the pile, and a guess, even by a genius, was still no proof. Indeed, Fermi guessed how to position the uranium metal inside the outer layers of graphite near the exact center of the sphere. (The uranium arrived from MIT as a metal and as an oxide. Uranium metal fissioned better than the oxide. To maximize its properties, it was placed into the exact center. The oxide would surround it higher up in the pile.) As he did not know the final dimension of the pile, he could only guess where its center would be. Fermi also had to guess where to stack the graphite, because it arrived in varying grades of purity.

At the end of each working shift, twice a day, Anderson took a blueprint of the pile to Fermi's office in Eckhart Hall to plan the strategy for the next shift. As the pile rose higher toward the ceiling of the squash court, they worried where to position the cadmium-coated control and safety rods that ran through the girth of the pile. If there were too few control rods, Fermi knew, the pile might become too reactive as it grew in size. The control rods were made of cadmium sheets nailed to flat strips of wood. After their insertion, they were padlocked into place, with Zinn and Anderson keeping the keys. Zinn designed the ultimate automatic safety rod, which he called the *zip.* Straightforward and simple, heavy weights were hung from one end of the rod and a simple pulley to the other. Once the rope holding the rod out of the pile was untied and released, gravity pulled the rod into the pile with a loud crashing sound, absorbing the neutrons and, thus, "cooling off" the reaction. Everything worked, as a guess, or what the physicists called "theory."

Before the twice-daily meetings with Fermi, Anderson and Zinn measured the pile's increased rate of neutron production. Fermi used their figures to estimate the additional layers the pile needed to reach criticality. Each layer produced more neutrons, a hopeful sign. The pile was building its strength gradually. If fifty-seven layers were an accurate estimate, the pile would fit into the squash court, with a flat top against the roof and only inches to spare. Fermi did not think that they could reach that height before the Reviewing Committee came, so he set a new date: December 2, 1942. Not coincidentally, the committee was scheduled on that day to return to Chicago from an inspection tour of California.

Meanwhile, Leona Woods connected the pile to a series of counters in the spectators' gallery, from which Fermi, scanning the graphs and dials, would shout orders to the crew below on the squash court floor. Somehow, he was going to have to "play" the pile. If he gave it too much freedom, it could run out of control; if he gave it too little, it would not go critical. And if the counter readings were inaccurate, they might find themselves in danger without knowing.

On the night of December 1, Anderson supervised the stacking of layer 57. Then he called a halt and told everybody to go to bed. He removed all the cadmium rods, except one, and measured the neutron production rate. Alone in the squash court, momentarily he felt tempted to pull the final rod and become the single witness to history. But he kept his agreement with Fermi, whom he had promised to wait until the next morning. Anderson walked around the pile, locking the rods.

It all seemed hopelessly amateurish, a rickety invention of wire and wood and strips and bricks and balloons, with the awesome purpose of unleashing the most powerful forces in the universe. It simply did not seem likely. Looking at it, squat and dark and silent, it seemed a joke. As a machine, it did not actually do anything that machines were supposed to do: heave and steam and clank and whine. It was not unlike a huge ball of hardened mud, or an immense, blackened, deformed egg about to give birth to the nuclear age, now resting in its stiff wooden nest. Yet, there could be no mistaking. Fermi thought it was beautiful, a sculpture as soaring as a Brancusi. If he had not been so totally unshakable in his belief that it would function according to elegant theory, the others might have laughed.

As usual, Fermi spent the night of December 1 at home with Laura and the children. They talked and ate a normal meal of pasta and bread, and then, by nine, he kissed them good night and went up to bed. Within minutes after putting out the light he was asleep, with the alarm set for four. Nothing about his routine that evening in any way suggested that the next day, of all the yesterdays and all the tomorrows, would not be just any other day.

A couple of hundred yards from Stagg Field in Jones Chemical Laboratory, lights beamed down through the night on the chemistry paraphernalia assembled there by Glenn Seaborg, whom Compton had recruited in May to continue experiments on the unpredictable element plutonium.

CP-1, everybody understood, would have no direct relevance to the war unless the plutonium it produced could be removed and separated from the uranium from which it derived. Plutonium, of course, held out the promise of easy access to bomb "fuel," certainly when compared with the separation process of uranium 235. Seaborg felt confident; everything that he had learned since his arrival had served to bolster his assurance.

Daringly he had recruited what might have seemed to anyone else an unusual research team: an entomologist (a specialist in insects), a microchemist, a physiologist, and an ultramicroscopist. The field of tracer chemistry by which elements such as plutonium were studied in their available submicroscopic "tracer" quantities was relatively new in America. Seaborg had recruited his team on the basis that they knew how to work with invisible things, such as the thirty-*trillionths* of an ounce of plutonium, far less than the eye could see with a microscope, that Seaborg had produced with the Berkeley cyclotron. The Manhattan Project, of course, would require pounds of plutonium. In Chicago the team had produced three micrograms of plutonium. That excited visitors from the Met Lab who stopped by the Jones Laboratory as "tourists" to gaze at the speck of man-made material. They had been thrilled by the sight, but when Groves had peered through the microscope, he had grumbled, "I don't see anything." Exasperated, Seaborg had tried to explain.

Plutonium is so unusual as to approach the unbelievable. Under some circumstances plutonium can be nearly as hard and brittle as glass; under others, as soft and plastic as lead. It will burn and crumble quickly to powder when heated in air, or slowly disintegrate when kept at room temperature. It undergoes no less than five phase transitions between room temperature and its melting point. Strangely enough, in two of its phases, plutonium actually contracts as it is being heated. It also has no less than four oxidation states. It is unique among all the chemical elements. And it is fiendishly toxic, even in small amounts.

Groves was not impressed; he did not care how plutonium behaved. Nothing intrinsic to the miracle of its existence mattered to him. He wanted enough of it, much more than that speck he had not been able to see, to pour into a casing and explode. Frankly, he had trouble understanding the "crackpots'" hushed expressions of wonder over a mere pinhead quantity of the stuff. He wanted Seaborg to find a means to extract the plutonium out of a pile, first out of CP-1, then out of the factory piles ready for construction at Hanford. He did not care either that one microspeck of plutonium, if inhaled into the lungs, would almost certainly result in a cancerous bone tumor.

Seaborg had spent most of his time in Chicago experimenting with chemical solutions that would "carry" the plutonium. He had searched for the right mixture to take out the plutonium, and leave behind the "slag" that had not undergone a transformation. But until now, all his efforts had failed.

Given its nature, nothing about plutonium surprised Seaborg. By all reasoning, bismuth phosphate would not carry the plutonium, but Seaborg tried it anyway, less with the expectation of success than to follow the method of testing all chemicals without exception. To his utter surprise, bismuth not only carried plutonium but carried it extremely well. He was still testing with tracer quantities of plutonium that might behave differently once it was produced in mass. But he took an unusual, daring step. He followed the theory, another guess, really, that plutonium responded in the same way as uranium. This theory held up consistently, and now, as Fermi had readied CP-1, Seaborg dared to state that factory piles would produce plutonium with bismuth phosphate as the carrier.

The stakes for CP-1's success were as high for Seaborg as they were for Fermi.

Puffing vapor, Fermi trudged through the crusted, blue-edged snow toward the entrance to the West Stands, where he said a cheerful good morning to the raccoon-swathed guards, who told him what was already obvious: the temperature had dropped and was expected to remain below zero throughout most of the day. There was no relief from the cold inside, either, where he greeted the team, who had assembled at eight-thirty sharp. He climbed the stairs to the spectators' balcony, replaced his overcoat with a butcher's jacket, took the familiar slide rule from his pocket, then looked over the balcony at his creation, CP-1. It was December 2, 1942: the day that Fermi brought man into the nuclear age.

Fermi had spent the dark hours of the morning in his study preparing for this final push, while the children and Laura slept in a silent house. Taking careful notes, he had calculated the degree of *flux,* the amount of fissioning, for each length that the control rod was pulled from CP-1. Presumably, since the rod absorbed neutrons, each foot it was withdrawn should allow the pile to "breathe" more and more until it could sustain its own life independent of the neutrons from the "starter" source in its center. What form that life would take, Fermi could not say. He only hoped that the birth of CP-1 would be smooth.

Fermi had already organized prearranged positions that the physicists would assume on the pile. Most would remain beside him on the balcony near the redundant boron trifluoride counters for measuring the low neutron intensities and ion chambers powered by dry-cell batteries and 110-volt mains strung inside the squash court. Other physicists would man the control and safety rods. The zip had been rigged to a solenoid on a neutron-detecting device; if the electricity failed or if the pile went out of control, the zip would automatically slam home, choking off the neutrons. Other safety rods worked at the push of a button. One last rod, connected to lead weights, was tied by a rope to the railing of the balcony. Norman Hilberry wielded a hatchet with which to cut the rope. Gravity then would pull the rod into CP-1. As a further safety measure, three physicists, who were calling themselves "the suicide squad," would stand on the portable elevator with three large commercial drinking-water bottles of cadmium sulfate solution. If all the other safety measures failed and the pile burst into nuclear flame, they would drench the whole pile in the liquid. One physicist, George Weil, would actually stand on the floor, at the end of the only control rod that would remain inside the pile. Weil would pull the measured rod out of the pile at lengths dictated by Fermi, depending on how quickly or slowly he wanted CP-1 to react. Like the accelerator of a car, pulling the rod out should make the pile go faster, and pushing it in should slow it down.

Fermi had placed most of the electronic components at one side of the gallery overlooking CP-1. The most crucial of these was a pen recorder on a scroll of paper to record the "flux" of the pile, much as an electrocardiograph records the beatings in the human heart. Younger physicists monitored the counters with Fermi close by to check for himself. He also relied on the slide rule in his hands; he used a lead pencil to jot down calculations on the slide rule's clean white reverse side.

He first checked the flux measurements of the night before. Then the instruments were calibrated against that standard. The speed alone with which Fermi scanned the instruments with his gray eyes betrayed his nervousness. Now, gesturing with his hands, he talked the team through the first stages.

"The pile is not performing now," he said in a voice that echoed off the court walls, "because inside it there are rods of cadmium which absorb neutrons. One single rod is sufficient to prevent a chain reaction. So our first step will be to pull out of the pile all control rods but the one that George will man." The team members removed the safety rods.

"This rod that we have pulled out with the others is automatically controlled," Fermi continued. "Should the intensity of the reaction become greater than a pre-set limit, this rod would go back inside the pile by itself." He pointed to the area of the electronics and measuring devices.

This pen will trace a line indicating the intensity of the radiation. When the pile chain-reacts, the pen will trace a line that will go up and up and that will not tend to level off. In other words, it will be an exponential pile. Presently we shall begin our experiment. George will pull out his rod a little at a time. We shall take measurements and verify that the pile will keep on acting as we have calculated. George will first set the rod at thirteen feet. This means that thirteen feet of the rod will still be inside the pile. The counters will click faster and the pen will move up to this point, and then its trace will level off.

He paused before saying, "Go ahead, George."

Over in an Eckhart Hall conference room, Arthur Compton was convening the Reviewing Committee that had arrived that morning from California. The committee chairman, Warren Lewis, looked around the room and asked, "Where's Fermi?"

"Fermi asked to be excused," Compton replied. "He has an important experiment going on in the laboratory and cannot join us."

Given the agenda, the committee wondered about his absence. They had already drawn up a preliminary report for General Groves, supporting continued plutonium research at Chicago but expressing disappointment at the speed of developments. In November when they had stopped in Chicago expecting news of positive results from CP-1, they had been given excuses. Crawford Greenwalt, from the du Pont Company, was skeptical as a result. Groves was pressuring du Pont to produce factory piles, but Greenwalt was not convinced that the results in Chicago so far warranted the outlay of personnel and capital that could be committed profitably to other pressing war-related work. If Fermi were at this meeting, he might allay some of Greenwalt's fears.

The telephone rang, and Compton picked it up.

"I thought you would want to know that Fermi is ready to start the critical experiment," the caller from Stagg Field said.

Compton looked around the room, then asked into the telephone, "Can I bring them?"

"No," the caller said. The balcony was already crowded with equipment and researchers. Any more people might disturb the physicists' concentration and upset the experiment. Fermi had told the caller to invite Compton and possibly one member of the committee.

"Gentlemen, Fermi is about to try the chain reaction," Compton said. "Tests show that the pile, only about three-quarters of the size that had been thought necessary, is ready to give a chain reaction."

Compton knew that Greenwalt, at forty, was junior on the committee, but he was potentially the most important to the future of the Met Lab work. Protocol suggested that Compton invite Lewis along, but he did not. He and Greenwalt left the conference room together.

"Pull it to thirteen feet, George," Fermi ordered. Weil cautiously exerted pressure on the control rod. It was ten thirty-seven.

"The trace will go to this point and level off." Fermi watched as the pen on the graph craggily moved upward. The sound of clicking in the counters increased from a lazy, random beat to a regular tattoo. Fermi put his finger on the paper roll of the graph. The line moved steadily upward.

Suddenly, a loud bang shattered the silence. Everyone froze, not knowing what had happened or what to expect. Fermi glanced over at Zinn. The pile was subcritical, but the flux had reached a preset point that Fermi had overlooked. The zip had released automatically, sliding back into the pile. The weights had crashed onto the wooden floor.

When the physicists had regained their composure, Fermi ordered the zip out again. The needle on the graph rose exactly to where Fermi had placed his finger, then leveled off. So far it was a virtuoso performance. Fermi scanned the indicators, calculated rapidly on the slide rule, and paused.

He looked at the faces around him. With a grin, he said, "I'm hungry. Let's go to lunch."

He saw the tension melt from the faces. The halt, which made the experiment seem like any other on any other day, helped them to relax. Fermi saw no reason to rush. He was enjoying himself. By "playing" with the pile, he was demonstrating his command, working it up and down toward criticality, the master of the machine.

Over in the Commons, the physicists did not discuss the experiment during the lunch break. They argued as usual about the war and gambled on the numbers in their checkbooks. Fermi went for lunch with Leona Woods and Anderson at the apartment of Woods's sister. She made pancakes with nuts in the batter, mixing the ingredients in such haste that the result contained bubbles of powdery, uncooked pancake mix. Just before two o'clock they walked back to Stagg Field where other scientists, having no connection to Met Lab who had heard rumors of what was happening, were gathering in the corridor outside the squash court. One of the physicists had rigged a loudspeaker so they could follow the experiment, as if it were an athletic event.

Once the physicists had resumed their positions, Fermi asked Weil to pull the rod out to the same length as before lunch. As a safety precaution, the zip was inserted while the control rod was pulled out the distance ordered by Fermi. Once it was set, the zip was removed. Now, he called for the zip to go in, and the control rod to go out a further six inches. The zip came out again. The clicking increased to a steady, constant sound.

Fermi looked over at the "suicide squad" with their bottles of cadmium sulfate solution. He warned them, "No matter what happens, unless you see me collapse, I do not want you to pour out the solution. If you do I'll come after you with an ax."

Fermi then looked at the graph. Everything checked out. He ordered "zip in," then to Weil, "This time take the control rod out twelve inches."

Leaning over Fermi's shoulder, Leona Woods asked, "When do we start to get scared?" Fermi thought to himself, "Well, all right, not yet, but in a short time we should begin to get scared."

Fermi turned to Arthur Compton. "This is going to do it," he said. "Now it will become self-sustaining." He pointed to the graph. "The trace will climb and continue to climb. It will *not* level off."

Seconds passed as counters rattled. The "suicide squad" gripped the bottles of cadmium sulfate solution, and Hilberry tightened his grasp on the hatchet, his eyes on the rope. These men and the others watching from the balcony were in a sense as primitively equipped to handle the power of the pile as were the people who first created fire in their darkened caves. Like those cavemen, these physicists were now entering a realm where no one had ever gone. As the counters rattled and the needle edged up and up and up on the graph, the pile produced neutrons at an incredible rate, entering, then splitting nuclei; loosing into the pile two more neutrons and on and on and on; flying out of the nuclei, bouncing off graphite, slowing, then entering further nuclei—a chaotic controlled explosion of billions of nuclei, transforming matter, as alchemists for centuries had dreamed of doing, into energy and precious plutonium. The needle on the graph climbed straight up, rolling around and around the graph, showing life that had never before sustained itself quite like this miracle, an endless series of chain reactions compared to the paltry few Fermi had produced in the goldfish pond eight years ago, almost to the day.

The scientists froze, not yet knowing how they should react and when or if they might raise the curtain of fear. They did not yet know whether they had succeeded or failed or, if they had succeeded, what it would mean.

Then, almost by imperceptible degrees, a smile started to form itself on Fermi's face.

He lowered the slide rule to his side. "The reaction *is* self-sustaining," he said.

And still nobody moved or said a word, waiting either to be blown into oblivion or to be witnesses to history. For the next twenty-eight minutes CP-1 operated on its own, feebly producing the energy to light a two-hundred-watt light bulb. Its power did not matter to the physicists. Life did. And inside its blackened shell the pile was churning the abundant uranium isotope into bomb-producing plutonium.

At three fifty-three, Fermi said, "Okay, zip in."

The clicking diminished and the needle traced a downward line on the graph as CP-1 went subcritical and then back to an inert lump.

"Lock the control rods into the safety position," Fermi said, "and come back tomorrow morning."

As the physicists were removing their coats, Eugene Wigner handed Fermi a bottle of Bertolli Chianti wrapped in the traditional Tuscan raffia. Wigner passed around paper cups as Fermi uncorked the bottle. They drank in complete silence. No one offered a toast. No one cheered. No one laughed. Only one person spoke. Referring to the Nazis, Leona Woods said, "Let's hope that *we* are the *first* to succeed."

Compton went to a telephone to call James Conant, the president of Harvard University and the chairman of the Combined Policy Committee. Their conversation was short and cryptic. He said, "You'll be interested to know that the Italian navigator has just landed in the New World. He arrived sooner than he had expected."

Conant asked, "Were the natives friendly?"

"Everyone landed safe and happy."

The physicists crushed the cups and threw them on the floor, then as one of them hung the empty Chianti bottle on a nail and turned off the lights, they wandered off, across the snow through shadows that were lengthening into darkness.

D
r. Samuel Goudsmit, a physicist and close friend of the Fermis, understood the problem only too well: until he captured Werner Heisenberg somewhere in the collapsing Reich, the Allied Command would not know whether Germany had maintained its lead in the race, perhaps even by producing at least one atomic bomb with which to force the Allies to sue for peace.

The Army had recruited Goudsmit as part of a special, secret Army unit, made up of 114 men, called *Alsos,* the Greek word for "grove," after General Groves, who had conceived of the idea as a necessary precaution. The Army had found Goudsmit on the campus of MIT, where he had spent most of the war working on radar. Neither his direct superior, Army Colonel Boris T. Pash, nor Groves told him anything about Allied atomic bomb research. But he had deduced certain facts; the concentration of his friends, all nuclear scientists, at the University of Chicago had to indicate one stage or another of an American bomb project. Groves had recruited Goudsmit precisely for his ignorance of the Manhattan Project, and beyond that for his fluency in German, French, and Dutch; his prewar acquaintance with several of the German physicists; and, last of all, his grasp of theoretical physics. Despite his ignorance, Goudsmit knew, as he said, that "somewhere in Germany, still hidden, there [might be] a group of men, whom we have never heard of, secretly manufacturing atom bombs even now." He had read top-secret intelligence reports and concluded for himself that "no one but Professor Heisenberg could be the brains of a German uranium project and every physicist throughout the world knew that."

Groves had conceived of Alsos less than a year before to "cover all principal scientific military developments and . . . to gain knowledge of enemy progress without disclosing our interest in any particular field." Italy was then being liberated, and Groves assigned Colonel Pash, a former California high school football coach who earlier had helped Groves investigate Robert Oppenheimer's Communist background, to search Naples, Taranto, and Brindisi for signs of German atomic research. But the Italians knew nothing of significance. The experience, however, was not wasted; it helped establish Alsos's lines of authority, its responsibilities, and its methods of operations. Its operatives soon took to wearing a special uniform arm patch, an alpha (for Alsos) pierced by a red bolt of lightning to signify atomic research. With this unique ensign Alsos became a force unto itself, answering directly to Groves, going where it pleased in the European theater, overriding standing orders and ignoring inconvenient military laws. Cleared by a letter from the secretary of war to Eisenhower that said, "I consider it [the Alsos mission] to be of the highest importance to the war effort. . . . Your assistance is essential, and I hope you will give Colonel Pash every facility and assistance at your disposal which will be necessary and helpful in the successful operation of this mission," Alsos was as close to a law unto itself as any Army unit would ever be.

Before Overlord landed Allied troops on the Normandy beaches in June 1944, Alsos had sought to discover where the German atomic scientists were working. The previous fall American censorship officials had intercepted a letter postmarked Hechingen, Germany, in which a prisoner of war mentioned "a research laboratory numbered 'D.' " At the beginning of the summer of 1944, Groves had ordered a constant aerial surveillance of Hechingen. The photos revealed nothing of particular interest at first. It was a small town with a cathedral and a *Schloss* (castle). But in the late summer, just after Alsos had set up offices in Paris, aerial reconnaissance revealed a change that alarmed Groves. The Germans had built a slave-labor camp around Hechingen and had broken ground on a new industrial site, which in a matter of weeks had become an impressive complex of buildings with power lines and a rail spur; trains supplied the site with tons of materials every day. Groves guessed "that something was being built that commanded the utmost priority." He guessed it was a bomb factory, although Intelligence experts were not so convinced.

In summer 1944, Alsos followed the Allied troops so closely that their jeeps had been fired on entering Paris. Sam Goudsmit joined Alsos there, ready to start the search for Heisenberg, as the fortunes of the Allies allowed. But first, Goudsmit went to the Collège de France of the Joliot-Curies, who had remained in Paris for the duration, living and working near the German physicists that Diebner had sent from Berlin. Frédéric Joliot-Curie had joined the *Maquis* primarily to fight for postwar Communist influence in the French government. He had actually used the labs at the college as a munitions dump and factory, a Nobel laureate surreptitiously making homemade bombs with which to kill Germans.

When they met at the laboratory, Goudsmit, warm-hearted, with a lively sense of humor, a healthy disrespect for authority, and passionate interests as far afield from physics as rare wine, Egyptology, and amateur sleuthing in the Sherlock Holmes vein, cracked open cans of K rations and shared a bottle of vintage champagne that Frédéric had saved to celebrate the liberation. Frédéric described to Goudsmit the fate of von Halban and Lew Kowarski, who he still thought had gone down with the *Broompark*. Goudsmit told him the happy news that they were safely in America, then he led the conversation around to the Germans. As far as Frédéric knew, the Germans had worked on the bomb. He himself had refused to cooperate, even forbidding them at first to use the college's laboratories. But as the occupation had lengthened, he had relented, he said. He had watched everything they did and listened to what they said. They had used the cyclotron on the understanding that the work was not related to their war effort, but he knew that was a lie.

When the interview ended, Goudsmit thought that Joliot-Curie had told less than the whole truth. He had been evasive, particularly on the question of the Nazis at the college, and Goudsmit did not trust him. When Goudsmit asked him about Heisenberg, Joliot-Curie said that he knew nothing, although he had heard a rumor that a number of German physicists, including von Weizsäcker, had gone to the University of Strasbourg. Maybe Heisenberg had gone there, too.

From all the disparate bits of intelligence he received, Goudsmit assumed that German work on the bomb paralleled what he had gleaned about the Allied effort. It was even likely that they were still ahead, and the thought made him "plenty jittery." In addition, Groves told Alsos that Hitler was boasting about "secret weapons" and that the German V project had been stepped up presumably to transport atomic bombs when and if they became available, and, even sooner, to deliver radioactive matter over Allied and liberated countries to poison troops and panic civilians.

Late in September, Colonel Pash sent out a probe with the Operation Marketbasket parachute invasion of Holland. As the Germans were counterattacking at Arnhem, Robert Blake, an Alsos agent, struggled to reach the center of the "bridge too far" over the Rhine. If the Germans were using the Rhine's waters to cool a plutonium-producing pile, traces of radioactivity would appear downstream, even as far as Arnhem. If this were true, only the faster-running water at the center of the river would give an accurate reading. As bullets flew around him, Blake threw a bucket tied to a rope over the railing of the bridge. To the astonishment of the troops huddled on the other side, he stood up and pulled it in; then he dashed for safety. The Allied soldiers, whom the Germans would soon repulse, never saw Blake again. They had not known why he was there, but he had provided them with a strange interlude. They might have tried to stop him from such an undertaking, but armed with the letter he had shown them from Eisenhower, Blake could have danced the hula on the bridge for all the power they had to interfere.

In Paris, Blake gave the Rhine water to Goudsmit, who included a bottle of vintage Roussillon from the south of France with the shipment to Washington, D.C. On the wine label he wrote, "Test this for activity too!" He imagined that the officer in charge of analyzing the Rhine water would thank him for his generosity.

Meanwhile, Allied troops swept through Belgium, liberating Brussels. As soon as possible afterward, Alsos interviewed Gaston André, the director for uranium of Union Minière in Brussels, who confirmed that Auer, the German chemical company, had ordered as much as seventy tons of uranium since June 1940. Another German company, Roges GmbH, had purchased 115 tons of refined and partially refined materials, 610 tons of crude materials, 17 tons of uranium alloys, and about 110 tons of rejects from the refining process. In January and May 1943, Roges had bought an additional 140 tons of refined uranium. Pash went with the British 21st Army group to liberate the area around the uranium storage site, where he found 68 tons of uranium oxide. Troops poured the uranium into wooden barrels disguised to look as if they contained whiskey, and dispatched them to America, via Britain.

Back in Paris, Army G-2 learned from the OSS and its own interrogation of prisoners about a German technical spy ring that had disguised itself as a chemical company called *Cellastic* in a house off the Champs Élysées, on 20 rue Quentin Beauchart. When Sam Goudsmit arrived there, the place was empty, but left behind were half-packed boxes of sample bottles and other technical equipment suggesting an interest in applied and pure science. The Germans had soundproofed some of the offices, and an intercom had been designed to prevent phone tapping. From carbon papers in the wastebaskets, Goudsmit learned the names and addresses of the French who had worked for the Germans or supplied them with materials or technical information.

He went to one of the addresses, a shop selling scientific books near the Sorbonne that was owned by a Mexican of European and Mexican-Indian descent. Goudsmit asked the man whether he had mailed technical books to Cellastic's employees, or whether they had ever visited the shop.

"There was one young physicist who came here frequently," the bookshop owner said. "I sent him some books recently, but they came back as undelivered. I got a letter from him the other day. He's a nice fellow." He searched the drawers of the desk. "Let me see if I can find it," he said. "I did not read it carefully and forgot what it was about."

A couple of days later Goudsmit went with the letter to the Pont Saint-Pierre, near Rouen, to the address of the "nice fellow," a young Dutch physicist whom Goudsmit hated on sight for his collaboration with the Germans. He told Goudsmit that the Abwehr, German Military Intelligence, had organized a group of physicists in Paris to keep an eye on French scientific developments to ensure that the French did not work against Germany. Any important French scientific discoveries, particularly at the Collège de France, were to be delivered to Berlin for use by the German physicists.

Everything that Goudsmit had seen so far pointed in one direction: the Germans had maintained the pace of their atomic bomb research despite the bombing of Berlin and the Allied invasion of the Continent.

Eventually, running down other Cellastic leads, Sam Goudsmit went to The Hague, Holland, the lovely coastal city in which he was born and his parents had lived until their "transport" to the German death camp. He dreamed that he might find his parents at home, waiting for him just as he had last seen them. He had received their farewell letter from the Nazi death camp in March 1943, nearly two years before. He knew that it was a dream, but one from which he hoped never to awaken.

He parked his jeep and climbed in through one of the windows. The house had been stripped of nearly everything, its furnishings, shutters, floorboards, banister. He climbed the stairs to the room where he had slept as a boy. He found the high school report cards and souvenirs that his parents had kept from his youth. He closed his eyes. "I could see the house as it used to look thirty years ago," he said. "Here was the glassed-in porch which was my mother's favorite breakfast nook. There was the corner where the piano always stood. Over there had been my bookcase. What had happened to the many books I had left behind?"

He wandered out of the house, wondering why he had come.

Everything that had been his formative life was now destroyed by the Germans. The visit only strengthened his commitment to find Heisenberg before the Germans used a bomb to do this on a massive scale to others.

Back in Paris, he read through raw intelligence from Union Minière. It identified a well-known German chemist who had worked out of Paris during the occupation for a chemical company called *Terres-Rares*. The German, according to Union Minière, had ordered a large quantity of thorium to be sent to Germany only days before the liberation of Paris, and thorium, Goudsmit knew, could be used in advanced atomic bomb research.

The French employees of Terres-Rares denied knowing why the German wanted the thorium; he traveled frequently and rarely stayed in Paris. They only knew a man named Jensen and his secretary who had managed the office.

"Did they leave anything behind them when they cleared out?" Goudsmit asked.

"Oh, no, nothing" was the reply.

That seemed impossible to Goudsmit. "Are you positive?" he asked.

"Just a couple of catalogues," they said.

But Goudsmit found on a list of registered letters the name of Auer, the German chemical company. He also saw that Jensen had sent a letter to his secretary, Fräulein Ilse Hermanns, in Eupen, on the German-Belgian border.

"I'll bring her back," Pash told Goudsmit.

Soon, Pash returned to Paris with Fräulein Hermanns and Jensen, the office manager, whom he and Goudsmit interrogated in their hotel suite. After a few hours they realized that Jensen either knew nothing or was lying. Pash continued the questioning without a break while Goudsmit climbed into bed to read the papers in Jensen's briefcase.

From canceled train tickets, Goudsmit realized that Jensen had visited Berlin two weeks ago. En route to Berlin, Jensen had made a wide detour to visit a place that was so far out of the way that Goudsmit became suspicious. He examined the train tickets again. Jensen had stopped in the town of Hechingen. It sounded familiar to him, and he asked Pash, who was still questioning Jensen. OSS reports from Groves in Washington indicated that Hechingen was the town to which Heisenberg had moved the atomic bomb research; the Germans were building a slave-labor camp near there. Goudsmit thought: Jensen, thorium, Hechingen, Heisenberg, the German atomic bomb. The pieces suddenly fell into place.

Jensen explained that his mother lived in Hechingen. He had stopped to visit her on his way to Berlin, and after leaving Berlin he had joined his secretary in Eupen. And what about the thorium? Goudsmit asked. The reply seemed unbelievable.

Terres-Rares represented Auer in France, Jensen said, and Auer had plans for the use of thorium after the war. The Auer and Company directors had noted the success of American toothpaste manufacturers' bizarre advertising claims for chemicals such as fluoride. Auer wanted to introduce in postwar Germany a new toothpaste with thorium called "Doramad—Radioaktive Zahncreme—Use toothpaste with thorium! Have sparkling brilliant teeth—radioactive brilliance!" It was true: all their apprehensions concerned a chemical that was to be used for toothpaste! Pash saw the irony, but Goudsmit dined out on the story.

Alsos was back to square one without a single German in its grasp with direct knowledge of the Reich's atomic plans and progress.

At about the same time, a "rocket" dispatch from Washington arrived at Alsos's headquarters in Paris. It said, "Water negative. Wine shows activity. Send more. Action." Thinking this was a tongue-in-cheek reply, Goudsmit thought no more of it, until a follow-up "action" cable demanded to know why he had not sent the wine bottles. It dawned on Goudsmit that the Roussillon wine had emitted weak radioactivity in laboratory tests. The analysts in Washington actually had diluted the lovely wine with chemicals. Embarrassed, Goudsmit cabled back, trying to explain, but Groves ordered Alsos to send a team to the vineyard in the south of France. An Alsos major and captain volunteered for the assignment without hesitation. Goudsmit told them before they left, "Do a complete job. Don't be stingy with the confidential funds. And above all be sure that [for] every bottle of wine you locate you secure a file copy for our office in Paris." The officers set out in a jeep on a tour of France's wine country, basking in the hospitality of growers who thought that they wanted to secure the export market of their wine when the war was won. Ten days later, their jeep loaded with crates of the world's best wines as "file copies," they were received by Alsos in Paris as conquering heroes.

When he heard, Groves could not seem to understand. He was dealing with civilian scientists, not career military officers. He rebuked Goudsmit sharply, but the affair was soon forgotten.

By November 15, 1944, General George Patton's Second Armored Division entered Strasbourg. Pash accompanied Patton's Third Army Group tanks, taking extraordinary risks out of a desire to capture the German physicists before they had the opportunity to flee east into the Reich, but when he searched the university buildings where he thought they were hiding he was unable to find even one physicist. He doubted that they could have fled through the German lines, but they could not be found. Pash found the house of von Weizsäcker, who had disappeared too. He cabled Paris for Goudsmit to join him to start translating and interpreting the thick research files left behind, while he continued to look for the physicists. The longer he stayed in Strasbourg the less he believed that all of them could have succeeded in slipping away.

A few days after the liberation of Strasbourg had begun, an officer of the Third Army Group's "T-Force Command," formed to search newly liberated cities for specified "targets" of interest to Allied Intelligence, informed Pash that he had interrogated medical doctors at the Strasbourg Hospital who did not seem to know much of anything about medicine. He didn't know who they were and had jailed them all. When Goudsmit finally arrived in Strasbourg, Pash asked him to check out the "doctors." Just seeing them, Goudsmit knew that these were physicists, the first German physicists Alsos had found. However, they could tell him very little, he soon realized, about the atomic program, except that von Weizsäcker and a few others had managed to leave Strasbourg well before the first Allied artillery shells were fired into the city.

Later, as the soldiers in his detachment played poker on the floor in von Weizsäcker's house, Goudsmit read the German's technical papers and diaries by the light of a candle, page by page. Most of the letters contained gossip and rumor; one letter had been addressed to "Lieber Werner." Goudsmit read it with special interest. Heisenberg had been having difficulty obtaining "special metal" in lumps and slabs, although the powdered form of uranium was available in abundance. Reference to Auer and Company and certain "large scale" experiments being carried out by the Army Ordnance's proving ground near Berlin tantalized Goudsmit but gave him little to go on.

Then he discovered one letter that made the search worthwhile. It referred to the Kaiser Wilhelm Institute of Physics and its director, Heisenberg, who had ordered the evacuation of the whole institute—the machinery, materials, and personnel—to Hechingen in the Black Forest. The letter gave the exact address and even the telephone number of the hotel in Hechingen where the physicists were staying. Obviously the bombing raids had forced the nuclear scientists out of Berlin and into the relative safety of the countryside. They had moved their bomb project, lock, stock, and barrel; by now, Goudsmit estimated by the date of the letter, the Germans had had enough time to create a complete nuclear establishment in Hechingen. As interesting and even tantalizing as the picture that formed in his head was, Goudsmit knew that Alsos would have to wait to reach Hechingen until the Allied armies moved into that area, perhaps a crucial period of months.

In the meantime, Alsos crossed the boundary into Germany on February 24, 1945, near the city of Aachen. Soon afterward, they occupied laboratories at the University of Heidelberg and captured Walter Bothe, Heisenberg's antagonist and the analyst who had declared graphite next to useless as a moderator. He provided Alsos with the information that Heisenberg had moved the underground bunker complex in its entirety to Hechingen with Max von Laue and von Weizsäcker; Otto Hahn had gone to Tailfingen, near Hechingen. What progress Heisenberg had made in Hechingen was anybody's guess.

In Thuringen, an Alsos team discovered a uranium pile in the cellar of an old schoolhouse occupied by a few scientists hiding there with their families. The scientists had dug a deep circular pit in which to stack the uranium and heavy water but had accomplished little else. On the whole, the schoolhouse reactor room seemed unused, even dismantled, as if they had not progressed very far in the construction of the pile, or a completed pile had been dismantled for transport elsewhere.

Searching around the schoolhouse, Pash found a pile of rocks. "What is this black stuff?" he asked.

"That's nothing but coal," a German scientist replied.

Pash picked up a chunk of the "coal." "It seems awfully heavy for coal," he said. It was uranium.

Pash did not want the captured German scientists to know which unit he represented. His careful line of questioning was meant to suggest to them that he was an ordinary American soldier. They told him that Kurt Diebner had been the director of this laboratory. He had cleared out, taking with him the better scientists and most of the nuclear research material, only a couple of days before.

Next came Celle, north of Hannover, where Alsos found a centrifuge lab for the separation of uranium isotopes in an abandoned parachute factory. The bolts of parachute silk that the Alsos team confiscated meant more to them than the physicists and lab equipment; nothing Alsos was finding compared with the bomb research operations in America at Hanford and Oak Ridge. The Germans had achieved the basics. That much was true. But they had not progressed with their project on an industrial scale. That deduction should have given Alsos confidence, but it did not. Germany did not have enough plutonium or U-235 to produce several bombs. But were German physicists making enough to produce one? Only the capture of Heisenberg and the occupation of Hechingen now seemed likely to give them those assurances.

In February 1945, the Yalta Conference split Germany into three occupation zones. As a footnote, the Allies decided to let France liberate a slice of the Reich with its army. Hechingen fell in that zone. Groves presented a convincing case for an Alsos raid, but the American State Department ordered him in no circumstances to poach on French "territory." Groves did not argue for long. He circumvented the State Department with plans for an operation he code-named *Harborage*, by which Alsos would occupy Hechingen only long enough to capture the German physicists, seize their equipment and documents, then get out before the French arrived. Secretary of War Henry Stimson was sympathetic to Harborage. The "assets" at Hechingen were worth a diplomatic fight, but first, before he gave his approval, Stimson wanted Groves to show him what was involved. Groves pulled down a large wall map in the secretary's office; Hechingen was a small town, Groves explained, but it couldn't be that small. Yet neither he nor Stimson could locate it. As great men sometimes do, they called in an aide, a younger man who got down on the floor to search the lower quadrants of the map. Hechingen appeared only inches from the floor. Stimson and Groves joined him on their knees, gazing at the dot on the map for several minutes as Groves traced for Stimson the route by which he wanted the American Army units to cut diagonally across the French Army advance. Later, Stimson gave his approval.

In Germany, Pash knew that the French were advancing toward Hechingen nearly without opposition. As things stood, Harborage would be too late. Pash now argued for a commando-style parachute drop on Hechingen and Haigerloch: in and out in twenty-four hours. But Groves did not want the Germans in Hechingen to stand and fight. Pash then offered an alternative, a traditional, swift ground assault employing the T-Force Command. He called the raid *Humbug*.

As soon as possible afterward, Alsos set out along the eastern bank of the Rhine in a convoy of the T-Force and elements of the 1279th Engineers Combat Battalion, consisting of two armored cars, several jeeps, transport trucks, and other armored vehicles. At a point directly west of Hechingen, the convoy swung sharply east. Sam Goudsmit, in a jeep beside Pash, his head sunk deep into an Army combat helmet, counted the hours.

The village of Haigerloch in the state of Württemberg in southern Germany had a unique distinction in the Third Reich. In January 1945, the physicists at the Kaiser Wilhelm Institute in Berlin-Dahlem had arrived there and unloaded their truckloads of equipment. Haigerloch, located in a gentle countryside, was suddenly the Third Reich's atomic city.

Each morning after their arrival Heisenberg and his colleagues mounted bicycles in front of the Swann Inn in Hechingen and then rode the ten miles through the farming country to Haigerloch and the equipment on which they worked throughout the day. The village had been selected for its unusual geology. It lay sunken in a depression formed by the Eyach River. The river made a sharp S-bend in Haigerloch. On one side of its banks, half-timbered houses of ancient construction looked out onto a massive limestone ledge around which the river turned. The villagers on Sundays crossed the Eyach River to attend services in the cathedral built on top of the limestone ledge. This storybook village served a very important function for the physicists: it was nearly impossible to hit with bombs.

The village also provided Heisenberg with a temptation that he rarely tried to resist. After reaching Haigerloch by bicycle he would climb 149 stone steps leading to the doors of the magnificent Schlosskirche, the castle church, on the flat top of the thumb-shaped ledge. The interior of the church had not been torn or neglected by time. Its decoration had originally been the ambition of optimistic and cheerful men. Gilt and pastel blue frets and fillets and soothing frescoes of biblical myths festooned nearly every square foot of the ceiling and walls in humbling swirls of movement and beauty. Colored light shot into the interior through fastidiously crafted stained-glass windows. This was a joyous space for marriages and baptisms and celebratory Easter Sundays, a place redolent of royalty when it was still important in Germany. It was not the beauty that particularly tempted Heisenberg, but the instrument on the balcony near the doors. There he would seat himself on the wooden bench before a complex, many-tiered, ivory-inlaid keyboard and fill the majestic space with the resonant chords of Bach fugues.

He realized more than once the irony of playing church music over what lay directly beneath him. About fifty yards from the thumb-end of the river two tarpaper huts nuzzled against the base of a limestone ledge, almost in direct line below the soaring bell tower of the church. The huts protected and hid from view the jagged mouth of a dark cavity, an old *Keller* (wine cellar), a veritable cave in which for centuries priests from the castle church had laid down their sacramental wines. The temperature inside the cave was noticeably cooler, and a heavy dampness pervaded the air there even in spring and summer. The cave extended for about twenty-five yards and had a uniform width of about ten yards. A beam was thrown across the twelve-foot vault of the cave. Below the beam the physicists had dug a deep circular well, into which they planned to sink their uranium reactor made of several score of tentacles made from two-inch-square uranium metal cubes that dangled above the receptacle for the precious heavy water.

Heisenberg had nearly completed his experiments with the cave pile by late April 1945. He had lowered the links of uranium cubes into the vessel and filled the well with the last of the heavy water that had reached them from Norsk-Hydro. Then as he had watched the counters in the huts, Heisenberg had reflected once again on the error that had doomed these experiments from the start, indeed, an error that had doomed the entire German atomic effort, without anyone's knowing, nearly from the start.

While the physicists were in Berlin at the institute, they saw no alternative to the heavy water, which had failed to arrive from Norway. They had waited, suffered endless delays, and waited some more. Perhaps Heisenberg's own pride had prevented him from trying other moderators. Perhaps his pride prevented him from rechecking the experiments and calculations on graphite. He had sponsored heavy water, and when Bothe had reported that graphite contained unacceptable absorptive qualities, Heisenberg had felt vindicated and had not investigated the matter further. If he had checked Bothe's research, he would have found a series of errors. Bothe had declared graphite unusable, and Heisenberg had agreed and had not questioned that result. It was too late to look back now; it was also too late to place blame. But, as Heisenberg watched the counters in the sheds beside the cave, he could not help but wonder. If Bothe had not failed, by now he would have achieved criticality in a uranium pile.

Perhaps the oversights were all to the good, Heisenberg had thought, as the counters started their telltale clicking. His honor and that of other German physicists was, he felt, intact. They still had their minds, and, as he often said, "Education for rational thought is certainly a worthwhile task, and we must do our utmost to bring it about after the war. . . . The Führer is no substitute for raw materials, verbiage no viable alternative to scientific and technical achievements." It was just as well that he had not given Hitler the gift of nuclear power, especially now that the war seemed to be over.

As he checked the counters, he saw that the neutrons had multiplied, but the pile had not created a self-sustaining chain reaction. It was obvious that further experiments were futile without the additional heavy water and uranium that he needed. The Reich was collapsing all around him. All that was left for him was to wait. The last of the German troops retreating east had passed through Hechingen days ago. The physicists heard the rumble of enemy tanks approaching from the west and the south. There was little that they could do besides bury the uranium, the heavy water, and their research reports.

That last night, April 22, 1945, Heisenberg gathered the physicists in the gloom of the air-raid shelter in Hechingen. It was almost three o'clock in the morning, and the room smelled of defeat. Heisenberg consoled them with the reminder of what they had accomplished under such appalling conditions. German physics could take credit for the theory of nuclear energy. The transfer of that theory into fact had eluded them, not because of anything they had done or failed to do, but because the Reich had not supplied them with the tools necessary to succeed. Yet, despite Heisenberg's remarks, the physicists did not try to conceal their disappointment.

Heisenberg said farewell without telling them where he was going. Then, just after three in the morning, he walked out of the air-raid shelter and climbed on his bicycle heavy with a knapsack with emergency rations and personal documents. He pedaled down the hill leading out of Hechingen. He did not need the road sign for GAMMERTINGEN—26 KM to point him to his destination 270 kilometers away. He would be lucky to reach it alive.

Pash, Goudsmit, and the engineers of Humbug encountered only slight resistance as they traveled east toward Haigerloch and Hechingen, with several towns along the route surrendering to them by telephone. They had spotted French Senegalese troops who they hoped would not notify their commanders of Americans in the French sector. They still did not know whether the Germans were defending their nuclear site. And they learned that the suspected slave-labor camp was a petrochemical factory the Germans were building in the last hours of the war.

As they entered Haigerloch, not a single shot was fired against them. At first the house shutters were bolted shut, but once the villagers understood that there was to be no fighting, curiosity prodded them out of doors. Strangers had come into the village only four months ago, they told the Alsos translators, strangers who had secreted themselves nearby in an old cave, telling the villagers to stay away.

The purpose of the cave was hardly a mystery to Pash and Goudsmit. They drove the jeeps over the bridge and along the wide, dry bank of the Eyach River. They stopped beside the two tarpaper huts. High above them was the bell tower of the Schlosskirche. They entered the huts cautiously, then peered into the cave. Back in the dark recess, as their eyes adjusted, the awesome shape of what they had come for slowly revealed itself: a machine, they saw, of deceptive simplicity.

They felt relief at finding the pile, but they had not yet found the German physicist who could answer their questions. Goudsmit guessed that the Germans had failed to make the uranium 238 "cook." Why they had not managed to go further, he could not say.

Goudsmit and Pash emerged from their initial inspection of the cave as the engineers were preparing to demolish some of the nuclear equipment with dynamite. Above them, high on the ledge, they heard a sharp cry and saw a head, barely visible, craning out a window of the Schlosskirche. Soon afterward the monsignor came pounding down the 149 steps and rounded the corner of the ledge. He blocked the hut's door, commanding the men of Alsos to leave. If they intended to demolish the cave, then they would have to be willing to blow him up, too, for damage to the cave would threaten the structural stability of his church, and if that was lost, he might just as well join his Maker. The monsignor stood his ground, and the engineers relented.

Later that same afternoon, as the engineers removed the uranium and heavy water and whatever equipment they could unbolt, Pash and Goudsmit drove toward Hechingen, where they met heavy resistance. The next morning they tried to reach the town again, and this time the resistance had completely disappeared. They found most of the German physicists waiting for them, like naughty schoolboys, in the lobby of the Swann Inn. They showed Pash and Goudsmit to a temporary laboratory near the inn, where the physicists said they would find Heisenberg's office. There on a desk was a framed photograph of Goudsmit and Heisenberg together that summer before the war in Michigan when Goudsmit had begged Heisenberg to stay in America.

Goudsmit returned to the inn to interrogate von Weizsäcker about Heisenberg, while Pash went to Tailfingen, another village where the scientists had set up laboratories. Pash asked the first man he found on the street where he might find Herr Otto Hahn. The German pointed to an old school building. Pash knocked on the door and asked for Hahn, and the building porter politely showed him to a makeshift laboratory and stiffly introduced him. It was "like a business call on a customer," Pash said. He asked Hahn where they had put their secret reports. Hahn replied, "I have them right here."

In the next four days Alsos rounded up almost all the scientists, destroyed the equipment in the cave, and captured most of the documents, the storage drums of uranium, and the heavy water. French troops were near by, and time was short for Alsos. As they were boarding trucks to leave, von Weizsäcker told Pash about a hiding place of other, more important technical papers. Engineers went to the garden behind his house. They tore open the lid of the cesspool and pulled out a sealed drum in which the documents were hidden.

Goudsmit had been careful to ask each physicist about Heisenberg. His frustration at not finding him had by now nearly reached its limit. Every other important physicist was in their grasp, but they did not know where Heisenberg had gone. The others had described his leaving on bicycle, but he had not told them his destination. He could have either fled west, to be captured by the French or Americans, or east, to be captured by the Russians. On the loose, Heisenberg posed no real threat now, but in the hands of the Russians he was a potential danger.

Alsos cleared out of Hechingen hours before the French Army arrived. Humbug had succeeded beyond expectation, but Goudsmit could not avoid feeling that he personally had failed.

The desolation sickened Heisenberg. He had been traveling three days and three nights, staying off the larger roads in daylight to avoid strafing aircraft. While he hid in roadside ditches and fields, he watched the passing of angry and confused German soldiers; marauding bands of foreign-tongued refugees from death camps in the east; boys fourteen and fifteen years old, drafted by the Wehrmacht in its final desperate moments, now lost and hungry. He had hoped to board a train at Weilheim, but when he had arrived there, the whole town seemed to be in flames. He pressed on, riding his bicycle. At one juncture, an SS deserter had threatened him with a pistol and probably would have killed him if he had not bribed him with a package of Pall Malls. Finally on the morning of the third day, starved and exhausted, he reached Urfeld and his "safe" house, where he fell into Elisabeth's arms, then later drank to their reunion from a bottle of champagne she had saved for the christening of their daughter.

After he slept, Heisenberg packed a suitcase, placing it near the front door. Fearing the reign of terror of SS members who were hanging Wehrmacht soldiers from trees for "desertion," setting fire to houses that displayed white surrender flags, and plundering food and drink in a final orgy of their special madness, Elisabeth and Werner and the children spent the daylight hours in the cellar of the house. An entire SS battalion was camped outside Urfeld, and Heisenberg feared a bloody final battle that might trap them between the SS and whichever of the liberating armies reached the village first. It was ironic that Heisenberg was ending his war as it had begun, in terror of the SS. He did not care who liberated his family. His liberators would treat him and his family in accordance with his stature as a Nobel laureate; at the least, they would treat him better than the SS would. For nearly a week, they hid in the basement; he ventured out when his mother, staying in a nearby house, called.

Colonel Pash, in the hotel lobby waiting for the reconnaissance patrols to report on their searches of the outlying houses, inspected the man before him. Pash had never seen a uniform quite like the one he wore. An American junior officer by Pash's side whispered "SS."

It was May 2, 1945, and this SS general, bivouacked outside the town, was surrendering himself and his entire division. He had heard fighting earlier in the day, he explained, but as far as he was concerned, the war was finished. Pash barely believed his ears. His Alsos raiding party consisted of only eighteen men. They had come here to Urfeld to find Heisenberg, who they had learned lived here. The problem now for Pash, though, was complicated by the surrender of the SS division. Pash's party was approximately twenty miles in front of advance elements of the Seventh Army. He was out alone in enemy country. The SS general probably thought that Pash's raiding party was the spearhead of a much larger force. But Pash didn't want this surrender. Heisenberg was worth ten SS divisions and ten generals. Yet, he could not let the general know the truth. Otherwise, he might want to fight.

Pash tried to act matter-of-fact. He told the general, as he could see, that it was late in the day. Pash didn't want to upset his own commanding general, only a few miles behind him at the head of a large American column, he said, suggesting that the SS general get a good night's sleep. The general seemed to understand perfectly.

Just as the SS general was turning to leave, another of Pash's soldiers brought in another German commander who wanted to surrender. Pash repeated the bluff, about tomorrow's being another day. His instincts told him to leave Urfeld fast and forget about Heisenberg this time around. If fighting did start between the SS division and the Seventh Army, there was no telling what would happen to him and his men.

He considered his options when a raider came to tell him that he had found Heisenberg's house. That was something, at least, Pash had thought, picking up his rifle. As he approached the little house minutes later, he saw lights in the window. His men covering the entrance and the back indicated to him that there had been no resistance. Pash walked in.

Standing there in the doorway was a woman of considerable beauty beside three children. By her expression, she was frightened and a little relieved. Pash asked, "Where is he?"

Elisabeth Heisenberg replied, "I'll call him." He was with his mother. Into the telephone, she said simply, "They are here."

Minutes later, the man whom Pash had seen only in photographs rushed into the room. He said to Pash, "I have been expecting you."

Sam Goudsmit felt uncomfortable interrogating enemy physicists. He had known so many of them before the war, when they were colleagues. And the difference troubled him. They were being held in jail cells. They wore cast-off military clothing, and they looked unfed, confused, and frightened. Here in Heidelberg as he was interviewing the last of them, he hoped that this unpleasant duty would soon be finished and forgotten. He agreed with the sentiment in a captured letter that Heisenberg had written to Elisabeth. ". . . In my emotions, the misery of the past and the sight of the human destruction are mixed with intensive happiness of making a fresh start and building anew. I hope that fate will allow me to be equal to the task."

A guard brought in Heisenberg. They were like strangers, Goudsmit and Heisenberg. Aside from the details of the Nazi atomic program and physics, there was very little for either one of them to say. Goudsmit recalled, though, that six years ago he had begged Heisenberg to wait out the war at the University of Michigan. He thought, too, of his parents and his visit to the house in The Hague.

Heisenberg told him that the German physicists in his opinion had not cooperated with the Nazis; they had done only the minimum work necessary to preserve their university positions and hold together what remained of the once-proud German physics. Goudsmit wondered whether he could ever trust anyone like Heisenberg again: There would always be the worry that the Nazis had reached deep into his soul, after all, regardless of what he said here. How much truth would he blend with falsehood to give the impression of an "inner exile," despite the evidence. It probably did not matter, Goudsmit thought. Heisenberg was too valuable a physicist for his past to threaten his future. In time, the memory of the war would blur as if these real events had been a dream.

Goudsmit asked, "Wouldn't you want to come to America now and work with us?"

Heisenberg answered automatically, "No, I don't want to leave. Germany needs me."

Goudsmit could understand that. Heisenberg had said precisely the same thing before the war. He did not try to convince him now as he had once done, and they talked, mostly about mutual friends. As the minutes passed, Heisenberg seemed to relax. He knew that the Allies would hold him in detention for several weeks, at least, and that this was his last chance to ask questions freely of a friend like Goudsmit. There was only one question that he wanted answered, and he asked it now.

Were the Americans working on an atomic bomb?

Goudsmit shook his head. "We made no efforts in that direction," he said. "We had more important things to do."

Epilogue

On July 16, 1945, in the hours before sunrise over the parched moonscape of the southern New Mexico desert called the *Jornado del Muerto,* the "Journey of Death" that early Spanish travelers had named as a warning to those who would follow, Enrico Fermi inspected the final preparations for the creation of a phenomenon that no man had ever seen, a replication of forces that had formed the earth.

It was code-named *Trinity.*

Ten kilometers away from Fermi in the darkness of the Second Air Force's Alamogordo bombing range, a high tower of spindly steel girders cradled "Fat Man," an implosion bomb containing plutonium. If he realized his contribution to this huge effort, it did not show.

It had been a long road from the squash court at Stagg Field to here, by way of Oak Ridge and Hanford and Los Alamos, the atomic city that Groves had built. After the success of CP-1, the Met Lab physicists had continued a long series of pile tests in the Argonne Forest. Fermi had transported this knowledge, first into a prototype pile at Oak Ridge; later, after millions of dollars had been spent on construction at Hanford, the factory piles had failed to operate as predicted, threatening to delay the entire project. Du Pont's Greenwalt, who believed in Fermi's genius, had explained to him that xenon, a by-product of the factory piles, was poisoning the plutonium. Fermi thought about the phenomenon for a while, then recommended a course of action notable for its simplicity. He had told the Hanford engineers to accelerate the pile to its maximum capacity, well beyond any limit tested before. Just as Fermi had predicted, the increased radioactivity in the pile had blown out the poison, just as the acceleration of an automobile's engine clears the valves of carbon.

In the early stages, Fermi had spent his time advising and recommending, solving problems of theory that cropped up weekly, but he did not move to Los Alamos until the summer of 1944, at Oppenheimer's insistence. Los Alamos provided a place for the reunion of old friends and colleagues from Europe and Columbia. Segrè, the "Basilisk," was there, along with Teller, Peierls, Frisch, Anderson, and Bohr, and so too was the newspaper reporter from *The New York Times,* William Laurence. Laura had joined him on the mesa; by now she knew that living in one place for the duration was only a wish. The Army had allocated the Fermis lodging on the "prestigious" "Bath Tub Row," but Fermi declined the privilege, preferring to live near lesser mortals than Groves and Oppenheimer. He took control of Section F (for *Fermi*), in which he acted as a general consultant, a sage to whom any of the physicists could bring their more difficult problems. Work on the mesa began at eight o'clock sharp, an hour after a siren that Fermi took to calling "Oppie's whistle" sounded over the camp. Laura pitched in with voluntary work at the hospital.

On weekends, they hiked in the Sangre de Cristo Mountains. Fermi fished along the Frijoles Stream with a bizarre assortment of hooks and lures that he had invented himself with the idea that he knew best what appealed to trout. In the winter he had skied with Niels Bohr on Sawyer Hill. It amused Bohr to watch Fermi trudge uphill on his skis, preferring the hard physical exercise to gliding down the trails. Together, the old man and Fermi had explored Pueblo caves and refreshed themselves under the tall ponderosas. In the evenings on weekends, the Fermis rarely missed the Los Alamos community square dances. With a red bandanna around his neck, a western Stetson on his head, khakis, and cowboy boots, Fermi called the dances with his Italian accent. The dancers could barely understand his calls, but few of them seemed to notice.

Fermi privately questioned the moral implications of his contribution to the atomic bomb, but while "the grim business of war," as he called it, was still being waged in the Pacific, he praised the destructive potential of the plutonium bomb, as he would later condemn hydrogen bombs. Beyond the war, "there was no choice," he believed. "Once basic knowledge is acquired, any attempt at preventing its fruition would be as futile as hoping to stop the earth from revolving around the sun."

In the secret code language of the Los Alamos physicists, the Trinity plutonium bomb was "the gadget." If it exploded as they predicted, the birth would be that of a "boy." The night before the test, on July 15, several of the physicists had discussed what they thought might happen. To Groves's dismay, they started placing bets on whether it would work, and if it did, on its explosive force. Fermi put his money in the porkpie hat on the table in the canteen of the Trinity Camp at Alamogordo and then raised a disturbing question. He wondered aloud whether the bomb might trigger the heavens, destroying every living thing on earth. Groves said no, but nobody really knew, not even Fermi.

Now in the predawn desert, Fermi heard someone near him in the dark say, "It is now minus five minutes." He prepared himself as he had been told, putting on the goggles against the predicted, blinding flash of the explosion. He reached into the pocket of his windbreaker for a small notebook. He ripped a couple of pages of the paper into small pieces and stood sideways to the distant tower.

At five twenty-nine, someone yelled, "Zero."

For a few seconds, nothing happened. Fermi continued to look away from the tower, gripping the little pieces of paper in his hand.

His first impression was of a very intense flash of light and a sensation of heat on the exposed parts of his body. Although he stared away from the explosion, he had the impression that the countryside was brighter than in full daylight. He turned his head briefly toward the rising conglomeration of nuclear flames. After a few seconds, the flash lost its brightness and appeared as a huge pillar of smoke with an expanded head like a gigantic mushroom, rising, he estimated, to an elevation of thirty thousand feet.

Forty seconds after the initial flash, Fermi started to release pieces of paper from his hand, raised several inches above his head. A gentle gust rippled his clothes, blowing the papers two and a half yards from where he was standing. He calculated rapidly in his head and then said to nobody in particular, "That corresponds to ten thousand tons of TNT." The birth, he thought, was indeed a boy, one of tremendous health and great vitality.

When it was all over, he did not share the elation of the others or the gloom of Oppenheimer. In a sense, this had been *his* boy. He was proud. But he was also shaken. When the time came later in the morning to return to Los Alamos, he found a driver and said, "It's not safe for me to drive. You do it."

On July 3, a Dakota lifted them into the skies over Liège and across the Channel to the Huntington Military Airbase, near Cambridge, England. They were "detained under His Majesty's pleasure" in a lovely, 250-year-old brick farmhouse called Farm Hall, with a garden, a lawn, and two towering trees. Hahn was there, as were Kurt Diebner, von Weizsäcker, and of course Heisenberg.

With nothing on their hands but idle time, they talked, argued, and thought. Heisenberg used Farm Hall's library, rereading Trollope and memorizing a different German poem each day. The British Secret Intelligence Service permitted then to wander the grounds at will, and a radio installed in the dining room provided them with the BBC news. With so little to do, they were mainly preoccupied about their families back in Germany. The Allies had cut the Reich into occupation zones since the final capitulation in May. Letters they wrote and received only partly assuaged fears that their families had been trapped in the Russian Zone.

Unknown to them, the British Secret Intelligence Service had bugged Farm Hall with electronic listening devices. On the day they had arrived, the hidden equipment had picked up Kurt Diebner's asking Heisenberg, "I wonder whether there are built-in microphones here?"

"Built-in microphones?" Heisenberg had replied, laughing. "Oh, no, they're not so sly. I don't think they know such Gestapo methods. In that respect they're a bit old-fashioned."

Groves in Washington had requested the bugging, to learn what the physicists really thought when they were alone and their guard was lowered. These men were potential assets. Once they were released, Groves could not force any of them to emigrate to America, and, given his natural suspicion, he did not want them to ship their knowledge to the Russians. The bugs were helping him to learn what they really knew and the way they really felt.

Naturally, they were completely ignorant of the successful Trinity test.

On the evening of August 6, 1945, three weeks after the Trinity explosion, they were seated around the small dining room table. As had become their custom, they switched on the radio for the six o'clock news report. As its lead item, the BBC reported details of an atomic explosion over the Japanese city of Hiroshima, resulting in the death of approximately 260,000 Japanese.

For a long moment, the German physicists sat in silence.

Otto Hahn was the first to speak. "If the Americans have a uranium bomb, you're all second-rate. Poor Heisenberg," he said.

"Did they use the word *uranium* in connection with the bomb?" Heisenberg asked.

"No," Hahn replied.

Angry and disbelieving, Heisenberg said, "Then it doesn't involve atoms." He could not seem to accept this ultimate defeat. He said, "The equivalent of twenty thousand tons of high explosive is certainly enormous though.... I can only think that some dilettante in America knows that the bomb is equivalent to twenty thousand tons of high explosive, and in reality it [the atom bomb] doesn't function at all."

Hahn turned his head away. "Anyway, Heisenberg," he said, "you're second-rate and can pack your bags."

"I'm ready to believe that it's a high-pressure bomb," Heisenberg persisted. "I don't believe though that uranium is involved. I think it's some chemical substance with which they've enormously intensified the explosive force."

Then they fell silent, waiting in deepening gloom for the nine o'clock news. Heisenberg thought, Well, people lie a lot. Who knows? The BBC reported that a tremendous number of people had worked for years to achieve the bomb. Hadn't Goudsmit told him that America had more important things to do? Had Goudsmit, his old friend, actually lied to him?

After the news, he said, "More funds were first made available in Germany in the spring of 1942 . . . when we . . . had absolutely certain proof that this business was possible. . . . We did not muster the moral courage to recommend that the government should employ one hundred and twenty thousand people in spring 1942 to develop this business."

Von Weizsäcker disagreed. "I think we didn't succeed because all physicists were in principle against succeeding," he said. "If we had all wanted Germany to win the war, we could have succeeded."

Otto Hahn, who had started the race for the bomb in December 1938, had the final word. "I don't believe that," he said. "But I'm thankful we didn't."

Notes

PROLOGUE

An understanding of the early influence of Plato, Thales, and Democritus on the early-twentieth-century physicists like Rutherford, Chadwick, Cockcroft, and Bohr was derived primarily from Hermann's biography of Heisenberg and Rutherford's *The Newer Alchemy*. The account given by Albert Speer in his *Inside the Third Reich: Memoirs* of the meeting with Goebbels and Hitler does not reveal the specific nature of the weapon, but by that date Hitler had been made aware of an atomic bomb's feasibility. Most probably he was referring to a bomb, although he did not subscribe until near the end to the long-range development of weaponry and particularly to the so-called X-weapons, such as rockets, an atomic bomb, the jet engine, and submarine sonar countermeasures.

PART I

The principal sources were, of necessity, Laura Fermi's *Atoms in the Family* and *Mussolini*, both of which are highly recommended, not so much for the scientific insight in the former or the historical depth in the latter as for a look into the mind of the author. She told what she knew through anecdotes; because of the private nature of her husband coupled with the imposition of secrecy by the American federal government, she could go only so far. For a better understanding of the lives of Jews in Italy under Mussolini, Michaelis's excellent *Mussolini & the Jews: German-Italian Relations & the Jewish Question in Italy 1922–1945* served as an excellent primer, telling what neither Laura nor Enrico Fermi ever told about the pressures that led them to their decision and what lay ahead in her absence for the family. Nella Weiner Fermi talked at some length about her mother and father, as did Albert Wattenberg and Robert G. Sachs. Segrè in his *Enrico Fermi: Physicist* contributed firsthand written views of Fermi as a man and a scientist, as did the soft-spoken and introspective Nobel physicist, Chandrasekhara, in an interview at the University of Chicago. Fermi's inner thoughts, however, remain a mystery to anyone who once knew him who is still alive today.

PART II

Perhaps too much has been made of the *Das Schwarze Korps* incident. Hermann made little of it in his flattering biography, and Elisabeth Heisenberg in *Inner Exile* minimized the relevance of his mother's recruitment to carry the letter, but Heisenberg wrote in *Physics and Beyond* about the incident as if it had been somewhat traumatic in nature. The quotes from the conversation between his mother and Mrs. Himmler were related by Heisenberg himself. In light of later decisions and the mind-set that embraced him in the war years, it seemed to me one of the keys to his character. Heisenberg devoted considerable energies to philosophical understanding and not only as it related to science in such essays as "Positivism, Metaphysics and Religion." He thought deeply about honor and correctness and, therefore, might have thought himself and his attitude toward the Third Reich in some deeper, philosophical sense vindicated by the Himmler letter. His character reveals itself in these same essays and monographs, perhaps in ways that he did not intend and that often seem at variance with the descriptions by Hermann and Heelan and the strained and sometimes illogical apologies of Elisabeth Heisenberg in *Inner Exile.* To reach an understanding of what life for a scientist was like under Hitler from 1933 onward, Beyerchen's *Scientists Under Hitler* was invaluable for its clear exposition—particularly of the political strains created by the German scientists who advanced such bizarre concepts as that of "Aryan" physics.

The dialogue among Dunning, Bohr, Fermi, and Laurence was recalled in detail by Laurence and documented on tape and transcripts at the Oral History Library, Columbia University. The exceptional dialogue between Heisenberg and Fermi in the summer of 1939 came straight from Heisenberg's "Individual Behavior in the Face of Political Disaster." Fermi and Pegram confirmed the meeting, although Fermi never documented precisely what was said except to mention that he had encouraged Heisenberg to stay. Much of the other dialogue came from the copious reminiscences of Szilard, the testimony of Alexander Sachs before the Senate hearings, and Hahn's *My Life*. The most precise and reliable overall picture of the buildup to the official government commitment was found in the highly recommended *The New World* by Hewlett and Anderson.

PART III

Robert Jungk and Ronald Clark provided material for the accounts of the French sweep of the Norsk-Hydro stocks and Tizard's attempt to convince Sengier. Much of the detail and dialogue, along with the account of Captain Sharp's discovery, Sengier related to Harald Steinert in *The Atom Rush*. Material on the early German project derived from David Irving and, to a lesser degree, Peierls's review of Heisenberg's *Physics and Beyond*.

PART IV

Fermi described the early efforts with the exponential pile at Columbia in a lecture to the American Physical Society the year he died, adding the ironic comments about Szilard's suggesting that their relationship in those years was not always smooth. Weart and Weiss also detail not just the work at Columbia but the struggle over censorship as well, which put Szilard in conflict with Fermi. In the absence of anecdotal accounts by the principals, Leona Libby's *The Uranium People* provided detail of the nonscientific experiences at Columbia. Descriptions of Seaborg came from an interview by Larry Collins for *The Fifth Horseman*.

PART V

The Bohr-Heisenberg meeting has been the cause of some controversy. Most of the account here is derived from Heisenberg's own recollections. He wrote that Bohr "was so horrified by the very possibility of producing atomic weapons that he did not follow the rest of my remarks. . . . I found it most painful to see how complete was the isolation to which our policy had brought us Germans, and to realize how war can cut into even the most longstanding friendships, at least for a time." The actual degree of anxiety the conversation caused Bohr is open to interpretation; he did not expound on the subject at length, although he felt compelled to relate the content and his reading of the conversation in the worst light to Tube Alloys.

The first institute meeting failed to attract leaders of the SS, the high command, and ministers like Speer, according to David Irving, because a secretary at the institute copied the wrong information, filling the envelopes with highly technical documents.

PART VI

The FRESHMAN account is derived from the official history published by His Majesty's Stationery Office under the title *By Air to Battle—The Official Account of the British Airborne Divisions* and from the monograph *The Heavy-Water Operations in Norway 1942–1944* by Colonel J. S. Wilson, who commanded the Norwegian section of the Special Operations Executive. Gowing's valuable and scholarly work, *Britain and Atomic Energy,* on the British diplomatic and scientific efforts provided a backdrop, supplemented by Clark, and the main elements of the Moe Berg anecdote came from Kaufman's delightful book and from Heisenberg's own account, related to and written by Elisabeth Heisenberg in *Inner Exile*.

The dialogue after the air raid on March 1, 1943, off the Potsdamer Platz, between Heisenberg and Adolf Butenandt, a biochemist at the Berlin-Dahlem Institute, was related in all its detail by Heisenberg in "Towards a New Beginning."

Elisabeth Heisenberg in *Inner Exile* gave one side of the story about the letter on behalf of the Goudsmits. Samuel Goudsmit, in his voluminous papers at the Institute of Physics in New York, wrote only briefly about the painful episode, confirming the request.

PART VII

Fermi wrote his own recollections for commemorative occasions about the life and times of the Met Lab at the University of Chicago. In addition, I interviewed several researchers and workers, including Herbert Kubitchek; William James Sturm; Robert Sachs, currently director of the Enrico Fermi Institute at the University of Chicago; Roger Holdebrand, professor of physics; Nathan Sugarman, and Albert Wattenberg in Urbana. The descriptions also benefited from the wealth of written recollections by nearly every other physicist who worked at Met Lab before December 2, 1942.

Information about the fate of Admiral Capon came from Nella Weiner Fermi and from a valuable paper written by Juan A. del Regato, M.D., Professor of Radiology, VA Medical Center, University of South Florida, who personally had interviewed Emilio Segrè and Dr. Perluigi Cova.

The dialogue of Nichols's meeting with Sengier in New York came from *The Atom Rush* and del Regato's interviews with Madame Hamoir, Sengier's secretary; Gaston André, his former associate; and F. Lekime of Union Minière, of Brussels.

The most valuable descriptions of "Gunnerside" came from

one of the participants, Knut Haukelid, in his *Skis Against the Atom.*

PART VIII

Research for the CP-1 drama came from interviews with participants (see Part 7), from Compton's *Atomic Quest,* and from Conant's *My Several Lives.*

PART IX

Pash and Goudsmit wrote copiously on *Alsos,* as did General Groves in his *Now It Can Be Told.* These accounts were supplemented by the author's visit to Hechingen, Haigerloch, and Tailfingen and an interview with Monsignor Gulde of Schlosskirche Haigerloch. Pash and Goudsmit offer conflicting descriptions of the extent of the German effort in early 1945, with Pash less certain than Goudsmit. Pash seemed to me less interested in retrieving the remnants of the German pile research than he was in locating and detaining the nuclear physicists before they fell into Russian hands. From a reading of his collected papers at the Institute of Physics in New York, it seemed clear that Goudsmit had reason to believe differently. He spent years after the war arguing in correspondence with Heisenberg about the extent of the German atomic development.

PART X

Pash and Heisenberg both described Heisenberg's capture, and Goudsmit provided the dialogue of Heisenberg's initial interrogation.

EPILOGUE

Fermi offered his views on Alamogordo, July 16, 1945, in "My Observations." Beyond these Laura Fermi reported as evidence of his emotional response his unusual decision to ride home to Los

Alamos; he otherwise always insisted on driving himself. The dialogue from Hall Farm came from *Now It Can Be Told,* which to the present remains the only part of the taped transcripts that has been declassified, as a result of the insistence of the British censors at the Public Records Office, Kew.

Bibliography

Abelson, Philip H. "A Sport Played by Graduate Students." *Bulletin of the Atomic Scientists* 30, no. 5 (May 1974).

Agnew, Harold M. "Early Impressions." *Bulletin of the Atomic Scientists* 38, no. 10 (December 1982), pp. 20–21.

Amrine, Michael. *The Great Decision.* New York: G.P. Putnam's Sons, 1959.

Anderson, Herbert L. "The Legacy of Fermi and Szilard." *Bulletin of the Atomic Scientists* 30, no. 7 (September 1974), pp. 56–62.

———. "Fermi, Szilard and Trinity." *Bulletin of the Atomic Scientists* 30, no. 8 (October 1974), pp. 40–47.

Bainbridge, Kenneth T. "Prelude to Trinity." *Bulletin of the Atomic Scientists* 31, no. 4 (April 1975), pp. 42–46.

Baxter, James Phinney III. *Scientists Against Time.* Cambridge, Mass.: Massachusetts Institute of Technology Press, 1968.

Beyerchen, Alan D. *Scientists Under Hitler.* New Haven: Yale University Press, 1977.

Blow, Michael. *History of the Atomic Bomb.* New York: American Heritage, 1968.

Born, Max. *The Born-Einstein Letters, 1916–1955.* New York: The Macmillan Company, 1971.

Brewer, Shelby T. *The First Reactor.* Washington, D.C.: Department of Energy, History Division, 1982.

Brode, Bernice. "Tales of Los Alamos." In *Reminiscences of Los Alamos.* Dordrecht: Reidel, 1980.

Brown, Anthony Cave, and Macdonald, Charles B., eds. *The Secret History of the Atomic Bomb.* New York: Delta, 1977.

Bush, Vannevar. *Pieces of the Action.* New York: Morrow, 1970.

Childs, Herbert. *An American Genius.* New York: E. P. Dutton, 1968.

Clark, Ronald W. *The Birth of the Bomb.* London: Phoenix House, 1961.

———. *Einstein: The Life and Times.* New York: Avon, 1971.

Compton, Arthur H. *Atomic Quest.* New York: Oxford University Press, 1956.

Conant, James B. *My Several Lives.* New York: Harper & Row, 1970.

Crowther, James Gerald. *Science at War.* New York: Philosophical Library, 1948.

Curie, Eve. *Madame Curie.* London: Heinemann, 1938.

Davidson, C. F. "On the Occurrence of Uranium in Ancient Conglomerates." *Economic Geology* 52 (1957).

Davis, Nuel Pharr. *Lawrence and Oppenheimer.* New York: Simon & Schuster, 1968.

Dawidowicz, Lucy S. *The War Against the Jews 1933–1945.* New York: Holt, Rinehart & Winston, 1975.

del Regato, Juan A. *Enrico Fermi.* London: Pergamon Press, 1982.

De Toledano, Ralph. *The Greatest Plot in History.* 2d ed. New York: Arlington House, 1977.

Evans, Medford. "My Observations During the Explosion at Trinity on July 16, 1945." *Trinity Test Reports.* Washington, D.C.: National Archives, undated.

———. "Physics at Columbia University, the Genesis of the Nuclear Energy Project." *American Physical Society* (January 30, 1954).

———. *The Secret War for the A Bomb.* Chicago: Henry Regnery, 1953.

Fermi, Laura. *Atoms in the Family.* Chicago: University of Chicago Press, 1954.

———. *Mussolini.* Chicago: University of Chicago Press, 1966.

Frisch, Otto. "Somebody Turned the Sun on with a Switch." *Bulletin of the Atomic Scientists* 30, no. 4 (April 1974), pp. 12–18.

———. *What Little I Remember.* Cambridge, England: Cambridge University Press, 1979.

Gallagher, Thomas M. *Assault in Norway.* New York: Harcourt Brace Jovanovich, 1975.

Goldsmith, Maurice. *Frédéric Joliot-Curie.* London: Lawrence & Wishart, 1976.

Goudsmit, Samuel A. *Alsos.* New York: Henry Schuman, 1947.

Gowing, Margaret. *Britain and Atomic Energy 1939–1945.* New York: St. Martin's, 1964.

Groueff, Stéphane. *Manhattan Project.* Boston: Little, Brown, 1967.

Groves, Leslie. *Now It Can Be Told.* New York: Harper & Row, 1962.

Hahn, Otto. *Otto Hahn: My Life*. New York: Herder & Herder, 1970.

Haukelid, Knut. *Skis Against the Atom*. Translated by F. H. Lyon. London: William Kimber, 1954.

Heelan, Patrick A. *Quantum Mechanics and Objectivity: A Study of the Physical Philosophy of Werner Heisenberg*. The Hague: Nijhoff, 1965.

Heisenberg, Elisabeth. *Inner Exile*. Stuttgart: Birkhäuser Verlag, 1984.

Heisenberg, Werner. *Monographs: The Physicist's Conception of Nature*. New York: Harcourt, Brace, 1958.

———. *Physics and Philosophy*. London: Allen & Unwin, 1959.

———. *Physics and Beyond*. New York: Harper & Row, 1971.

———. "Research in Germany on the Technical Applications of Atomic Energy." *Nature* (August 16, 1942).

Hermann, Armin. *Werner Heisenberg 1901–1976*. Munich: Inter Nationes, 1976.

Hewlett, Richard G. *CP-1 in the Race for the Atomic Bomb*. Washington, D.C.: U.S. Atomic Energy Commission, 1967.

———, and Anderson, Oscar E. *The New World*. Vol. 1, 1939/1946. University Park: Pennsylvania State University Press, 1962.

Hilberry, Norman. "The Birth of the Nuclear Age—December 2, 1942." *University of Chicago Reports* 13, no. 2 (December 2, 1962).

Hilts, Philip J. *Scientific Temperaments*. New York: Simon & Schuster, 1982.

His Majesty's Stationery Office. *By Air to Battle—The Official Account of the British Airborne Divisions*. London, 1945.

Hyde, Montgomery. *The Atom Bomb Spies*. New York: Ballantine, 1980.

Irving, David. *The Virus House*. London: William Kimber, 1967.

Jones, R. V. *Most Secret War*. London: Hamish Hamilton, 1978.

Jungk, Robert. *Brighter Than a Thousand Suns*. New York: Pelican, 1982.

Kamen, Martin D. "The Birthplace of Big Science." *Bulletin of the Atomic Scientists* 30, no. 9 (November 1974), pp. 42–46.

Kaufman, Louis. *Moe Berg: Athlete, Scholar, Spy*. Boston: Little, Brown, 1975.

Kellaway, F. W. *Splitting the Atom*. London: Crowther, 1945.

Kevles, Daniel J. *The Physicists*. New York: Alfred A. Knopf, 1977.

Lamont, Lansing. *Day of Trinity*. New York: Atheneum, 1965.

Lapp, Ralph E. *Atoms and People*. New York: Harper & Bros., 1956.

Laurence, William. *The Hell Bomb*. London: Hollis & Carter, 1951.

———. *Oral History*. New York: Columbia University Oral History Project, undated.

Libby, Leona Marshall. *The Uranium People*. New York: Crane, Russak, 1979.

Meitner, Lise. "Looking Back." *Bulletin of the Atomic Scientists* 20, no. 9 (November 1964), pp. 2–7.

Metropolis, N. *Enrico Fermi*. A Record of the Fermi Memorial Symposium, April 29, 1955. Washington, D.C., American Physical Society.

Michaelis, Meir. *Mussolini & the Jews: German–Italian Relations & the Jewish Question in Italy 1922–1945*. New York: Oxford University Press, 1979.

Moore, Ruth. *Niels Bohr: The Man and the Scientist*. London: Hodder & Stoughton, 1967.

Nichols, Robert, and Browne, Maurice. *Wings over Europe*. New York: Dodd, Mead, 1929.

Nielson, J. Rud. "Memories of Niels Bohr." *Physics Today* 16, no. 10 (1963).

Nininger, R. D. "The Genesis of Uranium Deposits." *Report of the 21st Session*, International Geological Congress. Copenhagen, 1960.

Oliphant, Mark. "The Beginning: Chadwick and the Neutrons." *Bulletin of the Atomic Scientists* 38, no. 10 (December 1982), pp. 14–18.
———. *Rutherford: Recollections of the Cambridge Days*. Amsterdam: Elsevier, 1972.

Page, L. R. "The Source of Uranium Deposits." *Report of the 21st Session*, International Geological Congress. Copenhagen, 1960.

Pash, Boris T. *The Alsos Mission*. New York: Award House, 1969.

Peierls, Rudolf. "Atomic Germans." *The New York Review of Books*, July 1, 1971.

Rabi, Isidor. *Science: The Center of Culture*. New York: New American Library, 1970.

Rabinowitch, Eugene. "James Franck and Leo Szilard." *Bulletin of the Atomic Scientists* 20, no. 8 (October 1964).

Rozenthal, S., ed. *Niels Bohr, His Life and Work as Seen by His Friends and Colleagues*. Amsterdam: North-Holland Publishing, 1967.

Rutherford, Ernest. *The Collected Papers of Lord Rutherford of Nelson*. Vol. 3. London: Allen & Unwin, 1965.
———. *The Newer Alchemy*. Cambridge: Cambridge University Press, 1937.

Sachs, Alexander. "Opening Testimony," Special Committee on Atomic Energy. "Background and Early History of the Atomic Bomb Project in Relation to President Roosevelt." U.S. Senate, 79th Cong., 1st sess. Washington, D.C.: Government Printing Office, 1946.

Sachs, Robert G. *The Nuclear Chain Reaction—Forty Years Later*. Proceedings of a University of Chicago commemorative symposium. Chicago: University of Chicago Press, 1984.

Segrè, Emilio. *Enrico Fermi: Physicist*. Chicago: University of Chicago Press, 1970.

Sherwin, Martin J. *A World Destroyed*. New York: Alfred A. Knopf, 1975.

Smith, Alice Kimball. "The Elusive Dr. Szilard." *Harper's* (July 1960).

———. *A Peril and a Hope*. Chicago: University of Chicago Press, 1965.

Smyth, Henry De Wolf. *Atomic Energy for Military Purposes, 1940–1945*. Princeton, N.J.: Princeton University Press, 1945.

Speer, Albert. *Inside the Third Reich: Memoirs*. New York: The Macmillan Company, 1970.

Steinert, Harald. *The Atom Rush: Man's Quest for Radioactive Materials*. Translated and adapted from the German by Nicholas Wharton. London: Thames & Hudson, 1958.

Szilard, Leo. "We Turned the Switch." *The Nation* (December 22, 1945).

Teller, Edward. *Our Nuclear Future*. New York: Criterion Books, 1958.

Ulam, Stanislaw M. *Adventures of a Mathematician*. New York: Charles Scribner's, 1976.

Wattenberg, Albert. "The Building of the First Chain Reaction Pile." *Bulletin of the Atomic Scientists* 30, no. 6 (June 1974), pp. 51–57.

Weart, Spencer R., and Szilard, Gertrude Weiss, eds. *Leo Szilard: His Version of the Facts*. Cambridge, Mass.: Massachusetts Institute of Technology Press, 1978.

Weinberg, A. H., and Nordheim, L. ". . . The State of the Art Known to the Germans in 1945." *Memo*. Clifton, N.J.: Monsanto Chemical Co., Clifton Labs, undated.

Wells, H. G. *The World Set Free*. London: Macmillan & Co., 1914.

Wilson, Jane. "The End of Youth and Innocence." *Bulletin of the Atomic Scientists* 31, no. 6 (June 1975), pp. 12–14.

York, Frank Herbert. *The Advisors: Oppenheimer, Teller and the Superbomb*. San Francisco: W. H. Freeman, 1976.

Index

Clark, Ronald W., 293, 295
Cockcroft, John, 121, 291
Collège de France, 68, 71, 115, 116, 120, 122–24, 132, 263, 266
Collins, Larry, 294
Columbia University, 8, 9, 54, 59, 69, 73–75, 81, 85, 90, 96, 142, 145, 147, 204, 210, 219, 220, 224, 245, 286, 293–94
    football team of, 138
    Oral History Library, 293
    Physics Department, 54–55, 63–65, 81, 139, 202
Combined Operations, 181–82, 184, 235
Combined Policy Committee, 257
Committee on Uranium, see Briggs Committee
Compton, Arthur Holly, 210–12, 218, 221, 223–24, 296
    and CP-1 experiment, 253–55, 257
    and isotope separation research, 204–205
    Oppenheimer and, 230
    relationship with Fermi, 216–17
    Seaborg and, 249
Conant, James, 257, 296
Concentration camps, 145, 193
Cook County Parks Department, 212
Copenhagen Institute of Theoretical Physics, 36
Corbino, Senator, 16, 21, 22, 25, 152
Cova, Perluigi, 295
Criticality, 184, 185, 216, 217, 221, 277
    of CP-1, 244, 247, 248, 255–57
Curie, Marie, 15, 50, 67, 73, 78
Cyclotrons, 62, 119, 126, 127, 145, 150
Czechoslovakia:
    German invasion of, 73, 74
    uranium mines in, 74, 77, 78, 80, 87, 89, 101, 109

Dachau, 40, 145
D'Agostino, Oscar, 16
Daladier, Edouard, 116
Dante, 145

Darwin, Charles, 37
Dautry, Raoul, 113–15, 118
Debye, Peter, 132, 141, 157
Defense of the Race (magazine), 11
del Regato, Juan A., 295
Democritus, 1, 291
Denmark:
    Frisch in, 42, 53, 61
    German occupation of, 117, 159, 175–76
    Heisenberg in, 35, 36, 160–61
    underground in, 173
Deuterium, 72
Deuterons, 151
Deutsche Allgemeine Zeitung (newspaper), 101–102, 127
Deuxième Bureau, 114, 115, 117, 120, 175
Diebner, Kurt, 102–104, 106, 108, 263, 271
    detained in England, 288, 289
    heavy water and, 126–27
    as provisional head of Kaiser Wilhelm Institute, 132, 141, 157
    uranium supplies and, 131
Donovan, William, 188
du Pont Company, 217, 244, 253, 285
Dunkirk evacuation, 124
Dunning, John Ray, 65–67, 293

E.I. du Pont de Nemours, see du Pont Company
Einstein, Albert, 1, 2, 32, 33, 37, 62, 65, 145, 191
    and government decision to fund atomic research, 95, 111
    Heisenberg and, 36
    interviewed by Laurence, 143
    letter to Briggs, 146
    letters to Roosevelt, 89–90, 141–42
    Szilard and, 57, 86–90
Eisenhower, General Dwight D., 262, 264
Electron, discovery of, 1
Elizabeth, Queen Mother of Belgium, 87

England:
   atomic research in, 62, 118–22, 150;
      see also MAUD; Tube Alloys
   Berlin bombed by, 188
   Bohr's escape to, 177–79
   declaration of war by, 195
   emigration of scientists to, 34, 63
   evacuation of French scientists to,
      122, 124–26
   Frisch in, 110–13, 119, 173, 201,
      230, 232, 235
   German physicists detained in,
      288–90
   Peierls in, 110–13, 119, 173, 201,
      230, 232, 235
   during Phony War, 108
   Szilard in, 55–59, 87
   uranium sought by, 78–81
   See also British *entries*
Enrico Fermi (Segrè), 292
Euler, Hans, 104–105
Exponential piles, 211, 216, 220, 245,
   293

Factory piles, 216, 217, 250, 253, 285
Federal Bureau of Investigation
   (FBI), 179, 203
Fermi, Enrico, xii, 36, 38, 40, 63, 73,
   129, 142, 292–97
   arrival in U.S., 54–55
   becomes U.S. citizen, 225
   at beginning of World War II,
      90–92
   Bohr and, 51–52, 60–62, 160, 179
   and British research, 175
   caution about publishing by, 69–71
   childhood of, 46–47
   code name of, 215–16
   and CP-1, 243–48, 250–57
   Debye and, 141
   departure from Italy, 45–49
   emigration to America, 7–10, 28, 45
   family life in Chicago, 224–26
   government decision to fund
      research by, 95–96

graphite in research by, 137–41,
   206–210
Groves and, 215–17
Heisenberg visits in U.S., 81–86,
   104
Hooper and, 73–76, 79
Laurence and, 64–67
at Los Alamos, 285–88
marriage of, 12–14
meeting with Briggs, 145–47
Meitner and, 49–51
at Met Lab, 210–12, 216–17, 219–23,
   229
modifier research of, 92–94, 137–41,
   147–49
neutron experiments of, 14–26, 41
Nobel Prize awarded to, 10–11,
   26–28, 45, 48, 49, 51
Oppenheimer and, 230–31
plutonium and, 152–54, 205
slow neutrons discovered by,
   24–26, 68
suburban life of, 59–60, 144–45
Szilard and, 57, 86–87
U.S. government restrictions on,
   201–203
Fermi, Giulio, 13, 45, 54, 59, 144,
   202–203
Fermi, Laura, xii, 21, 22, 63, 201–203,
   211, 221, 291–92, 296
   arrival in U.S., 54
   becomes U.S. citizen, 225
   at beginning of World War II,
      90–92
   in Chicago, 224–26, 248, 251
   departure from Italy, 45–48
   Jewish background of, 8–9, 11–12
   at Los Alamos, 286
   marriage of, 12–14
   Meitner and, 39
   and Nobel Prize, 10–11, 26–28, 49
   suburban life of, 59–60, 144–45
   Szilard and, 57
Fermi, Nella Weiner, xii, 13, 45, 47,
   48, 54, 59, 144–45, 203, 292,
   295